The Ghosts of Whidbey Island

The Ghosts of Whidbey Island

Victoria Ventris Shea

Protection Island Trading Co.

Contents

Contents

Contents

Dedicated to the First People and First Settlers
of Whidbey Island

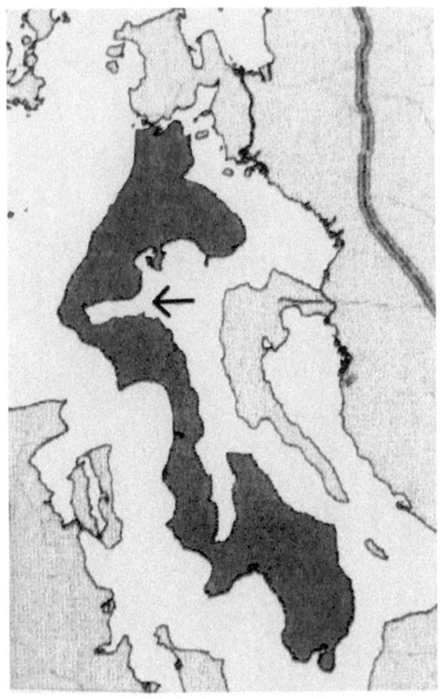

Arrow = Penn Cove.
Additional maps in back.
*Whidbey Camano Land
Trust*

Mollie's Poem

Learn to make the most of life,
Lose no happy day;
Time will never bring thee back
Chances swept away.
Leave no tender word unsaid,
Love while love shall last;
The mill will never, never grind
With the water that is past.

--Mollie Coupe, 1880's

{ 1 }

The Making of a Leader

They walk among us, not often seen but sometimes felt . . . those who came before. Adoring the natural beauty and abundance of their home, they stay as stewards over their island, entwined with the land and sea. I feel their presence in the early morning fog that crawls up from the water and dissipates into pink mist with the morning sun--the natives and first settlers of Whidbey Island. We should know them if we walk here too.

At Sunnyside Cemetery above Ebey's bluff, the first light of day accentuates the ridgeline of the Olympic Mountains, and I think about how each of my parents had talked to the dead before they passed. I wonder if that is why I find peace here, among the spirits. I ask them to help me understand how life used to be in this place.

Images slide into my mind: Penn Cove lined with beached canoes, a single log cabin on Ebey's bluff, a small schooner sailing towards Puget Sound. There is love and loss, and there is murder. The island was called Tscha-kole-chy.

* * *

No one can get Spirit power unless he is clean and his stomach is empty. Born of high blood, a young Skagit warrior who will become well-known as Snetlum has fasted and prayed, hoping to take his place as a leader of his village which sits at the longest point of beach at the south end of *New-wy-ey*, "quiet cove" (Penn's Cove). It is known as a place "where one goes into the woods," which is a good name since his people are running into the forest to hide.

That is what we do, he thinks to himself, seeing the backsides of his People duck between branches, their cedar bark aprons and blankets and hats blending in with the trees and shadows. *True to our Skagit name, we run and hide, like an invitation to be attacked.* He hardens his body like stone, dropping the cedar blanket from his shoulders, wanting to feel the rain, knowing his time has come.

Kwakiutl (kwak-ee-YEW-tul) raiders from Vancouver Island have returned. They have been seen in war paint acting bold, as if firewater and over-confidence will give them protection rather than their cedar armor. As his Skagit People run to hide, the invaders slip into a small plank house at the edge of the village to finish their drink, assuming they will be unmolested. Soon, they will grab more young Skagit sons to use as slaves, which is worse than death since they will be denied an after-life as a slave. They will kill anyone who gets in their way and take heads, leaving women to scream and wail. Fathers have tried to buy their sons back in the past, but the thieves are wicked. They will not trade except for muskets. His village has no muskets.

If they had them, they would not be foolish enough to trade them away.

Snetlum's fists tighten and his jaw grinds as he remembers the Kwakiutl raiders coming when he was a young boy. His mother swept him away deep into the woods even though she'd been shot in the arm with an arrow. From between the trees, he could see the great flames below on the beach reaching as high as the eagle's nest and roaring like the wings of the Snohomish thunderbird. When his People returned to their village, the buildings were gone. All was black and smoldering in the rain. Gone too were some of his friends. He remembered the months of living in summer shelters made of grass, reed and cattail mats while their winter houses were rebuilt. They worked together, families helping families.

Their over-confidence will get them killed, he thinks to himself. He rushes to his platform in the longhouse to grab weapons, singing a praise song to ensure their success. The dagger that hangs from his waist talks to his leg, and he says a prayer of gratitude for its quickness. Running back with a force powered by Wind Spirit, a hatchet in one hand and a whale bone war club in the other, he arrives at the house taken by the invaders and sneaks up to an outside wall. The raucous behavior inside tells him to wait while they finish their drink, especially since it will make them weak . . . and it will be their last.

As he waits, he quiets his breath and thinks of the Kwantlen people who live next to Hudson Bay Company's Fort Langley to the north. When *they* were attacked by the Kwakiutl from Quadra Island, the British "King George" men in Canada joined forces with their neighbor Kwantlen people and repelled them so dramatically that they have not had an attack since. Now the Kwakiutl from the north travel further to an easier target, to *his* Skagit village on Penn's Cove. He tightens his grip on his hatchet.

The people living along the Skagit River take care of each other. When the Lower Skagit people were raided and some were killed by a northern group, the Upper Skagit people took revenge. Their retaliation will not be needed this time. This time, Snetlum will get vengeance for them all.

Snetlum's mind moves into prayer to his spirit helpers as he waits. He has known his spirit helpers since he was a young boy. He had wandered cold and alone for several days during wind and rainstorms, taking many different paths from his fire. That is when White Deer found him along with Wind and Hawk, and he learned his spirit song. *Wind, give me strength and courage so I can protect my village. Hawk, give me power to wait and watch before I act.* In his mind, he uses the power of Hawk to fly with the Wind up to the sky and patiently look down on himself in wait.

When the group inside the house quiets, he springs without thought, throwing open the flap and swinging the hatchet into the neck of the closest invader along with his war cry, surprising them all. They try to get to their feet, but the liquor has slowed them and made them stupid. They slip in the blood beneath them, unable to get traction. Snetlum's hatchet slashes another neck and an ankle while his club cracks a head. He twirls and lunges at the taller men as the blood and spit fly and he sings his warrior power song until the only sound is the exertion of his own body. He stops, all senses alert, and meets Silence.

Silence brings exhaustion. His fury wanes as he drops, feeling as though Wind and Hawk who had invaded his body with Power have left him. The bloody scene will get worse, as he is expected to take their heads. They are misshapen heads, broad and flattened with long black beards. Snetlum's people flatten the heads of their babies also, but not to such extreme. These killers have thick hair coated with red ochre from ground up iron ore and bear grease, creating a metallic feral smell to mix with the coppery tang of blood. He forces himself to work, lifting his hatchet again and again with all the strength he can manage, fearing that he will suffer from the ghosts of these enemies in his dreams.

Wishing he was not alone, he once again calls on his spirit guides for help. He must finish the job. Resting between heads, he thinks how the Kwakiutl will not come back after learning of his wrath, and he hopes they will not seek revenge. *They were the invaders after all.*

A story is widely told about his People on the island being able to hypnotize themselves into seeing in the dark and becoming invisible to other people. Now he hopes the story will be mixed with his new story of revenge: how the Skagit people can seem peaceful, but if provoked, can turn mean and kill. They can even kill northern people who are larger and more aggressive. He begins to imagine the relief on the faces of his People as he cuts invader's necks and a safer future now that others will know that Lower Skagit warriors can be fierce.

Just before dark, he uses the last of his strength to exit the house. Broadly built and taller than his People, Snetlum draws a tether of heads behind him, ten in all. He had had no time for war paint before his fight but now he is covered in red and rust, his fingers sticking together. He feels as though he looks through a thick mask as he sees the relieved faces of his village which turn to pride. They had thought that he was dead. Now they rush to welcome and congratulate him.

Snetlum crawls into his sweat lodge made of twigs, brush and dirt over a frame that sits inside the tree line. It is the one he has been using during his months of preparation. His family's slaves prepare the fire outside and bring water for his cleansing process. After they roll the hot rocks from the fire into the depression in the ground in front of him and splash the first scoop of water, the shaman sprinkles herbs onto the rock. The white steam rises skyward, and Snetlum begins his praise songs to his spirit helpers and to Spirit Above.

He feels the silent strength of the giant oak trees nearby, along with fir trees that surround him standing straight and tall like sky guards. The nearest long-life maker, the cedar tree, drapes its branches. The temperature rises and steam fills his lungs, cleansing him physically and spiritually. He hears the shaman dancing with his rattles outside the sweat lodge, and his head begins to bob while he dreams.

He dreams of recovery, of peace and purity surrounding him like a white fog. He is content, White Deer standing by his side. It is White Deer that long ago gave him instincts to survive and strength that is underestimated by others because he can also use tenderness and grace. The fog becomes gray. It turns red and the severed heads float in a lake of blood and the sound of thunder wakes him to the smell of smoke and the crackle of another great fire. Scrambling to the flap to see, he realizes how hot and sick he is and drops to his knees to vomit, powerless.

When he can stand, he sees that the house of blood is being burned. His people sing and dance the ghosts away, adding red cedar boughs to be rid of bad energy. He cleans his body, removing residue from the battle by scraping away his sweat with old, softened twigs and fresh yew leaves that were left by the slaves. Then he submerges himself into the cold creek.

Feeling clean, hollow and light, he approaches the village center.

"A feast for you, my son," his mother says coming to meet him. "A celebration to honor your bravery." She wipes her warm hand down the side of his face, and he closes his eyes, appreciating her touch.

Turning towards the beach, he sees preparations in front of the longhouses. "It looks like we have guests," he says.

"Our long-time friends from across the water . . . the ones with the smiling daughter?" she teases.

Snetlum grins. "Tolo," he says. Her name is Due Ductivid, but she adopted the nickname he gave her when they were children: Tolo, which means "to win." As a child, she was competitive and fun, challenging him especially in races and hand games. Now that they are older, it is not appropriate for him to sit next to her, but he will sit nearby where he can see her.

Mats are arranged to receive long alder bowls and plates of fresh salmon which has been split and roasted on sticks. Smoked clams, roasted venison, camas root, sun-dried salmon berries and seaweed in seal grease make a bountiful buffet. Unable to use his fingers for ten days after a battle, Snetlum skewers his food with a stick and uses a shell spoon.

Tolo comes to serve him tea from a large shell. "Made of dried huckleberry leaves," she says.

They keep eye contact for ten heartbeats as he reaches for the tea, his hands on hers. A new sparkle in Tolo's eyes reflects the firelight.

{ **2** }

The Elders

At death, a person's soul or essence journeys to live in the Land of the Dead, but their second spirit could become a ghost. The People are wary of ghosts and will take care of their departed for generations to stay in their favor. –Coast Salish

Snetlum is invited by his father to smoke with leaders of the village, a great honor. Dried native tobacco mixed with kinni-kinnick fills the pipe and it begins its trip around the circle. Snetlum sits between his father and uncle, looking proud.

His father will stifle that pride. "You will help build a new house to replace the one that was burned."

Snetlum stares into the fire, disappointed by his father's first words, having expected words of praise. Silently, he considers his response as he examines his father's stern face, jaw grinding rhythmically like the beat of a heart.

"Yes, father."

His father's jaw relaxes. He does not tell his son that he has been proud of him since the beginning. That he has prepared Snetlum to be a leader ever since he climbed the highest tree the day that Snetlum was born to place his afterbirth closest to the sky. He did not explain that the People will continue to test him to know if he is fit to lead. They will watch for signs of wisdom, fairness and willingness for balance rather than self-pride.

His uncle speaks next. "Let us post guards to watch for future raids. Also, runners should be sent to our friends so they may be prepared . . . in case there is retaliation."

Snetlum tries to hide his pride with a blank face as he imagines the story of his bravery being told across the water.

An elder speaks. "Two Klallam killed King George men as they came north out of Fort Vancouver, through Nisqually territory. They were trappers for Hudson Bay Company. We know one of them killed, named McKenzie."

Heads nod.

"They were going north to the trading post called Langley on the Fraser River."

The elder waits respectfully, giving time for thinking and the possibility of a response as the tang of tobacco smoke swirls. "The Klallam say they had been mistreated."

The others wait, sensing that the story is not finished. "Hudson Bay Company at Vancouver sent a war party to retaliate. The village they destroyed and the families they killed were not related to the two who killed the trappers."

Silence.

"King George men do not know us. They do not care to know us," Snetlum's father says. "They do not understand that we live in many different villages and have family ties with many different peoples." He pauses in thought. "We are forced to know the Whites because of their power. It is the way now. The shaman sees no other path unless Spirit Above makes them sick."

"What is the white man's heart?" another elder asks. "It seems that he wants and wants. He wants furs for the smallest price, he wants fish and meat. I hear that he wants our people to work for a few potatoes and scraps of cloth."

Snetlum's uncle speaks. "Hearing their talk is like trying to listen from the other side of a great thundering river. Their message is broken and garbled. They are not interested in knowing our thoughts."

Smoke surrounds them and the pipe is passed again and again. "They are not generous like Whidbey was," reflects an elder. "He gave us iron and copper for only a few fish. I still have the clapper he gave me," he shows a toothless grin.

"They do not need to be generous anymore," Snetlum's father says, refilling the pipe.

As twilight softens the sky, fish runs are discussed. Snetlum thinks on the story of Hudson Bay Company. He knows that his people will need to make a decision about the white invaders one day and he will likely be asked for his thoughts as a leader of the oldest Skagit village. He thinks first of his own family and his extended family within their longhouse, then of his village at Watsak Point (Snakelum Point). *How do we prepare ourselves for what comes?*

He considers the other large Skagit villages around the cove: Bla-satts (Long Point), P't-sa-tl-y (Coupeville) where descendants of *k'ek'edib* (the first human live), and around to D-Gubal-hole (San deFuca) on the north side (and Monroe's Landing). He also thinks of the Skagit people living on the next two coves to the north of his own. *My spirit helper, White Deer, please help us have the instincts to survive.*

In his mind, he flies with Hawk to see the other villages on the island. The closest, over the island's back to the west side and a bit south is the Suquamish led by his friend, Tslalakam. *We will remain side by side*, he thinks. He sees the Klallam encampment to the north of the Suquamish. *They are unpredictable.* He hopes they will not bring trouble. On the northeast shore are the Swinomish. Snohomish villages dominate the south part of the island, one at Bush Point and the largest "Digwadsh" (Rugged Nose) at Sandy Point with six longhouses and a cedar palisade to protect against marauding groups. *They will protect themselves.*

Every day, different Salish people come to visit from other places because of the island's location between three great waterways and three great rivers that empty into the water on its eastern shore. The stories that visitors bring tell him that the future is uncertain. *If we do not fight, what choices do we have? Let us make the choice to live. Spirit Above, protect us all, protect our home.*

* * *

"Father, your idea of an alliance marriage must be forgotten." He looks down at his father who sits on a log on the beach, repairing a fishing net. "I want Tolo for my wife." He squints from the sun but holds his father's stare.

His father motions for him to sit. "The alliance marriage will be good for our village."

Snetlum sits. In his mind's eye, he sees Tolo smiling at him over her shoulder, the two long braids created by her grandmother always hanging down her back. "Our world changes, father. You know it. Allow me to have a few years of the life I choose before the unknown changes everything."

The face of Snetlum's father scrunches in pain. His chest hurts. He calls for his pipe, and once it is lit and he sees the smoke rising, he tells his spirit helpers that he does not like change from tradition. He does not like it at all. *What will happen to the young people without tradition?*

The wedding celebration and feast take place in winter as all ceremonies do. It is held at the Potlatch House of Tolo's family, and she has weaved her own hair into one braid. Together, they sprinkle tobacco into the fire to the north, south, east and west, then wash their hands in the same cedar bowl to forget their lives before marriage. The feast is a hearty one followed by dancing, and Tolo shows her husband how well her feet can dance because of him. Snetlum must tell himself that a warrior is not allowed to giggle.

* * *

Tolo stops drinking the tea that avoids having a child. Their son Kwass-Ka-Nam is born into the salt water of Penn's Cove, and a great potlatch is planned for the following winter. The added responsibility of being a father changes Snetlum's perspective. He prays that his family and people have long lives, content in their homes with abundance all around, and are able to adjust to a changing world.

He teaches Kwass-Ka-Nam how to live: to fish, to hunt, and to paddle in strong currents. He teaches his son how to bail a canoe, even in a storm, and how to get back into the canoe when it turns over. In the annual games, Kwass-Ka-Nam excels at several competitions, especially in running. He learns to hunt with a child's size bow and arrows. When he reaches twelve years old, Snetlum teaches him how to make an adult-size bow. They walk together through the woods listening to the trees and smelling the wet needles until they find the yew tree that waits for Kwass-Ka-Nam. It is the one with the perfect strength, width and natural bend for his new bow.

$$\{\ 3\ \}$$

Fort Nisqually, 1833-39

Like every year in June, the camas sends a stalk up out of the ground a foot tall and shows pale blue blossoms. The women get their digging sticks and begin their harvest, onion-shaped bulbs the size of a hickory nut. It's also berry-picking time, salmonberries and strawberries. The women work their way through the bushes and fields, folded baskets under their arms ready to fill. Some of the men go south to trade, along the bottom of Puget Sound.

It's 1833 and Snetlum leads a group, which includes his thirteen-year-old son Kwass-Ka-Nam, south towards a new Hudson Bay Company trading post in Nisqually territory near the mouth of Sequalitchew Creek. Its location provides a refuge for traders and trappers who travel north from Fort Vancouver on the Columbia River. Word has spread that they want otter and beaver hides. Snetlum's group paddle their six canoes packed with beaver pelts, relieved to be trading in the south away from marauding groups of the north.

The weather has turned warm. Snetlum folds his cedar blanket to store beside him and pulls his cedar hat lower over his eyes against glare from the water, the tops of his knees glistening in the sun. He wonders if he will get a fair deal for the skins they carry. Hopefully, he will be able to obtain muskets, their only means of protection in the new way of life.

At the bottom of Puget Sound, they pull up to shore and find a newly roofed storehouse that looks like a small longhouse, "Nisqually House." The surrounding area is populated with summer mat houses and campfires of the Steilacoom, Puyallup and Klallam people who have come to trade. Snetlum sees the nearly completed Fort Nisqually further inland and a third building under construction. It is a beautiful site with abundant trees and prairie for grazing stock and views of mountains all around.

As the hammers pound, Snetlum sees several members of the Sequalitchew bent over to tend a garden of tiny new sprouts and a King George man just beyond, examining wildflowers on the prairie. *It is good,* he thinks to himself. *They work together.* All the Hudson Bay forts are known to be neutral locations where people from different villages may get to know each other without fear of war.

He sees that the men have beards, causing him to remember the Kwakiutl having beards and the act of removing those bearded heads. He is dealing with the angst in his stomach telling him not to trust these men when a man called McDonald comes to speak with him. McDonald sees the beaver pelts in the canoes and uses trade talk (Chinook Jargon) and hand motions, waving the skins out of the canoes to examine them for cleanliness and lack of infestation. He is pleased to see that they have been stretched and properly treated and dried. "Hiyu?" (Many?)

Snetlum shows both hands six times and one hand one time. He makes motions as if shooting with a long gun. "Pop pop," he says to make it known that he wishes to purchase muskets.

"Sixty-five," McDonald says, making a motion to wait. He goes into the storehouse and a man called Ouvrie helps him bring out two long guns, two pounds of gun powder for each, two pounds of shot for each and a dozen flint.

Snetlum points with his finger at each long gun and holds up one finger, "Hiyu."

Ouvrie looks to McDonald.

"Keep him happy," McDonald says. "We want him to come back."

As Ouvrie goes to get another long gun, Snetlum's cousin points out a man sitting outside the storehouse wrapped in a blanket. His leg is naked, propped up on a stump. "How would your mother feel about such a blanket?" his cousin asks.

Snetlum approaches the man to touch the blanket. He sees that it is very tightly woven wool, thicker than his own wool blankets made of mountain goat fibers and special dog hair from the dogs that the Snohomish raise. He also sees that the man's leg has a gash that has been sewn shut, red and swollen. The young man from the wildflowers arrives to check on his patient and says, "Doc Tolmie," extending his hand with a smile. "Cultus axe (bad axe)," he says, nodding towards the man's leg.

Snetlum is aware of the white man's gesture and shakes his hand. He pinches the corner of the blanket and shows two fingers to the man Ouvrie.

As they pull away with their three long guns and two blankets, Snetlum thinks of how Fort Nisqually is so new. He imagines how it will change with more white settlers coming from the east.

At home, he enjoys the security of his village enclosure. It is a four-hundred-foot long wall of protection, thirty feet high. There is great excitement over the fire weapons. He sees the delight of the women who gather to inspect the blankets and then their envy. Thankful to be called away, he attends an elders' meeting.

"Now that we have guns, might we trade for some of their tobacco?" an elder asks. "Also, our women would like some beads and a mirror or two and we would also like more iron knives."

"We must take salmon and deer meat, grandfather, along with more hides," Snetlum says. "They said they would trade for as much food as we could bring to them."

Snetlum is suddenly weary, knowing that since there are more items available to trade, his people will want to trade more . . . and raids between villages to steal goods to use as trade will become more frequent. *Our traditions will change,* he thinks to himself. *Traditions have guided us since the beginning. Without them, we will be like the salmon who forgets its spawning home.* In the longhouse, he struggles on his sleeping mat that night, fighting the King George men in his dreams, and when the floor becomes a lake of blood with severed, bearded heads, he wakes with a start, knowing that their hauntings have begun.

He returns to the fort in August and finds three hundred camped on the beach, this time including Suquamish, Snohomish and Tillamook people. Hudson Bay Company at Nisqually is growing fast, and they have begun to accept some Native trade items such as baskets, mats, and strings of shells that can be used as money to trade with other Native groups.

When he returns home, he is told that King George men from Hudson Bay Company had been on the island while he was away. They walked the prairies with a long metal rope and left wooden sticks in the ground. Tslalakum had the sticks removed and burned.

And so it begins, Snetlum thinks. *How long do we have?*

* * *

The Black Robes, April 1839

Standing in the field outside Simon Plamandon's cabin on the Cowlitz River, Father Blanchet's heart thrums to the sound of his own voice singing Christian hymns that have been translated into Chinook Jargon. It is the accompaniment of the sweet Indian choir that has brought tears to his eyes. Father Demers is there, too. With a gift of languages, he has translated a dictionary and mission handbook of prayers and hymns into Chinook. Father Blanchet created a Sahale stick (stick from God) to use for instruction, also known as the Catholic Ladder. It is drawn on a piece of wood and is read from the bottom to the top like a totem pole, marked to indicate the centuries and years of history in the Bible from creation to present in a series of pictographs with Earth on the bottom and Heaven at the top.

The priests had been thrilled to see the first few Native people appear for Mass at the cabin of Simon Plamandon and his wife, Thas-e-muth, daughter of the great Cowlitz leader Scanewa. Twenty-two arrived, some from as far away as Whidbey Island. Now their summer mat houses on frames populate Simon's farm. The widespread respect for Simon had called them to come.

Simon Plamandon, a French Canadian from Quebec, had been a trapper at Fort Astoria since he was 16. Captured by the Cowlitz, he negotiated his release, became friends with leader Scanewa, and married his daughter. When Scanewa was killed, Simon inherited much of his holdings, including the expectation of leadership until Scanewa's sons were old enough to do it themselves. It was Simon who had first petitioned for Catholic priests through Hudson Bay Company. When he sent out word for the Indians to come, they came.

The regalia and symbols that the priests use in their ceremonies make it look like the Black Robes know about the unseen Power of the Spirit world. They come to learn about the secrets of walking with the Great Spirit as a friend. Snetlum, his son, and others from Whidbey Island including Tslalakum of the Suquamish and Witskalatche of the Snohomish come too.

Instruction is for a week. Bible stories, prayers, songs, and repeat and repeat until each of the leaders can teach their own people using the small Catholic Ladder they receive as a gift. The last day is baptisms, both priests standing in the creek, each with a helper for the dunking. Simon's wife is first, receiving her new name, Veronica. Then leader Sealth who will become known as Chief Seattle receives the name Noah. Witskalatche is named John, and Snetlum's son receives the name George. It is Native custom to receive a new name at important moments in life, and Snetlum likes the name George. It fits with his new plan for the alignment of his village with the King George men.

As Snetlum paddles home with his group, he thinks of the constant praise, prayer and singing over many days as something like the spirit quest of his youth, and he recognizes the Power of blending the practices of the Black Robes with that of his People.

At his village, the leaders gather around to hear about the Black Robes' secrets. His father and uncle do not sit as straight as they once did against the power of gravity. Snetlum reminds the council of their talk the first time he smoked the pipe with the leaders. "I remember that one of our elders said that he did not know the white man's heart."

Many heads nod.

"Yes," his uncle says. "We agreed that their words are confusing and sometimes not to be trusted."

"I have listened to the Black Robes speak," Snetlum says. "For the first time, white men seem to speak on our side of the river." There is pause as heads nod. "When they talk of the Great Spirit and know life after death and tell the stories from His book, it is as though our hearts understand each other."

"Will you tell us their secrets?"

"Yes. Their message is for all of us, including the women and children, and I have listened well."

Before sleep, Snetlum's eyes climb to the top of his precious Catholic Ladder, hoping to get above his bad dreams, praying for relief from the ghosts who continue to haunt him, those heads that float in the sea of red.

$$\{\ 4\ \}$$

Father Blanchet, 1840

The dead do not leave us. It is we who are in the darkness. We do not see them, but they see us. They are living near us, transfigured into light and power and love. --Karl Rahner, 20th Century Catholic Theologian

Snetlum's mother and aunts carefully dress his father in his best clothes and ceremonial hat and wrap him in his warmest blanket at death. The shaman has been to the Spirit world to find the elder's wandering soul and was unable to bring him back to the living. Now he fasts and prays and sings and dances to clear the path for the soul's travel. The leader's body lies in the longhouse for several days while the village mourns and fasts, then is taken from the house through a hole in the wall.

"I am too old to change," he had told Snetlum when he became ill. "I want to visit the Spirit world of our ancestors. I am not a bad man. I did not tell Jesus Christ to die for me."

The shaman officiates and the village drummer sounds the hollow echo of their loss as the family places his body in his small canoe along with his treasures so he will want for nothing in the Land of the Dead and will not linger for any valuables left behind. Snetlum's vision blurs as he places his father's adze and spear into the canoe, arranging them at his father's left side. "I have sharpened your weapons and tools, father," he says, "so they will be ready for use when you need them." He straps the knife to his father's waist and fits the club near his right hand, bow and quiver of arrows on his chest. His mother brings copper ornaments and shell beads, status items he has enjoyed as a respected leader, her gnarled fingers arranging them about his head.

The fishing net is placed at his father's feet, and Snetlum remembers he and his father stretching it across from this small canoe to his uncle's canoe resulting in such a large catch of fish that they could not load it. They'd had to drag it to shore through the water. His throat catches. He feels more vulnerable with his father's death, knowing that their way of life will come to an end, especially with the passing of their elders.

The canoe is hoisted up into the fork of a tree, safe from violation and so his spirit can fly away. Holes have been punched into the bottom to let the rain out and they put a smaller canoe upside down over the top for protection. The People are wary of ghosts and will take care of their departed for generations to stay in their favor. When the blankets or canoe deteriorate, the body will be rewrapped and the canoe repaired, but only with the guidance of the shaman for the sake of safety from ghosts.

It is a sad time in the village. They will not speak his father's name to ensure that his soul will not be confused and think he is being called and attach to the living. They will eat only dried foods during mourning and sprinkle a bit of his father's favorite dried salmon and a pinch of tobacco into the fire to sustain him in the Spirit world. The memorial potlatch will be held during the next winter.

Snetlum begins to waver in his teaching from the Black Robes. The old native ways feel familiar and right. It causes him to question himself as a leader. As he sits on the bank above *Su-suk-us*, the clam and mussel bed of his village, he watches the women and slaves digging clams as they always have and remembers his father's words from his childhood. *We must learn from our ancestors. They have shown us what works best.*

In his sweat lodge with his spirit helpers, Hawk and White Deer, he wonders how to prepare his sons. He cannot see a future. His father's teaching: *Always remember that the earth was your first teacher,* does not seem helpful at the moment.

* * *

On May 28, 1840, as Snetlum continues to battle his thoughts about the future, the Black Robe Blanchet arrives at Tslalakum's Suquamish Village on the west side of Whidbey Island. He has come at Tslalakum's request.

At his arrival, villagers run, frightened, calling "Qui vive! Qui vive!" (Who are you!).

Tslalakum wears only his apron and the wooden Cross that hangs from his neck to greet the priest. "We were attacked this morning by the Klallam. Two Klallam were killed, and most in my village have not seen a Black Robe before." Tslalakum helps the priest from his canoe. "These Klallam do not know God nor pray to Him." His hand goes to his Cross. "It is the Cross that hangs from my neck that protects me."

The next day is Friday. An altar is prepared using mats like an open summer shelter and a rough plank serves as a table for sacred vessels. A large Catholic Ladder 6 feet long and 15 inches wide is attached to a mat and hoisted up a pole for all to see. The priest makes the sign of the Cross and everyone who has gathered, women and children included, make the same sign, surprising him. He begins to sing the first couplet of a Christian song in Chinook jargon and the group continues the song to its end. Blanchet is amazed that they know the song. Touched by the beautiful innocent harmony, his tears tumble. He feels the greatness of his Lord who has done this work through the seeds that were planted on the Cowlitz.

When Snetlum and his group arrive, Father Blanchet has changed from his black robe into his surplice, a tunic of white that hangs to his knees with wide, wing-like sleeves. His black stole hangs from his neck like banners straight down to his knees with symbols of the Cross decorating the bottoms. Clearly, the teaching has begun.

Snetlum sits with a sea of Suquamish, Skagit and Snohomish. He looks at the large Catholic Ladder, impressed that the Black Robes know their history from six thousand years ago. There is Power in that. When the Klallam come, saying they want peace, Father Blanchet encourages the smoking of the pipe, and Snetlum feels the nudge of White Deer. *Could an alliance with whites protect us?*

Father Blanchet comes to see Snetlum the following day in his longhouse of split-cedar planks. It is two-hundred feet in length and located in the center of a row of longhouses with shed roofs, smaller houses on each end. The priest is led through Snetlum's private entrance near the center of the building, a space that indicates his high status. The insulating mats have been recently removed after their long winter, and the opening overhead displays a blue sky above their firepit. They sit on a pile of fresh folded mats. Father Blanchet prays for Snetlum and his wife Tolo, asking God to increase their faith and the reach of their influence to others. He praises Snetlum for having only one wife, the Christian way.

For Sunday Mass, four hundred people gather. A cry is heard, and everyone stands to look--a great wooden Cross twenty-four feet long is being carried to its hole in the ground. Once it is set, they all follow Father Blanchet's example and prostrate them-selves at its feet. The priest stays with his face pressed to the ground, so very humbled by the love of these people and the gift of knowing that his efforts matter after years of teaching.

During the baptisms, all but the babies repeat after the priest, "Yes, we believe in God who created all things. Yes, we believe in Jesus Christ, who came to redeem us." Women line up with their young children, wanting the medicine of baptism. One hundred twenty-two frightened, crying children are bap-tized on the exceedingly warm day. Snetlum hears a mother say to her son, "You have a Protector who is Jesus Christ now. He is the son of the Great Spirit."

Snetlum feels the possibility of a future because of Father Blanchet. When the priest gives him his own, larger Catholic

Ladder on parchment, he is honored and offers to transport the priest home in his own canoe. From then on, Father Blanchet's reports to Catholic authorities will include comments about the "mission" on Whidbey Island.

On the evening of Snetlum's return, a flock of ducks are busy eating the small fish along the shore. He watches as the village quietly erects poles and supports to hold up their duck-catching nets. When the ducks congregate closer together in the dark, fires are lit on shore and the people make noise. Ducks fly toward the fire, are caught in the net and fall into the water to be retrieved. Snetlum prays that if his spirit flies toward Heaven one day rather than to the Land of the Dead like his ancestors, he will not be lost or alone but will be retrieved by the glory of Jesus Christ.

{ **5** }

Ebey Wedding, 1843
Missouri

Movement in my peripheral vision, a wave of unexplained emotion, a confusing scent: these are signs that a ghost is nearby, a spirit who gains energy from the local environment. But the Ebey family tells me that it all began in Missouri . . .

A moment to herself, Rebecca runs her fingers over the precious headboard of her bed which was created and carved for her by her father. He had given it to her on her 16th birthday and painted it blue at her request. She treasures anything made by her Pa, anything that he made time to accomplish that was not a necessity, considering all the work that needed to be done on the farm from dawn to dark. It is a treasure made even dearer now that he has begun a chronic cough, a sure sign of the infamous malady so prevalent called consumption.

She tries to squelch her feeling of abandoning her family and bends down to kiss the headboard, saying goodbye to her youth. *It was actually gone awhile ago,* she thinks to herself. *I am 21 after all, just a few years away from being a spinster.* Shuddering at the thought, she kisses it again to say goodbye to her home and her life with her parents. She will be married before the day is over, never to sleep in this bed again. With one more stroke of her hand over the carved scrolling oak leaves, she tells her fingertips to remember and walks out the door.

Her parents, James and Harriet Davis, have the wagon packed with food items for the wedding reception on this brisk October 3rd, including two large cakes along with Rebecca's trousseau in several dust-colored carpet bags. While she rides in the front under a lap blanket between her mother and father, her older brothers James and John and younger siblings Thomas and Martha climb into the back. John has always been the serious one and has grown sensitive to others' behaviors since James' head injury. They had been felling trees when a branch hit a snag and grazed James as it fell. In truth, he was lucky to be alive. Now James has good days and bad days and can become emotional at times. Since their father's health is in question, John takes a larger role in the family which includes watching over his brother.

Young and wiry, Thomas is a funny, nonstop tease, often turning somber moments into a happy distraction. Even now while riding in the back of the wagon, he is busy poking through the bags. He sneaks a finger into the side of a cake for a taste of frosting and gabbles away at how they will be losing Rebecca. When James tells him to shut it, he takes the harmonica from his pocket and sticks it into his mouth without playing, his shaggy dark hair covering his face.

Martha rides along with starry eyes. Being the youngest, she has been allowed to be a romantic, often with her head in the clouds. Today is the most romantic she can imagine. She hasn't thought about how the chores will be different at home once Rebecca is gone. Their mother Harriet will let her enjoy the day, save the tantrum for tomorrow.

The wedding will take place at "The Cabins," known locally as "The Cabins of White Folks," the first settlers among the local Indians of Adair County, Missouri. A gentle breeze carries the first bite of early winter as Rebecca and her family step down from their wagon and enter the warmth of the log cabin of Jacob and Sarah Ebey (Eebee).

The cabin is full of well-wishers: parents, aunts and uncles, brothers and sisters, cousins, neighbors and their friends, the Crockett family, all inside. Rebecca is prim, dressed in white on the arm of her father as they walk together from Ebey's bedroom. Her dress, not entirely white because of it being hand-made of linsey-woolsey, was created by her with a fitted bodice and decorated by her mother with lace on the neckline and sleeves. She carries a nosegay of blue vervain and late purple asters tied in the same lace. Several asters peek out of the great bulbous knot of dark hair high on the back of her head which accentuates her long, elegant neck. Her pretty, heart-shaped face is aimed at her father until she looks away to find Isaac. He waits for her in front of the new Methodist Pastor Jacob Ebey, Isaac's brother. Rebecca's smile lights up her eyes and the entire room, enhanced by the rose color that happens on her cheeks.

Young Pastor Ebey greets everyone with a wide grin. The devout Methodist couple declare their intent to marry which is received with boisterous cries and statements of approval and support. After prayers, proclamations and a short sermon, vows are exchanged: "Rebecca Whitley Davis, do you take Isaac Neff Ebey to be your husband?"

Rebecca studies his face, such a handsome, intelligent, kind face. His dark mustache and beard are carefully trimmed, every hair in place. He stands patiently as if he already trusts that she will make the right decision. As if he knows her that well. For the first time, she notices that his left nostril is a bit higher than the right, surprised she hadn't seen that before. She wonders what else she will learn about him for the rest of her life.

"I do," she says.

Not big on ceremony, Rebecca is thankful when Isaac's rough hands finally slide a simple silver wedding band up the length of her finger. Pastor says, "They are no longer two, but one. What God has joined together, let man not separate." Isaac bends to kiss her which creates a frenzy of cheers. Embarrassed, she hangs onto him, refusing to let go of his hand. Somehow, together, they light a unity candle. The final blessing puts everything right.

A fiddler plays a merry jig and dancing begins while food is set out in the kitchen. Elders eat first, then a bottle is quietly passed between the men. Children scamper and skitter from the kitchen to the dancefloor and back again, not sure where they want to be.

Rebecca dances, feeling Isaac's arms around her. "Why does music turn children into little animals, do you think?" she asks.

"I suppose it does not happen often enough that they know how to react, and clearly, the attention of the adults is elsewhere."

He grabs a young cousin who is running by and sends them all outside where they attack each other at the old Fort Clark next door. It has been abandoned for ten years, ever since the end of native unrest in the area. Isaac's father had helped end that unrest with his participation in the Blackhawk War, having commanded a company in the same battalion as Abraham Lincoln.

After a few traditional Kentucky square dances are called and folks dance enough to reinforce their roots and memories of earlier days, the merriment inside the cabin begins to quiet and conversations turn to the most popular topic of the year--Oregon fever. The newspapers had been full of it just five months before the wedding when a thousand people had left from Independence, Missouri, to head west. The excitement had made the bottom of Isaac's feet itch.

Samuel Crockett clamps his hand onto Isaac's shoulder. He's a dark-haired, bearded young man with deep, close-set eyes and Isaac's closest, most reliable friend.

"I'm going," he says. "Headed West next spring, my friend. Have you heard about Willamette Valley? The richest, most fertile lands imaginable. There for the taking."

Isaac stares at him for a moment. "Well . . . that's a sorry . . . state of affairs." A slight stoppage in Ebey's words occurs when he is tired or emotional, and Samuel has surprised him. "Going without *me*. You'll probably get lost or shot in some dispute without *me*. We'll . . . never hear from you again."

"Why don't you and Rebecca come along?" Samuel smiles at Rebecca who sits next to Isaac. "You know, start your home in the promised land?"

Rebecca is already proud of her new husband, elected sheriff of Adair County for the past three years. She does not want Samuel to influence his thinking. "I suppose you want someone to cook and take care of you on the trip, Mr. Crockett," she says, hoping that she has put the idea to rest. She goes to join the ladies in the kitchen where they are looking for Thomas. Half of a cake is missing,

* * *

Isaac leans toward Samuel. "Between you and me, it crossed my mind to go last spring . . . but now I'm married, and well . . . it changes things. I'm an apprentice at the law office in town. Did you know? I'm learning how to draw up contracts and wills."

"And I thought your black suit and tightly trimmed hair and beard on that handsome shrewd face were just for the wedding. Now I know better. You look the part."

Isaac shrugs. "Also, father needs me to help with the farm." He shakes his head. "Rebecca changes everything. Marriage will keep me content at home."

Rebecca knows that her husband loves adventure. He has dreams about the future, lots of them, always wanting to make things better. He is thoughtful, honest and has good judgment. People trust and respect him even though he's only 25 years old. She hopes and prays that their plan to have children will be enough to keep him at home.

{ **6** }

Samuel Crockett, 1844-46

One in five Americans say they have encountered a ghost. –Science News Explores

Before his wedding, Ebey had tucked away several newspaper articles: *"Oregon Country is a land of pure delight in the woody solitudes of the West,"* and *"Oregon fever is raging in almost every part of the Union."* Now, when he receives a letter from Samuel who is on the trip and sits to read it, Rebecca plunks their newborn son Eason into the crook of his arm like an anchor.

Samuel's wagon train is led by Colonel Gilliam who fought along with Ebey's father in the Blackhawk War and served as Missouri State senator.

"They've got eighty wagons, Rebecca," Ebey says. "Over three hundred people. Can you imagine that huge train moving? At least six oxen pulling each wagon, people walking behind,

{ 35 }

followed by a herd of livestock with riders on horseback keeping them together."

"Seems like a great undertaking," she says, kneading enough dough for six loaves of bread. She means that it sounds like a huge challenge, but Ebey hears her meaning as a wonderful undertaking.

"Indeed! And Samuel is one of them, on horseback I mean. He's hired on with a Mr. Gerrish to help herd his stock."

"I imagine the trip would be quite costly if he hadn't," she says. *Don't say it,* she tells herself, but she can't stop. "Good thing he does not have a family to take care of."

The next few letters read like adventures from a book. Ebey is intrigued, imagining the scenes:

Gunfire woke us in the night, and I joined the posse to rescue horses and cattle that were stolen. We tracked the culprits for miles in the rain through the mud and into the rugged country and found the cows, or what was left of them. They'd been butchered. We continued to search for the horses, wading in mud up to our knees, getting more miserable with every mucky mile until we couldn't track anymore.

We all needed coffee and breakfast including the horses, and we headed back to camp covered in mud but feeling good about having made such a great effort. When we arrived, we came face to face with the missing horses. They had wandered back into camp on their own. It wasn't as funny as some folks seemed to think.

* * *

To make the large wagon train more manageable, Colonel Gilliam breaks it into smaller groups and appoints thirty-year-old Michael Troutman Simmons as leader of Samuel's group.

Originally from Kentucky, Simmons is a quick-tempered, big man who travels with his wife Elizabeth and four young sons and does not hesitate to speak his mind.

"Now that the Colonel has passed along his responsibility, he will be taking off to hunt buffalo whenever the urge strikes him," Simmons says. "Just watch."

Samuel can think of nothing better. "Maybe I should go with him."

"Not if you want to keep your job," Simmons says and rides to speak with George Bush.

Sometimes Simmons relies on the advice of 54-year-old George Washington Bush. Bush travels with his wife Isabella and five children in multiple wagons packed with nursery trees and seeds and a herd of livestock. An educated black man (half black) raised on a profitable farm in Missouri, he traveled extensively as a free trapper and had a relationship with Hudson Bay Company. He is a generous man, providing teams and supplies to some of the other families who want to go West but can't afford it on their own.

* * *

As the letters arrive, Ebey thinks that this is not the year to go West. Samuel writes that the spring weather is especially wet, and the wagons make unusually slow progress or no progress at all. Finding places to ford swollen rivers without losing livestock or wagons or people and constantly digging heavy, thick mud from under wagon wheels. It all takes time. Rain soaks them and their provisions though they are covered with oil cloth and double canvas covers the wagons. Dry wood becomes precious, and lighting a fire, though not always possible, is the greatest achievement of those days. Their ruined provisions and extra days on the trail require them to buy or trade for more supplies, forcing them to pay exorbitant prices.

In September, Ebey receives a letter that he does not share with Rebecca. Samuel writes on July 1 that they are only as far as Fort Laramie and are suffering with dysentery and rheumatism. The group leaders are now more focused on their destination than on trying to keep the groups together, and they are in bad shape, about to begin their struggle over the Rocky Mountains.

It is the last letter that anyone receives for a very long, worrisome time.

Snow comes early for Samuel's wagon train of six families, stopping it at the Dalles. They cannot continue. Dangerously low on provisions and Elizabeth Simmons soon to have their fifth baby, Samuel and the other young, unmarried men are sent ahead on horseback to get help. As the oldest in a family of six children, Samuel has grown up with a sense of responsibility, but having the lives of so many in his hands is daunting, and he rides with seriousness, thinking of those left behind. He reaches Oregon City on October 18.

From their makeshift camp, Simmons waits and watches, keeping one eye on Elizabeth. When he finally sees a series of canoes coming up the Columbia with Samuel in one, his throat catches. He allows himself a deep breath, not realizing how many days he has been holding it. The hired Indians beach the canoes and carry food up to the camp.

Simmons shakes Samuel's hand. "It's a hard thing, seeing your kids hungry," he says, his way of saying thank you.

"Gotta admit," Samuel says, "I was a little afraid we might find some of you dead by the time we got back."

"Can't be afraid," Simmons says. "As a Kentuckian, I'm not allowed to be afraid. Sick, starving, hurt maybe, but never afraid."

With help from the Indians and food in their bellies, they paddle down the Columbia River to Fort Vancouver, making one brief stop along the way for Elizabeth to have her baby on the riverbank.

* * *

British-owned Hudson Bay Company at Fort Vancouver is not allowed to assist Americans, but Bush persuades the chief factor, Dr. McLoughlin to help. He allows all six families to camp together at one of their cabins twenty miles east of the fort. They spend a year cutting cedar shakes to sell to the fort while looking for land to claim. With the help of local Indians and canoes, they travel from the Columbia up the Cowlitz River to the Indian portage between the Cowlitz and Chehalis Rivers called the Cowlitz Landing. From there, they work north using axes and ox-drawn sleds in nearly constant rain to cut a rough road through dense forest 58 miles to the Deschutes River and the southernmost point of Puget Sound. It takes them fifteen days of cold, wet exhaustion.

They build one house to share while building the others, and James McAllister, his wife and six children make their first house out of two gigantic cedar stumps growing side by side.

They burn out the middle and burn holes for shelving, scrape away the charcoal and put on a roof, making them snug in their cocoon. All the families settle within six square miles of each other and call their new home New Market, the first American settlement on Puget Sound, complete with a grist mill built by Simmons and Samuel.

Their closest neighbor is a village of the Steh-chass people of the Nisqually with three cedar-plank longhouses and about eight families in each. The Steh-chass believe that water has power and spirit, like all things. They call the series of water cascades 'tumtum' meaning 'heartbeat' since the water hitting the stones sounds like the drumming of a heart. The settlers appreciate the help they receive from the local Indians who include Nisqually leader Leschi and Duwamish/Suquamish leader Sealth (Chief Seattle).

Samuel writes home about the beauty, abundance and promise of the area, encouraging Ebey and his family to come. He explains that since 1818, Oregon Country north of the Columbia River and west of the Rockies has been called Vancouver District, jointly occupied by British and American trappers and settlers.

"It is a bit contentious between countries here. In fact, last year in '45, our government changed the name from Vancouver District to Lewis County, wanting to honor Meriwether Lewis, an American, rather than the British George Vancouver. It likely reflects the sentiment: British Hudson Bay Company trying to establish themselves everywhere they can, and Americans scrambling to make their own way."

{ 7 }

American "Boston Man,"
1841-47

Cedar, offered to the sacred fire during sweat lodge ceremonies and burned during prayers, eliminates evil spirits and connects the person with the spirit world. –a Native American belief

The Roman Catholic Church lists Whidbey Island as one of their missions on their roster and the priests come to lend support twice a year. Snetlum thought he would have constant support after bringing his people into the protection of the Church, and now he feels abandoned. He goes to his sweat lodge to pray for help. His prayer is answered with the arrival of Father Bolduc.

Filled with relief, Snetlum shows the priest the treasured Catholic Ladder on parchment left by Father Blanchet. "I have been using it."

"You have done well," Father Bolduc says, his hand on the leader's shoulder. "I can relieve you for a few days of lessons and prayers."

Snetlum is older now and enjoys the comfort of the fire, often dressed in a hide shirt with otter fur around the neck. Determined to keep Father Bolduc, he returns to his sweat lodge to speak with his spirit helpers. He feels the comfort of White Deer and the persistence of Hawk. *What does the priest need for him to want to stay?* As he warms, his head begins to nod, and the answer comes. He leaves the lodge with a quicker gait than normal, no time for the normal cleansing dunk in the creek, and he calls together the builders in the village. His son George is among them.

"We will build a house so the priest will stay," he says. "Put it on the hill near the Cross. It will be the Church of Jesus Christ. A priest will need to stay in such a house."

As the framework goes up and the outline of the future building is clear, Snetlum pulls the priest towards the Cross to the construction site. "It is your house, the church of the son of the Great Spirit, so you will stay now. We are building it like the King George houses at Nisqually, from logs, so you will feel at home."

Bolduc smiles, patting Snetlum on the back. "Very generous of you, Snetlum," he says, admiring the construction work. "I will ask the Church if I can be allowed to stay."

A few days later when the church is standing but unfinished, Witskalatche of the Snohomish arrives to speak with the priest. He was hired years earlier to run messages between the forts for Hudson Bay Company and comes with the message that Bolduc is needed in Victoria.

"I am sorry, Snetlum," Bolduc says. "I belong to the Church. They decide where I go." He gives a blessing and leaves in his canoe, headed north.

* * *

In June, Lieutenant Charles Wilkes, American commander of a U.S. Exploring Expedition, arrives in Penn's Cove in the tall ship *USS Vincennes* accompanied by the brig, *Porpoise*. From a distance, Wilkes sees the 24-foot cross perched on a hill and the beginning of a building that he thinks is a church. The homes of timber and planks are surrounded by large enclosures four hundred feet long made of planks placed upright in the ground thirty feet high like a fort.

Snetlum comes to greet him. He admires Wilkes' uniform and metal buttons and notices his long, narrow nose and chin. "Are you a King George man?" he asks.

"American," Wilkes says. "Lieutenant Wilkes to be exact, a 'Boston man.'"

They walk the beach, past fires burning in a ditch where fish and clams will hang to dry. "I see from marks on some of your people that you have suffered disease," Wilkes says.

"Yes, some of our people are at summer camps to collect berries," Snetlum explains, "but our population is diminished. There were many deaths here four years ago. I was told it is called flu."

The older men of the village gather to see the American "Boston Man" in uniform. Some wear only an apron despite light rain. Others wear a fibrous blanket over their shoulders attached with a wooden pin. Some leaders, like Snetlum, wear a leather shirt with fringe, decorated in beads and shells and leggings.

The women watch from a distance, not sure of the visitor's intent. Some wear cedar bark skirts and shawls. Others wear tunics showing embellishments of little brass bells, gifts from priests. A few have pierced noses decorated with a bone or wooden peg.

Lt. Wilkes looks out over the island. "I can see the influence of Fort Nisqually here," he says. "What are you growing in your fields besides wildflowers?"

"We did not plant the wildflowers. Camas grows among them. We plant potatoes and beans obtained from Fort Nisqually. We enjoy our potatoes." He leads Wilkes to the strawberry fields where he motions for Wilkes to help himself.

"Delicious," Wilkes says, his hands getting sticky with juice. "It is good that I left most of the crew on ship. They would have made short work of your strawberry fields."

As they approach the wall that surrounds the village homes, Wilkes asks about the need for such protection.

"We are attacked by people from the north, lately from those up the Fraser River," Snetlum says, leading him past the midden mounds toward the gate. "We have a few muskets to shoot between the planks." Snetlum's smile shows a few missing teeth. "Though we do not care to feel like prisoners." He points north and south. "We post a guard at each point of the entrance to the cove to give us warning and time to get inside. It gives us safety when we need it."

They walk inside the gate along the single row of cedar plank longhouses, each more than a hundred feet in length and approach Snetlum's house, larger than the rest. Wilkes admires the carved and painted cedar posts at the entrance, images of Salmon, Eagle, and Hawk. Inside, mats hang between family spaces with dormant firepits. The inside of the outer walls are lined with two layers of wide platforms, the top for storage of dried food, fresh berries, roots and such. The bottom platform is covered with mats for sleeping. During cold and wet weather, fish, meat and clams hang over some of the fires to dry. Posts in individual spaces are carved with images of the guardian spirits of family members.

Snetlum bends to open his bent-wood cedar box of treasures, also carved and painted. Reverently, he lifts a long roll of heavy paper and Wilkes helps him gently unroll it. He sees simple sketches of European houses, churches, and heavenly bodies.

"It helps me teach the way of the Black Robes," Snetlum says. "We follow the Black Robes and Jesus Christ, son of the Great Spirit."

Lt. Wilkes continues on with his exploring expedition, reporting that Whidbey Island is a viable agricultural site in the capable hands of the local Indians.

* * *

The following year, Snetlum watches and prays for the return of Father Bolduc or any priest for that matter and looks for evidence of them when he trades at Fort Nisqually but finds none. His enthusiasm fades along with his faith, and the church building near the Cross on the island sits unfinished. The day that Marcel Bernier arrives, a worker who had originally come with Father Blanchet, Snetlum feels a tiny ember of hope.

"Where is a priest?" he asks, looking across the water north and south for another canoe.

"There is no priest coming," Bernier says. "I have come alone to help you build your church."

Snetlum thinks, looking down at his naked foot on the beach. "If the church building is finished, will a priest come?"

"I cannot say. Priests are called to different places by the Church," Bernier says. "I am told you are doing good work here. The church wants to support you in your *own* efforts."

"I am not a priest," Snetlum says, looking away, "and I am tired." He walks away to his sweat lodge. Without his leadership, the villagers are not willing to work.

* * *

Mount Saint Helens blows her top on December 5, 1842, and ash and mud fill the Toutle River killing the fish. The Cowlitz people call it Lavelatla (Smoking Mountain), saying she is jealous again. Snetlum thinks the explosion of Lavelatla and the dead fish are a sign to stop trading at Fort Nisqually. Within a few months, a new Hudson Bay Company trading post open s in Victoria, north of Whidbey Island. He encourages his people to trade there instead. It is a much shorter trip. He would rather not be reminded of his disappointment in the priests by returning to Nisqually land.

* * *

Four years later, 1847, the unfinished church building stands in ruin and Whidbey Island has been removed from the Catholic roster as the location of a mission. Still, Snetlum walks to the Cross every day to embrace and kiss it. On the days when he lays prostrate at its foot, it is because the ghosts of the floating skulls have returned in his dreams.

A ship or canoe stops now and then, and a small group comes to shore for one reason or another: to stretch their legs, to build a fire, to hunt, to pick berries, to gather bird's eggs from the rocks. These visitors are tolerated because none of them stay. Snetlum is thankful that his island is not like the area near Fort Nisqually where settlers build houses.

When his grandson is born, George names him Helmits, and Snetlum becomes a respected elder of the village while George builds his influence as a leader. In the fall, when the berries have all been picked and the food stores have been processed and they are planning the winter potlatch to celebrate his grandson's birth, the dreaded changes begin. A white man arrives on the other side of the island near Tslalakam's Suquamish Village. He is quite pale, has a long beard and light blue eyes, and he builds a quick cabin of poles, plants some wheat among the camas, and is gone. They hope that he will not return.

His name is Glasgow, and he *will* return in the Spring at exactly the wrong time.

Leader Patkanim, 1848

The spirit world is more real than most of us realize . . . You should look at all things as Spirit, realize that we are family with all. –Floyd "Red Crow" Westerman, Native of South Dakota

Snetlum holds his grandson Helmits on his lap and tells their origin story to the children who have gathered around. He has always enjoyed telling the stories and now it feels like a responsibility. Who else will pass down the stories to help remember the old ways?

"There was a boy who did a bad thing. He was the son of a respected leader. These people lived across the water on the mainland. What the boy did was very bad, so he was put onto this island where no one else lived at the time. The boy lived alone here for a long time, and he became very lonely. He made himself a sweat lodge and prayed to his spirit guides and to

Spirit Above to bring him some friends because he was so lonely. In his dream, he was told to make a hedgerow of seaweed on the beach.

So, he gathered a big bunch of light brown seaweed and rolled it into a nice long row. The next morning, he found that the seaweed hedgerow had become ten young people, and a number of crows were there to teach them how to speak."

"Is that why some of us have brown hair instead of black?" a child asks.

Before he can ask the boy what *he* thinks, a runner comes with a message. "The white man is back. He is at his house."

Snetlum walks with his sons beyond the Cross and unfinished church over the back of the island to see the white man. Two white men are turning up soil to get ready to plant, a clear sign that they intend to stay. One is the man they saw earlier. The other is a stocky man with a trimmed beard and a heavy ridgeline of brows, making his eyes look badger-like, sunken into his head. A Snohomish woman comes from the cabin. Snetlum speaks to her.

"Who are these people?" he asks, nodding towards the whites.

"From Nisqually way," she says, waving south. Then she points at each one, "Glasgow, Rabbeson."

"Are they good men?"

The woman shrugs, looking away.

"I am Snetlum, of the Lower Skagit people on this island. You?"

"I am called Julia, a daughter of Patkanim, of the Snohomish and Snoqualmie. I know who you are. I have seen you at Fort Nisqually."

"Glasgow," Snetlum says, raising his hand toward the white man.

Glasgow stops working and turns to Julia. "Ask him about the Cross and the unfinished church," he says. "Is there a mission here?"

Snetlum has learned enough English to understand the question, and he turns away, not wishing to talk about it, especially with this man who seems to have no manners. *So it begins,* he thinks to himself.

Several days later, canoes begin to arrive on the island, a constant flow of them, group after group, people of the Duwamish, Snoqualmie, Snohomish, Klallam, Upper Skagit and most of the other groups from the area between Nisqually and the island. They camp as close to Penn's Cove as they can, 8,000 of them camped in their portable summer mat huts in a three-mile radius. Just like that, a huge village is formed. Although large groups have gathered here before, no one can remember ever having a gathering as large as this.

Snetlum asks one of the leaders why so many have come.

"We are called by Patkanim. This is the furthest location from Nisqually and a place without white settlers, until now." The leader nods towards Glasgow's tiny rough cabin.

Snetlum's gut tells him to be concerned and he speaks to his son George who has become more of a leader. "Patkanim is unpredictable, son. He is powerful. He wields his leadership influence over everyone from here to the top of Snoqualmie

Mountain. Listen well but hold back. He has been known to sacrifice others for his own personal gain. For him to call a group this large is a serious matter."

The visitors cut brush and add seaweed and nets to build a fence line for catching their dinner, the largest dinner ever known on the island. Their reinforced brush line reaches from Penn's Cove on the east side of the island over its back to the shore on the other side towards Townsend Land. A group begins in the south with their dogs and whippers. They drive the deer, running and leaping with every other living thing on the ground that can run into the brush line as the arrows fly. Sixty deer and their animal friends and a sea of red salmon roast on fires all along the beach, the blue and lavender flames of burning driftwood a comfort since time began.

Snetlum, wearing his cross around his neck and his ceremonial copper earrings, sits with other leaders and shamans from nearby villages and observes the scene. He wonders how his ancestors would feel about the large group, proud or afraid? Its power is infectious like a parasite, and he watches as it grows among the people. One thing he knows for sure, change is here, and he must decide if he is for it or against it. He would like to avoid making a stand against Patkanim. No leader wants to make a target of their village for Patkanim's wrath. Snetlum feels his spine tighten, his nerves on edge. His memory of the bloody cabin and all those severed heads flashes from his past. It was necessary at the time. He hopes it will not need to be repeated. The thought of adding to his nightmares makes him shudder, but it is a price he is willing to pay to protect his family.

Family and village groups gather at fires for their food. As with all gatherings, singing, drumming and dancing begin, each person dancing their own spirit dance. They dance with whale bone clubs or hatchets, sometimes lunging with their weapon. Here and there a long rifle is reflected in the firelight. Snetlum knows a war dance when he sees one.

When the drums change to call for quiet, leaders gather closer to the center. A few stand to speak about the strength of the People having come together, the joy of the ancestors and the presence of all their spirit helpers.

Patkanim stands and waits to speak. He has cropped hair with a flat beret on his head and a sharp sloping nose. When he has the attention of all the other leaders, he speaks out in a large voice. "The time has come to rid us of the white intruders," he says. "They come to make farms south of Nisqually at the Willamette. More and more come and stay. They will be here, in your village, soon. I say we attack Fort Nisqually now, drive away the King George men. Then we rid ourselves of the Boston men. Our acts will discourage newcomers. We will divide up their goods and go back to the old ways."

"We need to act now," says John Taylor of the Snohomish. "I have been to the Willamette Valley and have seen the American "Boston Men." I say we act while we still can."

"If they overrun us," Patkanim says, "they will send us away on fire-ships to a distant place where the sun never shines, and we will be left there to die."

Another leader stands. "Or become their slaves. I say strike fear in the white man's heart to avoid future troubles."

Patkanim continues. "If we take the fort at Nisqually, it will unite all the southern people and discourage others from coming."

Chew-see-a-kit, a leader of the Steilacoom known at Fort Nisqually as Gray Head stands. "We have always been attacked by the Snoqualmie and Snohomish. They have constantly made raids on us, killing, robbing and taking my people as slaves . . . It stopped when the Boston Men came with their cattle and planted fields. We will not attack them."

A Duwamish leader stands. "My people occupy the country between the Nisqually and the Snohomish, and *we* will protect you."

Chew-see-a-kit shakes his head. "I would rather have one rifle with a Boston man behind it as a protector than all of the whole Duwamish."

During angry debate, Snetlum's thoughts mirror those of Chew-see-a-kit. His people have learned much from the Fort Nisqually people and from the Black Robes. He thinks it is not possible to stop the Whites from coming no matter what they do. On the other hand, his people have not felt the desperation of being overrun that others are experiencing. Not yet, anyway.

"Let us prove our seriousness by killing the two who are here on the island," Patkanim says, nodding toward the cabin on the hill. "Chew-see-a-kit will see that we are serious and are able to protect his people."

Snetlum looks for Glasgow and Rabbeson, but they seem to be gone, along with a small canoe. Glasgow's woman Julia stands near her father, acting like she knows nothing. Torches are lit and Glasgow's house is burned to the ground.

* * *

As the sky begins to lighten, George Snetlum dunks himself into the cold water off the spit of Snakelum Point and swims a bit. It is his morning prayer and time with the Great Silence. He sees canoes beginning to leave the island in groups, causing his mind to swim like his body, thinking about alliances and enemies.

His father warms himself at the fire after having taken his own quick splash.

"Has there ever been such a large gathering as last night, father?"

Snetlum thinks awhile, gazing into the flames. "There was a large group that came together when I was a young man," he says, "nothing like this. A time when the Kwakiutl attacked the Lummi people, stole slaves as usual, but one was a young girl. She was a cousin of ours. Her father called for help from the Lower Skagit, the Upper Skagit, the Snohomish and all the Lummi people to get her . . . to get all those back who had been stolen, but his daughter was the real reason. We were more than twenty canoes, nothing like last night."

"Did *you* go?" George asks.

"I was known as a warrior then," Snetlum says. "I was expected to go. A woman stood on the top of a house at the Kwakiutl village, screaming in our language to kill the Kwakiutl. We knew she was a captive and wanted to be rescued."

"Did you get our cousin back?" George asks.

"No," Snetlum says. "We had only bows and arrows. The Kwakiutl had guns. We killed many, but some of us were also killed. We could not find the young Lummi daughter or save the woman on the roof."

That night, Snetlum hears the woman screaming in his sleep, but this time, she screams not just for herself, but for all of them.

{ **9** }

Going West, 1848

Other than murder, what makes a ghost? . . . a broken heart.
–Legends of America

Another son to keep Ebey at home is born in 1846, Jacob "Ellison." To Rebecca, the new baby seems just in time since Samuel continues to send letters about the progress in Puget Sound, activating Ebey's imagination. He reads that two Americans, Edmund Sylvester and Levi Smith have built a cabin eight miles north of New Market at Budd's Inlet. They have livestock and a garden, and their Indian neighbors have a village there, Bus-chut-hwud "frequented by black bears." A well-known, important Indian leader named Sealth (Seattle) spends his winters there. "This place will continue to develop," Samuel writes, "with or without you." It sounds like an ultimatum to Ebey.

In June, Oregon Country belongs to the United States through the Oregon Treaty with Britain. The dividing line is drawn at the 49th parallel. Hudson Bay Company can continue to do business as part of the deal and has rights to navigate the Columbia River and continue in the fur trade.

Ebey remembers Samuel's previous letter, how Americans are working hard "to make their own way." He wants to be one of those Americans "making their own way" on American soil. Rebecca feels his shift. He still works the farm, practices law, participates in local government, but as more friends go West, his spirit fades. Rebecca sees his energy wane and his attention wander. She hopes it will pass.

After Ellison's first birthday, when it's too late in the year for Ebey to begin a trip, Rebecca folds laundry in the living room while Ebey reads his letters from Samuel . . . again.

"Go," she says, snapping a pillowcase.

"Go where?"

"Head West like all the others. Go find us a dream," she says, turning away to fold a sheet and hide her worry.

Ebey's mouth drops open.

She looks at his face, waiting for a reply. "I can see that you are hurting," she says. "I have no right to keep you here. Go find us a home in paradise."

He stands to wrap his arms around her, his breath a bit ragged as he takes in her clean scent. "You have every right to 'keep' me," he says. "I love being kept."

"Well, I may not *want* to keep you if you do not go after your dream. You have turned into a shadow, Mr. Ebey. I want my energetic husband back, even if he will be far away."

"Let's . . . wait and . . . decide this winter," he says, but she can see his mind already working, planning the trip. Clearly, he is excited to go.

* * *

The following spring, as he prepares to leave, Ebey learns that gold is discovered at Sutter's Mill on American River near Coloma in California. He sees it as a sign that he is meant to go, to find gold and make a comfortable life for his family in a healthy environment. Everything he could want for his family is on the west coast, waiting to be claimed. He is determined with every breath to be successful.

He brings Eason up into his arms and feels the weight of him. Eason has grown husky at four years old. He's become quite a talker too, knowing that the word "Pa" will always get attention. Ebey wants to remember this moment, knowing that his son will be a different child the next time they are together. As he brings two-year-old Ellison up into his arms and feels Eason continuing to hug his leg, he grinds his teeth against the tears that want to flow. He hides his face in his baby's chest and feels little-boy pats on top of his head. He cannot move. It's not until Rebecca comes to put her hand on his back and take the boys that he can walk away. Their dog, Rover, whines as if he feels the emotion but stays home as he is told.

Being without his wife and children creates a vast hollow in Ebey's gut as he joins a small wagon train. He works to push his guilt away, filling every quiet moment with prayers for them, telling himself that his family and hers will watch over them. He remembers Rebecca's words of encouragement, tries to forget the tense lines that formed in her neck when they'd said goodbye.

The day that Rebecca began her cough, he'd lost the strength in his legs. *But she is young and strong, a force of nature, really, her heart and feet firmly planted in the precepts of the Bible to direct her every decision, Ebey tells himself. A healthy environment is the best medicine for her, which is exactly what is promised to those who make it to Oregon Country. He will make that promise come true for Rebecca. She had already felt better before he'd left. Perhaps to see the glory of an ocean sunset will cure her cough.*

He hires on with a family to help herd their livestock along the trail and take his turn at night to listen and watch for thieving bandits and wolf attacks. He knows the trip will become a way of life, a two-thousand-mile trip that will take five or six months if they can make about fifteen miles per day. He and his horse quickly develop a relationship and routine, starting their mornings together to round up the stragglers that have wandered away from the herd, then driving them along the trail to catch up with the wagon train.

On the trail, Ebey admits to himself that Ambition pushes him, has always pushed him. He begins to feel that his dreams of Adventure are within reach too. When he hears it said that pioneers are always looking forward, he knows that's him. He is a pioneer.

His trip is comparatively easy. No endless, week-long torrents of rain or Indian mischief or insect attacks or tsunamis of illness. Unavoidable potentially deadly river crossings, yes, along with the guilt of leaving Rebecca. They roll across the great plains on a fairly good road to the first supply post at newly established Fort Kearny in Nebraska Territory where the army protects emigrants from potential Indian attacks. It does not look like much of a fort, just a building, but Ebey gets a few supplies there to take care of his horse and the cattle, their hooves wearing down much quicker than he had anticipated.

They travel six hundred miles of Platte River country across Wyoming Territory with its huge granite rocks jutting out of the flat, dry terrain. In southwest Wyoming, in Sweetwater country, where only sagebrush and some prairie grass grows, Ebey sees a tall rock at a bluff on the west side of the Green River. He carves his name there, "I. N. Ebey, July 10, 1848."

They begin the gradual, barely noticeable ascent over South Pass to cross the Rocky Mountains into Oregon Country. It is hot during the day and cold at night. A few thunderstorms cause Ebey to get to know the Lord even a little better than before. He had been anticipating the crossing over the Rockies whenever he had thought of the trip, expecting to be lambasted by visions of icy peaks. Instead, it's a wide-open high plateau covered in sagebrush, and the only icy peaks are far to the north. Still, he is thoughtful as he begins the descent, knowing that he has entered Oregon Country which is now United States soil.

As he rides, he ponders the potential of his new life, hoping that his training in law from Missouri will help him make a manful rise above poverty and that he will keep his reputation of honesty and trustworthiness so that maybe his life will make a difference. He is itching to help develop Oregon Country, and especially the area that will become his family's home, wherever that is.

It takes a month to get from Sweetwater to Fort Hall and the steep, dangerous Snake River canyon. It is a challenge moving the wagons and cattle along the canyon through the Blue Mountains. They stop often to repair broken wheels and a few overturned wagons. It takes another six weeks to get to the Columbia River near the Whitman Mission, then several weeks more to the tiny settlement at The Dalles. That is where Ebey and a few others break from the group to take the newly established trail to Budd's Inlet while the others continue to Oregon City and the Willamette Valley.

* * *

On a brisk October day, Ebey finds his best friend, Samuel Crockett, splitting firewood at his cabin on a claim just south of Budd's Inlet. He looks different, a bit older, cheeks a bit sunken and very tan.

"Brother!" Samuel says, seeing him. He lays a heavy arm across Ebey's shoulders, then pulls back for a good look. "I'd say married life agrees with you."

"Not sure pioneer life agrees with *you!*" Ebey pounds him on the back. "Though you *have* . . . bulked up a bit. At least your beard is trimmed. Are you courting someone?"

"Naw, nobody to court, and I'm pretty busy just feeding myself. The beard's trimmed because of summer weather, but that's over now, so no promises. Say, did you hear? We're a territory now, not Oregon *Country* anymore, all the way from the crest of the Rocky Mountains to the Pacific Ocean. As Oregon *Territory*, we're ready to participate in the benefits of being governed."

Ebey rubs his hands together. "When did that happen?"

"August. Just got the word."

In the cabin, they talk long into the night like brothers sometimes do. Samuel tells him that Sylvester's friend Smith died in August, an epileptic seizure sending him out of his canoe to drown. "Sylvester has named their little settlement Smithfield in Smith's memory," Samuel says. "Sylvester works at Simmons' mill now and cuts shingles to send to Nisqually, but he's planning to head out to California soon, ya know, to look for gold."

"Let's us go too," Ebey says grinning.

"Don't you want to lay low for a time? Take a rest?" Samuel asks.

"No," Ebey says, "I want to make every minute count that I'm away from my family. Let's find a big load of . . . gold and build a couple houses and get our families over here."

"Yeah, it's been a long time since we seen 'em," Samuel says, "but I want you to meet Simmons at New Market first. He's someone you should know."

At New Market, Ebey meets tall, burly Michael Troutman Simmons, the epitome of "pioneer" always looking forward. His grist mill is producing coarse flour, thanks to Samuel's know-how to use metal parts from a wagon to work the stone wheel.

"I'm starting up a sawmill too," Simmons says, wiping his face with the kerchief from his pocket. "Been working on it since I saw an old upright saw for sale at Fort Nisqually. I am mighty pleased to meet you, Ebey, especially since you are a friend of Samuel's and a lawyer too."

"It looks like . . . you are establishing a nice little community here, Mr. Simmons," Ebey says.

"Thank ya. It is, yes, but I got a beef with Doc Tolmie at Fort Nisqually," he says. Only his eyes show above a bearded face, blond curls sticking out of his stocking cap like porcupine quills. "I got no patience for details or paperwork. Samuel knows what's going on, maybe you could help us out."

"Doc Tolmie is Chief Factor at the fort," Samuel says. "It's a British-owned Hudson Bay Company trading post. He's moved a herd of wild cattle across the Nisqually River, we think to expand their land holdings since their future is shaky with the territory being part of the United States now."

"Then as citizens, we should act on behalf of the United States," Ebey says. "It's probably . . . best to gather settlers from around the area to decide as a group how to handle it."

The group that Simmons calls together votes for a chairman, then agrees that a letter of protest reflecting their viewpoint should be delivered to Doc Tolmie at the fort. The chairman appoints Ebey to draft it. Samuel and a resident named Rabbeson will help him deliver it.

* * *

Ebey finds the fort to be a busy place and far more extensive than he had imagined. It is enclosed with fir logs 18 feet high to create a wall 150 feet down each side with a small bastion at each of the four corners. Inside is the house for Doc Tolmie, a store for trading, and several small buildings for the lodging of traders and travelers.

He enjoys meeting Tolmie. The two of them walk out to view the terrain together, Ebey wanting to negotiate privately without Rabbeson's ego getting involved. Doc Tolmie explains that they need range land for over two thousand cattle originally from Mexico and they have nearly six thousand sheep to graze as well. Hudson Bay Company has added an agricultural branch, Puget Sound Agricultural Company. Their purpose is to grow food. They also ship livestock and food to their other forts and to Russian America (Alaska), the Sandwich Islands (Hawaii) and Alta, California (San Francisco). Even so, Doc Tolmie agrees to move the cattle back across the river.

On their way back to New Market, Rabbeson tells stories of his experiences on Puget Sound. "A friend called Glasgow talked me and another guy, big guy called Carnix, to go with him north to a place called Whidbey's Island. He'd built a rough cabin there on land that looked good for farming. So we headed up Hood's Canal, the three of us along with Glasgow's woman who was Indian. When we camped overnight, we encountered a group of Indians. We had already decided between us who would do which chores, so when the head Indian saw big ole Carnix pack'n wood while we sat enjoying the fire, he thought Carnix was our slave and wanted to buy him from us."

"Having slaves is a sign of wealth with the Indians," Ebey says. "I suppose a big white man would be considered special."

"We thought it was a good joke at the time and said we'd sell Carnix for something outlandish, can't remember what now..." Rabbeson says. "We thought the price was impossible to get, that Carnix would be safe. But Glasgow's woman told us that the leader was very serious and would accept the offer and would eventually come up with the price." He laughs, shaking his head. "You should have seen the look on Carnix's face. Before we could turn around, he was out of there headed back south as fast as he could go."

"Have you seen him since?" Ebey asks.

"Come to think of it . . ." He laughs again. "Yeah, he's okay last I heard. But that Indian woman saved our hides more than once. When we got to Glasgow's cabin, planning to plant crops and stay awhile, there was a huge gathering of Indians from a lot of different tribes, thousands of them. Come to find out that Glasgow's woman was the daughter of the chief Patkanim, the guy in charge of the whole group. We kind of wanted to stay and watch, but she warned us that they were talking about killing us, so we grabbed a canoe and paddled out of there. You need to keep your wits about ya. We were lucky to get out alive."

Ebey's stomach drops. He has not heard of anything remotely as dangerous as this sounds. He can't possibly bring his family here. "Does that kind of thing happen often?" Ebey asks.

"Naw. They're usually too busy warring with each other . . . and disease is taking its toll," Rabbeson says. "I've never seen such a large group, and never one so angry."

"Whidbey Island is safe," Samuel says. "The local Indians are peace-loving. It looks like good farming there, not all forested, some natural prairies. The British at Hudson Bay Company surveyed it years ago as a possible trading post between the Columbia River and Vancouver Island. They'd been considering it as a place to grow crops for Fort Victoria too, with all those prairies already cleared."

But Ebey is not ready to look for a home. He wants to go with Samuel and the others on the well-traveled Hudson Bay Company trail to the gold mines of northern California.

The Orbit, 1849-50

Thousands died in the California gold rush. Survivors kept pushing forward, building a new city on top of the debris, a cemetery of forgotten people below their feet. The buildings, historical sites and tunnels are the most haunted sites in the United States. –U.S. Ghost Adventures

On horseback with supply mules and Sylvester's wagon, they travel south to Fort Vancouver then on through the Siskiyou Mountain Pass to Sacramento Valley. Despite the misery of constant rain, Ebey gets himself a gold pan and along the way, samples the riverbeds at the slow bends. The clouds break as he swirls and slushes his fines under the warm California sun, finding a little gold here and there. The site of those first flakes in his pan set the hairs on the back of his neck standing straight and his heart to thrumming in his ears. He feels the hook of the quest. He spreads his treasure out on a canvas and pulls it inside his makeshift tent to dry overnight. He finds Samuel already in his bedroll, with malaria.

After several weeks of Samuel sweating through his clothes with high fever, along with the shaking chills and muscle pain, Ebey sends him home, north to Budd's Inlet, with a group of friends. Then Ebey continues with a few others to the mining camps. He is surprised to see so many people already mining along the way.

Ebey smells the mass of people mining gold around Coloma before he sees them, such a dense population of men who have no need for cleanliness. They look like scavengers, clamoring for sustenance, a fierceness in their eyes that Ebey has only seen in a few who ended up in jail during his days as sheriff in Adair County. Men have come from the Sandwich Islands, Mexico, China, Chile, and Peru all looking for gold.

It's dangerous in the mining camps, liquor everywhere, laws and law enforcement nowhere, loose women, gambling, theft, sky-high prices for basic necessities: every way to take a man's money in a desperate, dense population of those whose dreams have been smashed. A man can be killed without provocation in such a place. The losers wonder how they will recover, feeling better only after a few drinks and a woman to tell them how wonderful they are before taking the last of their money. Then, it's back to the slurry again.

Ebey and friends give it their best. They find enough gold to begin a new life, but it's a tough game and the nuggets they carry quickly dwindle because everything is so expensive. Most of the surface gold has been removed, partly because the extra-wet spring has washed it away, and for them to go deeper into the ground would require a big investment and the purchase of equipment with no guarantee of return.

Summer wanes. Ebey is still working to find just a little more gold when he hears from several newcomers that Rebecca's family is on the trail, headed west. His mind scrambles, panics. He tells himself that it cannot be true, but the possibility continues to pick at him until he is worried. He hasn't heard anything from home, has no way of knowing about his family. When he hears that Dr. Redman, a friend of Rebecca's father, is at a mine 25 miles away, he closes up his own mining camp and goes there, unable to think of anything else. Dr. Redman tells him that he is sure that Rebecca's parents are on the road, but he knows nothing of Rebecca and the boys.

Ebey decides to return to Oregon Territory in case Rebecca's parents are there, though he knows it is highly unlikely. He goes into Sacramento City to find passage and finds a sea of people there. It seems the only ones making money are those who supply goods to the miners. The *Orbit,* a small brig on the Sacramento River, is needing repairs and it's for sale at a good price. Ebey puts his gold profits together with that of three friends, Sylvester, Shaw and Jackson, and they buy the thing, thinking it will be an inexpensive, easy trip back to Orgon Territory.

Always looking forward, they hatch a plan to bring commerce into Puget Sound. Their first cargo includes four ready-to-assemble store buildings, potatoes, butter and cheese. If they can sell it all at New Market and Budd's Inlet, they will bring spars and pilings back to sell in San Francisco. Everyone in the group is sick, and they hope to recover on the *Orbit.* Their only healthy friend, Alonzo Poe, volunteers to go ahead with funds to arrange for their return load so that no time will be lost in their new enterprise.

While waiting for final repairs on the *Orbit*, Ebey hears that people from his part of Missouri are camped 15 miles away, having just arrived. Feeling poorly, he drags himself there to ask about his family, but he is met with disappointment along with fever and chills and a gripping stomach. Back at the *Orbit*, he confines himself to the cabin, afraid of treatment from unscrupulous "doctors" on shore and the likelihood of being robbed.

By the time the tiny brig sails north, unfurling its square-rigged sails on both masts, Ebey is feeling better. He breathes the fresh salt air as they scoot and bob up the coast, seeing the rugged shoreline for the first time. His heart swells with the adventure of it as if he plays a role in his dog-eared copy of *Robinson Crusoe*. Two black and white orcas breach, their breath punctuating the air. Others join them, arching up through the water in harmony with such grace that Ebey wonders about the divinity of God's creatures.

On approaching the entrance to the Strait of Juan de Fuca, he feels a sudden cold, offshore wind against his right cheek. It comes up fast, plucking his hat from his head. The harder it blows, the more the sails strain. Clinging to the railing, he watches the sails tear. Soon, torn pieces whip in the wind, and the main sails split from top to bottom. He prays for God's intervention, wondering what a landlubber like himself is doing on the water. They are carried out to sea as if on a whim, far above Vancouver Island, and with waves coming in over the bow, Ebey feels certain that they are destined for Davy Jones'

Locker deep in the ocean. He wonders how Rebecca and his boys will get on without him.

But the little brig stays together, and Providence wears down the wind. They limp back, cold and weary, to the entrance of the Strait of Juan De Fuca on the first day of the new year 1850. They hope the danger is done, but at Neah Bay, the wind moves against them again, and they are stalled. Suddenly, Jackson announces that he will sell his interest in the *Orbit*.

Ebey helps the captain repair the sails. He becomes philosophical as he waits for the wind to change, wondering if Adventure always comes with Hardship. It takes two weeks of fishing and trading with the Indians to feed themselves before the wind changes its mind, and they sail through Admiralty Inlet between Port Townsend and Whidbey Island.

As they continue south through Puget Sound, Ebey sees canoes traveling the water, fishing with nets and close to shore and smoke curling up from Indian longhouses in villages surrounded by palisades. They pass through deep water by dense forests and prairies suitable for farming. He holds onto his hope to improve Rebecca's health in this beautiful green place, unable to imagine anyone ever being ill here.

Not having found Alonzo Poe at Smithfield, Ebey expects to find him at New Market with Michael Simmons, but Poe is nowhere to be found and no one has heard from him. Ebey's heart sinks, thinking his "cake is dough." They've lost their investment, and he remembers his goal of keeping his reputation. He asks about the possibility of Rebecca's family having arrived in the area, but there is no hint of them either. It makes him feel very much alone and vulnerable.

At Simmons' sawmill, he sees Rabbeson running the saw. A crowd of Indians stand at a distance, wanting to watch the mill run.

Rabbeson sees Ebey and stops the saw. "Hey Ebey. Welcome back."

Ebey nods toward the Indians. "How do you keep them standing far enough away from the saw?"

"I threatened 'em, of course. Told them to see if they could lift a log onto the carriage and when they couldn't do it, I used the kant-hook to roll it over by myself." He laughs. "Then I told 'em that with my magic hook, I could throw any one of them across the river."

Ebey smiles, wobbling his head back and forth, still worrying about his lost investment. He walks through the rain to see the grist mill, mentally adding up the bills that need paying. Simmons is there working.

"I have news," Simmons says, smiling from under a lean-to. "Come out of the rain, Ebey."

"Hope it's good news," Ebey says. "Don't want to think of what else can go wrong."

"I've bought Jackson's share of the *Orbit*," Simmons says. "And now that I'm a partner, I'm willing to supply the pilings, lumber, and shingles for the trip back to California."

Ebey is so relieved that he thinks he hears ringing in his ears. He shakes Simmons' hand with both of his own. "You're saving us, you know."

"Well, I've got a sawmill after all. Might as well make good use of it." Simmons shrugs.

The captain and crew are paid from passenger fares and the sale of cargo to the settlers, and the *Orbit* sails away fully loaded for its next round-trip with Ebey on board.

* * *

Lack of information about Ebey's family threatens to overwhelm him with worry during the sail back to San Francisco Bay. It has been more than a year and a half since leaving them and he is desperate to know that they are well. He writes to his parents on February 20: *"I have written so often without being favored with a single line from those who are dearer to me than life itself. I am almost persuaded to believe I am forgotten or only remembered as one who once was, a ghost perhaps."*

Four days later when he arrives in San Francisco, he discovers his first letters waiting for him at the post office, including one from Rebecca dated September 22. He holds it with tenderness as if it comes from a secret, precious world and touches it to his lips, inhaling. He walks from the chaos of Clay Street to the *Orbit* to open his letter. Carefully breaking the seal and unfolding the paper, he finds enclosed a lock of each of his boys' hair. She knew how much it would mean to him to receive actual evidence of their existence. Teary eyed, he tries to read. He reads her words slowly, listening for her voice as she describes the normal events at home. Feeling like he breathes real oxygen for the first time in a while, his worry fades, and he writes back that her words are *"a refreshing shower on the thirsting ground of my soul."*

As they leave San Francisco with merchandise for Puget Sound, Ebey feels that his troubles may be over. They travel north from California, feeling healthier and more optimistic to the mouth of the Columbia River, and run aground at Astoria. *Orbit* takes such a beating in the hard-hitting surf that Ebey, the captain and crew reluctantly abandon ship to save their lives. He stands on shore with both hands on top of his head as if to hold his brain together, searching for an alternative to the loss of his entire investment. Has he completely failed his family? Is his reputation lost? He prays for a miracle.

The wind changes. The little brig stays together and rights herself, floating freely. Quickly, before she can run aground again, they jump back into their small boat to battle the waves and return to her only to find that Astorians have boarded her first. Ebey's hands go back up to the top of his head. Anyone can claim an abandoned ship as well as its cargo.

A burly, red-bearded, weather-beaten face peers over the gunwale to Ebey below in the small boat where he bounces with the others in the rough chop. "Allow me to come aboard, sir," Ebey shouts over the howling chaos. "Let us discuss the possibility of a compromise."

Ebey is allowed to come aboard. Feeling hopeful in the small boat, his mates continue to fight the waves as they wait, chuckling and sharing stories about Ebey's gift of negotiation.

"I imagine that this sort of thing happens quite often in this location," Ebey says.

Red Beard slaps the gunwale, laughing. "It sure does. Happens *all* the time. A vessel comes through here with the wind and tide just right . . . well, this here's the result."

Ebey scratches his head as if thinking. "I suppose that in a court of law, this could look like a trap. Your group scurried on board so fast, I wonder if a judge might consider it an act of piracy."

Red Beard stops smiling, seems to grow even larger than before.

"Our eyes had not left the vessel, sir, as we waited to board it again ourselves."

"Then you should have left someone on board," Red Beard says, spitting over the side.

"As a lawyer, I feel compelled to tell you that your best choice here is to take the payment that I am about to offer you and leave this vessel, which was not truly abandoned," Ebey says, "in order to avoid spending time in front of a judge."

When they arrive at New Market, they are surprised to find Alonzo Poe there to meet them.

"I'm sorry I disappeared, Ebey. I was ill as soon as I left you," Alonzo says. "Too sick to send word. I'm just thankful to be alive."

Ebey squeezes Poe's shoulder. "I'm thankful too, friend. You . . . don't know how much. Of all the calamities we have overcome, finding you alive is truly the greatest."

* * *

Ebey takes another trip to San Francisco on the *Orbit*, hoping to make a worthwhile profit on a load of lumber but finds that other groups have beat him to it, temporarily flooding the market. He has his inventory held, not to be sold until the price goes back up.

The price change seems to be enough discouragement for Simmons to want to sell his mills at New Market. "It isn't just the business," he tells Ebey. "This area is not as safe as it used to be. I'd like to have my family in a more populated settlement."

"Has something happened?" Ebey asks.

"Did you hear what Patkanim did last spring?"

Ebey shakes his head.

"He had a hundred of his Indians go to Fort Nisqually with weapons. I was outside the gate and could see that trouble was coming. We asked why he came in such a warlike manner. You haven't met him have you?" Simmons asks.

"No," Ebey says. "Not looking forward to it either."

"Well, he said he was worried about his daughter being mistreated by her husband who was there. So, we let him inside but when we tried to close the gate to keep his friends out, a skirmish happened. Two were killed and some hurt bad."

"Do you think an attack was the plan from the beginning?" Ebey asks.

"Sure do. You can't trust that one. Somehow, he escaped. He's smart, I'll say that. Of course *he* didn't fire a shot himself. He had his people do it."

"Tolmie sent a report to Fort Vancouver, and I sent a message to Governor Lane. But get this: after a few days, Patkanim returned to the fort to turn in the Indians he claimed did the shooting. He thought he would collect a $500 bounty even knowing that his people would be hanged."

"Do you suppose they were slaves he turned in?" Ebey asks.

"Maybe slaves or people he wanted dead. Then he sent the rest of his men out to tell the settlers that they would be allowed to leave the country if they left their property behind."

"What? He is giving . . . ultimatums?" Ebey's stress is apparent in his speech. "How did the settlers respond to that?"

"How do ya think? They're preparing their defenses, of course. We're building blockhouses at New Market, same thing on the Cowlitz. The governor is sending arms and ammunition. There will be a U.S. army regiment garrisoned at Fort Steilacoom."

Ebey shakes his head. "I still hope for a peaceful transition. We can't really blame them with so many settlers moving here . . . but there's no excuse for killing."

"That's why I'm moving the family to Smithfield. I'm gonna build a store there, an *American* trading post. I've drawn the plan, a 25- by 40-foot, two-story building where we can live on the second floor and have the store on the bottom."

Ebey had thought about settling among new friends in South Puget Sound. He had even filed a claim there, but now he thinks it may be safer for his family somewhere else. He needs to know where.

{ 11 }

Home, 1850

"I scarcely know how I shall write or what I shall write. When I think of home, of father of mother, sisters and brothers, wife, children and friends, my heart sinks within me. I can scarcely find words to clothe my ideas, it seems so like writing to the dead, like addressing language to those who have passed the pale of mortality." –Letter from Isaac Ebey to his brother Winfield

Before leaving Smithfield to look for a new home, Ebey talks with Sylvester about the future of his town, and how it will grow quickly because of its location. He suggests "Olympia" as a grand name, like the majestic Olympic Mountains. Sylvester takes to the name immediately and calls everyone together to celebrate. Ebey offers poetic lines during the merriment, beginning in a loud, clear voice as the glasses are held high: *"Afar their crystal summits rise, like gems against the sunset skies ..."* and something about Olympian gods.

{77}

Ebey chuckles, remembering the evening as he paddles with Duwamish guides to investigate north in Puget Sound, up the Duwamish River and into Elliott Bay. While camped on the bank of a large lake that the Duwamish call At-sar-kal (Lake Washington), he writes to Michael Simmons about the pristine water and abundance of life, rich in natural beauty. Simmons sends Ebey's letter to the *Oregon Spectator*, enthralling its readers. If new settlers had not heard of Isaac Neff Ebey before, they knew of him now.

Remembering the encouragement of his friend Samuel Crockett who has been in the area much longer, Ebey continues further north. He had been intrigued with the land off Admiralty Inlet ever since he'd first seen it from the deck of the *Orbit*, knowing that every ship that sails into or out of Puget Sound will pass through that inlet. He'd noticed the prairie land on Whidbey Island suitable for farming. Rabbeson had told him about it. He remembers that Hudson Bay Company had even considered it for themselves as an agricultural property before the Oregon Treaty. His greatest concern is the character and state of mind of the local Indians.

This trip, they paddle up Saratoga Passage on the east side of Whidbey Island to the entrance of Penn's Cove. The distant eastern skyline is sharp and jagged with layers of mountain peaks, the Cascades. To the north looms Mount Baker (Komo Kulshan). At over ten thousand feet, its immense, snow-covered top mingles with clouds.

Penn's Cove is lined with Indian villages. Ebey wonders if these are the people who planned to kill Rabbeson and his friend Glasgow. He won't bring his family to live among such a dense population of Indians on an island no matter how strategic the location. They pull up onto the beach at Snakelum Point, Ebey's pilots assuring him that it will be safe. He has learned to trust his companions over the days but feels slightly vulnerable as he steps out of the canoe.

Children come to take Ebey's hands and lead him into the longhouse of the elder Snetlum. Snetlum sits by his fire, needing the warmth more than in the past. He waves the children away except for one boy of about ten years old who sits by his grandfather.

It has been two years since "The Big Talk" when Patkanim had tried to organize an attack on white settlers and one year since the Black Robes abandoned their mission on the island, abandoning Snetlum. It isn't often that a white man comes to visit, and it feels to him like an important occasion. He invites Ebey to sit.

The two men look each other over, hoping to ascertain some level of character by the other's appearance. Snetlum holds a blanket across his back, his belly relaxed over an apron. Ebey's clothes are worn homespun for his travels in the wilderness. Ebey sits, waiting to be acknowledged. Impressed by a white man who has the self-control and patience to be quiet, Snetlum lights the pipe. "How far have you traveled?" he asks, passing the lit pipe.

"I have taken the trail across the country." Ebey draws on the pipe and hands it back. "I am looking for a home." He sits, comfortable in the silence.

The smoke flows slowly from Snetlum's nose and mouth.

Ebey is quiet. He has spoken. It is not his turn to speak again in this man's home.

Snetlum notices an unusual stoppage to the man's speech and appreciates it. He speaks with sincerity and kindness, his blue eyes steady and calm. "Did they tell you that I am Snetlum?" he asks.

"Yes," Ebey says. "My name is Isaac Ebey." He extends his hand and Snetlum shakes it, noticing that Ebey's is a hardworking hand, rough with calluses.

Snetlum passes the pipe to Ebey and nods towards the boy. "This is my grandson, Helmits."

"Helmits," Ebey says, smiling at the boy. "You have a large village here."

"There is larger across the water," Snetlum says, pointing north. "You call it Oak Harbor, the village of Squi-qui . . . twice as large."

Ebey returns the pipe.

"Our village is the oldest. Do you think you want a home here, on our island?"

"That might depend on you," Ebey says. "I would never bring my family to a place that is . . . dangerous. I am told that you are a good leader here."

"Yes, I have influence here. That does not mean that I control anyone. We have always welcomed Whites here. Of course, we do not wish to share our island with anyone, but the future has become clear. It is unlikely that we will be able to keep this place for ourselves alone."

Ebey wonders how many in this village have died from disease, how large their numbers may have been before now. "Such change must be difficult."

"We pray that people who live here with us will be fair and can be trusted to not interfere with our way of life, people who will not attempt to take advantage of our good nature."

Ebey gives time for the elder's words to settle. "Yes, more white people are coming. I have no desire to change your way of life." He replays Snetlum's words in his mind.

"If I am among the first, I give my word that you can trust me to be fair and honest . . . if you give your promise that I and my family will not be molested."

Snetlum motions toward his bentwood cedar box and tells Ebey to open it. Ebey lifts the lid, revealing the Christian contents.

"We are Christian people," Snetlum says, "more likely to hide than to fight. The Indians from the north cause trouble for all of us. The Klallam at Townsend Land can cause trouble too, but not as bad as those from the north. If your people living on our island can protect us from them and treat us fairly, we would welcome you."

Ebey smiles. "It is an honor to meet you, Snetlum. I will think on what you say and not interfere with your day any longer." He wonders if he has found a home.

"Have you seen much of this island?" Snetlum asks.

"I am seeing this cove now and have seen the rest only from the water."

"You would do well to take a walk before you go. The forest, like the prairie, is alive with Spirit helpers, teachers, ancient reminders. Our family can help your guides carry your canoe over the back of the island, and you can see the land as you go."

As Ebey leaves Snetlum's longhouse, he sees his companions sitting at a fire on the beach for a meal. Women tend the fire, spreading it out and putting pebbles on top. Then they layer clams, then twigs and leaves and dirt on top. They motion for Ebey to sit down.

Ebey sits, seeing how large the cove is from their viewpoint at the entrance. "May I pay for my food? I have bread to share."

"Potlatch," a woman replies.

"What does that mean?" Ebey asks a guide.

"It means it is a gift, and you should repay it someday in the future."

In a short while, the clams are uncovered and served on a slab of driftwood. The bread is passed around, each tearing off a chunk, and Ebey learns a little more Chinook Jargon.

After their meal, Ebey helps paddle to the inside of the cove along with a canoe of young men sent by Snetlum. When they pass by the 24-foot cross that stands on the hill, it seems like a signal that he and his family belong on this island. He feels his heart thumping in his chest.

His canoe is beached, hoisted up by the young men and carried along the trail over the back of the island. As he walks the natural prairie, he remembers Samuel telling him that it is characteristic of the rain shadow to form intermittent prairies. He bends to squeeze handfuls of rich black soil that has been tended by Indians since the beginning. They follow a ridgeline along the prairie to a bluff where the trail winds its way down to the water's edge, and a small spring empties onto the beach. It's the same bluff that he had originally admired from the *Orbit*.

* * *

Having been away from his family for too long, Ebey is anxious to declare Puget Sound their new home. He writes to his parents: "*A great deal of improvement will be done on the Sound. Mills will go up, towns located, merchants flocking into the country and all things going ahead. The Sound is bound to be the second place on the Pacific Ocean. San Francisco will always be the first. The vast amount of timber that will be consumed in California and the Sandwich Islands, all of which have to come from Oregon Territory, make this a very desirable location for those who want to make money and enjoy good health.*

"*No country in the world can exceed this section of country for its commercial advantages. The navigation is perfectly safe and suitable for vessels of any size from a seventy-five-ton ship to a fishing smack. Anchorage is found all along from the entrance of the Straits to the head of the Sound.*"

Then, at age 32, Ebey makes his claim for 640 acres on the west side of Whidbey Island, the maximum acreage for a married couple. He is thankful for it, sees it as God's gift, especially after he hears that acreage claims will be cut to half the size the following year. This land is exactly what he wants. In fact, it's better than he had ever imagined. Only a fool would not make a good living off so much rich land. He stands on his claim, imagining crops everywhere he looks, anxious to tell Rebecca, "It's time to come."

Ebey's land is across Admiralty Inlet from the harbor of Port Townsend, the first safe harbor for ships entering Puget Sound. He appreciates the weather diversity the island provides. When the sea rolls, white-topped in the wind, roaring on his west side of the island, it can lie like liquid slate on the east side. Thick white fog can camp on Ebey's beach, blinding him from the water, while Snetlum's village on Penn's Cove is in full sun. And it can change by the hour. Its most important attribute is that his property fronts the water highway from the Pacific Ocean through the Strait of Juan de Fuca and into Admiralty Inlet, the entrance to Puget Sound. It is the route that sailing ships will travel, and commerce will increase with new settlers.

From the bluff of his property, he can see stately Mount Rainier to the south and the westward skyline of the Olympic Mountains with its wall of Hurricane Ridge reaching out towards the ocean. Across the water, a spiral of smoke climbs up out of the beach town of Port Townsend and the square chunk of Protection Island lies near shore to the northwest.

Whidbey Island itself is a joy of abundance. Its clusters of oak and evergreen stand among fields of meadow with camas, a field of blue flowers in the spring. The fields are burned periodically to keep brush and trees from growing there, and the Indians have cultivated potatoes as well. No wonder, the soil is rich and ready for farming. With the mild climate, Ebey will have a much longer growing season than back in Missouri. The berry patches, plentiful deer and rabbit all make him feel it will be a good home for his family. Maybe it is true that the sunset here can cure one's ailments, ailments like his lonely heart, or Rebecca's cough.

In his tent by candlelight, he writes to Rebecca, anxious for her and the boys to come in the spring. He knows that he will need proof of residence and proof of cultivation to make good on his claim. He will need an official survey within two years, and it will take several years for his ownership to be legal and final, but that is fine with him.

The next morning, he begins to cut trees to build his cabin with the help of Snetlum's people who will be paid in tobacco and a blanket and potatoes. He also turns the ground using hand tools to prepare it for planting while thinking of Rebecca and his boys.

He is notching a log when Witskatche, a friend of Snetlum, arrives dressed in his favorite outfit, a French uniform. He carries the mail on his rounds for Hudson Bay Company. Ebey shares dried venison and biscuits with him and then sits on a stump to open his letter. It comes with sad news. Rebecca's father has died of consumption. Ebey's brother, the Reverend Jacob Jr. who married them, has also died while ministering in a foreign country. Ebey is numb, feeling the loss without the comfort of family so far away. He writes again to Rebecca, knowing that her heart is broken and to his parents regarding the death of his brother. *"That intelligence has fallen on my spirit like midnight darkness. He will receive a crown of goodness for his faithfulness, but he was my brother. As David says, 'I will go to him, but he will not return to me.'"*

He thinks of the piece he read from his copy of the book, *Dream Life: A Fable of the Seasons* about the narrator losing *his* brother. How he forgives his brother for all the teasing he endured from him in childhood, even for being pushed out of an oak tree. But he cannot forgive *himself* for speaking harsh words towards his brother, even though the words were long ago. Ebey feels the pain of it in his heart.

* * *

As Ebey works his field, he finds the remains of a burnt cabin and is certain that it is the same cabin that Rabbeson and Glasgow had abandoned two years before. He is the only white person in the area, and regardless of Snetlum's assurance, the fact that Rabbeson and Glasgow had been forced to flee from that cabin in order to save their lives . . . It gives him pause.

On Snakelum Point, Snetlum's son George asks his father if they might offer Ebey the logs for his cabin that were prepared for their church. "The logs are still stacked there, ready to use," George says.

"No," Snetlum says, hugging his fire. "Those logs are for the house of Jesus Christ. Jesus Christ would not like us to give them away."

{ **12** }

Rebecca, 1851

It is a secret of the world that all things subsist, and do not die, but only retire a little from sight, and return again. Nothing is dead.
--Ralph Waldo Emerson, "Nominalist and Realist"

Rebecca remembers the past, before she had met Ebey. She had been foolish as a girl. At least that's what her mother said. She had loved spending time in books and wandering the forest and hadn't wanted to get married to be burdened with house, home and family. She was pretty, had admirers. Even so, when she was twenty, her mother warned her that she would become a spinster. Then, she'd met Isaac Neff Ebey, five years her senior. Handsome with dark, bushy hair, he was quiet, kind, confident and so very attentive, seeming to notice things about her without words as if they'd known each other for years.

He was well-read and could comment on nearly any volume she could mention. They'd both been impressed with Emerson's essay "Nature," regarding the study of nature as being a reflection of the Divine. Their opinions had differed regarding Emerson's attitude about society. Like Emerson, Rebecca believed society to be a distraction from nature and therefore, a distraction from God. Ebey held that society was necessary and a responsibility of believing citizens to mold and protect it with a moral compass. At first when they talked of these things, Rebecca saw intrigue in his eyes. Then she saw love.

Now on New Year's Day 1851, her thick, dark hair is tied into a tight bun at the base of her long, graceful neck, out of the way as she slides more bread into the woodstove oven. Still in her apron, she sits in the rocker near the fire, her wedding dress in her lap, remembering every moment of the day she was married in this dress. It's been seven years since she wore it to become Rebecca Whitley Davis Ebey. She tenses up with the memory of her father's stable arm leading her to her husband and marriage, her father who is gone now. Her throat tightens. She begins to cut, shortening the hem of the dress, not wanting it to drag through the mud on the Oregon Trail. Then she removes the lace to save for something special, too precious to be ruined during the work she will need to do. She's lost weight because of bouts of illness and the constant chores but is disinclined to take the dress in, hoping she might regain the weight.

Two Christmases without her husband, two Christmases for the children to be without their father, and to have experienced the death of their grandfather. Two Christmases of reading Dickens' *A Christmas Carol* alone. She shakes her head, thinking of her mother who has become melancholy since her father's death and unwell and quite dependent. *It feels like I have a third child, but how does a daughter separate herself from her mother who needs her? And don't the children need their grandmother? My sister Martha needs to help more.*

Rebecca does not know how she will get prepared in time to start her trip in early spring. There's everything imaginable to do including settling the finances at home with some property to sell and bills to finish paying. To be sure that the wagon will be sturdy enough for the trip seems to be a huge goal. Securing young, healthy stock and necessary provisions will take every moment she can find.

She looks over to her mother who is wrapped in a blanket by the fire. Her silhouette is framed by a window which provides enough light for re-reading her copy of *Jane Eyre*. Her wispy white hair has escaped its pins. Snow falls outside, quieting everything except the sparks from the fire and the creaking of Rebecca's chair as she sews.

"Mother, won't you please come with us to Oregon? You and Martha and my brothers can all come." She bends to her sewing, not wanting to plead.

Her mother looks up from her book. "Won't *you* please stay here with us? With me?"

"You know that the Bible says I am to be with my husband. The relationship between husband and wife is meant to be stronger than between parent and child."

"Yes dear, but it does not say that you should follow him across the world. He needs to come home." Her mother bites her lips to keep from repeating what Samuel Crockett's mother told her, that there had been a large number of drownings during the crossings over the Green River in Wyoming due to flooding, that the Platte River's muddy bottom hides pools of quicksand.

"He is doing his best to make a better life for us." Rebecca's chair rocks with quick rhythmic creaking, ". . . for all of us. He is embracing opportunity." The creaking slows. "Please come with us, mother. We can go together."

"You expect me to abandon everything your father has done for us here? Leave my home? Abandon his grave for goodness' sake?"

Rebecca searches for words. "I wish with all my heart that you would be willing to do that."

"You should not be taking those babies on that horrendous trip! It's well over a thousand miles for heaven's sake! You'll be traveling for half the year!" Her mother raises her book, blocking her face to end the conversation and hide her tears. She lowers it just long enough to say, "What if you become ill? Then what?" and raises it again.

* * *

Rebecca prays her mother's soul and spirit into the arms of Jesus for healing and comfort, and the strength to come to Oregon Territory once she and the boys are settled there. She tells herself that they will all come when her mother is stronger. In the meantime, her brother John will handle things well at home and James Jr. will help on his good days, being challenged from his head injury. She feels better knowing that Martha will still be home but a bit guilty for allowing Thomas to come with her on the trail.

Her younger brother, sweet, positive, goofy Thomas, with dark brown curly hair and green eyes and the lanky body of a youngster is certain that it will be a great adventure. He prepares for driving the wagon by securing himself a pair of goggles to protect his eyes from dust, wearing them about the farm like a disguise. It causes the dogs to bark.

Twenty-nine-year-old Rebecca reads her husband's letter again and again for his advice on preparing for the trip. What is needed to reset a tire, how to care for oxen hoofs, how there is need of livestock in Oregon Territory. *"It is better to drive your property than to haul it. . . Do not study how you can bring the most, but how you can get along with the least. . . Aim to cover about a hundred miles per week to not wear down the stock too much. . . Be the earliest to leave in the Spring so there will be grazing before the big wagon trains come through. . . Do not sell your provisions on the road but remember the duty of hospitality to provide a meal to a hungry stranger."*

She tucks the letter, a copy of "Parkman's Guide to the Oregon Trail," and the lace from her wedding dress into her things for travel. After securing their flour, lard, sugar, and salt, she packs bacon in a barrel of bran and fresh eggs into a barrel of cornmeal. She has a long talk with Blossom, their milk cow, about how it will be a difficult trip, but they will be relying on her to be strong. Then she fills the water keg and loads the little chicken coop into the wagon along with their bedrolls and covers it all with oiled canvas to keep the dust and rain out.

Rebecca, Thomas, Eason and Ellison, ages seven and five, along with Rover, travel with Samuel Crockett's family. Colonel Walter Crockett and his wife Mary bring Samuel's siblings:

John with his wife Ann and their three children Sarah, Sammie and Willie; Susan who is 28; and three younger brothers, Hugh, Charles and Walter Jr.

The first few nights on the trail, she lies awake in her tent unwilling to let go of her worry for her mother until the trials of the day wear her out. Knowing that she must focus on the matters in front of her, and that she has no power to help her mother, she gives it all into the Lord's care and falls solidly asleep.

Now and then along the way, they join other groups, creating a large, cumbersome wagon train. The slow-moving group is a target for harassment from Indians. They have become bold, tired of the parade of settlers tramping across the prairies, and callus to the problems of the whites. Realizing that many of the whites have no concern for them either. Colonel Crockett, a quiet, dignified, respected leader, sets the tone regarding the Indians. They should always be treated fairly but with a firm hand.

On the days when everything goes right, the routine of the road reveals itself. The cattle graze each morning until breakfast is finished, then the cows are milked into buckets with lids. The buckets are hung under the wagons to bounce and swing so that butter can be skimmed from the top for the evening meal. The drivers yoke teams of four or six oxen per wagon and the tents are stowed. To get them rolling, Thomas wears his goggles to ride through camp, making circles in the air with his hat and hollering an exuberant "Yeee Haw!" It is a job that he very much enjoys. Then he hops into their wagon to drive. Some ride ahead on horseback and many walk to save the oxen from extra weight, and to save themselves from a jerking, crushing ride. Lunch is a one-hour stop. Later in the day, a rider investigates ahead of the train to find the next good campground so they can stop an hour before sundown—just enough time to set up tents, get wood and water, and make the fire for supper.

During the evening, smoking pipes are lit and visiting begins. People are making new acquaintances and life-long friends. Sometimes, familiar songs like *Oh! Susanna* are sung. When the talk quiets and folks go to their bedrolls, they listen for the familiar harmonica of a lonely traveler playing *Roll on Silver Moon, guide the traveler's way.*

* * *

Just beyond Omaha tribal territory, a great storm hits in the night with thunder and lightning, stampeding the cattle away. Rebecca and the boys are kept in their camp beds until the rain soaks through two layers of canvas, making their wool blankets more precious than food. The sky flashes and cracks and the rain torrents down. Rivulets flow from the ditches they dig around their campsite. Cold and wet the next morning, even Rover stays curled up tight under the wagon. Rebecca's brother Thomas rides out with a group to find their vagabond stock. It is all she can do to help around the camp before crawling back into her soggy bed with her boys. They search for most of the day in the continuing rain and return with some, but not all the livestock.

Their misery continues into another night. Buffalo chips that were collected when dry to use as fuel for the lack of wood are moist now, more dung again than chips. It will not burn.

Rebecca and the boys had helped collect the chips but had not been able to eat food cooked with them anyway, even when they pinched their noses. They make do with crackers and milk for another night, longing for the warmth of a fire and the chance to dry their clothes and bedding. Huddled together for warmth inside their wool blankets, they pray for a new day.

Harassment from Indians comes in many forms, mostly the theft of livestock. When Thomas rides off in pursuit again with the cattle drovers, Rebecca re-reads her husband's letter, looking for the part that says not to worry about Indians. She has read the opening lines so many times that she has memorized them.

"Rebecca, my love, I write this letter with a better heart and pleasanter feeling than I have written in many a long day. Take good care of your health. I have suffered a great deal because I knew you suffered on account of my absence. At least keep in good heart, and when you pray, please remember me, who lets not an hour of the day pass but what I think of you and ask God to bless you and the children. Oh how I desire to be with the children to watch the opening of their youthful minds. . . Little danger is to be apprehended from the Indians and none after you pass the Pawnee on the Platte . . ."

Thomas returns, saying that it was white people who stole their horses, having lost their own. She wonders if the situation has changed since Ebey took the trail three years before. She has developed the routine of riding horseback up ahead of the wagon train every morning and letting the horses graze as Ebey recommended, much healthier for her and the horses. Sometimes she and the boys walk along the cut-off trails, the smaller trails that lead away from the main, often to a bit of water or to a cleaner, greener area with less dust and fewer gravesites to see. The cut-off trails eventually lead back to the main trail, but the terrain and distance are unknown when starting off.

It's a warm, lovely day when Rebecca and the boys walk a cut-off trail through the sagebrush that takes them further from the main trail than they've ever been. They have walked for hours with no sign of the trail returning to the main one and they are tired, especially Ellison who has begun to drag his feet. Rebecca worries whether they should turn back even though they would be nearly a day's distance behind the wagon train if they do. Thinking what to do, she points out the purple asters that line a trickling spring next to the trail. She thinks of the dust and evidence of death along the main trail and decides that the asters and lovely spring grasses are difficult to leave. To keep Ellison moving, Eason tells stories about what they might find around the next bend, "a snake, a prairie dog, a trading post. Hear all the people?"

They listen, but it's a galloping horse they hear, and their eyes open wide when an actual Indian on horseback comes around the bend galloping on a pony. He rides straight at them, his face decorated in black and red war paint. Rebecca's heart stops. She grabs the boys, pulling them into the bushes, but Ellison starts running and the Indian pursues him. Bending down low from his pony, he pats the top of Ellison's head and says, "We fight Sioux." Then he rides away.

Rebecca's knees are stiff as she herds the boys along quickly now, truly fearful of what might lie ahead. When the boys' shock wears off, it changes to joy, having had the greatest excitement of their lives. They can't wait to tell their story. Rebecca does not recover so quickly. In her sons, she sees their father's love of adventure, and she says prayers of thankfulness for their safety. It is the last cut-off trail she will ever take. The Colonel's expression, more critical than normal, and Thomas's worried one do not need to be repeated.

{ **13** }

Focused on Fort Hall, 1851

I think in a lot of cases, ghosts are history demanding to be remembered. –Jeff Belanger, Most Terrifying Places in America

Prairie dogs entertain the travelers along the Platte River. There are burrows and mounds as far as Rebecca and the boys can see. The pups gather together in the cool evening to watch the settlers. When the moon comes up, they bark and yelp their chorus.

Well-known landmarks help Rebecca see their progress. Chimney Rock tells them they are getting close to Wyoming. Independence Rock, like a giant beached whale, is where migrants sign their names as evidence of how far they've come and for encouragement to loved ones who will come along behind. Next comes Devil's Gate.

On Holden Hill on the west bank of Green River, Rebecca finds her husband's name, *I. N. Ebey, July 10th, 1848*. She follows the lines with her finger before carving her own name between his lines. Feeling a special loneliness for him that muggy August evening, after Bible reading and prayers, she yields to her one distraction on the trail and lights a candle to read her mother's copy of *Jane Eyre* and spend time with Mr. Rochester.

At Bear River, the grass is waist high. It camouflages grasshoppers that invade everywhere, clicking, chirping, scraping. They sound like a storm. Thomas wears his goggles in defense while the others continue forward in a jerking dance of swats. Grasshoppers are shaken from clothes and pulled from hair.

Approaching Fort Hall, they are greeted by prairie chickens running about, larger than sage hens, and they catch a few for dinner. Rebecca's health has wavered during the trip, but with Fort Hall in sight, her spirit, and therefore her health, soars. She will see her husband soon and the boys will have their father. It has been too long without him.

That evening, as campers sleep under a full moon, Rover barks, the horses agitate, and gunfire wakes Rebecca. She hears more shots and holds her breath to listen, wondering if she will need to protect her children. Thomas arrives at her tent. "It's John," he says. "He was on guard duty. Gave a warning shot to stop Indians from stealing the stock. They shot back at him."

"Where are the Indians now?" she asks.

"Gone."

"Stay with the boys," she says and goes to see for herself. John's family is gathered around him, a lantern lit. "Is he shot?" she asks, her heart racing.

"Yeah, he's shot," Colonel Crockett says. "Well, not so much him as his powder horn that hangs from his chest. It saved him this time. We better have more guards at night from now on."

Back in the tent, Rebecca lights a candle to read Ebey's letter again, the part saying he will meet her at Fort Hall. *"I know these words on paper are a poor substitute for the words of the heart. I shall be there to meet you at Fort Hall or east of there. I hope you will find us approaching each other from different directions. From your ever faithful husband, I. N. Ebey. Postscript: Our property is known as the best in Oregon Territory. I think it is the very best in the Pacific. 'Lo an a whong' is the Indian name. It signifies a portage."* Rebecca cannot think about their property right now, only about the welfare of her family and seeing her husband again.

* * *

Headed east on horseback, Ebey's chest hurts in anticipation of seeing his family. When his arms begin to remember the last time that he held his sons and the painful Empty returns, he looks for distraction. He turns to his best friend Samuel Crockett who goes to reunite with his family as well. Their heads are full of recent events.

Independence Day had been a great celebration in Olympia for settlers north of the Columbia River. It was a resplendent outdoor meal supplied by their own hands. Ebey can still see the tin cups raised and hear the toasts "to the future state of Columbia." The reader's strong, firm voice declares every patriotic sentence of the *Declaration of Independence*. He can still see the faces of Simmons and Bush and Plamandon taking it all in.

"We are being ignored in the north by the Oregon territorial government," Ebey says as he rides. "Oregon Territory is too vast. We need separate representation for our area. Now that more settlers are coming, we should have mail service, roads, law enforcement, even lighthouses one day so vessels are not lost on the rocks."

Samuel lifts the front of his hat to scratch and scans the horizon. "What about military protection? If northern Indians attack, who would come to help?"

"We help each other for now, but the population will grow," Ebey says. They come to a stream and let the horses drink. "That lawyer John Chapman sure gave a fiery speech."

"Got us riled up enough to write that petition to Congress asking for a separate territory," Samuel says, deciding to walk. He needs a break from the saddle. Walking along, he's happy it's just the two of them, no wagon train with all their problems. "I thought Simmons County would be a good name."

Ebey tucks a plug of tobacco into his cheek. "Yeah, but Simmons wanted Thurston's name on it. Thurston earned it, I guess, first delegate to Congress from Oregon Territory. He pushed through the Donation Claim Act that got us our land claims, among other things."

"If the fever hadn't gotten him, he'd still be watching out for us. We need someone from our neck of the woods to keep at it."

Ebey spits to the side. "The petition is a step forward. If the territorial governor Joe Lane endorses it, that'll be important. Twenty-four delegates including Plamondon, Simmons and Alonzo Poe are meeting to organize a northern territorial government. We'll be ready."

Samuel rubs his backside. "We wouldn't need to travel all the way to Oregon City to exercise our rights of citizenship."

Ebey pats his copy of the petition from *The Oregonian* in his pocket, having brought it to show to Rebecca:

"Those portions of Oregon Territory lying south and north of the Columbia River must, from their geographical position, difference in climate and internal resources, remain in a great degree distinct communities, with different interests and policies in all that appertains to their domestic legislation, and the various interests that are to be regulated, nourished, and cherished by it.

The communication between these two portions of the Territory is difficult, casual and uncertain, although time and improvement would in some measure remove this obstacle, yet it would for a long period in the future, form a serious barrier to the prosperity and well-being of each, so long as they remain under one government." – Isaac Ebey to Congress

* * *

Rebecca watches down the trail for the silhouette of her husband, and with each group they pass, her heart tightens. Eason has a concerned look too. To Ellison, his father is a bit of a mystery man who loves him through his mother's words.

Camped at Fort Hall, she begins to worry that something has happened to him, even wonders if he has changed his mind. She opens his letter that his brother Winfield had shared with her for her trip. *"The great desire of my heart is to get my own and father's family to this country . . . Whidbey Island is almost a paradise of nature, a good land for cultivation. If Rebecca, the children, and you, Winfield, all were here, I think I could live and die here content."*

Their wagon train continues west out of Fort Hall, Rebecca having fashionably fixed her hair in the hopes of meeting her husband. It's parted in the middle, combed strait down over her ears, then up in the back to a knot. She battles her thoughts as she rides out ahead, butterflies in her belly. They stop along a pretty little creek off the Snake River for a midday meal of cold biscuits and jerky. Rebecca is making sure that everyone has food when she sees two riders coming up to camp, pack horses following behind, faces hidden in shadow beneath their hat brims.

As Ebey slides off his horse, Rover jumps on him, and he has Rebecca in his arms before she knows it's him. The boys stand back, unsure, and Eason's eyes fill with tears remembering his father, realizing the emptiness that he has tried to ignore. "Pa!" Eason cries.

Ebey grabs his eldest boy's face, pointing it up to his own. He wipes away the tears, seeing the lopsided grin, a front tooth just coming in next to an empty gap. Eason's face is covered in freckles from months of sun on the trail. "I love you, son. I've missed you." When his own vision blurs, he bends to pull Ellison up over his shoulder. "I've got you now, my boy. You're all mine!" and he twirls around, bringing him back down into his arms as Ellison laughs. Then, he holds Rebecca, feeling her in his arms while his sons' arms are around his legs.

Rebecca nearly swoons, feeling as nervous as she was as a bride, while her husband kisses her in front of everyone. It causes her heart to race. When she hears Samuel Crockett and his family whooping at them, she hides, red-faced, behind his back, her arms around his waist.

It's the first time that Samuel's mother, Mary, has seen her son in seven years. She declares that she will not be letting go of him anytime soon.

Being together calls for celebration, and it is such a pleasant spot that they stay for the night. Ebey and Samuel have come prepared for the reunion, knowing that provisions would be low at this point on the trail. They unload a large ham, along with potatoes, onions and carrots that have come from Ebey's garden. After coffee and a tin of cookies, they talk the evening away, pass a bottle, have a chew.

Asked about his gold-mining adventure, Ebey says, "It didn't pan out," with a wide grin, not wanting to talk about it. When the voices begin to quiet and eyelids begin to close in the firelight, the harmonica begins to play. Folks turn in. Ebey and Rebecca move their tent away from camp that night.

"Should I feel afraid out here away from the others?" Rebecca asks, feeling a bit shy. Her hair knot, normally perfect, is loose and askew.

"You are with your husband, my love, my brave, smart, wonderful woman." He kisses her neck and removes the pins from her hair. "You don't need to be afraid." He unties her apron. "My greatest wish is to make your days easier . . ." he releases her hair, "to provide the blessings that a little wealth can provide . . ." He holds her close, his nose deep in her hair, taking in her scent. ". . . provide . . . our children . . . a good situation . . ."

She smiles, sinking to the blankets.

In the morning, eyes around camp remain on the fire where the biscuits cook, and smiles hide behind the rims of tin coffee cups.

$$\{\ 14\ \}$$

Together, Winter 1851-52

Ghosts never speak until spoken to. –*The Ghost,* 1837, Thomas Ingoldsky,

Arriving in Olympia November 8th, the emigrants are among new friends, safely tucked into warm cabins for the coldest winter months. The budding town of Olympia has become the new northern extension of the Oregon Trail where they can transfer from foot and wagons to canoes and ships to continue north through Puget Sound to Whidbey Island.

At the beginning of the new year, the settlers learn that their request to Congress has been approved. The area north of the Columbia River which includes all of Puget Sound and the Olympic Peninsula is now officially named Thurston County. Their celebration is great.

In the evening, Ebey and Rebecca sit in front of the fire, holding hands. To Ebey, life seems simpler now. After three years apart, he is on the verge of taking his family to their new home. The civic responsibilities he has felt as a new, educated settler in the Olympia area do not seem so important now. He feels the tiny bones in the back of Rebecca's thin, hard-working hand and rotates the silver wedding band she has worn for eight years. As he describes their new home, she closes her eyes, trying to imagine his description of the feeling of salt spray on his face from choppy water and wind and how the beaches are always changing. "Most important," he says, "we can farm nearly year-round."

To prepare for the move, the group removes the wheels and lashes together the bases of three wagons, two side-by-side and one centered behind as a type of tail. Sealed together with tar and pitch, it creates a water-tight, reinforced, flat-bottomed scow. Ebey and Samuel create a mast and sail, hoping that the wind will cooperate. They plan to also take Ebey's canoe and hire another canoe to be paddled by Indians to help pilot the way and in case they need saving if the scow falls apart.

At first light on a crisp March morning, the Ebey family, Thomas, and Colonel Crockett with the Crockett sons Samuel and John begin their voyage north while the Crockett women and youngers stay in Olympia. It's a clear sky and thankfully, no rain and a little breeze.

"Can I ride in the canoe with the Indians, Pa?" Eason asks. Ellison perks up, wide-eyed with excitement. Rebecca's head pops up, alert. She looks to Ebey, tension on her face.

"I know them well, Rebecca. You can trust them," Ebey says. "They have paddled me all over Puget Sound . . . for weeks. The boys will be safer with them in their canoe than in a canoe with any of us." With his nod, the boys climb into the canoe and sit where the Indians indicate. Rebecca steps into Ebey's canoe, paddled by Samuel and the Colonel.

With all the provisions the scow can hold, and Rover tied securely inside, they push the flat-bottomed scow out into deeper water. Their good milking cow Blossom, who is still re-covering from the long trip, stands centered in the back, her tail hanging stiffly over the end in concern. The tide is going out, and to their relief, the scow stays together. With long poles and paddles, Ebey, Thomas and John Crockett manage to steer their clumsy craft north. Thomas and John know nothing about navigating through Puget Sound. Just to prove it, Thomas puts on his goggles and leans far out over the front of the scow, one hand above his goggles as if to shield his eyes from the sun like an ornament on the bow. It gets a good laugh, even from the Indians who are more likely to see a carved totem there. Still, they are able to avoid the rocks, reefs, shoals and thick beds of kelp thanks to the canoes that lead them.

A colony of seals bark from their rocks and splash into the water as they pass. Rover barks in return, wanting to jump ship. Rebecca looks at her own colony, all from Missouri, and won-ders how this land-loving group ended up in this new, beautiful world of water. *By the Grace of God,* she thinks. She's never seen so much water and forest. From time to time, Ebey's sail moves them along without much effort, and Thomas is able to lower a fishing line out the back. When the tide comes in, they get the boat to shore and wait until it goes out again.

Every stop is a new adventure. Eason and Ellison scour the shoreline for new shells and kelp they can use as whips of slime while Rover races about. Ebey puts the boys to work digging clams. He shows them his new skills as he roasts the clams in the fire, the flames turning blue and white from the driftwood. When cooled, they eat with their fingers off pieces of driftwood. Their Indian guides join them, and Rebecca learns that she is called a *klootchman* (woman) in Chinook jargon and they would be called *siwash* as men. Camped at night, they sleep hard and take turns at watch to dissuade any quiet visitors who may have thoughts of theft. On their way again, they pass by Indians who stop and stare, watching Blossom in the heavy contraption float by, propelled by the sail.

"You would think they have never seen a good milking cow floating in a box before," Ebey says, chuckling.

They come to rest with the incoming tide at Ebey's property on the western shore of Whidbey Island. Ebey leads Blossom while Thomas twists her tail, coaxing her up the path to the top of the bluff and the cabin. Before the boys can grab Rover, he takes off, oblivious to being called back. Rebecca stares at the little cabin that waits for them northeast of a small ravine then turns to take in the unbelievable view. On the other side of Admiralty Inlet, smoke swirls upward from the darkening woods of Port Townsend. The sun is beginning to sink, lighting the jagged peaks of the Olympic Mountains.

Ebey waves across the water. "The Klallam over there require the settlers to pay in order to live there. That's Alfred Plummer and Charles Batchelor over there. Our Skagit Indians just hope that our presence will protect them from the raiding parties that come from the North."

Rebecca covers her mouth with her left hand and points with her right. "What is that huge ridgeline of mountains?"

"That's Hurricane Ridge," Ebey says, wrapping his arm around her. "Part of the Olympic Mountains. To your left is Mt. Rainier reigning to the South."

She turns to look, her mouth still open. The mountain is stately as if it truly does reign. Ebey turns her toward the cabin. "This is temporary," he says. "We will have a larger house . . . soon, more than one. I thought we would call it *The Cabins* like in Missouri. It will help it seem like home. What do you think?"

"Well, Mr. Ebey," Rebecca says. "I think that you have thought of everything."

The gulls compete for their final meal of the day, creating chaos in the sky, as the scow is quickly unloaded and belongings are packed up to the cabin, wet boots squeaking along the way. As the sky turns orange, water is collected from the stream that is steps away in the gully. Inside, the fire is started in the woodstove that Ebey purchased at Fort Nisqually. Gulls gather together to nest for the night, and the tide crashes against the shore as if to celebrate their homecoming.

They all appreciate that it's warm and dry as they squeeze into the cabin, and Rebecca smiles to see a bedroom framed into one corner. Ebey lights a lamp for the evening meal, beans and salt pork one more time, heated on the woodstove, and the last of the bread. After dinner, with the warmth of the snapping fire, everyone is ready for sleep. Bedrolls are laid out. Ebey carries his boys to their bedrolls on the floor in the bedroom. He pulls a small mattress from the corner for Rebecca and himself.

"Where did you get this mattress?" she yawns, lowering herself as if to Heaven.

"I bought feathers from the Indians and used an old sail from the *Orbit* as the cover. A couple of klootchmen sewed it up for me."

"I love it," she whispers, letting her head down. "I'll sleep like a baby . . ."

The next morning, after cooked oats with blessed Blossom's fresh milk and cornbread, Ebey and Samuel lead the Crockett men to investigate the island while Rebecca rests. They come back with a deer to dress.

"It seems like a hospitable island, Ebey." The Colonel is supervising Samuel as if he needs guidance while butchering the deer.

"There are three settlers about ten miles north," Ebey says. He sharpens some long sticks to use as skewers. "They call the location Oak Harbor for the trees. Garry Oaks, I guess."

Samuel scratches his nose with the back of his hand, his fingers sticky with butchering. "Good to know. What sort of men are they?"

"Well, Lansdale is a widower, a medical doctor. His wife died 14 years ago, He's been on the move ever since. He started out on the Columbia, had a medical practice in Vancouver, even drew out the plan for the town. Then he came here, was living northeast of us, named it Oak Harbor, but now he's moved to the head of Penn's Cove. He calls his new place Coveland."

"You need to see the cove before you choose your land," Samuel says to his father.

"*New-wy-ey* the Indians call it, Quiet Cove," Ebey says. "Lansdale's gone a lot. He leaves in his canoe to tend to business . . . and to take care of the sick."

"Why would he live up here if he wants to tend the sick?" the Colonel asks.

Ebey shrugs. "He just keeps moving. Came across in '49. I told him about the Indian Pass above Snoqualmie Falls, and he left immediately with a guide to go and see it. Then he described it in the newspaper as a new route across the Cascades. He is intent on helping establish new settlers. You'll like him."

"I do like that property a few miles south of you, Ebey," the Colonel says. "It reaches right down to a marshy area for great duck hunting for one thing, and beach access as well."

Samuel pokes the air with his knife. "See Penn's Cove before you decide, father. Then, if you still like this side, okay." They thread the meat onto two hefty skewers.

"Most of the traffic will be on this side." Ebey points west. "Port Townsend across the way there is the first safe harbor ships will find when they come into Puget Sound . . . It will be good to have you as neighbors wherever you all land."

As the sky darkens, they take turns turning the spit outside over a fire, both hindquarters going round and round while Rover stands guard, drool dripping on his paws. When the meat is golden brown and the juices run clean, they slice it up to eat with potatoes cooked in the coals and apples from the underground root cellar.

The next morning spits rain while the Crocketts and Thomas are off looking at land. Ebey gets to work in his fields and Ellison and Eason help, anxious to be with their father. They plant potatoes and onions and carrots and parsnips. "We'll plant barley and wheat next," Ebey says. "Cabbage and peas later." He holds up the black dirt and rubs it between his palms as it falls to the earth. "This black dirt will feed us well, sons. Good thing you're here to help take care of it."

Once the Colonel's original choice of land is confirmed, he and sons Samuel and John prepare to go back to Olympia to get the rest of their family. Lansdale comes over the island's back to accompany them, bringing his canoe and Indian paddlers with him.

"I need to check on some things in Olympia anyhow," Lansdale says, "and I can help you arrange to get your stock here."

"Much obliged," the Colonel says, shaking hands. Bags have formed under his eyes, a sign of a sleepless night.

Ebey and Thomas shove the scow off the beach with the tide. "God willing, it'll stay together and get you back," Ebey calls. "Rebecca will be happier when the other women folk are here," *and we need the oxen for farming,* he thinks to himself.

He stands at the beach until they are out of sight, thinking of the wharf he wants to build below his cabin. He knows he must concentrate on the farm and house first, but he imagines the regular traffic and visitors who will come. He wants to encourage mail delivery and shipments, too. After all, *A pioneer must always be looking forward.*

The white population grows quickly around the Ebeys with the addition of the Crockett family and others soon to come.

$\{$ **15** $\}$

The Welcome, 1852

These shores will swarm with the invisible dead of my tribe, and when your children's children think themselves alone in the field . . . or in the silence of the pathless woods, they will not be alone. –Sealth (Chief Seattle), 1855

As settlers move into Oregon Territory and Puget Sound, their diseases come too, killing the young, the old, the weak and especially the Indians who have no immunity. Overlanders bring sickness but so do the sailing ships that trade with foreign lands. Wagon trains are sometimes stopped for weeks while they bury their dead and hope to recover enough health to continue. Cholera, mountain fever and scurvy are the biggest killers on the trail. Smallpox, measles, whooping cough, typhoid fever, flu—It all arrives eventually, and it is deadly.

* * *

Snetlum's eldest son George comes across the island with a group that carries a gift in a large basket. They walk up out of the thick fog of Penn's Cove and onto the island's back where they break through above the fog and squint from the sun that bounces off a new fogbank ahead, lying below them. The crystal-clear Olympic Mountains greet them in a blue sky. Then they continue down into the new fogbank that sits on the water between Whidbey Island and Port Townsend, where Ebey's cabin is wrapped in a white wet blanket.

Ebey and Thomas are outside splitting firewood. The sound of the axe striking wood seems dull in the fog. "I'm thinking of claiming land on the northeast corner of yours," Thomas says. "That would save the piece northwest of you for your parents when they arrive." Rover barks once before George's group comes through the fog as they descend the hill. The dark bodies look intimidating in the white background. "Company," Thomas says, gripping his axe handle.

Ebey stands and puts his axe aside. "George!" he says, shaking his hand. "How is your father?"

"He is well . . . fine. He is waiting for his new canoe to be finished. You come see it one day. Your family here now?"

"Yes, let me bring them out. I want you to meet them. Rebecca!" he calls, "bring the boys outside."

Rebecca comes out, wiping her hands with her apron and calling the boys. A lock of hair has escaped her bun and fallen down the side of her face. She tries to tuck it in, anxious to meet their Indian neighbors. They appear very relaxed, one dressed in western clothes, the others with cedar blankets over their shoulders. The ends of their long dark hair float as the fog moves, pulling the air.

"Come down off the porch, dear." Ebey waves her closer. She stands next to him, and he puts his arm around her. "This is my wife, Mrs. Ebey and this is her brother, Thomas. Tell the others that they are to be respected as I have been respected."

George keeps eye contact with Ebey and gives a gentle nod.

Then Ebey stands between his sons, his hand on each head. "These are my sons, Eason and Ellison. They are not to be molested."

"My father wishes to welcome your family to our island since he believes you have our best interest in your heart. He had me bring you more feathers for your beds." George hands Ebey the large basket filled with feathers pressed tightly together.

"That is very generous. Please thank him for us. I have something for him, too." Ebey ducks into the house and returns with a leather pouch of tobacco. "To his good health," he says, handing it over. "Please tell him that I will come and see him soon."

* * *

The Crockett men return from Olympia with family and cattle, and they claim land next to each other at the Colonel's first choice near Admiralty Head. Their son John's property is closer to Penn's Cove. It touches the northeast corner of Ebey's. The Crocketts build a camp to live in while constructing their first cabin. More important than the cabin, they get the farm started.

John, with a gift for farming, and his youngest brother Walter Jr. dig up three-foot-high fern bracken which has edible roots for the Indians but is in their way for farming. Plowing requires a good plow and four yokes of oxen to get it cleared, necessitating the borrowing of oxen from Ebey to have enough to get the job done. The mutts that Walter Jr. brings from Olympia help keep the oxen moving.

Walter Jr. is comfortable with the local Indians who watch them plow. He had worked with Black Hawk's sons as a carpenter's apprentice in Iowa and had learned the Algonquian language of the Sauk people then. Now he visits with Snetlum's people and some of the other 1,200 Skagit living around the Cove, and there are other languages to learn.

Whidbey Island has always been a stopping place. People from the Skagit River and the Suquamish and Snohomish and Swinomish all come to fish and hunt, many of them also using the trail above Snetlum Village to go further inland for hunting. Ebey's beach is a frequent camping spot. Klallam Indians can often be found there with a canoe for hire to transport a paying customer to Port Townsend and back or beyond. Several Indian families have specific plots on the prairies of central Whidbey Island where they plant their potatoes. Chinook Jargon, trade talk, is what gets them by.

Being able to communicate is especially important when cattle graze themselves right onto Old King George's potato fields. Old King George is the son of Klallam leader Lach-ka-nam from Port Townsend. Old S'lalack's family from Victoria are not happy either. Their potato fields have been nearly destroyed. Ebey explains that he will help them file a grievance with the United States government and they will be paid for their loss. He does not tell them how long that might take.

He also does not tell them that there will be more cattle. The settlers have always let their cattle graze freely, knowing it's easier to fence their produce fields. Horses and sheep and pigs can be kept closer to home, but cattle gotta graze. Everyone, Indians included, will need to fence their growing fields, even if they don't like it.

* * *

Rebecca appreciates the clear sky and the soft, early June breeze. Still wearing her old wedding dress as a house dress now, she and the boys bend to poke more potato eyes into the ground. She sends them to get more water and stands to straighten her back. Crops have turned the fields green. The klootchman (Indian woman) she hired to weed the onions is bent with her work in the next field. Looking toward Port Townsend, she sees another ship coming into the harbor, a sign that her husband's hope of commerce is coming true. The vision of a majestic vessel silently floating into view with all sails flying never ceases to thrill her, something she had never seen before she came to Whidbey Island.

"Yo the house!"

Rebecca turns inland to see tall Captain Eli Hathaway walking towards her, a lean man with a forbidding face until he smiles. His callused hand lifts in greeting. She wonders if the calluses are from handling ship's ropes or from working his farm. His serious smile is that of a Master Mariner, weathered and protected by a thick mustache and beard, but he looks like a farmer today, carrying a worn jacket over his shoulder to reveal suspenders attached to his homespun trousers. He has walked from the claim he shares with Captain Holbrook on the northwest bank of Penn's Cove next to Lansdale's Coveland. His blue eyes smile at her from under a wide-brimmed hat.

"How do you do, Captain Hathaway." Rebecca's hand goes to her eyebrows to reduce the glare. "I thought you sailed everywhere you went in your ship's boat."

"Well, I thought I would walk my legs a bit today, such a pleasant one. Been liv'n in a tent over there among the rosebushes on the Cove since March, ya know, when I'm not on a ship, of course. Farming suits me almost as much as the sea, I guess, until I get restless. Let me help." He bends to plant more potatoes.

"Thank you, Captain." Rebecca continues to visit as they plant. "Will you stay on the island then?"

"I'll stay through the summer anyway. Captain Holbrook took out the claim last month. Just thought I'd come by for a visit."

"That's good. I see your ship over there, *Damaris Cove*," she straightens to point at Port Townsend, "but do you know the other ship that came in?"

"Yes Ma'am, a Hudson Bay Company ship from Nisqually. You'll see it often enough, I expect."

"And how is your wife, Captain Hathaway? Have you heard from her recently?"

He stands, being thoughtful about his answer. "Clarissa has written that she is feeling a bit under the weather, Ma'am, rendering her hesitant to leave Massachusetts at present. Our twin daughters are well, but it is possible, I suppose, that they may be disinclined to leave the comforts of home and family and friends."

"I am sorry to hear that, Captain. I hope she is better soon and up to the trip. It *is* rather an undertaking to come to Oregon Territory, the trip as well as living here, but we have the opportunity to make a new community among all of this beauty," she says, turning her palm upward.

The captain nods and looks away, his eyes glistening.

"Well, Captain, my husband and my brother Thomas are splitting boards on the beach for fencing and the boys are off to get water, but they will all be back soon for midday meal. Will you stay and join us? Mr. Ebey will be happy to see you."

"I'd be much obliged, ma'am, if it's not too much trouble." He helps her gather the remaining potato eyes to carry back to the house. "Eating my own cooking gets a bit tedious."

During their meal, Captain Hathaway talks about his idea to build himself a log cabin up against a great boulder above his tent, giving the impression that he might be thinking of settling down. Rebecca wonders if he will do that or return to his wife. With all the attention he gives the boys during their meal, she feels that he must miss his family very much.

{ **16** }

Therein Lies a Tale, 1852

Our feet are planted in the real world, but we dance with angels and ghosts. –John Cameron Mitchell

In June, the schooner *Mary Taylor* that runs between Portland and Puget Sound comes into Port Townsend and the Ebey cabin fills with friends. Captain Richard Holbrook and Samuel Howe stop by for a visit in time to escape a big wind and rainstorm. Colonel Crockett and family are already there as well to talk about raising their house in the morning and enlisting help from Ebey and Thomas. After roast venison stew with a rich cream gravy and biscuits for all, everyone gathers, most sitting on the floor, to catch up on news. Soon, the heads of children begin to bob. As the dark skies grow even darker with evening, lanterns are lit to golden the room. The closeness of hardworked, damp bodies mixes with the fumes from the oil lamps, and for diversion, the storytellers begin their entertainment.

"How about a seafaring story tonight, Captain Holbrook?' Ebey says. "You have a room full of landlubbers here who would dwell upon your every word. I understand you have been on ship since you were a child, spent years whale hunting, have seen foreign countries."

At 31, Captain Holbrook looks full of mischief, the typical full beard and mustache of a sea captain, his wind-blown light brown hair chopped to cover the tops of his ears, twinkles in his blue eyes. "Well, sir," he says, "whale hunting is a misery of boredom and foul food for months on end . . . until you see a whale, of course. I did that for ten years, since I was 13 years old. My most memorable trip was to sell whale oil to China. We did not think much of Japan and Russia since they would not let us land. Four of our crew starved to death off Russia . . . We did not get aid until we reached Hawaii. I was the only one able to stand at the helm by Honolulu."

"How were you treated in China?" Charles Crockett asks.

"Tolerated us, I would say. Much more hospitable than the cannibals who stormed us in the South Seas, but I did not think I should speak of it with the children and ladies present.'

Rebecca and Susan Crockett and her mother Mary look like they have swallowed poison.

"Another time for that one, then," Ebey says. "How about a story closer to home?"

"Well, it was San Francisco gold that brought me to this side of the country in '49," Holbrook says, "but I did not go into the mines like I had planned. When I saw people starving there like we had starved on ship, I went looking for food for them. Bought a sloop and sailed down to Monterey and returned with produce. Off the cost of San Francisco, I found a huge supply of gull's eggs. Folks ate 'em up."

"I came up here to Port Townsend a year ago. Got my claim now on the Cove, between Dr. Lansdale and Mr. Howe." Holbrook tips his head towards Howe. "I'm using ship's rigging to get logs out of the woods for San Francisco at the present . . . and happy to have neighbors such as yourselves."

His listeners nod. The rain and wind beat hard on the cabin roof as Ebey fits another chunk of wood into the woodstove. "Mr. Howe," Ebey says. "I've heard you have stories as well and a reputation for telling them."

Samuel Howe smiles, loving to be asked. He lowers his long, pointed nose, accentuating the bags below his eyes, and despite his crimped forehead, he continues to smile under the beard and mustache as he looks around the room. "Well, it was last winter, November 19of '51 when the Haida had us. We were prisoners. A group of us had chartered the *Georgiana* to go up to Queen Charlotte Island and see about the gold up there."

"We got blown onto the rocks off the island and our ship broke up. The Haida swarmed us, got everything of value off the ship, of course. We tried to figure how to not get killed or become slaves and get hidden away some place where no one could find us. So, we convinced 'em we were worth big money in trade."

"Clever," the Colonel says.

"Wouldn't someone come looking for ya?" Thomas asks.

"Sure," Howe says, "if they knew we didn't all drown. And if we got killed, I'm pretty sure our deaths would have been avenged, but that's not much consolation when you're still liv'n."

Ellison's eyes open where he leans against his uncle Thomas on the floor.

"Anyway, they got us."

Ellison sits up, alert.

"It's the dead of winter, no warm clothes or blankets and we're freezing to death. They had us 18 long, cold days and nights during snow and cold rain in a flea infested plank house. . . and I'm talking away at 'em best I can in Chinook about how we're worth something in trade. Finally, seven of 'em took the captain, the cook and myself to Fort Simpson across the water in Canada there for a ransom. Fort Simpson kept us, but after four weeks, they had done nothing for the ones left behind! Not one thing! The more I pleaded, the more they ignored me. Those shifty English at Fort Simpson were gonna just leave those poor wretches behind!"

"Don't tell me," Ebey says. "They didn't want to help Americans who were trying to get gold from British land."

Howe nods. "Evidently that was it, but they wouldn't admit it. Thank god the *George Emery* saw what happened and went for help. It was Simpson Moses, customs collector, who saved 'em. He chartered the *Damaris Cove* in the name of the U.S. government with Captain Hathaway at the helm. Outfitted it with four cannons and issued a letter of credit to get the ransom. Twenty-five American volunteers went too."

Rebecca's appreciation for Captain Hathaway grows, seeing him in her mind's eye as he pilots the ship in rescue.

"Moses is a brave man," Holbrook says, having heard the story before.

"He is very much against Hudson Bay Company," Ebey says. "I cannot say that he is fair about it in some situations."

Howe nods in agreement. "Saved lives in this case, anyway. Had to pay five blankets, a couple shirts, a bolt of muslin and two pounds tobacco for each prisoner. But then our government refused to sanction it. The rescue was six months ago, and no one's been reimbursed."

Heads wag in disgust. John Crockett winks, his children sleeping on both sides of him. "I'd rather have it end with the happy ending of rescue, I think."

* * *

The next day dawns with a breeze blowing away the last moist air of the storm. It is time to raise a house, a Crockett house. "I'll take the helm!" the Colonel says, clearly excited and affected by the storytelling of ships the night before. "All hands on deck!"

The logs are already prepared, and the first run is laid out on hefty stones. There are twelve men to work. It is a momentous day, the day that Ebey will see the beginning of the community that he has dreamed about, and the Crocketts will get their first home. He and Samuel cut saddle notches out of the ends of each log on the ground with axes while the others heft them into place, getting them to fit.

The next day, the roof is framed, and the rock fireplace is built, rocks having been hauled up from the beach a few each day since they arrived. Chinking with mud between the logs begins while the women keep the food coming out of Rebecca's stove. Samuel begins to split cedar for roofing shakes.

"Something I can do in my sleep," he says. "I did this all day long for many months to sell to Fort Nisqually when I first arrived years ago with Simmons."

To George Snetlum and his family, it looks and feels like an invasion.

Sailing Ships, June 1852

"The ghostship of the wrecked Flying Dutchman crossed our bow in a strange red light all aglow, her sails full though the wind was still. She came up on the port bow, where also the officer of the watch saw her, as did the quarterdeck midshipman, who was sent forward to the forecastle; but on arriving saw no sign of any material ship." --Prince George of Wales, ship's log on the *HMS Inconstant, 19th Century*

Two hundred and fifty ships sailed from the Boston area in 1849 for the six-month trip around Cape Horn below South America to San Francisco to find their dream of gold. It was very crowded on those ships. Everything that could float was filled with passengers. Many ships were chartered by large groups who pooled their money to get themselves to California by any means possible. They knew there was a high probability of sickness on those over-packed ships, but did they really know?

The 15-year-old elegant, three masted Duxbury charted by the Old Harvard Company was one of those ships. It was awkward, 95 feet long and requiring all of Massachusetts Bay to make a turn. With more than a hundred onboard, food and water were rationed, and it made for hard feelings. The passengers nearly mutinied. Some left the ship at the first stop, already sick of salt pork or fish, potatoes or unsalted hardtack. The now and then special treat, plums boiled into a pudding known as plum duff, did not make enough of a difference.

For six months of ocean travel they either weathered storms in the hold with all the others, elbows out to protect the bit of breathing space around them as the air grew fouler from sickness, or when the wind died away, they sat languishing on deck, praying for wind. Distraction came in the form of card games, storytelling and music. They fished and caught birds, firing rifles at anything that moved. Tensions built as they waited, crammed too tightly together on ship, waiting for Mother Nature.

Whether by ship or overland, ninety thousand immigrants got themselves to California. By 1850, over thirteen thousand lived in Oregon Territory, providing a serious market for commerce and an invasion to indigenous communities.

* * *

Penn's Cove, The Port of Sea Captains

Ship captains, pilots and Master Mariners come to Whidbey Island, some after trying the gold mines, some having been raised on ship, and some having spent years on whale hunts or trading with China, India, France, Hawaii or Alaska. Penn's Cove is attractive to sea captains because it is a safe deep-water harbor.

With sandy hair curls and muttonchops, kind-hearted Captain Thomas Coupe belongs to the sea, though his wife Maria would argue with that. He has been sailing since he was twelve years old along the Atlantic coast. Coming up through the Straits of Magellan to San Francisco, he buys half-interest in the fully rigged bark *Success* and develops the reputation of pushing through difficult situations. To prove the point, during the slack between tides and with a commanding breeze from the west, he sails right through Deception Pass without steam power, the first to do so. Then he sails into Penn's Cove.

He carries with him the story of his meeting his match in a great windstorm on the high seas. He told the crew to keep full sail even though the wind was so high that it tore off the heads of steep waves all around them. When it became so fierce that the main mast was likely to break and the sails had to come down to save the ship, the crew refused to go up the rat lines, not wanting to risk their own necks. Coupe thought of his wife's warnings about his high level of stubbornness as he climbed up the lines himself. The wind was so intense by the time he got near the top of the main sail that it tore his canvas pants completely away from his body, whipped away like a feather. He clung to the rigging, his white, naked legs nearly numb with cold, and he considered that it may not look dignified for a captain to be up there in that condition for all to see. He hung on with every ounce of strength, and in his stubbornness, he brought the sails down.

He always ends the story with a genial laugh. "I may have lost my pants that day," he says, "but the story will live forever among my crew."

He is 34 years old in 1852 when he comes to Penn's Cove, and he writes to his wife Maria to tell her that he has found the Garden of Eden. He tells her that if she and the children would come and join him on Whidbey Island, he would leave his seafaring voyages and stay closer to home. He chooses 320 acres at the water's edge of Penn's Cove with John Crockett's land to the south.

Sensible Maria, with her hair typically gathered into a proper bonnet, has always made the best of things, raising their children while her husband is at sea. She is not sure that she wants to trapse across the world to follow her sailing husband from New York city into the wilderness. Yet she is touched by his description of the island and his promise. Her friends and relatives advise against it, but as a good Methodist wife, she hardens her jaw and decides that her place is with her husband.

* * *

The first Sabbath in June, Rebecca wraps herself in the beauty of quiet serenity, a pristine substitute for her Methodist church. She and Ebey and the boys read from the Bible. They stand on the bluff looking out over the water as the sun begins to slide toward the horizon, and she leans back against her husband. "No bustling crowd as in the city to mar our peaceful happiness," she says.

"Yet one day, my love, we will see even more ship traffic out there bringing commerce to our shores." He wraps his arms around her against the sea breeze.

"You were right in foreseeing the future here, Mr. Ebey." She turns to nuzzle her face into his neck.

"And fortunate to have met up with Samuel and Simmons and the others at New Market when I arrived." he says.

"I pray for the day that our families join us. It is lonely without them." The chaos of gulls dropping clams on the beach to crack them open is softened by a loon's echoing call. "I would have preaching this day, if I could, to make it even more complete . . . and Sabbath school for the children." She smiles up at him. "Wouldn't that be perfect?"

"It will come in time." Ebey pats the top of her head, knowing it will raise her ire. "Be patient, my task master."

She squirms away from him. "You know I hate that! Leave my hair alone!" She picks up a split piece of firewood and chucks it at him before he chases her around the corner of the house.

Mail comes to Ebey through Port Townsend, forwarded from Olympia where Michael Simmons has become Postmaster. It's an official looking letter that comes, and he carefully breaks the seal and opens the folded paper. The words tighten his spine and constrict his breathing. He feels a mixture of pride, excitement, determination, and dread. He reads that he has been admitted to the bar in Oregon Territory and has been elected district attorney for the 3rd district which is north of the Columbia River. He has serious duties now, to the people of his community, to his Indian neighbors, to the territory, and to future generations.

He is excited and ready to do the work but dreads the necessity of leaving Rebecca and the boys in order to do it.

In the meantime, it feels good to be busy on the farm. He continues to plow and plant. As he gathers the first of the cabbages that he planted in cold weather, he thinks about boiled cabbage, cabbage salad, stuffed cabbage rolls and sauerkraut, making himself hungry. Then he walks to find the cows that wander off to graze and to bring the water since the little boys have done enough for the day. There will be frequent visitors coming, and he is anxious to build the larger house, make it as easy for Rebecca as he can.

Knowing his time is no longer entirely his own now, he hires Thomas Bartlett with his Indian friend John, and a sea-captain named Bell to help work the farm and to get wood from the forest and the beach. It's needed to build the new house and for fencing and firewood. Even though Bell has built a small cabin for himself on the Cove, Ebey knows that Bell's help is short-term. He is a sea captain after all, and the sea will surely call.

Having given up his plan for the day to raft timber to his beach because of the wind, Ebey hoes potatoes. He is looking at the square-rigged brig in Port Townsend Harbor when Dr. Lansdale walks up the bluff. "You've come just in time for a coffee break," Ebey says. They stand together to watch another vessel travel the Straits.

"Much obliged," Lansdale says turning toward the house. "We're having an election meeting at my cabin tomorrow. Hope you can be there."

Inside, Rebecca has hot coffee and warm bread and butter. "Thank you, Mrs. Ebey," Lansdale says. "I couldn't think of a warmer welcome than this hot food and coffee on such a blustery day. It's a wonder my paddlers could get me across from Townsend."

"You are always welcome, Doctor," she says.

Lansdale talks about the happenings in Olympia and the new settlers coming in. When he leaves, Ebey follows him out. "Doc," Ebey says. "Rebecca has a cough that comes and goes. I'm fearful that she may have inherited the affliction of her family. Her father passed away from consumption over a year ago."

Landsdale nods, putting his hand on Ebey's shoulder. "I can examine her if you want to know for sure. There are some quack remedies to avoid. The best thing for her is clean air and rest. A happy attitude can help, too. When she needs to rest, she should rest. Consumption advances very slowly in some people. Try to stay positive, Ebey."

* * *

A few days later, *Damaris Cove* is back in the harbor. Ebey is setting out the next batch of cabbage seedlings when Simpson Moses, the customs collector who saved Howe from northern Indians, arrives with two sailors for room and board. The two Indians who paddled them from the ship are happy to camp outside. Rebecca is well-prepared to house and feed them. The next day, she accompanies Moses to visit Crockett's new home. As they walk, they see the schooner *Chalborough* has also anchored in the harbor. "Have you seen a lot of ship traffic through here?" Moses asks.

"I'm not sure what 'a lot' would be, but we see about five or six per week. Some sit for several days waiting for the wind and tide to be right so they can move on. Most are carrying spars and pilings to San Francisco."

"I would say that is a big increase since the *Orbit* sailed through here with your husband only two years ago." Moses smiles.

It had been years since Rebecca had blushed, but this did it. She was proud of her husband. "Thank you for saying that, Mr. Moses," she says, still pink in the face. "It means a great deal."

On June 14, the evening before Ebey leaves for Olympia, he and Rebecca sit on the bluff to watch the quiet sunset together, his arms around her. A few gulls squawk on the beach. An eagle flies overhead, then another. She relaxes in his warmth. He smells like clean dirt and the sea. She feels his hands, rough from work and sees the red roughness of his face, baptized in the intermittent sea breeze of their new home.

"I'm so proud of you, Rebecca" he says. "You have been brave and have worked hard . . . I'm proud of the boys, too."

She pats his hand and snuggles her head up under his chin. "What takes you away from us?"

"Twenty-four delegates met in Olympia last month to form a state constitution before asking for admission to the Union," he says.

Rebecca's eyes grow. "Such important work you are all doing," she says, cupping his bearded cheek with her hand.

"You know some of the delegates: Michael Simmons and Alonzo Poe. I don't think you've met Simon Plamondon yet."

"It seems that everyone I meet is a character from a book, each so different. Mr. Simmons is so loud and direct, and Mr.

Poe is so diplomatic and careful. I wish I could be a little bird on your shoulder to watch and listen."

"It is quite a show, to be sure. They have asked me to help move things forward. I wish you could be my little shoulder bird, whisper your wisdom into my ear." He grabs her, knowing how much he will miss her, feeling like they have not had enough time together. Seven months is not nearly enough.

"There will be more and more visitors coming for meals and to spend the night," he says. "Do you think you can manage?"

"Yes, as long as I am well and can get some help. I told you I could do it. Don't worry, husband. Your work for our new community is important too."

"It will pull me away for a few weeks, I'm afraid. I truly wish I didn't need to go."

"Tsk, Tsk," she pats his hand again. "It's not like we'll be alone. Thomas is here and the neighbors if we need them, but we will miss you terribly."

He kisses her goodbye the next morning causing her to become teary-eyed, and although he says he will be gone for several weeks, her search for him on the horizon begins as soon as he has left. For Rebecca, whenever she must wait for her husband's return, she will be searching the horizon for him, if not from the bluff, then from her heart.

{ **18** }

Ladies' Days, June 1852

What makes ghosts? Love, thieves, and fear. –German Proverb

Rebecca distracts herself from her husband's absence by focusing on her work. Eason and Ellison haul as much cut wood as they can carry, as instructed by their father before he left. Rebecca writes in the journal that the schooner *George Emory* is in the Straits so that her husband will have a record when he returns home.

Her spirits are lifted when Mary Crockett, the Colonel's wife, comes to visit. "I've escaped," she says. "I swear, the cooking never lets up. It's one thing when you have all the comforts of home back in the states, but another thing entirely out here in the rough."

"It sounds like we should have some tea," Rebecca says. "I'm so glad for your visit." She brings her China teapot down from its display shelf to warm by the stove before adding hot water from the tea kettle, not wanting it to crack. It's one of the few special items that she brought from home, a treasured wedding gift from her mother-in-law.

"At least you've got a crew of men to bring water and firewood," Rebecca says, "as long as you don't need to ask them constantly. Do they do it on their own, I hope?"

Mary laughs, which causes Rebecca to laugh. "Why did I even ask?" Rebecca admires her white porcelain pot, its handle shaped like the outside of an ear edged in gold, tiny pink nosegays painted around the top. She cups her hands around it for a moment, remembering how she had tucked it into the barrel of cornmeal along with the fresh eggs to get it across the country safely.

"Is John's house nearly up?" she asks, scooping tea into a tiny strainer.

"Soon," Mary says. "When John and his family move into it . . . well . . . it will be a blessing. Two adults and a passel of kids for *them* to control and feed, not me."

"I imagine it's crowded," Rebecca says. "I hope you stay as long as you like and come often. I truly enjoy your company."

* * *

On her first Sabbath without Ebey, Old S'lalack and his family from Victoria arrive to work the ground around his little, rough-skin potatoes that grow on the prairie. Rebecca watches them young and old, bent over with sticks to loosen the ground. Ebey told her that they have been working this ground and growing potatoes here for generations, and they must be left to do it. She feels especially lonely as she watches the family together, missing Ebey and her family in Missouri, and she misses the preaching on Sabbath. She hopes that Eason and Ellison, who are inside reading their Bible stories, will be able to carry on her family tradition and have Sabbath school one day.

The following week, Rebecca welcomes the women and younger children of four families from the schooner *Mary Taylor* while the men and older boys stay on ship to manage their cattle: the Alexanders, the Bonsels, and two Smith families with twelve children in total. *Enough children for a school,* is Rebecca's first thought.

She enjoys seeing Frances Alexander and her two-year-old son Joseph again after meeting them in Olympia the previous winter. Born in Ireland, Frances and her husband John had lived north of the 49th parallel and had come across from Missouri in a wagon train in '51, the same year as Rebecca. Rebecca embraces her warmly and notices that Frances has a new bump of pregnancy.

She recalls that Ebey had been impressed with John Alexander when they'd met in Olympia, a good man who had lost a leg on the trail. It had become infected and was taken off with a carpenter's saw while Frances had refused to leave his side. Their 14-year-old son William had taken over the duties of the family with the help of his 12-year-old brother John Jr. In Olympia, John seemed to manage well without complaint with a wooden leg. Ebey had encouraged them to come to Whidbey Island.

At The Cabins, all the women help like a group of sisters. Soon, a stew simmers on the cookstove, salt pork, onion, carrot, cabbage and potato. Bread sops up the remaining broth from the pot and fills every nook and cranny of hunger. Rebecca sees the women nearly fall asleep on their feet with the warmth and comfort of the cabin, yet Mrs. Bonsel and the two Mrs. Smiths rally themselves into taking care of the dishes and clean-up while Rebecca visits with pregnant Frances.

"Thank you for putting us up, Rebecca," Frances says. "This is a lovely place. I thank God that we met you and learned about Whidbey Island."

"It is beautiful here, isn't it? How far along are you in your pregnancy?"

"About four months I think," Frances says. "Between you and me, it seems that having children over a sixteen-year period should be enough, don't you think? I'm hoping that God will decide that this is enough."

"Well, you'll be happy to know that we have a doctor nearby should you need one, Dr. Lansdale."

"We met him in Olympia," Frances says. "He also told us about Whidbey Island. A very nice man. He wanted to inspect John's leg when we were there, see how it was healing."

The next morning, Mrs. Joseph Smith hires one of the Klallam paddlers camped on the beach to take her in his canoe back to the *Mary Taylor* to get her belongings. She is back in time for breakfast. Samuel Crockett also arrives for breakfast with Ellison in his arms and Eason pulling at his shirt tail as they tumble in the door. He sits on a bench at the table with one boy on each side. He smiles at the ladies, then sees Rebecca's stern look. "Your husband *asked* me to check on you," Samuel says innocently. "I'm part of your family, after all."

With the word 'family,' Rebecca puts her hand on his shoulder. "Of course you are welcome at our table, Samuel. You will always be welcome here. Eason, get up and fetch Mr. Crockett a plate."

When Dr. Lansdale, Samuel Howe, and Captain Fay all arrive together, Rebecca thinks she might as well be running a boardinghouse in one of the populated states that she left. She sends the children outside, all twelve of them except for two-year-old Joseph.

"I've brought the mail," Dr. Lansdale says, handing it over.

Rebecca nearly melts, hoping for something from Mr. Ebey. Suddenly, she is free from all distractions, excited and fearful of what she might read. One letter is from Isaac's younger brother, Winfield Ebey, dated March 5, and the other is from her sister Martha still in Missouri, dated March 29. Rebecca sits alone in her bedroom to read, savoring each word, then rushes outside to find her boys. "Eason, Ellison, come here!"

Ellison arrives, his shirt askew from playing tag, followed by Eason. "We weren't do'n anything wrong, Ma."

"Your grandmother Harriet and uncles John and James and Aunt Martha are coming! This letter is dated three months ago. They have been on the trail for the last several months! We must pray for them while they are on their way to us."

The boys jump up and down. "Should we go tell Thomas, Ma?" Eason asks.

"Yes, go tell Thomas. He will want to know as much as we do."

Rebecca's heart is light as she enjoys the company of the women. They pitch in with the chores along with some singing and gossip, knowing that they will all be neighbors. It is the closest feeling of family she has had since leaving home, a pre-view of what's coming, she hopes. With several days of rain, the children's chaos becomes too much, and Mrs. Smith herds them into the bedroom to get them out from underfoot, but they are louder and more unruly in there than they were under their mothers' thumbs.

Rebecca hires six Indians to work the potato fields though she does not know them. Thomas is not available since he and Alexander's son William are working to finish Thomas's cabin so the Alexanders can stay there until they get their own home built. The Alexanders have claimed a long, skinny property between Ebey's and Penn's Cove, a piece that has a huge cross on it and receives regular visitations from the Indians.

Colonel Crockett comes by to check on things, having seen workers in the potato field. A light breeze blows, moving puffy clouds through the sky, perfect for work. He ducks his head inside the Ebey cabin and sees it full of women and children.

"I suppose Mr. Ebey asked you to check on me," Rebecca says, meeting him at the door.

Colonel Crockett steps back out of the doorway, away from all those women. "The truth will follow me to the grave, madam." He gives a formal bow.

"Well thank you for checking in, Colonel Crockett. We are fine. Would you be willing to part with some fresh venison for our dinner tonight? It would be a lovely treat for the ladies."

"Hugh brought in some fresh last night. I'll have a grandson bring it over to you."

Rebecca's hired workers come at the end of the day for their pay, and she goes out to inspect their work. Seeing that they have not covered as much ground as she had hoped, she offers them some potatoes and onions for their pay. A large Native man wearing a farmer's hat throws words at her and waves his arms in the air, though she understands none of it. She backs away, afraid for the first time as she hurries back to the house, glad that she is not alone there.

The next day, wild strawberry hunting brings the women merrily out of the house despite darkening skies. They swing their empty baskets and scour the fields, looking further and further. It takes persistence, and near the end of their energy, when they finally find a lovely patch, it begins to rain, the rainbow in the northeast sky offering no promises.

"Not now!" Frances Alexander says as her two-year old stuffs berries into his mouth. "We just found these!"

They pick as fast as they can and compete against each other but mostly against the rain as it comes faster. The chatter stops, and within minutes, they are drenched. Rebecca is chilled after the long walk home, yet she carries on. Wet clothes are hung all over the cabin to dry, reminding her of her visit to Snetlum's longhouse in rainy weather where food was hung from the rafters to dry. With some sugar, a biscuit, Blossom's rich cream and a few strawberries, a fresh-fruit treat is their reward, along with a moment of silence from the children while they eat.

Captain Bell arrives from *The Eagle* the next day bringing two letters from Mr. Ebey. Rebecca is hesitant to open them, afraid of what they might say. He writes how much he misses her and the children and of the importance of his being in Olympia to represent the settlers in the northern county as decisions are made, and the necessity to remain a few more days. To her, his words seem tired and lonely.

After nine days with Rebecca, the ladies each give their good-byes and appreciations. Mrs. Alexander moves into Thomas's cabin with her husband and children while Thomas continues to dig his well. Mrs. Bonsel moves into her own cabin with her husband and daughter. Mrs. Joseph Smith moves into Captain Bell's cabin on the Cove with her husband, and Cordelia Smith returns to Olympia with her husband.

Rebecca and her boys are alone. The absence of energy from the other women nearly echoes in the silence, and Rebecca suddenly feels exhausted. Two visitors stop from a schooner to hunt deer and she sells them 3 pounds of butter but has little energy for anything else. It has been an additional two weeks beyond Ebey's promised return. The only thing she wants to do is stand on the bluff and look south to see him coming home.

On Sunday, Independence Day, she writes in the journal: *"It is quiet except for the sound of cannon firing from Port Townsend or from a vessel, a great violation of Sabbath. It is cloudy with a little mist falling in a light wind. The water surface is calm, not a ripple or a wave except the surf which is slowly gliding to the shore as regular as the pendulum of a clock, gently."*

She and the boys are hoeing potatoes when Thomas Bartlett and his Indian friend John come. She is thankful to be able to hire them to help in the garden. John Crockett arrives supposedly to borrow tools, but she wonders if it is his unwritten turn to check on her. When a letter from Ebey arrives, she is downhearted. She wants no more letters, no more assurances. She wants her husband to be home. His assurances do not make her feel better. It has been three weeks. She is bone tired and lonely. As she prepares for bed that night, he walks in the door.

Rebecca flies into his arms and holds him, wet and cold. He is exhausted, having come by canoe until the high winds caused the Indians to insist they go ashore. He had left them and walked the long distance home in the storm, needing to get home to her. She stokes the woodstove to get him a hot meal and heats water. He changes into dry clothes. Rebecca cannot wipe the smile from her face, and he cannot take his eyes off of his wife. He holds her around the waist.

"I'm sorry, darling. I'm afraid that I need to hurry off to Salem again in a few days. That is why I needed to get home to you tonight."

Rebecca pulls away and turns away, not wanting him to see her immediate tears. She does not say that it is cruel. She does not tell him that he cannot possibly leave her again so soon. She does not say that she needs him, truly needs him, she and his sons need him. She will not make him feel worse than he already feels.

Bonsels on the Beach, Late Summer 1852

Our common sense is nothing more than the voices of thousands and thousands of ghosts from the past. –Zen and the Art of Motorcycle Maintenance

In addition to rapid killing diseases, the settlers bring consumption or tuberculosis, the slow death that wears down its victims over many years. It is so common in the white population that the deep, hacking cough becomes an indication of old age, like wrinkles. Named "the white plague" in Europe, it is considered a romantic disease there, painted as an indication of heightened sensitivity and spiritual purity so that young ladies strive to be thin and pale like those who are ill while it spreads across North America.

* * *

Rebecca lies awake, remembering her last moments with her husband. He had been home only three full days before he'd left again. She remembers what he said:

I had to get home to you quickly, despite the storm, because I am called to a term of the legislature. It could be a long one, maybe even two months. I will come home at the first opportunity.

Nothing he could say after that could make a difference except holding her as she sobbed into his chest. She had pushed herself to be strong during his absence, waiting for him to be home, and the thought of his leaving again was just too much.

The day before he left, they went to visit the Crockett family in their new home for the first time, a very pleasant visit. They arrived holding hands, but when Ebey explained to the Crocketts that he would be leaving again soon, all eyes turned to Rebecca causing her to hurry to help in the kitchen. Everyone agreed that it was a difficult time of year to be gone, especially for a farmer with so much to do.

She is thankful for her younger brother, Thomas, who stays close. He hauls poles for fencing their crops. The boys watch over the new calves, wanting to give them names. Within a few days, Rebecca feels a debilitating pain in her side, sending her to bed. She cannot lie or standup straight and can scarcely sit up in bed. In the evening, Thomas takes the children to John Crockett's home, and Susan Crockett comes to spend the night. With no improvement the next morning, Thomas goes to Coveland to fetch Dr. Lansdale.

The doctor arrives with his calm confidence and tells her, "You need to rest, dear Rebecca. Do not push yourself to get up. Decide to rest. This could be quite serious if you do not."

Privately, he wonders if he should send word to Mr. Ebey. It might be her appendix as well as consumption.

Several days later, Thomas calls from the living room to Rebecca in bed. "The first steam-propelled vessel in Puget Sound is here! Hudson Bay Company's *Beaver* is passing through!"

She pulls herself up and out of bed to see it. From the distance, it doesn't look terribly different than other vessels except for the big smokestack and fewer masts.

"I've heard that it burns forty cords of wood a day," Thomas says, "which is all it can carry, so they will use the sail whenever they can."

As soon as she gets back into bed, another steamer, the *U.S. Active* is in the harbor. "I don't know why it's here," Thomas says. "It is supposed to be surveying the Oregon and California coast . . . I guess we might be part of the Oregon coast?"

"I will need to see it another time," she says. "When did you grow up and get so serious?"

Thomas shrugs.

"Is it July 23rd?" Rebecca asks. "Mr. Ebey has been gone for ten days, and Eason is eight years old today."

"A worthy milestone," Thomas says. "I'm going back out to work. I'll call him in to come and sit with you when he gets his chores done."

And I will tell him how much I treasure him. It is all I can do on this birthday.

Men arrive on the island for deer hunting. Rebecca must turn them away, unable to cook. No sooner does Mrs. Bonsel arrive, bake bread, make pies and get supper ready than Dr. Lansdale and a survey engineer arrive from the *U.S. Active*. Dr.

Lansdale has brought medicine. "I think you are out of danger now but take it easy," he tells Rebecca. "Rest in bed as much as you can. When you are fully recovered, I will go with Thomas to meet your family as they cross the Cascades."

Rebecca feels her body relax. "That lightens my heart, doctor. Thank you."

"My daughter can stay with her until she's better," Mrs. Bonsel says. "She's old enough to fetch things, make tea and such."

Cordelia Smith returns for a visit at the end of July and runs the house for a few days. Dr. Lansdale wants to hear from Ebey about his schedule for returning home before leaving Rebecca. In the meantime, Thomas continues to work at Ebey's and dig his well on his own property. He finds water at 26 feet. Mr. Alexander, however, finds no water, only fine sand no matter where he digs on his property, no matter how deep.

Melancholy comes to visit Rebecca, and she writes in her journal, "*I cannot expect good health. I am resigned to the will of a Higher Power.*"

In August, she receives another letter from Ebey and one from Winfield in Missouri. Winfield confirms that her mother and brothers are indeed on the trail, but Martha is not coming. She was married last April. *Three months ago*, Rebecca thinks. *My sister is married, and I was not there. I may never see her again or her children yet to be born.* Her melancholy grows roots, yet she pulls herself from bed when she can to scan the horizon as if Ebey and her family will appear before her.

Thomas Bartlet works during the day at Ebey's and stays nights, camping on the property. Rebecca thinks the women neighbors could not know how lonely she is, or they would come to visit her. She writes in her journal: *"I always feel lonely when Mr. Ebey is gone. It makes me think when I had doting loving relatives all around me, a kind mother, aunts, sisters, brothers, cousins, would spare no pains to make me happy. I write to sister Martha to congratulate her on her marriage. She is my only sister as one is in Heaven. I am alone."*

Early on the morning of August 11 before breakfast, Ebey unexpectedly arrives home. Despite Rover wiggling violently between his legs, he sneaks in, not wanting to wake the children. He looks like he's slept rough for nearly a week, which he has. Rebecca is startled, having thought that she would need to wait another entire month. She nearly collapses into his arms.

"Do you forgive me?" he asks. "I *need* to know." He grips her with too much strength, as if desperate.

"I forgive you," she says, whispering near his ear.

He pulls back to see her face, wanting to see if she means it. He kisses her forehead, each eye, under her jawline. "Am I *fully* forgiven?"

"We are still here," she says. "I still love you. I know you are trying to make a good life for us."

He kisses her mouth and sweeps her up into bed. An hour later, the boys are up, wondering about breakfast. They are surprised and happy to see their father home. Blossom complains, wanting to be milked. Rover barks the arrival of the mail carrier, and Ebey looks like he has just been reborn.

The mail carrier reports that his boat is broken up on the beach, and he will be there for a few days while he mends it with the help of a few Indians. After a late breakfast, Ebey goes out with an engineer to survey claims, and a steady stream of visitors come to the cabin, including Doc Tolmie from Fort Nisqually with his half-Indian lady who was educated at the fort, her brother and two other ladies with a little boy. When they continue on to Victoria, Tolmie leaves the gift of a large cut of fresh beef.

Thomas and Dr. Lansdale go to meet Rebecca's mother and other brothers on the trail. Rebecca feels anxious, certain it is past time to meet them. She is reading a letter from her brother John which tells her that the Oregon trail is crowded, when Mrs. Bonsel and her daughter appear at her door, covered in soot and ash, looking ghostly.

"Oh! What happened!" Rebecca says.

"Indians burned down our house," Mrs. Bonsel says, looking lost, "though it was probably an accident."

Rebecca leads them to sit on the bench at the table. "Are you hurt? Are you okay?"

"Not hurt," she says, shaking her head. "I just don't know how we will recover from this."

"I smelled smoke, but thought they were burning a field."

"It got away from them." Mrs. Bonsel covers her face with her soot-covered hands. "I called 'Fire!' again and again but no one came, and I had to pull all our belongings out of the house myself. Now I'm worried it will all be taken."

"Mr. Ebey will talk to Snetlum's people. He can get assurance that nothing will be taken, especially since they are probably the ones who did the burning in the first place. Where is your husband?"

Mrs. Bonsel shrugs. "Victoria, I think."

After a meal and bath, Mrs. Bonsel is persuaded to stay with the Ebeys, "for her daughter's sake," though it takes some convincing. She stays only a few days, refusing to be a burden, especially on Rebecca Ebey who has always had her hands full and struggles with her health. Mrs. Bonsel moves herself and her daughter down to the beach and sets up camp, leaving their horse with Ebeys. It's a day of rainfall, and Rebecca cannot stop imagining how miserable they must be.

"Mr. Ebey," she says at mid-day meal. "What can we do about Mrs. Bonsel and her daughter? I worry for them so. If something happened, we would never forgive ourselves."

"We have already asked her to come as sincerely as we can, several times," he says. "I'm afraid the only way to get her to change her mind is to attack her stubbornness . . . and that may be all the strength she has left. I don't think we want to take that away from her. She must be allowed to make the choice . . . but I will speak to her husband when I see him next."

Ebey finishes his coffee and puts the tin cup down with a thud as if to announce *back to work*. "He's not likely to beat her, is he?"

"I don't think so. Besides, you will know how to speak to him. It is our Christian duty to care for our neighbors."

* * *

Ebey escorts Rebecca out to survey their crops. When she sees two of the Indians who had done poor work in the potato field, one being the angry man in the farmer's hat, she moves to stand behind her husband.

"What are you hiding from?" Ebey asks.

"Those two," she points. "They did not earn their pay in the potato field and then the siwash in the hat sassed me when I didn't pay them as much as they wanted. I gave them some potatoes and onions. It really was all they earned, and they disagreed. It was probably my fault for hiring six at one time, especially since I did not know them. They were feeling brave, I suppose."

"Wait right here," he says. Ebey walks over to the two Indians and pulls the hair of one and kicks the backside of the other, saying, "Cultus!" (bad). He points to Rebecca. "Klootchman! My wife!" he says, hitting his own chest. Then he waves them away, saying "Snetlum!"

He comes back to Rebecca. "I will not have you feeling afraid on our own property. I will speak to Snetlum tomorrow and find out about those two."

The next day, Rebecca takes to her bed, not feeling well, while Ebey goes to visit Snetlum. Lying there, she remembers meeting Ebey at Fort Hall a year ago when they camped on that beautiful creek, so lovely and romantic. She hears the rolling of the surf against the shore, the pebbles' cascading echo. It seems especially loud and poetic. She lies in a dreamy half-sleep, feeling safe with her husband at home. Suddenly, she sits up. "I can't be pregnant! Can I?"

{ **20** }

Captain Coupe, August 1852

Truly, the universe is full of ghosts, not sheeted church-yard spec-ters, but the inextinguishable elements of individual life, which having once been, can never die, though they blend and change. –H. Rider Haggard, *King Solomon's Mines*

Ebey rides to Snetlum's village, enjoying the quiet ride on horseback, his saddle squeaking beneath him. The morning sky is blue and the water calm. As he rides along the cove, he gets a peak at fluffy white icing on the water up against the opposite shore, a fog bank. It's thick, looks impenetrable and grows vertically in peaks like white mountains rising. Then he sees a three-masted ship at anchor languishing in the cove. Above the beach is a crew working to build a cabin.

"Yo, the cabin!" Ebey calls. He dismounts and walks towards the construction.

The ship's captain approaches, his hand out. "Thomas Coupe here, sir."

"Isaac Ebey. Pleased to meet you, Captain. I heard you were here. Impressive . . . vessel you've got there."

"It's the *Success*," Coupe says. "I plan to have a claim here, hoping to entice the family to come and join me."

"It's good to have you on the island. I won't keep you from your work. I'm on my way to visit with Snetlum in the village on the point. Have you met him?"

"No, but I've met his son George. It seems they are an amiable bunch."

"Yes," Ebey says. "Another fortunate aspect of this island, if we treat them well. You might get to know them when you have the time. Drop by our place for a visit at your convenience. We are on the bluff over the back of the island, across from Port Townsend."

Ebey points his horse east along the beach since it is low tide. The village dogs announce his arrival at Snetlum Village, making the horse skittish until George comes out to calm things down.

"Thank you, George. I've come to visit with your father, but I would like it if you were part of the conversation."

"He's there," George points toward the beach. "Admiring his new canoe. He talks to it like a friend."

Ebey sees the 28-foot canoe painted black on the outside, blue on the inside with a red line its length just below its top edge. Snetlum wears a traditional cedar bark cape and apron, running his hands over the sleek lines. "Snetlum," Ebey says, extending his hand. "A beautiful canoe you have."

"Red cedar," Snetlum says, shaking Ebey's hand. "This mighty tree took seven hundred years to grow this canoe for me. I honor it, it's sacrifice, and I am thankful. We are getting to know each other. I am afraid that I am remembering days gone by."

"A handsome vessel, Snetlum. Your canoe maker was one of the best, I'm sure."

Snetlum smiles. "Sam Wick is his name. It is good to see you, Ebey."

"I wonder if we could visit a bit."

"An opportunity to fill a pipe?" Snetlum asks.

"Yes, and I've brought the tobacco."

Snetlum, George and Ebey sit outside near a fire to visit and pass the pipe. Snetlum's joints talk to him, telling him that he would like to have a blanket. "More people come, Ebey," Snetlum says. "More think they may hunt on our land, the land of our ancestors."

"It will not be easy, the changes," Ebey says. "You thought good settlers could give protection against northern raiding parties."

"Yes, but what if the Whites are the raiding party? Our potato crops are being disturbed by your peoples' cattle."

"We are fencing our crops to keep the cows out. The cattle need to graze. Fencing will protect the potatoes."

Snetlum draws on the pipe.

"It is good that we can talk and work out our situations," Ebey says. "I have a situation with some of your younger men. Six were hired by my wife, Rebecca, to work in the field, and one was disrespectful to her. He did not think he was paid enough."

"Was he paid enough, Ebey?"

"My wife is an honest person. She only tells the truth."

"Do you know who it was?" Snetlum asks.

"The one who wears the farmer's hat. I kicked him in the backside. If he disrespects my wife, I disrespect him."

Snetlum smokes.

"Perhaps you could let them know that they should not come to my property unless I am home."

Snetlum nods. "I can only influence, but I will speak to them."

"Thank you, Snetlum. Our laws should protect you as much as they protect us. I am doing my best to have good laws here for all of us, and I will do my best to influence my people as well, to protect you and your village, your way of life."

As Ebey rides away from the village, he thinks about how the plight of the local Indians will require more attention. Difficulties are bound to arise.

* * *

Ebey helps John Crockett break ground to plant wheat. The tall grass is burned before plowing. Then John drives the oxen while Ebey hangs onto the plow handle and John's father, the Colonel, rides the plow beam to keep the plow in the ground. It is more work than they had expected as the ground is dry and hard. It will take several goes before they can make much progress. Captain Thomas Coupe arrives at their field when they stop for a midday meal on their third day of work. He has brought a stack of magazines to pass along.

"Looks like you're making progress," Coupe says. "Say, I heard your missus is under the weather, Ebey. I thought she might like some new reading material."

"Thank you, Captain. I'm sure she will. I should tell you that she calls you Captain Thomas even though she has not met you yet. Her brother is also named Thomas."

"That is sweet. Maria and the family are sailing around the Cape right now, on their way here. I suspect that my Maria and your Rebecca will enjoy each other."

"We were just talking about enlarging the trail into a road from the bluff to the cove." Ebey points with his arm. "It would help unite this area, make travel easier, especially for moving a load in a cart or wagon or to transport a canoe."

"That sounds like a good plan," Coupe says. "Our families will want to attend church one day. A road will make that easier. I would like to help if I am home."

* * *

In the late spring of '53, Captain Coupe sails the *Success* into San Francisco harbor with a load of lumber from Puget Sound as usual. This time, he will meet his wife and family who have traveled around the Cape from New York. He hopes that Maria will love Whidbey Island as much as he does.

After several weeks, they sail into Penn's Cove. Maria is intent on watching the shoreline. The sun is beginning to set, and the Captain watches her face, concerned that she may not be willing to stay. She seems interested in the Indian village at Snakelum Point when they sail past, the canoes lined up on their beach. It's when they get into the ship's boat to row ashore toward a line of dense forest and the tiny log cabin that her face constricts, her lips disappearing into her mouth.

"Captain Coupe! Have you gone crazy to bring me all the way from New York, from family and friends to such a place as this? In the middle of nowhere? With far more Indians than white people?" she says.

He carries each of the four children from the boat to shore, wading through the surf and hoping that Maria will not insist they stay on ship. He goes back for Maria, but she has turned to stone. She steps out of the boat and into the water, soaking her shoes and the bottom of her dress and stomps to shore. "Come children. It will be a difficult night, but we will manage."

Twelve-year old Sarah Elizabeth helps usher the younger children up the hill to the cabin.

Early morning is dark and dead quiet. Maria is bundled in a blanket, sitting on the stoop wondering what she should do. Coupe brings her hot coffee without a word. He lowers himself beside her and says nothing. That is one thing he has learned in his marriage. There are times when the best approach is silence. As the sun begins to lighten the sky, the woods become alive with bird song and the trees become black barriers to blinding light that hits Maria in the face, causing her to squint. It warms her face, and it warms the mist that floats across the cove like soft lace, sending it on its way. Maria looks up from the mist to see the focal point of it all. Mt. Baker covered in snow is lit up like an enormous ice cream cone, and suddenly, she feels small and insignificant, thankful for her husband and the chance for a healthy life for her children away from the filth of a large city.

Coupe sees her body and face relax and takes his cue. "We will have a framed house, Maria, a large one, as large as you like. I can hire the Hill brothers to build it right away."

She asks questions about the activities at the Indian village and about the neighbors, and about a church, and a school for the children.

"We have enough land to donate some for a Methodist Church and for a school, Maria. The community will grow quickly. We already have wonderful neighbors here for you to meet. They are good people."

"I guess I should be thankful that you've found a place you want to settle, Thomas," she says. "I was beginning to lose hope."

Coupe feels his breath grow shallow.

"If you truthfully promise me that you will not take long voyages anymore and we will be a whole family, the children will have a father to guide them here as they grow, we can try."

"My promise was and is to not go to sea in the winter, Maria. If I must go in the summer in order to take care of the family, then I must. We must be practical. But I will not go in the winter when you will need me to be at home."

"I suppose that is so. That's what I get for marrying a sea captain" she shrugs. "Now, let's talk about the new house."

"After you learn how to milk the cow." He pulls her up to standing. "An important morning chore." He pulls her around the cabin. "The children will learn as well, but first, we need to find the cow."

$$\{\ 21\ \}$$

The Cabins, Fall 1852

Fog ghosts are mysterious entities that haunt amidst the fog. They show up as wispy apparitions in the air, weightless and without any human form, coming and going quickly. –paranormalemissaries.com

Rebecca feels well enough to get out of bed to do the washing, but that is all she is able to do, and the little voice in her head continues to ask, *Could I be pregnant?* She realizes that she doesn't feel ill as much as tired. Two visitors come in a canoe from Port Townsend hoping to buy butter. She sees their anticipation but must turn them away. She has not had the energy to make butter in a week.

Rebecca's Journal: *Feeling melancholy this Sabbath. The beautiful green trees and clear sunbeams make everything delightful although we are far from our native land and in country where the gospel is not preached. We live in hopes of realizing religious ceremonies.*

Two days later, two Catholic priests arrive and tell Rebecca that they are looking for a location for a mission. She turns away for a moment to cover her smile, acknowledging that her Lord has a sense of humor. The priests travel to the Cove and return to Ebey's after baptizing several Indian children. That night, she is specific in her prayers for a "good *Methodist* preacher."

The fog is too heavy for Ebey to burn off more grass to prepare a new field, so he helps Hugh Crockett plow his field which has already been prepared. Ebey needs his oxen to be finished at the Crockett properties so he can have them back to work in his own fields.

Rebecca has been waiting for her tomatoes to become ripe enough to harvest for seed, and the day has come. She cuts the tomatoes into wedges to collect the seeds and drops the slippery kernels into several jars, adding a little water, then sets them in a cool corner with a cloth over the top to ferment. Everything else goes into a pot on the stove and she cooks the tomatoes with onion and salt to make a good sauce for canning. The house is full of steam and hot jars when Susan Crockett arrives, bringing a picture of a fruit basket she painted as a gift to hang on the wall.

Rebecca notices a few freckles that have popped up on Susan's nose. "What a lovely picture," she says. "Thank you! You are becoming quite talented, Susan. Apples, peaches, grapes. I can almost taste them."

Susan laughs. "I was hoping you would say that." She steps outside and returns with the actual basket and fruit, exactly like the picture.

It is the first time that Rebecca has laughed out loud in a long time, the laughter of joy. "Where did you find all this fruit?"

"Mr. Alexander returned from Olympia with it. I had to paint quickly so the actual fruit would be fresh for you."

"Well sit down. We will share an apple right now."

Sunday, September 12, Rebecca's Journal: *The sun rose this Sabbath from a bright and clear horizon and continued her journey through a beautiful clear pale blue sky. Everything looks pleasant and happy as though the smile of Heaven was upon it. The song of the blackbird this morning sounds sweeter than usual. I think our friends and family by this time are crossing the Blue Mountains.*

The following week, six sets of hands help Ebey raise his smokehouse, notching each log and lifting it up to fit. The comradery feels like the kind of cooperation that Ebey has longed for in this new community. He hires Captain Bell and Thomas Bartlet to help roof it with long cedar shingles and to do the chinking between logs. Bartlet needs his chinking tool which he left at home, and Ebey suggests that he ride Mr. Bonsel's horse which is boarded there to speed up the trip. Inexperienced with a horse, Bartlet saddles her and climbs aboard, but the saddle is loose, and it rotates, dumping him on the ground which upsets the horse. The horse takes several steps, one of which is onto Bartlet's arm, breaking it between the wrist and elbow.

Ebey knows that Dr. Lansdale is away. He sends Captain Bell to get Nathaniel Hill, and together, they set Bartlet's arm with sticks and strips of cloth. Rebecca volunteers a dishtowel for a sling.

The third week of September, Ebey begins his day surprised to find early morning frost. Fog sits on the water below the bluff looking so thick that he wonders if he could walk on it. He watches the rising sun in a clear sky accentuate the Olympic peaks then climb higher, sending light down the mountains to attack the mist. He knows he should be working. John Crockett is waiting for him to help plow today in exchange for a share of their produce. The smokehouse is finished, but there are logs to cut for the new house and the cookhouse. They need another outhouse. A pier needs to be built on the beach, but he is having trouble getting himself going this day. He stays to watch the last skinny cloud fly from the water in a streak.

Pushing to get through the day, he drags himself home in time for dinner. Susan Crockett is there, having spent the day with Rebecca, and her brother Samuel arrives to take her home.

"You don't look so well, Ebey," Samuel says.

Ebey sits at the table to eat, his head feeling heavy. It seems cold in the house, though the fire is roaring. "Let's hope it passes," he says.

"I have pronounced him 'sick,'" Rebecca says. "He will go straight to bed after he has eaten."

"John Alexander and I are going to Olympia and Fort Nisqually in a few weeks, so when you feel better, let us know if you need anything brought back from there."

"I will." Ebey chews and lifts a hand as Susan and Samuel go out the door.

The following morning, Rebecca finds ice in her tea kettle and shivers as she stokes the woodstove. She wonders what her first winter will be like on Whidbey Island, not expecting it to be so cold so soon. *It cannot possibly get as much snow as Missouri. The growing season is much longer here, and the livestock graze year-round,* she reminds herself. She makes a pot of oatmeal with Blossom's good cream, and toast with butter, and soft-boiled eggs and fried tomatoes for Ebey's breakfast. He and the boys have a quiet meal together while Rebecca sits with her coffee.

"Aren't you eating?" Ebey asks her.

"I'll eat later," she says.

He looks at her through squinting eyes, hoping it will help him determine the truth of her level of wellness. "It seems odd," he says, "to be here with just our family for breakfast. I like it."

"Me too," Ellison says, spooning his oatmeal.

"Eason," Ebey says, "I depend on you to be a good role model and get the chores done around here so I can work in the woods again today. We're close to getting the next house up."

Rebecca's heartbeat quickens. They have dreamed and talked about the new house for quite a while. Soon they will be living there. "Are you up to working today, husband?"

"I feel better, slept hard last night." He puts on his hat and coat and gloves. "I'll be somewhere between the woods and the new house site if you need me."

With the boys off to do chores, Rebecca is cleaning up the dishes when Captain Bell stops by.

"Would you like some breakfast, Captain?"

"No, no, just wanted to pay my respects. I'm on my way to Port Townsend harbor to see Captain Coupe. He is there at anchor in the *Success.*"

Rebecca had been so preoccupied with her husband's health that she had not bothered to notice the harbor. "I would love to send him some milk and butter. Would you be willing to carry it with you?"

"Surely, Mrs. Ebey. It would be my pleasure."

"Thank you, Captain, and please stay to dinner on your way home if it works for you."

Captain Bell returns at the end of the day for a home-cooked meal and time with family, precious things to a man living alone in the wilderness. He delivers fresh pork and matches and tobacco, gifts from Captain Coupe.

With the dawn of October, Ebey has two houses to raise: their new home and their cookhouse. It takes twelve men and a long, hard day's work. Frances Alexander, who is exceedingly pregnant, Mrs. Joseph Smith and John Crockett's wife Ann spend the day with Rebecca to help cook dinner for the crew. It is a festive, cheerful time of celebrating their community.

The next day is Sabbath and Ebey and Rebecca's wedding anniversary. They have an extra cup of coffee in the morning after breakfast with their Bible reading to celebrate.

"I will make a cobbler for dessert tonight to commemorate our nine years of marriage," Rebecca says.

"I am sorry, Rebecca," Ebey says. "I know they have not been easy years. I had hoped to have the new house ready for us to move into for our anniversary."

"You have been working harder than anyone I know, Mr. Ebey," she says. "The day we move in will be just as good whether it is today or some other day. I still love you."

He smiles with those loving, sincere eyes that always warm her heart, wraps his arms around her and kisses her fully. "It seems that I cannot make you swoon anymore, however." He feigns disappointment, as if his feelings are hurt.

"I don't have the energy for swooning any longer, but I love you just the same."

He ruffles her hair to prove that she has plenty of energy when it comes to defending herself.

October 10th, Rebecca's Journal: *We are spending this Sabbath in reading. All around seems beautifully adorned in quiet serenity. Although we have no towering churches yet, we can spend our time in training the young minds of our children in the principles of Christianity and creating within them a thirst for moral knowledge. The liberty of training our children in the way they should go is a blessing.*

* * *

William Engle is a kind and positive person behind a long, straight nose and mutton chops that meet a mustache. He grew up in New Jersey knowing about the duty of caring for others and not making a fuss about himself. Since he was eleven years old, he and his brother earned money for their mother and four siblings after their father's death by working for their uncle who was a farmer, lumberman and had a shipyard. He learned to be a ship's carpenter and practiced that trade until he was pulled away by the promise of gold in California like so many others. He traveled there via the Isthmus of Panama.

After a year's hard work in the mines, Engle decides to join Nathaniel and Humphrey Hill aboard the *J. S. Cabot* piloted by Captain Thomas Coupe. It is setting sail for Puget Sound.

Both Nathaniel and Humphrey Hill are attractive with dark hair and long well-proportioned faces except that Nathaniel's explosive beard and unkempt mustache are practically shocking, as if struck by lightning. He is a serious man, known for understatement and never hesitant to speak his mind. Humphrey, on the other hand, presents himself well. Neat and trimmed, he has a sparkle of fun in his eyes.

They are each in their twenties when all three arrive together at Ebey's bluff. They walk up the trail to The Cabins, having known Ebey previously through the *Orbit* when Nathaniel worked at the Customs House in San Francisco. Ebey welcomes them with information about the island, including the fact that there is a resident doctor, Dr. Lansdale. Lansdale is another name that the Hill brothers know. Sons of a doctor themselves and educated in pharmacy, they are aware of his good reputation.

From there, they continue to sail on the *J. S. Cabot* with Captain Coupe around the island and into Penn's Cove where they visit the Alexanders and buy bread, milk and butter. Meeting the good people of the island is part of the reason that they decide to stay. Before they know it, they have agreed to cut timber to load aboard the *J. S. Cabot* for the San Francisco market. It is work that allows them to become acquainted with the local Indians.

William Engle, who goes by "Bill," and the Hill brothers take claims along the bluff south of Ebey's, Bill's property being the closest. They work together to build a log cabin for Bill and live there together until the other cabins can be built, bachelors all three.

The wind increases until it becomes dangerous to cut trees, but Ebey does it anyway. He hopes to be spry enough on his feet to get out of the way if the wind should send a falling tree in the wrong direction. Rebecca told him that he is foolish to go out there, especially because of the accident that nearly killed her brother James. Now that he *is* out there and the wind has become fierce, she will not send anyone to get him. It would put them in danger too. She prays that he will have the common sense to quit on his own.

It is nearly dark when Ebey arrives from the woods, still alive. Ellison is asleep in his chair with a book in his lap. Eason is resting his sore foot on a wooden chest while studying his lesson when there is another tap on the door. John Alexander and Samuel Crockett are there just returned from Olympia and Nisqually. They have learned that Thomas is still waiting on the Umatilla River for Rebecca's family and Dr. Lansdale is on his way home. Rebecca had hoped for weeks that every knock on the door was her family. Now she must accept that her wait will be much longer, and Thomas is alone.

Life continues to be busy at The Cabins. Skagit friends bring cranberries to Rebecca as a regular routine in October when they are plentiful. She makes apple and cranberry pie and cranberry sauce to go with everything. A siwash (Indian man) who was hired to dig potatoes taps on her door. When she opens it, Rover is there waiting beside him, having become a friend. His tail wags and his ears flop about in the wind. The elder has come for his pay, his long gray hair streaming sideways. Rebecca is happy with his work and pays him with one of Ebey's shirts which has become too snug and some produce. He seems satisfied, showing a smile and a nod, and Rebecca must call Rover back to keep him from following his friend home.

Dr. Lansdale arrives, bringing new immigrants for Rebecca to welcome and feed. He tells her that he heard her family was in Grande Ronde Valley not far from Salem to buy live-stock. Thomas has gone to meet them. The weather has turned cold. Despite reports of unusually deep snow in Salem that has stopped all travel, Rebecca wants to linger on the bluff to watch for her brothers.

{ **22** }

In the Night, November 1852

The first settlers are buried in the town's graveyard, but they are also, along with every other citizen in the town's history, as present as the canopy of stars." –Dani Shapiro, *Signal Fires*

Every time Rebecca sees a ship harbored, or a small boat or canoe paddling to the beach, or people walking up the trail, her heart stops, hoping it is the moment that she has been imagining for months when she will first lay eyes on her family . . . her mother.

When Frances Alexander's birthing pains begin in the middle of the night, the two older Alexander boys are sent on horseback for Dr. Lansdale at Coveland. They carry huge torches as they gallop through the woods along Penn's Cove, knowing they could be chased by big gray timber wolves in the night. Calves and sheep are attacked every now and then and drug away for a meal. For the moment, they are more worried about the wolves than their mother's need. They had heard of the man on his horse who had been chased by a wolf pack. The man had climbed onto the limb of a tree, hoping his horse would escape on its own. He had spent the night in the tree and the poor horse had lost his tail, never to be the same.

Having been rousted in the wee hours, Ebey saddles his own and Bonsel's horse and leads Rebecca to Alexander's. They arrive before Dr. Lansdale and find the family already prepared for both the doctor and the baby, whoever arrives first. Rebecca holds Frances's hand, telling her how well she is doing, how her new baby will bring joy to everyone and will take care of her in her old age. When he arrives, Dr. Lansdale's calm and joyful countenance and expertise is a great comfort. He delivers a handsome little boy to the world. The first white baby born on Whidbey Island, Alexander's fourth son, is named Abram Lansdale Alexander.

Rebecca holds tiny Abram as Frances sleeps, finding it difficult to not fall in love. She gives each of the children and John a chance to do the same. God's presence feels near with the family gathered in golden candlelight. It causes her hand to move to her stomach. Her morning sickness is over. It is time to tell Ebey.

They ride home in the quiet as the sky begins to lighten, the east slowly giving light to the west. The air is still, but cold. Rebecca pulls her wool scarf up over her head, wrapping the ends around her neck inside her pulled-up collar.

"That whole family is a blessing," Ebey says, as if he reads her mind. He turns to look at Rebecca who rides behind. "I admire John tremendously. Not every man can lose a leg and then carry on as if he still has two."

"And how do you feel about the baby?" Rebecca asks.

"Beautiful. A gift from God himself."

"I am happy that you feel that way," she says.

Ebey stops, then turns his horse. "Do you mean to be telling me something?"

"Yes, husband. We are about three months along I would say."

Ebey has trouble swallowing through his tight throat. *What have I done?* "A blessing for us?" he asks. "Are you happy?"

"Yes, of course, Mr. Ebey," she says. "God's gifts are always a blessing. Maybe he will bless us with a little girl this time. We are safe in His hands."

Please let that be true, Lord. "Then I am happy too." He rides close and stretches out to kiss her but nearly pulls her off her horse. As they continue along the Cove, each in their own thoughts, the lightest, most fragile lemon mist rises from the water on the opposite shore and reaches toward them in long, swirling fingers.

Back at Alexander's, the Skagit neighbors are very interested to see a white baby. They line up at the house, patiently but persistently waiting. They wait for hours, even after the Ebeys and the doctor have left and continue to wait. Finally, despite his wife's protests, regardless of her fear, John gives each of his older boys a gun and plants one on each side of the doorway. He opens the door to let them parade one by one into the house and through the bedroom to see his wife lying in bed with the baby, hoping they will then go home.

* * *

In mid-November, Rebecca is cleaning up breakfast dishes when John Crockett brings turnips, venison and cabbage in payment for the use of their oxen. She marvels at the mild climate that allows cabbage to be harvested in November, the cattle able to graze all year. She is certain that people in Missouri are hovering inside around a large fire to keep warm and maybe hauling feed to their livestock.

Ebey comes back into the house from work. "How would you like to do something special today?" he asks.

Rebecca is intrigued and suspicious. "What?"

"Something I think you will like . . . "

"Mr. Ebey," she says, hands on her hips. "I do not have time for such games. Just tell me what you are thinking!"

"I thought you might like to move into our new house today, but if you're too busy . . ."

"It is ready? Why did you not tell me! Where are Eason and Ellison? Boys! Come and get your things! It is time to move! Our new house is ready! You can move into your new bedroom!"

Their new log house is larger than their first cabin. It has a main room, dining room and parlor, the parlor providing access to the main bedroom. There are two small rooms on the front porch, one for storage and one serving as a small bedroom for the boys. The dining area is large enough for several tables and benches. Two fireplaces, one in the main room and one in the parlor as well as the cookstove in the cookhouse. The cookhouse is separate with its own entrance and connected to the main house.

At three months pregnant, Rebecca has regained a little of her energy, and spends it on moving into the new cookhouse. The boys carry her mattress between them into the bedroom and they settle into their little bedroom on the porch that opens to the main room. That evening, with fire popping in the beautiful rock fireplace that Ebey built in the main room, Rebecca enjoys the comfort of her new home.

"How do you like the new cookstove?" Ebey asks. "It arrived just in time."

"I love it, of course," Rebecca says. "I love everything about our new home, but I do hope it can clean itself."

"What?"

"Look at the mud that has been tracked in all over the floor! I do not suppose it will disappear by the time I wake up in the morning."

In the morning, as Rebecca suspected, the house did not clean itself and the fairies did not come, and she needs to scrub the floors. While Ebey is gone to the Cove to get the one-hundred pounds of flour he ordered, she prepares the house for Sunday and guests the next day. When Ebey returns, John Alexander, John Crockett, Dr. Lansdale and Captain Coupe all arrive and spend the afternoon talking with Ebey about his upcoming trip to Salem in a few days. As their representative, Ebey listens to what is important to them. Captain Coupe and Dr. Lansdale stay for supper, the doctor spending the night in Ebey's old cabin.

Rebecca is restless that night, unable to sleep, but she will not complain to her husband. His responsibility goes beyond his immediate family, and he has worked his hardest to provide for her and the children.

Aware of her distress, Ebey tries to soothe her worries as he prepares to leave. "I have hired the Indian "John" to stay and make the fires and get wood and work around the house and property while I'm gone. He knows how to work. He is reliable," Ebey says.

Rebecca nods.

"Mr. Engle has agreed to stay at The Cabins every night until Thomas gets back. I do not want you to be alone at night."

She smiles, but her eyes do not hide her truth.

"He is our closest neighbor, living with the Hill brothers. You have said that he is kind and jovial." Ebey grinds his jaw, wishing he did not need to leave. "Your mother and John and James will be here soon, and then you won't give me another thought."

At that, her tears flow. "How can you say that?" she cries, hitting his chest. "Will you promise me that you will be back before the baby comes?"

"Yes, Rebecca. I promise. If I must leave my responsibilities to be back in time, I will do it. I promise."

Rebecca does not want to see him walk away from the house or leave the beach in a canoe. She wants to pretend that he is still there, working in the field or in the woods. She busies herself with candle-making, saying that she cannot leave her hot wax to say goodbye and sends the boys instead. *Dread,* she thinks. *I dread his leaving.* That evening she writes in her journal: *I am very much distressed at seeing Mr. Ebey start out for Salem this morning.*

After Ebey leaves, Rebecca clings to happy thoughts to fight against the melancholy that lurks. It is the first time that she feels panic rising. She is well aware of the fragility of life, having lost her sister and her father. Even though there are neighbors within a few miles and Bill Engle is there each night, she feels alone. She holds onto the thought of her mother and brothers being with her soon and the happy winter she will have with them. She tells herself that she has no time for anything other than her duties--her two boys to raise and educate, a farm to run, room and board to offer visitors when she is up to it. She must be mindful of her health, especially now that she is pregnant, especially since she is older with this pregnancy, thirty years old.

* * *

In Ebey's mind, when he leaves home on November 23, the memory of Rebecca's teary face and her unwillingness to say goodbye work at his gut. He remembers Bill Engle's sincere face, feels his reassuring hand on his shoulder, "I'll watch over her, man. Not to worry." His goal is to get his work done quickly and get back home.

Ebey joins 43 other delegates at the convention at Monticello just north of the Columbia River. They meet in a private home and sit in groups on blankets on the floor to draft an even stronger petition to Congress than they wrote the previous year, demanding the "right to legitimate representation," stating that the Oregon Territorial seat of Salem is too far away for the northern territorial residents.

From there, he will continue on to the Oregon Territorial Legislature as the only representative from Thurston County. It meets in Salem, another 140 miles beyond Olympia, an arduous trip. Everyone who lives north of the Columbia River depends on him to represent their best interests, and he is determined to do that.

* * *

At The Cabins, Skagit Indian John chinks the cookhouse and shaves the boards that need shaping like a master carver. He nails the cracks closed and cuts firewood. Neither John nor Rebecca are comfortable with the Klallam campers on the beach who come to watch the construction and the behaviors of the white woman with two children.

Five days after Ebey leaves, there is heavy frost. Rebecca is kneading bread dough, hoping it will rise despite the cold, when a letter arrives. Thrilled and worried at the same time, she wipes the dough from her hands and takes the letter. It is from Thomas. Her heart pounding, she sits at the table and notices her hands shake as she breaks the seal. Carefully, she unfolds the paper. Her breath is shallow as she reads. Then her eyes stop, her breath catches. The letter slides from her hands. Her mother has died on the trail.

{ 23 }

Alone, November 1852

Losing a parent is one of the most harrowing experiences that a person can go through. Sometimes, deceased parents aren't ready to leave. Maybe they want to impart more wisdom to their children or offer kind words, or just want to say 'I love you' one more time.--Jacob Shelton, ranker.com

As the letter flutters from her hands, emotional Pain causes her to hold her stomach, protection for the baby. Willing herself to breathe, she floats and loses herself in darkness, her head on the table. She regains consciousness but continues to float. "Jesus, the anchor of my soul," she says aloud, her prayer reaching skyward. She waits for that Anchor to bring her back, to feel the bench beneath her. Shock does not allow tears, but when truth strikes, and she doubts that she will ever forgive herself, tears become wails and the boys come running.

"What's the matter, Ma?" Eason asks. Ellison grabs her around her neck and hangs on.

Rebecca's Journal entry that night, November 28: *Oh, the distress of my heart. My dear mother has died on the Plains of the Oregon Trail. How can I ever get over it? I will reflect upon myself as long as I live that I did not persevere a little more and bring her with me when I came.*

The next day is Sabbath, and she will not stain a Sabbath with negative thoughts even though she has had no sleep or rest. *"Another beautiful day has dawned upon us. I know it is wrong for me to grieve. My mother's spirit has left this earth, but I have hope of meeting her in a far better world than this, which is the only consolation I have."*

The Skagit worker John daubs mud between the logs of the house. John Crockett brings a load of firewood, and the boys stay close to their mother after their chores are done. By the end of the day, she is vaguely aware that her face is swollen on one side and her tooth aches.

Dr. Lansdale raps on the door. "Rebecca, I am going to Port Townsend. Is there something that you need?" He notices Rebecca's low affect and swollen face, and the boys act like they are in trouble. "What is wrong?" he asks, leading her to a chair.

She has not spoken the words except to cry with her boys. She has not written about it to Ebey. It dawns on her that she has been thinking that if no one knows about her mother's death, maybe it will not be true. She looks at the floor. "My mother," she says. Unable to continue, she looks up with teary eyes.

"Is she sick?"

"She has passed," Rebecca says, feeling her throat tighten. "On the trail . . . on her way to us . . . to me. It is my fault."

Dr. Lansdale puts his hand on her shoulder. "No, Rebecca. You are not to blame. Every person who begins that trip knows the risks. She could have gotten sick or had an accident at home." He pours hot water from the kettle to make tea. "I am so sorry," he says, setting the cup in front of her. "You have had your share of challenges. How did you learn about it?"

"A letter from Thomas," she says. "He met our brothers in Oregon south of the Columbia River. He wrote that our mother died from illness," she begins to sob. "They buried her along the trail."

"They did not have a choice," Lansdale says. "Drink a little tea, please. Then I would like to look inside your mouth."

Rebecca's hand goes to her jaw. "I woke up with it swollen." She sips her tea.

Dr. Lansdale examines her mouth and tells her that she must rinse with warm saltwater frequently and he will check back tomorrow. "I will stop at Colonel Crockett's house to ask Susan Crockett to come for a few nights," he says. He takes her hand and squeezes. "Losing a mother is difficult. You are hurting . . . and lonely without Ebey. Try to hang on to your faith and the fact that your brothers will be here soon now that they are in Oregon."

Susan Crockett comes, but Rebecca does not have the energy to be good company, and after two days, Susan wants to go home, worried for her father who has been ill. Rebecca leaves eight-year-old Eason home while she and Ellison escort Susan to Susan's brother's house which is the closest Crockett house, knowing that John will get her home to her parents. As the sun drops, the temperature plummets and Rebecca is afraid to start home. She stays until morning, worrying about Eason, not wanting him to feel abandoned like her mother must have felt. When she and Ellison rush home in the morning, she finds Eason having breakfast with Bill Engle, enjoying amiable conversation.

When Skagit worker John is called to Port Townsend, Rebecca hires an Indian named Sam, but he comes only one day. She is thankful that Bill Engle spends the next day hauling firewood for them.

Rebecca rallies herself and decides that she and the boys will clean the yard. They work all day, even continue in the cold rain and again the next day until they are too tired to feel sad, with no energy for anything but sleep. Even then, she sits by the fire to sew a new pair of pants for Eason. He seems to have grown an inch a month in the last four months since he turned eight.

* * *

After the Monticello Convention, Ebey continues on to Salem to attend the 4th and Special Session of the Oregon Territorial Legislative Assembly on December 6. He is the representative from Thurston County. At the Assembly, he drafts a memorial to separate the territory north of the Columbia River from Oregon Territory, calling it Columbia Territory. It takes time, and he must stay to voice the hopes and expectations of those he represents. He is also making progress with the legislature to create new counties for Columbia Territory explaining that the current Thurston County is too large. Then he receives a letter from Rebecca.

Rebecca is always careful to present an optimistic attitude in her letters. Ebey is anxious to read it but keeps the letter in his pocket until after his meetings of the day and reads privately in his room. As soon as he opens the carefully folded paper, he sees that her handwriting looks different. The shapes are not round as usual, as if her hand would move only up and down rather than to the right. His eyes skim over the sentences about the island until he finds the trouble. Rebecca's mother is dead. His heart twists. *Oh to be with you now, my Rebecca. I am so sorry.*

He writes to her, saying that he is sorry, so sorry. He would be home if he possibly could, but he cannot. He is making progress for the establishment of new counties: a smaller Thurston County and additional counties to be named Pierce, Jefferson, Island and King. He is sponsoring a statute to name King County after William Rufus DeVane King, senator from Alabama and newly elected Vice President under President Pierce. *"If I leave now, I fear that all will be for nothing. I have given my word to the territory to represent them, and this is when I must do it. The results affect us all. Please be strong my love. Thomas and your other brothers will be there soon. I love you. I pray for you and the boys every day. I am yours, your ever faithful husband."*

* * *

On Whidbey Island, the talented Hill brothers help Bill Engle build his house, a house they will share for a while. At the same time, they build Captain Coupe's house. They also work in the forest to bring out logs for spars used for masts of ships and for pilings for wharves in San Francisco to be transported on the *J. S. Cabot* by Master Mariner Captain Coupe.

Nathanial and Robert Hill work together with axes and wedges to fell the trees. They instruct two Indians from Snetlum's village with the two-man cross-cut saw, the misery whip, to saw back and forth to cut the tree into long lengths, mostly Douglas fir and some Sitka spruce. Ox teams skid the logs out of the woods to float in the water where they are loaded onto the *J. S. Cabot* using a crane from the yard boom.

At the end of the day, they are tired and hungry, but being bachelors, their menu is meager, sometimes only meat, sometimes no bread. Nathaniel Hill cannot abide living without bread, so he hires a few Indians and a large canoe to take him to Victoria for provisions and most important, flour. It was to be a quick trip. He had not planned it taking nearly three days to get there, stalled by weather and tide, and he decides that sitting in a canoe that long is not an experience well-suited to a white man, no matter how large the canoe. Wet, cold, cramped, and determined, he manages to return after a six-day trip with a thousand pounds of hard-earned flour, thinking all the while about bread.

He delivers 250 lbs. of flour to Rebecca and sells 100 lbs. to Colonel Crockett. Bill Engle tells Nathaniel that he has accepted an order on their behalf during his absence to supply another load of logs for Captain Coupe to take to San Francisco. Not ready to work in the woods after his ordeal, Nathaniel takes Bill's place with Rebecca while Bill goes to cut boards and timber for his own place. Nathaniel is hoping that some of that flour will become bread, or anything baked or fried, in the hands of Mrs. Ebey.

After a hearty breakfast of eggs and pancakes, of which Nathaniel Hill eats enough for three people, the boys come in to say that they cannot find the cows. Nathaniel goes out to look for them, and searches all day, but they are not to be found.

"I don't suppose some wolves got them." Nathaniel says.

"All of them?" Rebecca says. "Without leaving any signs of attack? No bones, nothing?"

"I will look again tomorrow. They must be out there somewhere. It is an island after all. I doubt they swim well enough to attempt an escape." Nathaniel smiles at his own joke, a rarity.

Rebecca and the boys giggle. It is the lightest moment she experiences since learning of her mother's death.

That evening, Nathaniel stocks wood for the evening fire and for cooking in the morning. As he works, he tries to predict the morning meal, something with flour. *Maybe biscuits and gravy,* his mouth waters, *and coffee of course.* Coffee is another thing he cannot do without. Boiling parched peas like some people use when there is no coffee is no substitute at all. He will not drink it.

There is a rap on Rebecca's door. Joseph Smith is there to make a confession. He borrowed Ebey's old scow, the one that had miraculously stayed in one piece to transport Ebey's and Crockett's belongings and livestock to Whidbey Island from Olympia, but he has accidentally run it ashore on an island in a windstorm and it has broken all to pieces.

Rebecca doesn't think to ask if he is hurt or about the cargo on the scow. She only thinks of how her husband is gone, the cows are gone, the scow is gone, and her mother is gone.

{ 24 }

Snetlum, December 1852

A person with Deer as their spirit totem is a strong, intuitive protector who can be gentle and appreciative of others. –spiritanimals.org

The weather is especially cold. Snetlum has the sense that it will get even colder, much colder than most winters. Still, he makes his way to the Cross as often as he can, asking George to paddle him deeper into the Cove to the beach where John Alexander builds his house. He has met John Alexander there, a man with a wooden leg. He is a good man, a man who can be trusted, who welcomes Snetlum when he comes to visit his Cross.

Snetlum hobbles up the beach to put his left hand on the Cross and makes the sign of the Cross against his face and chest with his right. He caresses it with both hands and lovingly says the Lord's Prayer in Chinook the way he learned it from Father Blanchet as his eyes travel up to the top, nearly twenty feet from the ground. Then he kisses the Cross, crosses himself again and returns to his canoe. As he helps paddle the canoe home, anxious to get back to the fire to warm his joints, he sees that Komo Kulshan (Mt. Baker) towers over him in a clear blue sky.

In winter, especially during cold weather, when everyone is inside the longhouse around the fires, it is an important time for storytelling. The elders must continue to tell the stories to keep their culture alive. Snetlum is inspired by his vision of Komo Kulshan. He calls the children to come near if they wish to hear a story before his nap today. George Jr. is the quickest to settle next to his grandfather, and his cousins come to join.

"Would you like to hear the story of Komo Kulshan again?" Snetlum asks.

"And his wives?" George Jr. asks.

"Yes, grandson," Snetlum's hand lands on top of the boy's head.

"In the beginning, before Vancouver named Mt. Baker, it was called Komo Kulshan, "white shining mountain," Snetlum begins. The Cross on the rawhide around his neck vibrates when he talks. The children settle in, showing respect for the story and the storyteller.

"Kulshan was a handsome man who had two wives: one beautiful but jealous," he snarls his lip, *"and one amiable and kind,"* he smiles.

"Jealous wife wanted to be the favorite. She wanted more attention, so she left, leaving her children behind, hoping that Kulshan would call her back and show he loved her." His eyes grow wide. *"But he did not call her back."* He shakes his head.

"*The further away she traveled, the more she grew tall in order to look back and see if Kulshan might be calling her.*" Snetlum stretches his neck tall and looks over his shoulder. "*She finally traveled so far and grew so tall that she became Tacobud, the mountain named Mt. Rainier by Vancouver!*" He points in the direction of Mt. Rainier and the children do also.

"*The amiable wife was pregnant and wanted to see her mother, so Kulshan had all the animals dig a ditch for her so she could travel by canoe. They created the Nooksack River.*" He travels his hand through the air like a winding river.

"Grandfather," George Jr. says, "What kind of animals dug the ditch?"

"What kind do you suppose?" Snetlum asks.

"Animals that dig good?"

"Yes, what animals do you know that are good diggers, Grandson?"

"Dog!" George Jr. says.

"Wolf!" another child says.

"Ground hog! Rabbit! Bear?" All the children join in.

"Yes, yes, yes . . . Ready for the rest of the story?

Amiable wife lies down so people can walk over her easily and not need to climb. She became Spieden Island to the north of San Juan Island.

"*Kulshan grew lonely without his wives and stretches up to see them. He stretched and stretched as tall as you see him now. His children did the same and they grew tall to see their mother, creating the mountains south and east of their father Kulshan, creating the peaks that you see now around Mt. Baker."*

The children are quiet, waiting to see if the story is finished. "Go and see," he says.

The children scramble out of the longhouse.

Snetlum's hand goes to his throat. He wonders if he has gotten so old that he cannot tell a story without soreness in his throat, and he goes to his bed for his nap. He wakes in the evening feeling feverish and his throat feels like it is cut with a knife. His wife Tolo gives him willow bark tea to calm the pain, wraps him in his favorite dog-hair and mountain goat wool blanket and calls for the Shaman.

The Shaman comes with his totem rattles and herbs and uses cedar smoke to clear the bad energy that would make Snetlum sick. He chants and sings and dances and finally, Snetlum sleeps.

The next day, Snetlum's fever is high, and he can barely speak. His neck is swollen, and he struggles to breathe. For several days, he rests and sleeps as the shaman works. Snetlum travels through the Inbetween where he is held in the arms of a warm cedar tree, wrapped in its soft green boughs. He floats in the blue sky over the Cove where Hawk flies to tell him that he will be fine. He rests his fevered hand on the cool white head of White Deer that nuzzles his neck as Tolo washes him with cool water. When the shaman tells George that he has seen Snetlum's spirit, and he will not come back, George goes for Dr. Lansdale.

The doctor comes into the warm, stifling building with his medicine bag. The space is lit by the family fire, and he asks for more light to see inside Snetlum's mouth. George brings a burning stick and holds it close.

"There is an abscess growing in his throat, big," the doctor says, feeling the swollen glands on his neck. "It is cultus (bad). His tonsils are big, swollen, also cultus." He turns to face George and Tolo. "It is called quinsy, an infection of the throat, like poison."

"Can you take it out?" Tolo asks.

Dr. Lansdale shakes his head. "It is all through his body now. I am so sorry."

Snetlum's spirit stands with White Deer beneath the tall Cross on the hill. As the doctor examines him, he feels the shadow of the Cross on his face and neck and chest. It feels like love, warm, like a Heavenly touch. He hears Father Blanchet's Christian songs being sung, the songs that he himself taught to his village. Their singing voices are heard throughout the village and across the Cove. The people of his village sway and dance, not wanting to imagine their future without Snetlum. Tolo holds his hand, willing him to breathe as he struggles in his sleep. One deep, final exhale releases Snetlum's Spirit to fly with Hawk.

It is December 16. The world looks solid gray, without water or sky.

The gray day becomes dark. It begins to snow, hard and thick, flakes the size of small clams. It falls for hours, covering everything in white like White Deer, bringing Silence and Purity until two inches of cold fluff has settled on the ground.

It seems right to the People of Snetlum's village. The world changes without Snetlum. It *should* look different. They cannot imagine being without his guidance. George sends messengers to the Klallam people at Port Townsend to tell them what has happened and to invite them to come pay their respects.

Snetlum's body is prepared for viewing. George brings fragrant boughs of cedar and spruce. Tolo dresses him in his best ceremonial robe decorated with beads and deer hooves and shells, his Cross lying on his chest. They arrange his valuables around him, his large Catholic Ladder which was the gift from Father Blanchet and his carved bentwood cedar box of treasures.

The next morning, it is 19 degrees, snow and thick ice everywhere, yet the Klallam people come, each wearing as many layers of animal skins as they can for warmth under their ceremonial hats and capes and robes and blankets. They come to honor a leader who was respected by all.

* * *

Rebecca wakes to the sound of Nathaniel Hill stoking every fire that can be made in the new house and she cannot get dressed fast enough. In her heaviest coat, she realizes that the water in the teapot is solid and will need to be melted. Even the potatoes in the Cookhouse are frozen. It should not be this cold on Whidbey Island.

She sees the harbor full of canoes, the large war canoes and small canoes, all full of Indians, coming together across the water, and she wonders what has happened. Watching them beach their canoes and appear at the top of the bluff trail, it looks like the entire tribe of Klallam have come on such a frigid day. The tyees (leaders) come to her door. She recognizes the Klallam leader Lach-ka-nam from Port Townsend and his son who has been on the island frequently to tend their potato fields. They peer out from their layers of animal skins and blankets, looking like a village of bee hives on the move. "We must come in to warm ourselves," the son says. "Then we will continue on to Snetlum's village."

Rebecca knows that she must let them in but there are too many. "Only the tyees," she says. Soon, the house is filled with cold bodies, having arranged themselves to sit on the floor, and the temperature inside the house drops. Within minutes, those outside start fires with the smudge pots they carry and erect temporary shelters close together across her yard.

"What has caused you all to come on such a cold day?" she asks Lach-ka-nam's son.

"Snetlum has died. We come to honor him."

Rebecca feels pressure in her chest. She knows what a stabilizing influence Snetlum has been with the entire area and how much her husband has enjoyed knowing him. Ebey's absence seems even more acute than before. She must represent him well.

"That is sad news," she says. "Mr. Ebey liked him very much." She wonders if the Klallam people truly are there to honor Snetlum. It could be that it is to reinforce an alliance with George, or to make a show of their numbers when the Skagit are feeling vulnerable. Not being of their culture, Rebecca is unable to understand.

As the air warms inside her house, she wonders if some of the animal skins they wear have not yet been completely tanned, and clings to the promise that they will be leaving as soon as they are warm enough.

At Snetlum's village, the Klallam guests are received into the Potlatch house which is large enough to accommodate them, and smaller groups are allowed to visit Snetlum's longhouse to view his body. His treasures are also displayed, including his hatchet, bow and arrows, fishing net, and canoe paddle, each representing stories of Snetlum that will be remembered and retold. George explains that Snetlum will be buried in a box in the ground as Father Blanchet taught, as Snetlum wanted, rather than in a canoe in the arms of a tree. The Klallam visitors invite George's family to come to Port Townsend when their ceremonies are done. "We must continue with talks," Lach-ka-nam says.

As is custom, the Skagit people want to distance themselves from Snetlum's ghost while the casket is being created. The elders oversee the process, including the carving of a Cross into the front of Snetlum's box. Having little fear about an attachment of Snetlum's ghost because of their age, they are the ones to manage to lift Snetlum's body into the casket when it is finished.

The burial place is chosen on the crest of the hill above Snakelum Point where his spirit can see his family and his village below, and where White Deer will visit. There will be a memorial potlatch for Snetlum the following winter. They will spend their time until then getting ready.

* * *

Christmas arrives in a world of white. Dr. Lansdale and John Alexander come through the snow with a jar of pickles and a box of mincemeat, presents for Rebecca and the boys. She makes an excellent mincemeat pie for dinner, surprised at how good it is. Hot pie on a day that is 16 degrees is a welcome treat. Still, the temperature continues to drop, and Samuel Crockett and Nathaniel Hill haul more firewood to Rebecca when it is eight degrees.

Samuel wonders about the extreme cold as he unloads the wood, his fingers stiffening inside his gloves. He inserts a hand into his coat for a warmup. "How do we appease Snetlum so the cold will stop, do you think?" He looks at Nathaniel, not entirely joking.

"How do you know it's Snetlum?" Nathaniel asks, tossing an armload. "Maybe the world has grown bitter and cold without him. I know his family feels that way. They seem lost."

Samuel bends to clear his nose. "He brought a great deal of prestige to his village, to be sure."

"Respected by all, I'd say, Indians and Whites . . . and me," Nathaniel says. "That's enough wood for Rebecca for a few days. We can do more later."

Rebecca's loneliness continues. Despite the men's short visit, she is alone with her boys in the house. Her women friends are nowhere to be seen. She thinks of Christmases gone by, the happy times with family, baking cookies, making candy. The big family meal with turkey or goose, pies for dessert. She thinks if the women nearby knew of her loneliness, they would come to visit.

In the morning, it continues to snow, and the cows disappear again. By afternoon, the sun is shining. In the evening, George Snetlum raps on the door. He and his family are back from Port Townsend and ask to camp in the smokehouse overnight before continuing to Snakelum Point. Rebecca agrees with no concerns about George. It is 28 degrees.

On Rebecca's birthday a few days later, she allows herself time to grieve for her mother, but when it is time for her to enjoy her birthday plum duff, she is unable to stop weeping. It turns into puddles of purple.

{ **25** }

Taking Turns, January 1853

I heard that kind of sound that a ghost makes when it wants to tell about something that's on its mind and can't make itself understood, and so can't rest easy in its grave, and has to go about that way every night grieving. –Mark Twain

On New Year's Day, Rebecca coughs and shivers as she tends to Old Captain Coffin who sits in her parlor most of the day as if it is his own. This is one of the times when she misses her husband most, when an overly proud, disgusting guest thinks he can make demands on her. He treats women as if they are servants. She had turned him away on his previous attempt to stay when she was quite ill. This time, she manages to produce dinner for him, though he indicates no appreciation whatsoever.

Rebecca's Journal, January 2: *"We are very lonesome on this first Sabbath of the New Year. I wish Mr. Ebey was at home. I would feel much better. This beautiful evening the sun is shining very bright. The snow is thawing some. How thankful we should be to our Creator for preserving us until another New Years Day in health and bodily strength. May He enable us to spend this coming year more to His service and in performing our religious duties. In the end we will be happier."*

Eason reads to Ellison from his primer, then switches to the New Testament, trying to find something to occupy his thoughts. "Ma," he says, "when will Pa come home?"

"I do not know, Eason. I cannot read the future, and he has not told us in a letter . . . that we have seen anyway. Sometimes letters get lost, and the Port Townsend people have not been good about sending the mail on to us." She has had no news from Ebey in over a month and has written to him but has been unable to find someone willing to carry the letters for delivery. "It is our first winter and everything is new here. Think of the ship's captains. They are gone for many months across the ocean sometimes. We have no choice but to be patient."

"When will Uncle Thomas be back then?" Eason's voice sounds like a whine and he squirms in his chair as if he is trapped.

"You know the answer to that as well," she says. "When your Pa returns, he can help you be more industrious and not sit about to whine. I get tired of reminding you of your chores and the importance of a good attitude."

She has heard nothing about Thomas. Snow has fallen south of the Columbia River to three feet deep, causing new emigrants there to lose their provisions and cattle. She is afraid that her brothers, who were supposed to be in that area to buy livestock, are suffering from exposure and that they will get sick . . . like her mother.

A week into January, the temperature shoots up to 50 degrees. Rebecca is washing laundry and scrubbing the cookhouse floor with the leftover water. Joseph Smith from the cove comes to borrow a yoke of oxen to plow at his place, and she thinks about the last thing he borrowed, the scow. That did not end well, but she lets them go, hoping for the best. As Mr. Smith walks off with the oxen, Nathaniel Hill arrives.

"Mr. Smith is using our oxen," Rebecca says.

"Thank you, but I don't need them. I bought a yoke of oxen from Colonel Crockett this morning. Just checking on you and the boys."

"Is there a reason that you carry your gun today, Mr. Hill?"

"I had a little run-in with some Indians wanting to harass me at home. Since I was alone, I did not want to engage with their tomfoolery, so I scared them off with this." He shows the gun at his waist.

"Thankfully, I have not seen any Indians today," she says. "Dr. Lansdale was here, though, to see if I have any news from Mr. Ebey. I can assure you that I am more anxious for news than anyone."

"He is doing important work. I am sorry that it means sacrifice for you and the boys."

"It would be much easier for me if I could hear from him," she says. "I have written two letters to him that I cannot seem to mail, there has been so little traffic through here lately."

"Well," Hill says, scratching his head. "I just bought a small old canoe from George Snetlum. It's a calm, warm day. I should be making use of my new cattle, but I can spare a day to take your letters to Port Townsend for you, if you like."

"Mr. Hill, I hate to ask you, but it truly would help me gain a measure of peace if you could also see if there are letters there from Mr. Ebey or from my brothers. I have no idea if they are even alive."

"I will check for you, Mrs. Ebey. I know you must be hankering for a word by now."

But when Nathaniel Hill returns, he brings no reassurances, only that he has sent her letters on to Ebey.

With no choice but to continue her daily work, Rebecca hires a klootchman (Indian woman) to help scrub the floors. Skagit worker Sam comes back and digs beds to set out onions. Over several days, he creates three long beds and has three more to dig. Rebecca thinks of her mother as she sews a coat for Ellison and ticking for a mattress for the boys. She remembers hours of sitting with her mother in front of the fire to sew back home in Missouri.

Samuel Crocket stops in for a few minutes, but Rebecca is hoping to see his mother Mary or his sister Susan. She writes in her journal: *I do not know why they cannot come to see me in my distress. They are happy or ought to be happy, no deaths among them. Yet, they know not when their time may come. I do not envy them their happiness for no doubt they think they have their troubles.*

Rebecca spends Saturday ironing and baking bread in preparation for Sabbath as she does each week. The fog rolls in on Sunday, along with her companions: Loneliness and Melancholy. She reads to the children about Christ's crucifixion which seems to interest them. A great many klootchmen come, some to dig potatoes, some to trade. She tries to explain that they may not work or trade on this day, it being Sabbath, but she doubts they understand.

The following day is still fog, then the sun finally appears. The children dig up onion seedlings for Sam to plant, and he sets them out into the new beds he has dug. Rebecca is cleaning up the morning dishes when she sees a canoe of Indians coming across the water. Her heart thrums with the possibility of their delivering mail. She hopes and prays there will be word from Ebey or from Thomas on this sun-filled day. But there are no letters for anyone, and the fog returns. Still, she writes a letter to her husband to send along with them when they return to Port Townsend, hoping that it will remind them over there of their neighborly responsibility to forward the mail.

Fog rules the damp mornings toward the end of January. When it breaks apart into separate puffs and drifts away, Bill Engle and Humphrey Hill borrow Ebey's oxen and herd them onto a scow to float down the beach. They need the oxen in the woods where timber for pilings must be brought out of the forest.

John Crockett also comes to Ebey's to borrow some tools, chisels, and a wood plane. He can see the distress that clings to Rebecca. Her Skagit worker, Sam, sits in the corner, saying that he is sick and unable to work.

"How are you fairing, Rebecca?" John asks.

In truth, she feels abandoned. "Thank you for asking. The boys and I are fine."

"Susan is at our house right now," he says. "She and mother have been talking about coming to see you."

Rebecca just smiles. *Why would they come now after all this time?*

Two days later, the children finish setting out some fine raspberry bushes and go with Sam, who feels better, to get gooseberry bushes to transplant in the yard. Rebecca tries to think about the berries to come, but she feels sick and full of grief.

Rebecca's Journal, January 27: *I cannot get this load of grief away, yet I know it does no good and is a great injury to me. I think if Mr. Ebey was here, I would not take my mother's death so hard. I am alone, with no person who is interested in my welfare to converse with. I pray to the Lord to uphold me and enable me to bear it with more patience, lest I wear my body down and become unable to raise my family.*

* * *

After a winter of confinement, Eason and Ellison are off to visit John Crockett's family. The morning had been cloudy and windy, but the afternoon is calm as they trek towards the cove. Eason practices his whistling now that his mother is not there to be annoyed. Ellison runs here and there to kick anything above ground, usually the top of a plant or a cow pie. The wet ones are not as much fun. By the time they arrive at the Crockett's home, their wiggles have been tamed and they can behave as they should.

Rebecca is home, with Sam for company. Not feeling well, she enjoys the quiet and spends the day knitting and reading, part of the time in the *Bible* and part in *The Life of Olympia Morata,* about the 16th century Italian scholar who worked to advance Protestant Reformation in Italy through her writings, despite being a woman. Olympia's story gives Rebecca encouragement.

She is feeling better when the boys come back with turnips and cabbage from their visit.

The next day, she attempts to do the laundry and is thankful when a klootchman chances to come along who is willing to work and help her finish. Hugh Crockett comes to visit. *It must be his turn,* she thinks. They are sharing leftover stew and bread when they hear two cannon shots from the harbor.

Hugh's eyebrows rise. "Distress signal?"

"That vessel is just announcing its arrival," Rebecca tells Hugh, picking up the dishes. "Captain Hathaway explained it to me. The other ship has been there for several days. They cannot get up the Sound for the wind."

"You have cannons going off all the time?" Hugh asks.

"No, thank goodness. It's such a small harbor, easy to see unless there is fog."

During the last night of the month, Rebecca wakes to the hardest, loudest wind she has ever experienced, as if Mother Nature tears her hair out. She calls Eason and Ellison to her bed, and they cover their heads together as protection from the fury while the house jerks and creaks and the wind roars. Keeping one hand on her stomach, she prays them all into God's hands and hopes the roof will still be there by morning. Then she prays for the poor souls who have no shelter, especially those who might be traveling like Ebey and her brothers.

{ **26** }

Potato Problem,
February 1853

Our dead never forget this beautiful world . . . and yearn in tender fond affection over the lonely hearted living, and often return . . . to visit, guide, console, and comfort them. –Sealth (Chief Seattle)

February begins with pleasant weather and a good westerly breeze for vessels to sail in through the Straits. Captain Coupe's *Success* is anchored at Port Townsend, and Rebecca learns that Captain Fowler's brig *George Emery* is anchored in Penn's Cove. Captain Fowler himself arrives at her door with the mail, straight from Olympia. She watches as two letters are laid in her hands that are from her husband. It's as if she is sucked out of the dark. Carefully, she opens the first letter and sees the writing from his hand. As she reads, it is as if he is there, speaking to her, in his voice.

She reads of his heartfelt distress at being away and his greatest desire to be with her and the boys. He has had success: Four smaller counties out of the previously too-large Thurston County are now created, and their county seats have been assigned. Whidbey Island is now part of the newly named Island County with Coveland as its county seat. Olympia is the county seat of the reduced size Thurston County. Steilacoom is the seat for new Pierce County, and Seattle is the county seat for the newly created King County. She is proud of him. He has attended to his duty faithfully. He also sends a copy of *The Columbian*, Olympia's newspaper:

"Three cheers for Colonel Ebey, our talented and untiring representative in the House. Colonel I. N. Ebey has been wide awake to the interests of his district during the present session of the legislature and certainly deserves the warmest thanks of his constituents for the success that has attended his efforts in procuring the passage of acts for the creation of four new counties from territory of Thurston and securing the recommendation of the Legislature to Congress asking for an appropriation of $20,000 for a military road to be built from Fort Steilacoom to Walla Walla. He has done more in the Legislature than any other member and has endeared himself to all parties of Northern Oregon."

Ebey writes that in addition to the creation of counties, the territorial Governor Joseph Lane has endorsed Ebey's memorial to establish a separate territorial government north of the Columbia River, calling it Columbia Territory. The governor has sent it on to the United States Congress where it is being introduced as Bill HR348 to the House of Representatives in Washington D.C. by Charles Stuart and the Committee on Territories. He hopes for news of a good outcome.

The next morning, Rebecca serves breakfast before daylight, knowing that Captain Fowler will want to be on his way. Skagit worker Sam tells her that he will be leaving also. Captain Fowler had hired him a long time ago and needs him back. For Sam's pay, Rebecca gives him a blanket, a good used coat and boots and two good used shirts, which she feels is quite generous. Privately, she is relieved to be done with the prodding that Sam has needed to complete his work. As daylight breaks to dark clouds, they see two vessels coming up the Straits which sends the men out the door to the *George Emery* to take advantage of the wind.

Within a few days, a new northerly wind clears the skies and freezes the ground. Ice forms in the house. The cattle stomp through the crusted soft dirt in the onion field, but it is not as concerning as it would have been before receiving the letters from Ebey.

Expecting their father home soon, the children suddenly become industrious and study their lessons well. Rebecca does laundry with a little more energy and scrubs the floor over her six-month belly, hoping Ebey will be happy in his pleasant island home. When thoughts of how long he might be able to stay sneak in, she sends them away, refusing to think about that. She is exhausted that night and is still resting the next day when Samuel Howe and Captain Holbrook come.

They stomp and wipe their feet and remove their hats before coming into Rebecca's clean house. "We were wondering if the Indians have brought over the Island mail from Port Townsend yet," Samuel says.

"They have not," she says. "It is wrong of them. Captain Fowler brought letters to me directly from Mr. Ebey. They must know in Port Townsend how important the mail is to us, especially in winter, especially when our loved ones are not with us." She holds back tears.

"I imagine your husband will have a word to say about it when he returns," Samuel says. He is sorry to have caused more anguish for Rebecca.

* * *

Days go by with clouds that bring a little snow falling on flat water. Eason and Ellison are tired of walking every day, across the prairie to find Blossom before she can be milked, to the spring and back with water, to various neighbors on errands, to Bill Engle's house to feed the cat and dog when no one is home. When the ground thaws, they are outside, helping their mother dig in the onion beds. Mount Baker and the Olympic Mountains nearly vibrate in the cold, clear sky. Rebecca looks toward the bluff now and then, imagining the appearance of her husband, but it is John Alexander who shows up.

"A beautiful day," he says, riding up on his horse. He dismounts as if he didn't have a wooden leg. "We just butchered a pig. I have, oh, I'd say about 13 pounds of fresh pork here to share."

"You have! I thank you, Mr. Alexander." Rebecca leads him into the cookhouse. "I can't remember the last time we had fresh pork."

"It is a bit scarce for now. I am replacing Bill Engle here this night, Mrs. Ebey," he says. "The bachelors are at Oak Harbor tonight."

"Thank you for that." She smiles. "I have extra butter. I will wrap up three pounds of Blossom's best for you when you go."

"Yo, the house!" She hears Dr. Lansdale in the yard.

"Well, I guess it *is* a pretty day when so many are out for a visit," she says.

"Mrs. Ebey, Mr. Alexander," Lansdale nods. "I brought some newspapers to exchange if you're finished with the last bunch, Rebecca."

"Yes, thank you, Dr. Lansdale."

* * *

On Saturday mid-February, she wakes to fog and heavy frost. After the warm task of ironing, she completes her Saturday cleaning and baking. She is mending the children's clothes when Mrs. Alexander arrives, bringing three-year-old Joseph and baby Abram.

"I am so happy to see you!" Rebecca means it. "And you brought the baby!"

"Thought you might not mind some overnight company to distract you. You probably have your neck in a crick from peering around, hoping to see your husband any minute." She hands the baby over to Rebecca and gives Joseph his carved wooden horse which he takes to explore the room.

Rebecca feels the small life in her arms, hoping she will be able to hold her own healthy baby in a few months. "What well-behaved children you have, Frances," which is Abram's cue to fuss.

Frances takes him back to nurse him. "It looks like you will be having another one of your own before too long."

Rebecca's hand goes to her stomach. "Three more months, I think. I hope my husband is not shocked to see how large I've grown."

"I doubt he will hardly notice," Frances says. "He will be so anxious to see your face and the boys and be home again." She pats Abram on the back, and he gives a hearty burp. "He is happy about the baby, I assume?"

Rebecca nods. They visit the evening away. For Rebecca, it is nearly as if her sister or her mother were there. Frances helps with dinner and dishes and creates her own bed, and Rebecca thinks how nice it is to not need to do everything herself. The following day, Hugh brings Susan Crockett, but Rebecca cannot persuade her to stay. Still, she is less lonely that night as she peers out at the bright moon, thinking of Ebey. She wonders if the extra attention and visits are because her husband is coming home soon.

Rebecca sends Eason to tell Nathaniel Hill that the firewood is nearly gone. He and Hugh Crockett spend the day cutting firewood that they cannot haul until the following day when they can access some oxen. Feeling weak, Rebecca does not offer the men supper at the end of the day. Hugh has his meals at his parents' house, but Hill is a bachelor. He sees the lack of a cooked meal as a great hardship, a personal affront and does not come to haul wood the next day. Hugh comes alone, bringing several pheasants he shot, and she stuffs them and invites him to stay for dinner.

She is alone the day when the Klallam group from Port Townsend come to her door. "We want our pay now for the potatoes. Agent Starling will not pay. He says settlers will pay. We need pay or we will take your cattle for the meat."

Rebecca tries to remain calm. She is not used to Indians being demanding. "We understand. Mr. Ebey will be home in a few days and will pay."

The leader nods. He understands and knows that Ebey can be trusted. They go to camp on the beach and wait. Still, Rebecca wishes that her night-time company could be closer during the day.

The next day, six large young Klallam teenagers crowd in through Rebecca's door, intimidating her. "Out!" she says, waving them away with her hands. "Out!" but they stand like stone, unmoving and speak to her with angry voices until she gives up and collapses into a chair. They continue to provoke her, but she does not respond. Eventually, they become bored and leave. For the first time, Rebecca is angry, frustrated and afraid, wondering what so many large Indians might do with her alone there, her and her children.

The next day she feels unwell with barely enough energy to do simple tasks.

"Ma," Eason says. "Three of 'em are outside, and they won't let me go to the outhouse. I need to go, Ma."

"What do you mean 'they will not let you go'?"

"They push me and laugh. One has a rifle, Ma."

Rebecca's fury gets her to her feet. She opens the door and yells, "Get away! Go!" waving them away with her hands, but they only laugh and talk back in their language. She gets a stick and comes at the young aggressors with it, trying to run them off.

They run a short distance, then the one with the rifle stops and points it at Rebecca. Rebecca stops, shocked. The rifle is pointed at her for several minutes, taking her breath away. She turns to go into the house but is followed by two of them who push in behind her, including the one with the rifle.

"Take that pow pow out of my house!" she says, pointing. "Eason, go get Mr. Hill!"

Eason takes off. The Klallam culprits go too because of the threat of Mr. Hill. Rebecca feels faint and puts her face on the cool tabletop, trembling.

Rebecca's Journal entry: *I hope it will not be long before Mr. Ebey will come home. I am becoming weary with anxiety for his return. I am continually looking and cannot see nor hear of my dear husband. I am not afraid of the savages if he is in the neighborhood.*

Though she is still shaken the following week, warmer weather and sunshine entices Rebecca to her garden for a little work. She keeps one eye on the bluff where some Klallam families camp, but it is the young Skagit children who come to play. She hasn't seen them in a long while. A little girl comes to stand in front of Rebecca, taking her hand. She talks sweetly in her Skagit language, and Rebecca listens, wondering what the child's tender story is about. She looks into those beautiful brown eyes, seeing her sincerity and innocence. As she pats the little hand in hers to show that she is listening, she feels the touch of her Savior and her fear and anger slipping away.

$$\{\ 27\ \}$$

Washington Territory, February 1853

I am the sunlight on ripened grain, I am the gentle autumn rain. When you wake in the morning hush, I am the swift, uplifting rush of quiet birds in circling flight, I am the soft starlight at night. –Author Unknown

The early morning of Saturday, February 19, is cloudy with some gentle showers of rain until 10 o'clock when the mighty sun breaks through, shining in a bright sky. Along with it comes Isaac Ebey. He arrives home having caught a ride on a brig from Olympia to Penn's Cove, the last part of a long, cold, wet trip, after a three-month absence. When Ebey wraps his arms around Rebecca, and she says "my dear husband" three times into his chest, he feels in his gut how much he has been missed. He pulls back to look at her and sees clearly how pregnant she is, the length of his absence made clear.

"I have been praying for you, for us, nearly constantly," he says. "I have a gift for you."

"Nothing will seem like much of a gift now that we have the gift of you," she says, holding on to him.

"This might," he says. "We received a letter from your brother John. They are still near The Dalles and expect to come on soon."

It is as if the tightness that has been creeping up Rebecca's spine is released. "So they *are* alive," she says, teary eyed.

Rebecca's Journal: *I had, all morning, been wishing to the children that their Pa would come home and felt more desirous of seeing him than usual. I feel truly thankful to the "Giver of all good and perfect Gifts" that he was spared to return home safe to his family who stood so much in need of his assistance and company. May the Lord bless and sustain us and make us humble and grateful servants unto the end.*

The following day is Sabbath and Rebecca and Ebey are thankful for a quiet day together. Ebey needs a day of, it feels like weights hang from his arms and legs. The stressful work in Salem and the hard push to get home quickly nearly wore him out, but there is joy in his heart. John Alexander comes for a short visit about the Legislature. Nathaniel Hill comes and calls Ebey "Colonel" as he confidentially delivers his personal report about the goings on of the neighborhood during Ebey's absence, the wavering health he observed of Rebecca, the prickly moments with the Indians.

"Colonel?" Ebey says. "Not sure I have earned that."

"I would say so, Colonel." Hill repeats. "It designates the leader of a community, like this farming community. A term of respect, an honorary title in the South, you know. I'd say you've earned it."

That evening, Rebecca tells Ebey about the death of Snetlum.

"An infected throat?" he asks.

"Yes, Dr. Lansdale said that he might have been able to do something if they had called him sooner."

"He was a good man, Snetlum. If he had not been so well-respected here, we may not have been able to enjoy the peace of this place. It is important that I speak with George, maybe take some potatoes with our condolences."

It is a quiet morning as Ebey rides his horse to Penn's Cove. He has fruit trees to pick up off a brig and wants to see Snetlum's son. He watches the sun rise in ribbons as it works to break through a dark cloud, the progress reflected on calm water. Overhead, two eagles call as his horse picks his way over the rocky trail, two burlap bags of potatoes hanging behind the saddle. Ebey's mind is jumbled with work still to be done with the legislature, concern for Rebecca's health and upcoming birth of another child, the farm to manage, and his hopes that his own family will come from Missouri.

At Snakelum Village, he sees Snetlum's widow Tolo and her grandson, George Jr. on the beach, smoking strings of clams. He dismounts and brings the bags of potatoes.

"Good morning," he says. "I am sorry to hear of the death of Snetlum. These potatoes are to show respect for him. We miss him already." He lays the bags near Tolo.

Tolo grabs his wrist with both hands, understanding the gesture more than the words. She smiles and nods though her eyes glisten.

"Is George nearby?"

"He is out fishing," George Jr. says.

"Please tell him that I am sorry. I will come back to visit with him."

Having returned to Coveland, he loads his bareroot fruit trees onto his horse. Strapping them onto and behind his saddle, he is thinking that his horse looks like a long-legged porcupine when three men come to shake his hand.

"C. H. Ivans here," the first one says. "We want to congratulate you on your success in Salem."

"Thank you, Mr. Ivans. What brings you . . . to the island?" Ebey asks.

"Well, sir, we are waiting for the arrival of the brig *J. S. Cabot* into the Cove here. We chartered it to bring a number of families from the Columbia River. Seems they want to live on Whidbey Island. I myself have my eye on some land just around the Cove." He points toward the south side of the Cove.

"That is good news," Ebey says. "More families will lead to schools and churches, a real community. Did you know there are plans here for a . . . grist mill and a sawmill?"

"Yes, we have heard of that," Ivans says. "Folks won't need to travel to get their flour anymore."

"Attitudes surely get tense when there is no flour," Ebey says, chuckling. "Makes a person feel like he's being punished."

* * *

At home, Ebey sets out his fruit trees, telling Rebecca what each one is. They imagine their future orchard: apple, pear, peach, cherry, and plum. Rebecca is thrilled. She stands with her hands on her hips imagining the future.

"If the trees do well," she says, "and we live long enough, we will have our choice of fruit which will be a great luxury indeed."

"In about three years I would say. I bought some grape slips, too. What do you think about growing grapes for wine?"

"I think not, Mr. Ebey, but they will be a lovely treat as grapes."

"We need to take good care of them if they are to live at all."

Rebecca's Journal, February 22: *Some of the Klallam Indians are camped in the lower part of our garden again. I do not intend to be troubled by them as much as before. My health is some better today than it has been lately. I hope it may continue so that I may attend to my family and my household duties without suffering all the time. The children are studying their new books which their Pa brought them.*

The next day, the vessel *Franklin* comes into the Port Townsend harbor from Olympia and sits at anchor while Mr. Gilmore Hays takes a small boat across Admiralty Inlet to Whidbey Island. He walks up to Ebey's house and introduces himself, explaining that he is a widower and has come to pay a visit to Susan Crockett.

Ebey takes him inside for a cup of coffee and to learn something about the man before he leads him anywhere. "How have you come to know about Susan Crockett?" he asks.

"Well, anyone who sees me with my four children can see that I need a wife," Hays says. "The folks in Olympia encouraged me to come and meet Miss Crockett."

"How did you come to Olympia, Mr. Hays?"

"I led a train of emigrants across from Missouri last year in '52. We encountered a great deal of illness on that trip, came across a wagon all by itself. Nobody around except a baby still alive." He stops to rub his face. "Well sir, my wife and I could not walk away from that child. We took her with us, my wife nursing her and caring for her, hoping she would live." His head drops. He blinks his eyes and swallows hard. "Thing is, whatever the poor little tike had spread to my wife and three of our seven children, and we lost them all."

Ebey's breath catches. They hear the fire spark.

"A . . . very heavy toll, I must say," Ebey says, rubbing his forehead. "It seems that the . . . greatest threat on the trip now is disease. I am sorry for what you've lost."

"I admit that I am struggling to create a home and raise my remaining children. They are hurting so. Like I said, friends in Olympia sent me here. Would you be willing to make the introduction?"

"I would," says Ebey. "Stay in the little cabin tonight, and we will go tomorrow."

Dr. Lansdale comes to visit Ebey after dinner. Rebecca enjoys seeing the two men together, talking like long-lost brothers. Ebey laughs as he pours them a dollop of whiskey. She writes in her journal before going to bed: *May the Lord sustain my husband, assist him, and support him by His all-saving grace and help us both tread this earthly path together in happiness and affection and as good examples to our children.*"

The morning is pleasant and clear with no wind as Ebey walks Mr. Hays to Colonel Crockett's house. "Looks like you will not need to worry about leaving right away with the weather so calm," Ebey says. "Your vessel will not be able to leave until the wind picks up."

"Thank you for the introduction," Hays says.

"I am very . . . close with the Crocketts, Mr. Hays. They are like family to me. They will know that I approve of your character, or I would not be introducing you."

The next day, Ebey is hard behind the plow with Bill Engle's help. They take turns directing the oxen or riding the plow. The calm weather and smell of rich, turned dirt bring new life and energy into Ebey as if spring is around the corner. This is what he has longed to do since first coming to Whidbey Island, to work on his farm. He thinks of the cabbage, lettuce and tomatoes he is about to plant, how they will look and taste when they are ready to eat. There is nothing as satisfying as a well-tended farm.

The raising of John Alexander's first house is set for the next day. Frances spurs them all to action, having lived with her large family in the tight space of Thomas's little log cabin since their arrival the previous summer. With the help of Ebey, Gilmore Hays, all the Crockett men and Hill brothers, it goes up quickly. At the end of the day, Ebey comes home chatting away with Samuel Crockett who stays over after they talk together late into the night.

Ebey is finishing his breakfast with Samuel when John Crockett delivers potential suitor Gilmore Hays. He has been with the Crockett families for three days. Ebey raises his eyebrows at Mr. Hays, wondering how it went with Susan.

Hays rocks his head slightly. "She seems to be interested in someone else," he whispers, "though no one let on who it might be."

On their heels arrives John Alexander.

"Thought you'd have a lot to do on the new house today," Ebey says.

"I do, but I want to talk about the problem with the Klallam potato farmers while you're all here," Alexander says. "Frances told me how one with a long gun tormented Rebecca."

John Crockett scowls. "It has been causing us trouble since last summer. We need to decide what to do, calm things down."

"You know," Samuel says, "it is somewhat their own neglect in not fencing their field, at least through harvest."

Ebey clears his throat, thinking of Snetlum. "We must remember," he says, "their way of life has changed . . . rapidly. There were no cattle here before we arrived. They have never needed to fence anything before, apart from their own village for safety. Fencing land probably makes no sense to them."

"Could we pay half of the $300 we supposedly owe now and get them to wait for the balance?" John Crockett asks.

"And see them build fences around their potatoes this next season so the same does not happen again," Alexander says. "I could pay $20."

"I can also," says John Crockett.

"Considering that I don't have a family to feed," Samuel says, "I have $30 to contribute."

"If I contribute another $30, we will need $50 more," Ebey says. "Each of us should talk with other neighbors to see if more are willing to contribute. I volunteer to deliver the payment to the Klallam camped on the beach. I would like to have a few . . . words with them since they are so near our home and have evidently felt the right to . . . confront and intimidate my wife." The veins in Ebey's neck stand out as he talks.

"Would you like company?" Samuel asks.

"No, I do not want to seem confrontational, just . . . clear."

On the final day of the month, Rebecca recognizes Klallam men in the yard, King George, General Taylor and Clonason. She watches her husband pay them the money for their lost potatoes. He seems stern, but by the looks of their reactions, they are pleased. She hopes there will be no more trouble about ruined potatoes.

The *Columbian* newspaper arrives from Olympia, reporting that Bill HR 348 has passed the House of Representatives, but the name was changed from Ebey's proposal of Columbia Territory to Washington Territory on the argument that there is already a District of Columbia on the east coast. The territory will extend east from the Pacific Ocean to the crest of the Rocky Mountains. The Bill has now been sent to the Senate for approval.

Ebey reads the article, then shakes his head. "Lawmakers," he says. "They need to make some sort of change to prove they are doing something. I wonder if anyone asked how changing Columbia Territory to Washington Territory will reduce the confusion with the Washington District of Columbia?"

Samuel laughs. "Oh well, at least it passed the House, thanks to you. I hope the Senate does likewise."

{ **28** }

Magic Gun Hancock, March 1853

It is a beautiful warm day the first of March when Ebey puts his Sweet Jane apple trees into the ground. The others will be planted later: Ernest's Favorite, Avery's Early and Red Rareripe. He grafts the peach trees himself and tucks them into a nursery to be planted next season. The peach varieties are Nectarine and Admirable. He and Bill Engle keep the plow going. Inside, Rebecca sews herself a lead-colored dress to fit around her growing middle. She feels more relaxed and secure since her husband has promised that he will not leave again until after the baby is born. The boys run errands, including a search for Blossom's missing calf, and they do their studies.

Fog builds the next day. Rebecca is excited to try her new laundry soap, Excelsior Family soap, which takes the dirt out without boiling. She must soak them for three hours, rub a little, ring them out and rinse, far less work than before. Ebey and the boys spend the day on the beach, having found a large supply of drifted cedar timber there. He cuts it for rail timber to use for fencing. The first of it will be to corral Blossom's new calf if they can find her. He hopes that the Indian dogs have not killed her, or the wolves.

Virginian Sam Hancock, a 35-year-old with bright red hair, arrives on Ebey's beach in a canoe with several Klallam paddlers. He is there to visit Ebey and to look for a land claim. He is well-experienced in the area, having lived among the Makah at Neah Bay the previous year when they were decimated from smallpox, and having been a prisoner of a northern tribe, among other tribulations.

He is known among the Indians on the Olympic Peninsula as "The Red Hair Man with the Magic Gun." It is one example of his quick thinking having saved his life. Knowing some of the languages, he understood when a group was talking about killing him. Secretly, he put four loaded six-shooters into his large pocket inside his coat and told them that he had a magic gun that could fire continually without being reloaded. They told him to prove it. He pulled out a six shooter, fired it six times and put it back into his pocket. They challenged him, saying it ran out of bullets. So he pulled what looked like the same gun from his pocket and shot six more times. Still with no believers, he pulled a third gun and began firing, fully aware that there was one more loaded gun in his pocket if he truly needed it, but the Indians had been convinced by then and left him alone.

"Welcome to the island, Mr. Hancock," Ebey says, having met him previously in Tumwater with his unforgettable red hair.

"I was here on the island in '48 you know," he tells Ebey. "Hired seven Indian paddlers to help me look for coal, and they brought me here."

"Did you find any coal?"

"No, but I got to know the local Indians a bit. There was a battle going on at the time, or so I thought. Indians in war face paint were attacking each other, so I hesitated to come ashore."

"I can imagine," Ebey says.

"But my paddlers said it was just practice since there was no blood. They were *preparing* to go to war. A leader's wife had been stolen by the Snohomish and they asked me and my paddlers to help get her back," Hancock says. "I told them no, that I came to be friends with all Indians. I was able to negotiate to get the woman back for two blankets and two weapons. Then they were friends again."

"An admirable . . . resolution," Ebey says. "Well done. It does seem that they do not hold grudges once they feel that a balance has been reestablished."

"I noticed the natural prairies then." Sam looks at the fields that are planted behind him. "Food was easy. My paddlers speared fish. I shot a white deer."

Ebey's heart drops. He knows that Snetlum had a reverence for the white deer and he himself would not shoot one.

"Well, we are happy to have you on the island," Ebey says. "If you are looking for land to claim and you want . . . prairie, you may want to look south. The land around me has been claimed. Follow the bluff south past claims by the Hill brothers and the Crocketts and you should find something."

He has just said goodbye to Sam when his Skagit neighbors bring Blossom's missing calf to The Cabins. The poor little thing had fallen into a hole. They said that Blossom had been there at the hole for her, but there was nothing she could do to help. Ebey pays them eight yards of calico for finding the scoundrel, then begins to sink fence posts for her corral.

* * *

Having scouted the area, Sam Hancock finds himself at Colonel Crockett's home. It is Sunday evening, and he is invited to stay for dinner. The entire family is there, and he has the full attention of a pretty young woman named Susan who seems interested in what he has to say. He knows an audience for a story when he sees one.

They sit in the parlor after dinner for a visit, many getting comfortable on the floor near the fire as the wind whistles outside. "Did you come across on the Oregon Trail?" John Crockett asks.

"Yes sir. I led one of the early trains in '45.

"Any trouble with Indians then?" the Colonel asks.

"Well," Hancock says, crossing his legs Indian style. "Groups were stealing cattle was all. We had two hundred Sioux with horses pulling travois coming up behind us once. They traded deer skins and buffalo robes for western clothes, and all was fine. Next day, they traveled too close behind us and unintentionally spooked our mules. They bolted, of course. That caused the cattle to run, and then everything was running, impossible to control." He looks down, remembering. "Women and children were screaming. Some of the wagons turned over, throwing provisions everywhere. Oxen broke away from the wagons. Some people got their legs broke."

Susan Crockett's mouth is slightly puckered, imagining the broken legs and broken wagons everywhere, the screaming.

He sees Susan's brows pulling together. "That was when we used the term 'leeverites,'" Hancock says, laughing. "All the broken family keepsakes and furniture was left behind. We told folks to leave it right there. Two days of repairs, we were on our way again with the women driving the teams and herding the cattle. The weight of the injured riding in the wagons replaced all those leeverites left behind."

Susan smiles, relieved, enjoying the story. Her mother notices.

"A worthy ending," John Crockett says.

"There is some unclaimed prairie further on if you are interested," the Colonel says.

Mrs. Crockett speaks up. "Mr. Hancock, you are invited to stay with us for a time while you are here. You might help the boys with the plowing and planting if you are so inclined." She sees Susan blush the tiniest bit and knows that her instincts are correct.

Sam is an observant man, which has saved his life a few times. He is aware of Susan's interest, and he appreciates her dimpled smile, the hint of auburn in her dark hair, but he has no idea if he is capable of staying in one place for any period of time. Even though he might be looking for land, it is more of an investment for his old age than for settling down anytime soon. He thinks that no woman should be interested in him at this time of his life.

* * *

Rebecca's Journal, March 5: *Today our new president, General Pierce, takes his seat. I hope and trust that we will have a good President in Mr. Pierce. I have an Indian hired today to clear off the yard. Mr. Ebey is finishing harrowing in his wheat. The crows are very troublesome on it. A vessel sunk in the Straits today, the same as last month.*

Spring brings activity. The aroma of roasting clams and fresh meat lingers around the Indian villages. In addition to farmwork, there is more trading. Nathaniel Hill buys four bushels of potatoes and a white blanket from George Snetlum. Klallam groups come and go, trading with their Skagit neighbors. Visitors stay the night and get meals at The Cabins. Rebecca cooks, cleans, irons, does laundry and wears herself out until she is ill. When she hears that John Alexander has traveled up the Sound for provisions, she hopes that he might return with her brothers.

Rebecca's Journal, Sunday, March 13: *Another beautiful clear and warm day has dawned. I would like to hear a Sermon preached this beautiful Sabbath which makes a person feel so happy. We do not want proud hypocritical Ministers in this new Country. Let us pray to the Lord that He may send us purehearted laborers to help preserve our faith in Christ and make us thankful for all His kind and tender mercies.*

John Alexander returns with mail and newspapers but not her brothers. They learn that the U.S. Senate has officially accepted the new Territory of Washington, which causes Ebey to realize that he is out of port for a celebratory drink. He goes to Coveland for it and is gone most of the day, returning in the evening with Dr. Lansdale. They are joyous with the news. Lansdale continues to John Crockett's house to spread the word.

Island County's first officers are temporary appointments: Dr. Lansdale as County Auditor, Hugh Crockett as Sheriff, Humphrey Hill (a third Hill brother recently arrived) as Assessor, and John Alexander, John Crockett and I. J. Powers as County Commissioners.

None of them predict that their island would have a problem with witchcraft.

{ **29** }

Witchcraft, March 1853

The wind textures the water. As a gust approaches, you can see it roughen the surface, a stampede of hastening ghosts, footprints skipping over the swells and disappearing. –Amity Gaige, *Sea Wife*

A cool, blustery mid-March morning with a strong south wind brings a group of Klallam Indians carrying rifles over the hump of the island to Penn's Cove. They confront the Skagit there with the accusation that their Shaman has been practicing witchcraft and has used it to kill four of their People, including a leader. They shoot four Skagit to restore balance, killing them, and threaten that if the witchcraft does not stop, they will be back to kill more. Then they return to their camp on Ebey's beach.

Ebey is away from The Cabins, showing visitors potential property that is available for land claims. Rebecca is unaware of the trouble between the Klallam and Skagit people but sees a group of Skagit on the bluff above the beach. They holler and wave their rifles, and fire them a few times as if to threaten the Klallam camp below, then return to the Cove.

The next day, the Klallam leader known as King George comes over from Port Townsend, slips up behind a Skagit man who is secretly standing near their Klallam camp and shoots him. Then he throws the body into the water. Rebecca hears the gun shot and thinks it is another moment of the Skagit making harmless threats, but the Indian children tell her otherwise. When Ebey comes home at the end of the day and learns what has happened, he goes down to the water to investigate. A Skagit body floats back and forth in the surf.

"What has happened here?" he asks King George.

"The Skagit shaman is killing us, Ebey! He uses witchcraft. Killing is the only way to get rid of their evil spirits," King George says.

"There can be no killing. The Indian Agent, Starling, will help solve problems. He will know about this," Ebey says, knowing full well that Starling is busy elsewhere.

"Like payment for the ruined potatoes? No help at all," King George says.

"Then come to me for help. I will try."

King George gives a curt nod, but Ebey can see that he is still angry.

"Let the Skagit come and get the body from the beach," Ebey says. "Leave them alone. Remember when Snetlum died, and you all came to pay your respects? How can you . . . kill them now?"

The Klallam leader's eyes soften. "You do not understand, Ebey. We would do the same to our own people if they use witchcraft. We would kill our own. It is the only way to kill the evil. Our people understand it. It has always been this way. That Skagit was in our camp to hurt or kill us, maybe to get hair to use for more witchcraft. I must stop them. It is my job as a leader to protect my people."

Ebey shakes his head as he walks back up the bluff to The Cabins. He had read about the Salem witch trials in Massachusetts from 150 years ago. *How do we speed up their understanding?* he mutters to himself. *We do not have 150 years.*

When John Alexander hears about the trouble between the Indians, he borrows Nathaniel Hill's bullet molds.

* * *

Rebecca is cleaning up the breakfast dishes and Ebey is about to start his day when Samuel Crocket arrives. "I am going across to get provisions off that brig, the *Williamsburg,* out there in the harbor." He points toward the window with one hand and steals a biscuit from the kitchen table with the other. "It just arrived from California."

"Put some butter and honey on that biscuit, you thief," Rebecca says.

"I would not dream of contaminating your perfect biscuits, Madam, but if you insist." He spreads the butter and waxy honey across the top where it glistens. "I plan to hire a couple of Klallam paddlers to take me across to Port Townsend," he says, eyes on the biscuit. He bites quickly before the honey drips.

Ebey relates the recent events with the Klallam killings. "They will charge you $4 over and back, you know," he says. "Maybe we should demonstrate our distaste for their recent behavior."

Samuel swallows and licks his lips. "What do you have in mind, friend?"

"Well, I have my own canoe over at the Cove . . ." Ebey says. "How about if we go get it and you use it to paddle yourself across the inlet and save yourself some money? If King George loses our business, it might help him understand that we cannot abide by killing."

Together, they hook up the oxen to the wagon and head out on the narrow trail over the island, aiming to get to the Cove. As they cut, chop, break and smash vegetation from the path in order to get it wide enough for the wagon to get through, they come to the same conclusion: This path must become a road for wagons.

"The last time I built a road," Samuel says, grunting with effort, "it was from the Cowlitz Landing to Olympia . . . at least eight years ago now." He stops to breathe for a moment. "But that one was more than fifty miles long, and I never, ever want to do anything like that again. We were young and didn't know any better. It was miserable, I am telling you. It never stopped raining for a moment. We wallowed in muck the whole time."

Ebey saws at a skinny tree that is too stout to bend or break and shakes his head as he stands up straight. "I believe you. I am happy to have missed that adventure." He wipes a kerchief across his face.

"This road will be what, three miles maybe? There's already a trail and some of it is along the natural prairie. I bet we could do it in one day if everyone helps," Samuel says.

"We will get county approval for it before we ask for volunteers," Ebey says. *Pioneers are always looking forward.*

The next morning is calm, and canoes are launched from Ebey's beach: Samuel Crocket in Ebey's canoe and Hugh and Nathaniel Hill in the canoe that Nathaniel had purchased from Snetlum's son. They spend the day at Port Townsend and the night on the *Williamsburg* in the harbor, then return with a hundred pounds of flour for $10 and two hundred pounds of corn meal for $8 to be divided among the families. Everyone is disappointed that there is no pork to be found, anywhere.

Nathaniel Hill goes across the water again the next day to get more cornmeal before the brig leaves, and he struggles to get back to the island because of a storm that builds quickly. He lands on Whidbey Island much further south than he had wanted, thankful to have landed at all, and carries the cornmeal on his back, walking north up the beach for miles in the wind and rain. Then it begins to snow fat wet flakes. He moves on, knowing that stopping could be disastrous, miserable at the least, even if he *could* start a fire. When he gets to Ebey's Landing, an Indian dog dares to attack him before he gets up the bluff to Ebey's house, and with his patience entirely gone, he shoots it and continues walking, knowing he will pay his dues for it later.

Rebecca lends him a towel and dry clothes and gives him hot food and hot coffee. She thinks about how they must plan their days according to the weather. A storm on the water is not to be challenged. Everyone on the island knows that it is better to spend the night or several nights where you are rather than to gamble with the wind and waves in a storm.

As the storm continues to increase, two Klallam siwash (Indian men) who are coming across are capsized. They lose their canoe and everything in it, but they manage to get to Ebey's beach. They come to Ebey's door with six other Klallam from the beach, all afraid to stay down there overnight, wanting protection from the Skagit who they think will attack them. Ebey lets them stay together in one room.

When the storm is finally over, Ebey harrows his potato field while Eason and Ellison cut potatoes to plant. Rebecca does not feel well but does the housework and sewing that she is able to do. The Indian children tell her that the Skagit people around the Cove have all moved together to Oak Harbor to have safety in numbers from the Klallam.

It has been more than a month since Rebecca has had another woman to visit and when Ebey says he will take her and the boys in the wagon to John Crockett's farm to visit Frances and the children, she gathers several jars of her canned tomato sauce and loaves of bread and is ready to go. After a carefree visit, they return in a light rain and find Thomas in their house, drinking a cup of coffee in front of the fire. He is in serious need of a haircut.

Rebecca gasps, looking around for John and James. She grabs Thomas by his shirt at the shoulders. "What has happened to our brothers?" She can barely breathe.

"They are fine," Thomas says, patting her back, surprised to see her pregnancy. "I left them at the Columbia River. They lost all their cattle in the hard winter like everyone else except four which they intend to sell before coming here."

She buries her face in his shirt for a moment, continuing to hold on. "I have you now, Thomas, my sweet brother. I need you to stay close so I can look at you." She squeezes his arms and shoulders to see if he needs to be fattened up. "When will they come?"

"Soon," Thomas says. "They need to sell those cattle first."

"I know you want to see your place, Thomas, but will you stay with us for the night, please? For me? I need to have my brother under my own roof."

"Of course," Thomas says. "There is a surprise for you in the bedroom."

Rebecca's eyes are wide as she peaks through the doorway of the bedroom. She looks around the room, seeing nothing new, no boxes, nothing on the bed, then she gasps, not believing what she sees. The blue, hand-carved, precious headboard made by her father for her 16th birthday sits at the head of her bed. She treasured it before she left home, had willed her fingers to remember its carvings. Thomas and Ebey stick their heads in and see her running her hands over the carved scrolling oak leaves.

"How did you get this here?" She turns toward Thomas, tears blurring her vision.

"John gave it to me. He told me that Ma said he had to get it to you, even if he had to carry it on his shoulders. She told him that you needed it, so he passed it to me to bring."

"So it was Ma's idea?" she sobs, feeling like her mother's ghost has just arrived for a visit.

* * *

Ebey plants potatoes whenever the weather allows. When the ground is too wet for planting, he takes Eason and Ellison three miles into the woods to learn how to make rails for fence. They use cedar logs, cedar being easier to split and long-lasting in wet weather. They pound a wedge the full length to split it. The boys tucker out pretty quickly.

Eight months pregnant, Rebecca washes clothes and tends to the parade of visitors who come to The Cabins to the limit of her energy. She is thankful to have Thomas home. He works at his own house to create a new door and build a chimney.

Rebecca's Journal: *I am thankful to our Heavenly Father Who is so much better to us than we deserve. We do not praise him enough for all His tender mercies. I feel better today than usual but have no hopes of continuing so longer than one day at a time. I pray God to make me content with my situation and happy under any circumstances whatever.*

She hopes that her brothers John and James will be there before she delivers the baby. She would like to see them and hug them and know they are safe on Whidbey Island before that fateful day arrives.

Community Road,
April 1853

A grieving ghost is a spirit who remains to comfort a loved one during a period of mourning. --Jake Rice, Ghost Hunter, ghostly-activities.com

The first elected Board of Commissioners for Island County, Samuel Howe, John Alexander and John Crockett, meet at Alexander's new cabin in Coveland on Penn's Cove April 4th. The Justices of the Peace are appointed: Isaac Ebey, Nathaniel Hill and Thomas Hastie. Hastie is a new arrival, a woodcutter with family, hoping to escape the illnesses that have emerged in south Puget Sound. Dr. Lansdale is Probate Clerk and Ebey is Probate Judge. Hugh Crockett serves as Sheriff until elections for that position can be held.

The commissioners approve the creation of a county road from Ebey's beach to Coveland. The approval is based on a proposal from Ebey and Samuel Crockett that includes a petition signed by twelve settlers. That very day, Ebey and Crockett lay out the road, marking the areas that need extra work so that the road will stay wide enough for oxen and wagons for several years.

For four days, the weather is cool and breezy with fog and rain, and Ebey and the boys plant potatoes and onion and turnip seed. At last, when the rain stops, the roadwork begins. The volunteers come at dawn, a group on each end of the proposed road, carrying axes, saws, picks, and shovels clinking as they walk. On Ebey's end, he and Thomas join the Crockett men, the Hill brothers and Bill Engle and the cutting, chopping, digging, joking, swearing, laughing begins. Lunch is bleak for the bachelors. While Ebey and Thomas have biscuits and cheese, the poor bachelors like Engle have cold sandhill crane and potatoes to eat. Before dark, the laboring groups on each end meet in the middle and are too tired to celebrate, saying they will celebrate each time they use the road. They trudge home with tools that are much heavier than they had been that morning.

Saturday is as industrious as usual. Rebecca pushes herself to do the ironing and cooking, having done the laundry the day before in preparation for Sunday. Ebey builds a chimney in one of the rooms they rent and makes a bookcase. A vessel arrives in the harbor and delivers a stack of newspapers from Olympia along with a letter from Winfield Ebey, Isaac's younger brother in Missouri.

Ebey carefully opens the letter and is shocked to see that it is dated August 15 of last summer. "Mailed eight months ago? Who knows where this letter has been!" he says, clearly agitated. "We are lucky to have seen it at all. We might as well be on the moon."

Rebecca looks at the address on the outside of the paper. "It was sent to Salem," she says. "You were home August 11. That is what happened. Even so, it should not take eight months to receive mail."

Ebey reads the letter. "Winfield says that all is well except that mother was feeling poorly. They are upset that they have not received more letters from us. Well, hopefully they received my letters shortly after writing this. I will write back before that vessel leaves the harbor for Olympia and they can take it with them."

Sunday arrives with clear, pleasant weather. The Ebey family is late getting up, each of them bone-tired from a week of hard work. After family time around the breakfast table with eggs and fried potatoes, biscuits and milk, Rebecca shares her common Sunday thoughts about wishing for a church service. Rover barks once, a happy bark, and there is a quiet rap on the door. Ebey goes to open the door and sees Rebecca's brother John with James standing behind.

"At last," Ebey says with a big exhale. He opens the door wide and steps aside to get out of Rebecca's way.

Rebecca's bench falls backward as she launches herself at her older brother John. She comes at him screaming and he braces himself. "You are finally here," she says, pulling away to look at his face. "So much like our father." Then she turns to embrace James us well. "How are you feeling?" she asks, looking at John for a reaction to her question.

John curls up one side of his mouth and moves his hand back and forth, meaning good days and bad days, same as always since his head injury. He nods toward her pregnant belly and raises an eyebrow.

"One more month," she says. "I'm so glad you are here before the baby comes. It gives me more strength, your being here."

"Congratulations, sister," John says. He shakes Ebey's hand, but there is tension around his mouth.

Ebey thinks how difficult the trip must have been for John needing to take care of everything by himself including the burial of their mother on such a long, difficult journey, especially with some days undoubtedly devoted to the care of his brother. He must have been thankful to have had Thomas with them for a time.

Rebecca's Journal, April 10: *"No one on Earth can describe my feelings when I saw them. I was truly glad, but fresh thoughts of my dear mother came into my mind and O the anguish of my heart but for giving vent by screaming as loud as I could it seemed my heart would break. I thought I had gotten over her death, having been resigned to it, til I saw them and the sight of those who saw her leave this world and buried her brought her fresh to my memory. Lord assist me and enable me by grace to be content. John has such sound judgment and is so steady that he seems almost like father. Hereafter I will not be so lonely when Mr. Ebey is gone.*

No time to waste, Ebey leads John all over the center of the island, looking for prairie land to claim for him and James. They spend a week looking while James helps Thomas plant potatoes at his farm.

Rebecca hires a klootchman to help with laundry and scrubbing floors. By Saturday, she manages to do the ironing and prepares for Sunday and falls into bed early. Before she is asleep, the whole house is roused by gunfire. A group of twenty or thirty Klallam have come from Port Townsend to Ebey's beach with guns and knives to make war with those Klallam who are camped there. Guns are fired, knives are flashed and in a little while, all is quiet. They seem to be friends again. Still, Rover does not settle down for quite some time.

Rebecca's brother, John Davis, goes to work on Captain Bell's claim on the Cove, thinking he might want to offer to buy Bell's interest. When he is ready to investigate Port Townsend, there are no Indians on the beach to take him. In fact, there have been no Indians anywhere since the recent skirmish between the Klallam groups. Charles Crockett offers to go with him in Ebey's canoe.

Ebey hauls rail timber to his fence line and swings by John Crockett's farm at midday to take their yearling calf away as they requested. It has been getting all the milk from its mother, and the Crockett family need that milk. It is time for the calf to be weaned. After he makes a door to the little bedroom that Eason and Ellison share, he writes to his brother Winfield.

"Thomas and his brothers John and James are here at last— They had a hard time of it owing to illness and bad winter. Rebecca is well. The trail has been opened on this side of the Cascades directly to Puget Sound, so emigrants do not need to go to the Willamette first before coming to Puget Sound now. Fifty vessels engage in commerce with regularity in the

Sound now, a big improvement since my first ship Orbit two years ago."

Rebecca's Journal, April 20: *John Ross (a half breed) and his wife (half French and half Indian) are here this evening. Mr. Ross brought us a letter from the Colonial Schoolmaster of the Hudson Bay Company at Victoria inviting us to send our children to school under his charge. He promises to do a great deal by them. The schoolmaster was Master of the Leeds Moral and Industrial Training College in England.*

As Rebecca cleans up after breakfast, she thinks about the idea of sending her sons to Victoria for their education. She feels that in time, there will be a good school on Whidbey Island but that might be years away. The school in Victoria seems like a good opportunity and she is willing to consider it. Before she has finished washing the dishes, her brother John drags himself into the house. He is wet, bedraggled, and exhausted, having learned about the dangers of travel by water.

"What happened to you!" Rebecca asks. She mops at him with a towel and pours hot coffee, setting him next to the fire.

"Well, I guess I learned respect for the water last night," he says, holding the coffee cup in both hands. "Spent the whole night feeling powerless while it roughed me up, anyway."

"How did *that* happen?"

"Charles and I left Port Townsend after dark. Won't do that again. Now I know, even if it seems calm in shore, it might not be that way further out . . . and we had the canoe overloaded. Didn't know what a bad idea that was. We tossed a lot overboard to keep afloat, but we couldn't bail fast enough to be able to paddle. Waves came right over us!"

"Thank the Lord you survived." Rebecca feels shivers run up her spine. *He just got here, dear Lord. Please keep him safe.* "We follow the Indians," she says. "If they don't go, we don't go."

After a big swallow of coffee, John says, "Just the same, I think I will stay to dry land for a time now."

{ **31** }

Chloe, April 1853

"The people you love become ghosts inside of you, and like this you keep them alive." –Rob Montgomery, Actor, Producer, Director

Two Methodist ministers arrive at The Cabins to stay on Friday night, Reverend Benjamin Close from Olympia and Reverend Morse from the Willamette. Though Mr. Close intends to preach on Sunday morning, they go to Port Townsend for the day on Saturday, planning to be back before evening.

Also on Saturday, six families come off the brig *J. S. Cabot* which arrived the night before in the Cove. The brig was chartered by residents of Whidbey Island to bring the families of men who are already on the island as well as new settlers from Portland. Families are met by relatives or are directed to The Cabins for a place to stay. The brig will continue on with those who want to go to Olympia.

When visitors arrive at The Cabins, Rebecca sees a look of anticipation on their faces and wonders what is afoot. A widower named Reuben Doyle with two little girls, ages two and four, asks if there is a pastor on the island. There is a marriage to perform.

Rebecca nearly laughs, thinking that the Lord is in control. *We can never see His Plan but must have faith.*

"It just so happens, Mr. Doyle, that a preacher, Brother Close, should arrive at any moment who could perform the rite," Ebey says. "Your request is certainly good timing. He is in the area to perform church services in the morning."

Rebecca sees the pretty young woman with blond curls holding hands with the two little girls.

"Very good. I would like you to meet my betrothed, Miss Chloe Terry," Reuben says, "and her sister, Carolyn Kellogg with Carolyn's little daughters, Florence and Alma. Carolyn will continue on to Olympia to meet her husband, Dr. John Kellogg, a medical doctor. Chloe and I and my two girls intend to make our home here on Whidbey Island."

Ebey extends his hand. "Welcome to The Cabins, Mr. Doyle, Miss Terry, Mrs. Kellogg."

Rebecca thinks of what flowers are available and sends Eason and Ellison out to cut anything with a blossom to brighten the parlor. They return with light blue camas, red columbine, red currant and mock orange, all fragile blossoms. Rebecca creates a large bouquet and a small nosegay for the bride, hoping it will last through the ceremony.

When Brother Close arrives from Port Townsend that evening, he is surprised to find the congregation waiting for him. The wedding is performed April 23rd in the candlelight and firelight of Ebey's parlor, witnessed by other passengers from the *J. S. Cabot*. Chloe's sister, Carolyn and Carolyn's two little girls stand with the bride as Ebey stands with Reuben. Reuben's two little girls, Helen and Emma, stand with very pregnant Rebecca.

"This is a special moment," Rebecca says to the girls, holding their hands.

Helen and Emma nod their heads in seriousness, and she squeezes their hands, secretly hoping that the child she carries will also be a girl. As the couple is pronounced married and have their first quick kiss, Rebecca is struck with how lucky they are to see their blossoming community grow.

It rains the following day. Still, the Crockett households come for church service in Ebey's home, filling the parlor. Before the preachers leave, they express their intention to come back every month to preach, and Rebecca's prayers seem to be coming true.

The new Reuben and Chloe Doyle family stays at Ebey's house until they can raise their own cabin. Rebecca is thankful to Chloe for her help, especially when a new parade of potential settlers arrives the next few days, looking for land. Chloe is efficient, doing a large washing of clothes which dries well in a brisk wind. She takes on as many other duties as anyone could.

"How did you meet Mr. Doyle?" Rebecca asks as she folds laundry, hoping for a romantic answer.

Chloe is peeling potatoes. "We met on the *J. S. Cabot*," she says. "I was supposed to go with my sister to Olympia, but then I met Reuben. I have known him for only ten days!" A giggle erupts.

"Oh my! Is he *that* charming?"

"He is a good man, a printer by trade. He lost his wife on the Oregon Trail, and I lost my good sister and niece on the trail as well. When I told my poor brother . . . he met us on the trail, you see . . . when I had to tell him that his wife and daughter had died, well, it was quite difficult." Her eyes glisten. "Is this enough potatoes do you think?"

Rebecca nods.

"Then on our voyage here, I saw Mr. Doyle suffering the same loss as my brother, and his little girls took to me like honey on a biscuit . . . well, I guess I felt like I was home. I was needed, and instantly loved."

Rebecca holds back tears. "That is a very sad and very romantic story. I am sorry that you both lost loved ones on the trail. I lost my mother as well. We have sacrificed a great deal to be in this new wonderful place on Whidbey Island."

* * *

Rebecca is surprised to find George Snetlum at her door wearing a tan western shirt and trousers. His eyebrows seem lower than normal, the corners of his mouth turn down. She calls Eason to show George where his Pa is working in the woods.

A tall fir tree hits the ground with a thud that vibrates through Ebey's feet when he looks up to see George standing on the edge of the small clearing. Ebey is breathing hard, and he wipes his hands together before extending one to shake. "Hey

George. Have a seat," he says, pointing to a couple of tree stumps.

George lowers himself to the soft ground instead, crossing his legs.

Ebey matches George's move. "How are you doing, George? How is your family?"

George wipes away some fir cones from under his legs. "We are losing our home, Ebey. Houses are in our hunting area. Clams are taken from my family's clam bed without permission!"

Ebey wipes the back of his neck with his kerchief. *I should have checked on George earlier,* he thinks to himself. "I'm sorry, George. New people don't know your customs . . . but we can teach them. Let's go get pay for your clams."

They walk over the back of the island and paddle in Snetlum's canoe to Snakelum Village. From there, they walk up the hill to the closest cabin which belongs to Joseph Smith.

A tall, angular man comes around the corner of the cabin, gray eyes squinting with questions below a heavy ridgeline.

"Mr. Smith," Ebey says, extending his hand. "You probably know your neighbor here, George Snetlum."

Smith nods, waiting.

"We all try to be good friends to George and the others from his village," Ebey says, seeing the gray eyes flinch. "They have always hunted this entire island. Now there are cabins here."

"All of this is true, Ebey," Smith says, thinking that he has chores to do. "What's your point?"

"My point, our point," he says, nodding toward George, "is that they need to continue to hunt on this property."

"Well, no one's stop'n 'em, Ebey," Smith says. "Everyone hunts all over these woods without care about boundaries. So far, anyway."

"That's good," Ebey says, seeing George's tension relax a little. "Also, you may not know that George's family has a private clam bed, like most Indian families. No one, not even people from his own village, may dig clams there without permission. You will need to pay George for the clams you've dug."

Joseph Smith looks at George, a slight grimace on his face.

"If you want to keep good relations with your neighbors," Ebey adds.

George's body hardens. He keeps steady eye contact with the taller Smith.

Smith's bushy eyebrows rise. "How much?" he asks.

"An equal portion of food," George says.

Smith goes into his smokehouse and comes back with a haunch of smoked venison. "I did not know, George." he says. "Maybe next time you could show me where I can dig clams."

George nods, extending his hand, and they shake on it.

Ebey's stomach growls as he and George get back into the canoe.

"You can eat with us, Ebey," George says.

"Thanks, but I need to get back. They will wonder where I am."

Ebey is delivered back to Coveland and walks the community road alone, thinking about roasted clams and smoked venison. His mouth waters and his stomach grumbles. His only worry for the moment is whether he will get home in time for dinner.

Confinement, May 1853

Ghosts are all around us. Look for them, and you will find them.
–Ruskin Bond, Author from India

President Franklin Pierce appoints Ebey as *Deputy* Collector of Customs for the Puget Sound district and Inspector of Revenue at the port of Olympia. He is thankful for the position and wonders how he can fit his duties into his busy life. The month of May at The Cabins could not be busier with farming and the steady stream of visitors who come for a meal or to spend the night or several nights.

Mr. Ivans, the man who Ebey met at the cove when he was collecting his new fruit trees is at The Cabins with his wife, intending to file a claim on the Penn's Cove. They are musicians, she on the guitar and he on the violin. Their playing in the evening is a treat for everyone, especially Rebecca who thinks of the child she carries. The music seems to help her and the baby both relax despite a head cold and cough that she has developed.

Chloe cooks and sews and irons while minding the two little girls, allowing Rebecca to rest while her husband, Reuben Doyle, works on their claim. Ebey borrows Thomas to help get the fencing done, hoping to keep the cattle out of the wheat. By the end of the week, Rebecca feels stronger and thinks it is due to warmer weather until she learns that Eason and Ellison will be helping their father raft timber, which gives her back cramps. Even though the weather and water are calm, it is serious, dangerous work.

Mr. and Mrs. Ivans move onto their claim May 10th before their roof is up despite it looking like rain. It does rain all night while Rebecca worries for them. "What would cause them to move in so hastily?" she asks Ebey.

"Maybe they are afraid that someone else will claim it before the paperwork can be processed and they want to be able to say that they have been living on it," Ebey says. "The prime land is getting a little bit scarce now."

Unlike Rebecca, Ebey has no energy for worrying about Mrs. Ivans getting wet. He and Thomas continue to put up fence, this time around the potatoes. Ebey's arms feel like lead by the end of the day after digging all those post holes. When a vessel arrives with mail and newspapers, they sit together at the table to go through it. At the same time they read that the creation of Washington Territory was officially approved by the Senate on May 2, they hear the old rusty cannon in Port Townsend fire a big *kaboom*. It reverberates across the water.

"I guess they have heard the news over there as well," Ebey says, grinning. "I bet they whooped it up in Olympia, too." He is anxious to spread the news all over the island but must read a letter from Winfield first.

"Winfield says that they are all well and wish to come to Oregon but cannot make the outfit this season," he tells Rebecca. "We will need to wait another year."

Rebecca sees his shoulders droop. "I am sorry, husband," she says. "I know you were hoping for them to be here by fall, we both were. We have good news and not-so-good news. Maybe we could enjoy the good news?"

Ebey's face changes instantly, showing the smile of his younger self. "You know the great rush now will be to Washington Territory with its mild climate. There are more advantages here than in what remains of Oregon Territory. It should organize quickly now, and we need to make sure that it is done properly." He grabs his hat. "I am off to spread the news!"

When red-headed Sam Hancock and Samuel Crockett come to The Cabins carrying a big chunk of pork that they purchased in the harbor, Rebecca wonders if Sam Hancock has become a member of the Crockett family. The sparks in Susan Crockett's eyes were obvious when they first met. She sends the men home with a jar of vinegar for Ann Crockett and a hand-me-down dress for Susan Crockett that Rebecca thinks she will never wear again.

Ebey's letter to Winfield, May 20:

"We have now a separate political existence in Washington Territory which will give new impulse for good for the whole

country. I have been appointed Deputy Collector of Customs for the Puget Sound district and Inspector of Revenue at the port of Olympia. I am hoping to advance from the Deputy position to the Collector position and move the Port of Entry from Olympia to Port Townsend so that I may be home most of the time and keep improving the farm. There is a need for cattle here. It is best to bring them with you. They are expensive here. The Crocketts are doing some calving, but it will take time."

Rebecca's Journal, May 21: *I am very weak today. Can scarcely do my cooking. I am very lean and sometimes feel like my stay on this earth will not be very long. The Will of the Lord be done in all things. If He thinks it best for me to leave this earth soon, it is all right. I will leave all I hold dear here, into His special care. O, may He watch over them and protect them and not let them neglect the Soul's Salvation.*

Dr. Lansdale comes to see Rebecca. Then he talks with Ebey in whispers about holding an inquest over the body of a man named Judah Church who has been found dead on Church's claim in Oak Harbor where he had a little trading post. The cause is unknown since he has been dead for more than a month. Hugh Crockett as Sheriff suspects that he may have been killed for his watch and gold rings. Ebey serves as judge in Oak Harbor for the Inquest. The little jury agrees that the cause of death is unknown, and they bury the remains by shoveling dirt into a mound over the top.

Rebecca takes to her bed for her period of confinement, using the time to finish the baby's gowns, one of which is from the final remnant of her own wedding dress. Ebey stays close to home, but when she is sleeping, he takes a quick trip to Colonel

Crockett's for a cask of salted pork. It is a pleasant, warm day as he rides. Praying from the back of a horse, or while in his small canoe, has become a routine for him—a time when he is alone but does not feel alone, when there is nothing else to say or do. He prays for an easy delivery for Rebecca and a healthy baby for them all.

The following morning, he is splitting rails in the yard when Chloe calls him into the house for an early lunch. "Rebecca says that her pains are beginning," Chloe says. "She said that I should give you your lunch before you go to fetch Dr. Lansdale."

Immediately, he goes into the bedroom to see Rebecca. She is asleep, but he takes her hand and feels her forehead. Normal temperature, a good sign. Her eyes flutter and her whole face smiles. "Not to worry Mr. Ebey," she says. "I am just storing up some extra sleep to get ready for the work ahead."

Once he returns with Dr. Lansdale, he goes to get Frances Alexander, knowing how it will comfort Rebecca to have her there. Thomas arrives with Ann Crockett and Mrs. Ivans. It is a houseful of helpers, and newlywed Chloe Doyle is relieved that they have come.

Rebecca grabs her headboard as she feels her stomach sieze, the carved oak leaves making impressions in her palms. She hears the women's encouragement and feels Ann Crockett rub her back. After a memorable pain, Rebecca says, "I remember this now. I suppose it is too late to change my mind."

Frances chuckles. "Funny, Rebecca. You have a good situation here in your home with the doctor and all. You can do this. For heaven's sake! Take down your hair! Get comfortable."

As Rebecca releases her thick knot of hair, Ann Crockett tells her the story of how Simmons' wife had *her* baby. "It was when they were at the end of their ordeal coming across on the Trail. There was a great deal of snow and they had to camp, even got hungry for several weeks. When canoes arrived and they headed down the Columbia, they had to stop along the way so she could get out and have her baby in the snow on the riverbank."

"Oh my," Rebecca says. "I thought that Samuel came across with Simmons."

Ann laughs. "Yes he did. Maybe that is why he hasn't found a wife yet."

Dr. Lansdale comes in to check on progress. "It will be awhile," he says. "You are doing fine, Rebecca. Try to stay calm, your body knows what to do. I will come check on you again in a bit." He goes back to the parlor to sit with Ebey and the boys and everyone else who is hanging around, waiting.

The women are telling their stories while Rebecca silently speaks to her Lord: *"Your will be done, dear Lord. I pray that my husband and all of my children will be well in your loving arms, and if it is Your will, that I might be able to see them grow."*

After the pacing and the praying in the parlor, the clock ticks into May 26 and Rebecca births a perfect baby girl into the arms of Dr. Lansdale at 1 a.m. The birthing crew tends to Rebecca and the baby, and then Ebey comes in.

He holds his tiny newborn in one arm while holding Rebecca's hand. The candlelight reflects in Rebecca's eyes where she half-lays, propped up in bed. She feels the warm, rough hand of her husband and his strength as they talk about their daughter.

"Did you know that I have always hoped to have a girl one day?" she asks.

"No, you have never told me that, my love."

"Let's name her Sarah." She makes an effort to squeeze his hand. "Sarah after your mother and our sisters Sarah who are in Heaven now."

"That sounds perfect."

"I would like her middle name to be Harriet after my mother. Is that alright?"

"Yes." Her hand turns clammy is his. "You should sleep now, Rebecca. Sarah will be brought in if she needs you. Rest now."

Ebey carries the baby out to the main room to meet her young brothers who are foggy without sleep. They each show angelic smiles and touch the tiny face with one finger and kiss her forehead. "There," Ebey says. "Now she knows that she is loved by her brothers. You can go to bed."

Then everyone who is awake rallies around the breakfast table for a very early meal before heading home. Ebey is a little shaky as he eats, thinking that Rebecca looks mighty thin and frail lying in that bed.

{ **33** }

Collector of Customs,
May 1853

Ghosts linger round the places where our happiest and saddest hours have been spent, where the commonest items or the most trivial sounds carry us back to those bygone days to stand in the presence of the almost forgotten. –E.M. Archer, *Christina North*

Rebecca holds brand new Sarah when her three brothers come into the bedroom to visit. Thomas takes her first, feeling the lightness of her, rocking her in his arms like in a swing. "Such a tiny thing," he says before passing the bundle to John.

When James holds her, he cries. "New life," he says, feeling strong emotion.

"We are happy for her," John says, always trying to help James avoid bouts of depression. He returns the baby into Rebecca's arms.

"You have a great many uncles, my tiny daughter," Rebecca says in a groggy voice, her finger sliding over the baby's fuzzy cheek.

"There is another uncle coming next year," Ebey says. "Winfield plans to come with the grandparents . . . and then there's all our adopted family all over the island."

The birth of his daughter is also the day that Ebey learns that he may drop "Deputy" from his title. He is Collector of Customs now, which is what he wanted so that he could arrange to be closer to home. The bad news is that he is expected to go to Olympia to begin his new role. He knows that he will need to go as soon as Rebecca is out of danger.

Ann Crockett comes in the evening to stay with Rebecca and baby Sarah through the night, and Ebey, his head swimming, sits down to write to his brother Winfield:

> *"Rebecca was delivered early this morning of a fine daughter. She suffered a good deal but not so much as we expected. Our little daughter we conclude to call Sarah Harriet for Rebecca's Mother and Sister and for my Mother and Sister. She is quite comfortable. I have received my appointment as Collector of the Port of Puget's Sound."*

Dr. Lansdale comes to check on Rebecca over several days and brings news that Isaac Stevens has been appointed as Governor of Washington Territory and Superintendent of Indian Affairs. President Pierce named him within two weeks of the approval of Washington Territory. Neither Ebey nor Dr.

Lansdale are in favor of the appointment. At John Crockett's house, the neighbors discuss it.

"I understand that Isaac Stevens is a military man, graduated from West Point," John Crockett says. "That does not sound so bad."

"But he only sees his own goals, which I suspect are to make a name for himself," Ebey says. "Because his expertise is war, he sees the Indians as a . . . problem to conquer, like an enemy. He is a small, power-hungry man."

"I agree," Lansdale says. "Isaac Stevens was a big supporter of Franklin Pierce when he ran for President. They served in the Mexican-American War together. This appointment is President Pierce rewarding Stevens for his support rather than him being qualified for the position."

Samuel Crockett has heard of Stevens as well. "I hear the man is politically ambitious and conceited, will do more harm than good with the Indians . . . a military man without troops to command."

"For now, he is surveying the eastern part of the territory, looking for a northern route for a transcontinental railroad," Lansdale says. "He plans to meet with Indians along the way as he crosses the territory."

"What . . . can we do to have him replaced?" Ebey asks.

* * *

Guests come to The Cabins two days after Rebecca gives birth. Chloe Doyle is thankful that she has had some experience when Dr. Lansdale brings Indian Agent Colonel Starling and some soldiers to stay. Ebey escorts them to Colonel Crockett's house in the morning for a hunting trip and returns home to relieve Ann Crockett since Rebecca's recovery seems steady. When he finds Rebecca and the baby asleep, he leaves Chloe on alert and goes out to haul rails to continue fencing his fields.

It has been five days of Rebecca saying that she feels a bit better each day. When Colonel Starling offers Ebey a voyage back to Olympia for his Customs duty, he knows he must go. Before he leaves, he holds his daughter and rocks her. Her eyes open wide when he calls her "Sarah."

"I am sorry that I must leave, Rebecca. I will come back as early as possible and one day soon, I will only need to go across to Port Townsend," Ebey says. He looks at Rebecca, so prim and thin in bed, her long brown hair spread like a fan on the pillow. "Do I have your understanding? . . . your permission to go? I will need to withdraw from the position if I do not go."

"Yes, Mr. Ebey. You do not need my permission, but you have it. You have my heart and my love and the love of our children for their Pa . . . who is doing right by them and showing them how a respected member of the community behaves . . . I am surrounded by those who will watch over me, and the Lord is with me and with you, and you will come home as soon as you are able."

His throat constricts. "I *am* doing my best, and I love you," he says. He puts his hand beneath her head, his fingers through her loose hair, and kisses her tenderly on the mouth and on her forehead and on the back of her hand.

In Olympia, within two days of accepting the position of Collector of Customs for the Puget Sound district, Ebey writes to President Pierce to recommend a move of the Customs House from Olympia to Port Townsend.

Rebecca's recovery seems slow but steady for several weeks after giving birth, though she has occasional fever and cough. She prays that baby Sarah has not inherited her illness and spends much of her time in bed under the headboard of her father's carved oak leaves. Chloe cares for Sarah so that Rebecca may sleep.

{ **34** }

Hettie, Summer–Fall '53

Spirits don't hunt, nor trap, nor fish, nor do anything that vain men undertake, since they've none of the longings of this world to feed. –Hetty Hutter, James Fenimore Cooper's Deerslayer

Chloe's sister, Carolyn Kellogg, comes on a warm summer day with her two little daughters to visit Whidbey Island, having left her husband, Dr. John Kellogg, at home in Olympia.

"You look well," Chloe says, embracing each of them. She looks like her sister: long, sloping nose, blond curls escaping their pins. "How is your husband, the doctor?" She thinks of how she had relied on him during their time together on the Oregon Trail. There were so many illnesses, graves everywhere. A snowstorm had caused them to camp for three weeks while some of their cattle had died from starvation and cold, and they had stayed in Vancouver together for the winter.

"My husband is fine. I just came to see how you are doing, being newly married to a man you knew only ten days." Carolyn sees the stricken look on Chloe's face. "What's wrong? Did you not want me to come?"

Chloe's face changes immediately and she grabs another hug from Carolyn. "I'm afraid that I was remembering the loss of our good sister and niece and our poor brother's face when I told him of their death on the trail."

The little girls go off to play with their new cousins who are the same age. "I am so very happy to see you, sister. I have come into quite a family and community here," Chloe says. She picks up Rebecca's baby Sarah in her swaddling and whispers. "She is a very quiet baby. She rarely cries. Sadly, her mother Rebecca spends most of her time in bed. She is having a very difficult time recovering."

"So, Mrs. Chloe Terry Doyle, my beloved sister," Carolyn says, "you manage this household including Rebecca's two boys and baby Sarah here and your two new little daughters and I assume that you take care of Rebecca and your own husband and any guests who appear without warning as well." Carolyn takes a long breath. "I've never known you to be so . . . industrious."

Chloe nods seriously. "Mrs. Alexander comes from the Cove to nurse the baby since Rebecca is having trouble, and Reuben is a wonderful husband and father, and such a good storyteller. Listening to his stories is like reading a book."

Within a few days, Carolyn Kellogg meets all the neighbors and returns home to Olympia starry-eyed about the island, which causes Doc Kellogg to buy a canoe.

* * *

Nathaniel Hill returns home from San Francisco on the *J. S. Cabot*, having been gone for more than three months while waiting to get paid for the pilings he delivered. He returns with goods for the island as well as a yoke of oxen and feed. His brothers help him unload his cargo in Penn's Cove, hoisting each ox into the water with ship's rigging. After corralling them on shore, they update him on local news: a small trading post has opened in Coveland, and the first hanging at the county seat is about to occur.

He sees the scaffold that has been erected south of the courthouse in preparation and learns that acting Sheriff Hugh Crockett pursued the Indian suspected of killing Mr. Church all the way to Fort Steilacoom in a canoe. He brought the accused back for trial, which resulted in a conviction.

Nathaniel sees a crowd gathered for the hanging, mostly Indians. He watches as they come forward around the scaffolding, their arms raised, chanting a prayer to God in Heaven. Hugh Crockett lets them continue for a time, knowing that their ceremonies are long. After an hour, he gives the signal, and the hanging is done. As the Indians move away, 18-year-old Tom Hastie Jr. comes out from an unfinished storehouse with his rifle in hand.

"Were you the protection detail?" Nathaniel asks.

"Yeah. We didn't know what the Indians might do, and we didn't think it would be good for them to see me with the gun," Tom says. "I guess I was back-up, really. The Sheriff was there in front of them."

"I heard an Indian say that he wondered if the man in the noose might have been a slave substitute," Nathaniel says.

"I guess that does happen," Tom says, scratching his head.

* * *

In Olympia, Ebey receives word from Dr. Lansdale that Rebecca is not doing well, and he comes home on the next vessel headed north. He ignores the condition of the farm, determined to spend time with his wife. As soon as he walks in the door, Chloe puts Sarah into his arms, hoping it will help bolster him as he sees Rebecca who has become terribly thin.

Rebecca sobs when she sees him, the Truth written across her face. Her words flow as she confesses her greatest worry. It is for Sarah. "She is so tiny and frail," she cries. "I left my mother behind, and she died on the Trail. Now I'm afraid . . ." her coughing takes her words, "our daughter . . . may die too."

He is thankful for the weight of little Sarah in his arms as he sees Rebecca's weakened state. "We are all safe, Rebecca." Ebey kisses the back of her hand. "We are all in God's hands, you know that." He kisses her warm cheek. "How about if I sit and we read the Bible together?"

"I would love that very much. To hear your voice and the Word of God . . . it makes me feel safe."

Ebey reads aloud from the Bible and sees her relax, and he continues to read until she is asleep.

In the afternoon, Rebecca wakes to see Ebey still in a chair beside her, reading a book. He hears her sigh and helps her sit up a little, arranging her pillows. "Hello there," he says.

She ties her hair back loosely. "I am happy and surprised to see you are here when I know how much you need to do, Mr. Ebey. Where is our baby?"

"She is with the Alexanders. Mrs. Alexander will bring her back to you this evening."

"You are supposed to be in Olympia," she says, "on behalf of our new territory . . . and our families." She sits up taller, wanting him to think she will be fine.

"I am allowed to spend time with my wife, and I would rather be here with you."

"Tell me about your office in Olympia."

"I hope my office will be in Port Townsend soon, but for now, it is just a small room on the second floor of Edmund Sylvester's new building. There is a store on the first floor that Michael Simmons runs."

"I thought that Michael Simmons and his family were at New Market," Rebecca says.

"They moved. He sold his grist mill and sawmill. The name New Market has been changed to Tumwater."

"Oh my! How will we ever keep up with the changes? Tumwater?"

"Tum tum is Chinook for heartbeat. The Indians say the water sounds like a heartbeat at the falls. I suppose it should be tumchuck since chuck means water, but it seems a nice compromise."

"I like using the Indian names. We are the newcomers after all." She closes her eyes, imagining Ebey in his office for a few moments. "What are you reading?"

"*The Deerslayer*, James Fenimore Cooper. I found it on your nightstand."

"Thomas has been reading it to me," she says. "I love the person Hetty in the story. She is so young and sweet, armed with only her Bible when she faces her father's captors . . . She thinks that God will be more apt to remember a sorrow for something we have done, rather than the wrong itself."

"I like that idea," Ebey says. "She seems a likable character, to be sure."

"What do you think about Hettie as a nickname for our Sarah?" Rebecca asks. "She will need a nickname with so many Sarahs in the family and in the neighborhood."

"If it pleases you, Hettie will be perfect." He hands her a glass of water and tucks her in the covers with a kiss.

Rebecca feels comforted, safe and loved, and shows her happiest smile of many weeks.

{ 35 }

An Appointed Time, September 1853

*"Spirits can see, especially the spirits of parents who feel anxious about their children. --*Hetty Hutter in James Fenimore Cooper's *Deerslayer*

September is the beginning of harvest for farmers. Ebey travels between home and Olympia as often as he can to see Rebecca and to oversee work on his farm. He hires Indians to do much of the work and is thankful to Chloe and his friends and Rebecca's brothers who take charge when he is not there.

Maria Coupe has put up long enough with the tiny cabin that her husband, Captain Thomas Coupe, has provided for her and the family. She wants a larger home, the one that he promised her before she had agreed to stay, and she wants it now. She feels her jaw jutting out more than normal and her hair bonnet vibrates. "There is another child on the way, for heaven's sake!"

Coupe hires the Hill brothers to build their new house and asks them to make it a top priority. "If I need to live through another winter with my wife being this unhappy, well, I am telling you boys, it will not be good. I might need to live on the brig."

* * *

In Olympia, Ebey works quickly as if a clock ticks inside his head in an attempt to complete his work and hop on the next brig or schooner headed north to home. Sometimes it is a quick trip, but sometimes the wind dies, and his vessel sits for days. That frustration is the hardest thing for him to manage as he does not do well with idleness. Those are the times when he dwells on Rebecca's poor health the most, and his anxiety builds.

Ebey's letter to Winfield written at the Custom House in Olympia, September 28, 1853.

"*My Dear Brother, I have been sorely afflicted. Rebecca was confined about the 20th of May last and since that time she has not been able to be out of her bed or me leave her bedside except when business that could not be put off forced me from the house. I fear she has that scourge of her family, the consumption. Little hope now is entertained of her recovery. Yet still while there is life, there is hope. And I yet hope the best medical aid the country affords is in attendance on her.*"

We have a beautiful little daughter who appears to be as healthy as could be desired. We call her "Sarah Harriet." Rebecca has not nursed her since she was a week old. The baby is in the care of a very kind-hearted motherly woman who has been living with us. Rebecca has expressed a decision that if she should not recover, thatourMother should be a mother to her little one. Still, I hope for the best and trust so mournful a duty will not fall on my mother . . .

Friends think I should become a candidate for Delegate to Congress, but I declined. I promised Rebecca that I would leave her no more and I will keep my word. I will be able to move the Customs House from Olympia to Port Townsend in three months and can get across the water from my home in an hour . . . May God in his infinite mercy bless and watch over you all and make us once more a united family on earth as my hope is we shall be in Heaven where sickness and parting and death is no more. Your Brother, I.N. Ebey"

* * *

Meanwhile, it has been nearly a year since Snetlum's death. His son George remembers the bitter cold that lasted for weeks when his father died and how they had needed to take refuge with Rebecca Ebey. His father's Memorial Potlatch will be early this year to avoid such frigid weather. Villages practice their songs and dances, and as the time draws near, everyone fasts to ensure the success of the potlatch, an important part of their culture.

The guests arrive at the mouth of Penn's Cove, some in a stately show of large war canoes lashed together side by side, a richly dressed leader standing in the bow of each. This is how the Lower Skagit, Upper Skagit, the Swinomish and the Lummi people come. They sing their arriving song from the water, and Snetlum's Village sings their greeting song.

* * *

When a Methodist preacher comes to The Cabins to preach, Rebecca's spirit is lifted. She often remembers the scripture in her dreams. She also dreams of all those worrisome times of waiting for Ebey to come home, of the Indian children holding her hands, of her laundry flapping in the wind.

The Klallam and some Snohomish people beach their canoes at Ebey's beach. Before passing Ebey's home, Old Grayhead, dressed in his best regalia for the potlatch, takes a short detour, having heard that Rebecca Ebey is not well. He knocks at the door and gives Chloe a braided length of shredded cedar, telling her to burn it in the house, especially in Rebecca's room to clear away the spirits that make her sick.

Lying in bed, Rebecca remembers her boys' wide eyes on the Oregon Trail, Ebey's happy, expectant face at their wedding, their reunion near Fort Hall, their trip up Puget Sound with Blossom's tail twitching nervously over the back of the scow. She sleeps, dreaming of beautiful Puget Sound, the dense forest, mountain peaks, the smell of the ocean, her husband's rough, comforting hands. And there is cedar smoke.

* * *

At Snetlum's Village, Old Grayhead sees all the canoes lined up on the beach, great war canoes, side by side and announces his group, "We are Klallam from Townsend Land. We have come to honor your great leader, our friend, Snetlum."

Mourners gather inside the big Potlatch House. George wears his ceremonial coat decorated with abalone shells, his small wooden cross dangling from his neck. He bends to lift the large Christian Ladder. "This is what Snetlum treasured most," he says. "It will be preserved for future generations."

"My father had Wind Power," George says. "You may have heard the story: A group of Snoqualmie came in shovel-nose canoes to kill us. My father said, 'Get into your canoes. We will fight them on the water.' My father led them deep into the cove, calling, 'If you want to fight, come along, come along.'"

"Those shovel-nose canoes could not stand much wind," George says. "My father stood tall in his canoe to call the Wind, and the West Wind came up, blowing hard. One Snoqualmie canoe was broken up and lost, the other Snoqualmie scrambled across to Oak Harbor. Not one of our people was killed, because my father had Wind Power. I feel him still, in the Wind."

George is proud of the Potlatch. It teaches people to respect each other, to honor the givers who will then rely on the good will of others. Through the potlatch, all are thanked, and relations are strengthened. The power of their traditions will help them through changing times. He will always feel his father in the Wind.

* * *

Rebecca wakes, a swirl of fresh air massaging her face. She thinks that someone has let Rover into the house. He drops his head, heavy onto her bed and looks at her, staring. A tiny nose whine. She lifts her hand to the top of his head. "Hey boy. Did you come to say goodbye? You have been a good boy." Then he licks her hand and hurries out the door.

She sees the wind sway the tops of the great elms back in Missouri and create waves through the new field of wheat above the cabin. She hears it rush, shaking the fruit trees in her yard that will produce apples, pears and peaches. "In three years," her husband had said.

* * *

Eason goes into the bedroom to say goodnight to his mother before going to bed. He finds her cool to the touch, her mouth slack, and his mournful cry brings his younger brother Ellison followed by Chloe. "Oh Ma," Eason cries, laying his head on her body to sob. He feels his brother's arm across his back. Chloe is there with them, holding a candle, letting them be with their mother. She knows death, knows the emptiness it brings. When the boys have cried and cried, she leads them from the room.

The boys hold hands for the first time since they can remember and sit together near the fire while Chloe reads the Bible aloud for them all, her curls reflecting the light like a halo.

"Ma always said that Jesus was the Anchor of her Soul," Eason says. "Where is that in the Biblble?"

"I believe it is in the New Testament," Chloe says. She thumbs through, finding something in Hebrews. "*We have this hope as an anchor for the soul,*" she reads. "I guess it means that

God is unchanging. I believe your Ma would say that our faith in Jesus will keep us secure, like an anchor to the unchanging God. What do you think?"

Both boys solemnly nod their heads.

* * *

From Isaac Ebey,

On night of death of my dear wife, I was at Olympia. I had worked all day to be ready to start home the moment I completed my business. I was constantly thinking of the low state of her health... the anguish of my mind.

... at that moment her loving spirit had quit the frail tenement of clay that bound it to earth and was dwelling in worlds of light and love where friends meet to part no more. I fancy her spirit was at that moment hovering around me. The influence of her love was upon me.

In morning's life when hope was young
And strewed our path with flowers,
Thy smile of love, thy loving songs
Bade earth a heavenly tower.
Then cares of life had clustered 'round
My path; and darkness hid my way
Thy words of love dispelled the gloom,
Thy love, my light, made day.

Rebecca Whitley Davis Ebey departed this life on the 29th day of September AD 1853 at about 9 o'clock PM, aged 30 years, 9 months and one day and in the ninth year eleventh month and 26th day of wedlock. –Isaac Neff Ebey

* * *

The Ghosts of Whidbey Island

Obituary from The Columbian: Rebecca Ebey of Whidbey Island-- the first white woman to settle on the island. Her Christian values enabled her to endure with patience a lingering and severe illness and to meet death with calm resignation.

* * *

Reverend Benjamin Close presides over Rebecca's funeral. The large group gathers at her graveside in the garden northeast of The Cabins, a grave dug by neighbors. It is a warm, breezy day, and the boys stand between their distraught father and their Uncle Thomas. Chloe uses one hand to settle her dress which has lifted in the moving air and snuggles baby Hettie in the other arm. Hettie is dressed in the gown that Rebecca made for her from her own wedding dress.

Ebey looks at the group of friends who have gathered, each clearly grieving, and has a moment of clarity about the majesty of life and the grandness of their community. He looks around at the beautiful abundance of their island, feeling connection with the Living Spirit. Just that morning, he had walked through the garden and a turtle dove had fluttered nearby. He had called "Rebecca" and the bird had allowed him to come quite close as he had talked to his wife.

{ **36** }

Harvest, 1853–54

"On the night she died, I believe her spirit Hovered around me. I dreamt of her. I saw her as plainly as in life." --Isaac Ebey

Ebey finds his only solace in hard, physical work and seeing his farm thrive. If his farm thrives, his family will thrive, and he fills his head with every minutia of making it so. The rhythm of the place has changed ever since Rebecca took to her bed so many months ago. Ebey hires workers, and friends and uncles lend a hand, especially when he must be in Olympia. In the late fall, when the harvest is in, he invites the whole neighborhood for a meal, and they come carrying their own gifts of harvest from their own hard work.

When the light begins to fade and the candles are lit and precious coffee is poured to accompany a piece of apple pie, they look around for an uplifting story. Red-headed Sam Hancock is there. He has been working Colonel Crockett's farm.

Most folk think it is to be close to Susan Crockett, but he stands firm with not being the settling-down type. They ask him for a story, and he has one to tell, "but I certainly cannot say it is an uplifting one," he says. "The plight of the Indians is heavy on my mind as of late, so if you want uplifting, maybe John Crockett there could help you out or Chloe's husband, Mr. Doyle. I hear his stories are like reading a book."

"Perhaps we need to hear your thoughts regarding the Indians, Mr. Hancock," Ebey says. "We should know them now that the new governor will be in our midst soon, wielding his power."

"My thoughts are sympathetic," Hancock says. "I was at Neah Bay with the Makah when the Smallpox broke out there. They hadn't wanted me there. I had set up a small trading post to take advantage of the traffic up the Straits, and they didn't trust me, threatened to kill me if I didn't leave. When the smallpox arrived, I thought I was a gonner to be sure, for they thought I had brought it, ya see. But I was able to have them understand the truth. The smallpox had come on a brig from San Francisco that put off two of their own returning home, and a white man. They all had the smallpox. As you can imagine, it spread like the plague it was. They died in vast numbers day after day."

"Why would you stay there with that going on?" Susan Crockett asks, eyebrows curling in interest. She remembers seeing him come into Port Townsend harbor. He had three long canoes strapped together with several layers of cedar planks piled on top and everything else he owned on top of that. It had looked like a permanent move.

"I could not leave them. They were suffering so and coming to me for help. They lay on the beach, begging me for some kind of relief, even promised to be my slave for life if I could help them. All I could do was give them food and water." His eyes and red hair glisten in the candlelight.

"Of course, a few tried to escape from it and took the pox with them to Vancouver Island."

"Within two weeks, the beach was covered with dead bodies. I swear, the bodies littered the beach for eight miles. The sick started to come to my house, laid right down in my yard to die . . . I felt like they were saying, 'See what you have done?' to be doing that."

Ebey pours him a whiskey. "Thank ye, sir." It is so silent in Ebey's parlor that they hear him swallow when he lifts his glass.

"There were so many bodies . . . I dug two big holes, put, I don't know, maybe twenty bodies in each one. But they kept coming and I had to haul them to the beach at low tide, so they'd drift away . . . and o' course the dogs came. I could not do anything about it. It didn't feel right to shoot all those dogs for being dogs."

"How long were you dealing with all of this, Mr. Hancock?" Thomas asks.

"It ran its course in about six long weeks of hell. I'm sorry to use the word, but there is no other to describe it. Thought I'd lose my mind. The poor wretches who managed to live through it were lost without their families. They didn't know how to live anymore. There was an old man who climbed up into a tree, to get away from the disease, I guess. He was still there a month later, all wrapped up in his blanket. He hadn't moved: he was dead too, of course."

"I would say that he prepared himself for death," Ebey says. "The Makah people practice tree burial. He knew there would be no one left to get him up there once he died."

Hancock has another swallow of whiskey. "Hadn't thought of that. A happier end for him, then, maybe. Thank you for this," he says, referring to the whiskey. "Guess I'm just melancholy as winter's around the corner, but I thank ya all for listening. Haven't shared that one before and it's been heavy on my mind."

"They have all had their lives changed dramatically," John Crockett says. "The ones who are still alive need someone to speak for them. Some have tried to adopt our ways. Sealth and Leschi to name a few. I've heard that Leschi supplied food to some of the settlers around Tumwater when they first arrived. Saved them from starving."

"True," Samuel Crockett says. "I was one of those settlers."

Colonel Crockett clears his throat. "Now they all see how their lives are changing and the Indians north of here are becoming more aggressive."

"Unfortunately," Ebey says, "I do not think we can solve the future for the Indians tonight. Let us be thankful that those on our island are peace loving and willing to work for pay. We are thankful for harvest and this bountiful meal. And let us give thanks for each other and for the . . . memories of those we have lost."

Every head lowers when Rebecca comes to mind as if she smiles at them while walking in from the kitchen.

* * *

Ebey receives approval to move his office for Collector of Customs from Olympia to Port Townsend. Every vessel entering Puget Sound from any foreign port now is required to make its first stop at Port Townsend for inspection and to pay taxes on imported goods. More than fifty vessels trade in Puget Sound and pass in front of Ebey's home. He has a wharf erected below his home to make travel back and forth easier for him and for others. In the local *Pioneer and Democrat* publication, he announces himself as Attorney and Counselor-at-Law with his office in the new location of the Puget Sound Customs House.

As he gets organized in his Port Townsend office, he thinks of Rebecca, wishing that the change could have happened sooner so that he would have had more time with her. At least he is with his children more now. He thinks Rebecca is happy in Heaven when he appoints her brother, John Davis, as Collector for Penn's Cove.

* * *

Governor Isaac Stevens and family arrive in the town of Vancouver on the Columbia River in November 1853. From there, he and his wife Margaret and children travel to the Cowlitz Landing, sitting on mats in the bottom of a canoe paddled by Indians in the pouring rain. Margaret has been stoically quiet in the canoe, her face revealing her discomfort. It changes to horror as they walk in ankle-deep mud to a small log house full of untrimmed, unwashed men. The men are camped on the floor in blankets, their steamy air full of human stink. The governor says goodnight as she and the children are sent into a room for the women. When he is told that his bed is up through a hole in the roof, he is also horrified. The air is unbreathable there, and he spends the night sitting on a stool.

The next day, they travel up the Cowlitz Trail on their way to Olympia, often in mud up to their knees. Margaret begins to talk about the dry forts east of the Cascades that could make a better capital. "Why did you name Olympia as the capital of the territory before seeing it?" she asks. "Their newspaper says they only have one hotel, a livery stable and a saloon."

Stevens hears her criticism and does not respond, knowing that he would be opening the door to a public argument if he did.

In the cold and wet, they ford streams to get to Olympia. Margaret and the children remain in the wagon to stay out of the water, but it still soaks them up to their ankles and the horses fall into a hole. Toward the end of the trip, a guide tells her that it is the rainy season, not a good time to travel. "The place becomes an impossible bog," he says. From that moment on, the governor knows that he himself, rather than the terrain and weather, is to blame for his family's misery.

George Gibbs, a short, round ethnologist and lawyer who speaks Indian languages, comes with them. He had written the first treaties for the Territorial Governor in Oregon two years earlier. However, the treaties were not immediately ratified by the Senate because some believed that the tracts of land for the reservations were too large. This time he has been instructed by the Senate to decrease the size of reservations for Washington Territory.

In Olympia, Governor Stevens gets to know about thirty of the local settlers and collects information about the Indians west of the Cascades. He appoints Michael Simmons as head Indian Agent for Washington Territory. Simmons is known for being direct with the Indians, and Stevens believes he will be the right man to enforce the Treaties that will come.

* * *

On a frosty January afternoon, Bill Engle rides his horse up the bluff from Ebey's Landing, having taken delivery of the mail for the island. It comes weekly now from Port Townsend on the mail boat *Peter Thompkins* from Olympia, and Bill delivers it on the island. Ebey is working on the fence and walks over to accept it.

"Thank you, Bill," he says. "Are you headed to Cranney Store in Coveland to deliver the rest?"

"Yep, there's some mail for that side of the island too."

Ebey thumbs through the mail as he walks into the house, finding a letter regarding the Washington Territorial Legislature.

Their first session of the legislature meets on a blustery day that would thrill a ship's captain at the end of February. In Sylvester's Gold Bar Store in Olympia, they sit close together on the floor as Governor Stevens stands to address the assembly. Stevens is a small man, standing his tallest in boots at 5 feet, 3 inches, his head appearing slightly large on a small body. It is a well-trimmed head with thick dark hair, mustache and goatee. His dark, alert eyes watch for the group's reaction as he declares that the settlers' land claims through the Land Donation Act are not valid.

It gives the legislators pause.

"The Northwest Ordinance of 1789 promised that no Indian land would be taken without tribal consent," Stevens says. "We need that consent, and quickly. Indian title must be voided so that the land claims of the people you represent can be certified. We will extinguish Indian rights to the land with treaties they will sign and provide them with reservations . . . if the settlers you represent want to have legal rights to their properties."

Governor Stevens is ready to use any means possible to make a difference in Washington Territory, even if it means using intimidation and force, and it will be swift.

{ 37 }

Doc Kellogg, March 1854

"The loving heart from whence flowed the passages of this journal is forever stilled. But the spirit that emanated and pervaded all I trust still lives. A spirit perfect, rejoicing around the throne of God and our Savior forever." –Isaac Ebey

Dr. John Kellogg is a short stocky man with a froggy voice due to the ever-present cigar in his mouth. He has a tough, nearly cranky exterior but is a compassionate doctor for his patients. His kindhearted eyes echo illness and loss, a look he acquired as he crossed the country on the Oregon Trail. He, his wife Carolyn Terry Kellogg and their two little girls move from Olympia to Whidbey Island at Carolyn's insistence. She loves the island and the people there, including her own sister who was married recently at Ebey's home, Chloe Terry Doyle. It will be rough living in their island cabin for a while.

"It's not much," Doc Kellogg says as they arrive at their new home.

"Not much?" Carolyn asks. "It does not have a floor, John! Or a cookstove!"

"Well, it has a roof now," he says. "It didn't have a roof the last time I saw it, so we have made improvements already." He smiles, but her heavy breathing sounds like a threat. "We can cook in the fireplace." He tries to make his gruff voice sound light-hearted.

"Fine, you can do the cooking then," she says, hands on hips.

Fortunately, the neighbors help make up for her hardships. Colonel Walter Crockett and his wife Ann, who live on the other side of a marshy lake north of them, are wonderful neighbors. They sell their milk and Ann Crockett often puts a lump of butter in the bottom of the pail for Carolyn.

Doc Kellogg orders boards from Olympia in his attempt to fulfill his promise of improvement. A schooner delivers them by tossing them overboard, forcing him to wade into the surf to get them. As he hauls them up the hill from the beach on his back, he thinks there must be another way.

"I wonder how the sow will be delivered," he says as he comes in the door.

Carolyn is on her knees to stir a pot of stew that hangs in the fireplace. She blows away a blond curl that has fallen into her face and waves the spoon at him like a weapon. "I paid my valuable paisley shawl for that pig, you know. I loved that shawl, probably my most prized possession, carried it all across the country for goodness' sake."

"Yes, I know. We should have seen the sow by now. Let's hope the same schooner that delivered the boards didn't put her over the side and she drowned."

Carolyn turns back to her pot. "The settlers here are so hungry for pork . . . They wouldn't steal her, would they?"

"No, but we have drifters who come through here too . . . and there are wolves . . . and plenty of bear."

Several days later he receives a written note that the schooner delivered their sow. "Two weeks ago! Gawddammit! Don't you think they might have let me know when she was actually delivered? Not two weeks later?"

Carolyn grinds her teeth as she kneads dough, afraid to open her mouth.

"It says they dropped her over the side below our place, saw her swim to shore. I'll take Flora with me. Maybe she can help sniff her out . . . if she is alive somewhere. I hope Newfoundlands are a breed that can hunt." Flora wags her black tail as they set off together.

Just before dusk turns to dark, Carolyn hears him making a ruckus on the porch.

"What have you done!" Carolyn says. "You are mud from head to toe!"

"Found her," he says, stomping mud from his boots. "She was nested under a log and had ten little ones with her! Can you believe it? I've been herding them all the way home. It had to have been six miles." He gives Flora a good rub as she wags her tail. "It's a wonder we found them. I used the little ones for bait best I could to keep the mamma coming." He leans against the door frame, realizing how exhausted he is. "It's probably the hardest thing I've ever done, Carolyn." He pulls off his hat. "Come see how big she is, Carolyn, even after two weeks living on her own!"

"I believe they eat the camas roots," Carolyn says going out the door.

* * *

Sam Hancock has been farming Crockett's prairie for a time now, adopted into the Crockett family. It's like having parents and a bunch of brothers. Despite his being certain that he is not the settling-down type, he has come to love Whidbey Island . . . and he can no longer deny that he loves Susan Crockett. He is 36 and she is 31 when they are married. The Colonel tells him that he can always use another son. Everyone wonders if their children will have hair as red as Sam's. In addition to farming, Sam builds a brick kiln.

{ **38** }

Customs Clerk, May 1854

Like the ghost of a dear friend dead, is Time long past. A tone which is now forever fled, A hope which is now forever past, A love so sweet it could not last, is Time long past. –British Poet, Shelley

When the United States and Britain agreed on the 49th parallel "through the channel" between Vancouver Island, Province of Canada, and the United States as a boundary line, it was unclear as to which channel, Haro Strait or Rosario Strait. British Governor Douglas of Vancouver Island is not happy to have lost Washington Territory in the first place and is determined not to lose another square foot of land. When an American citizen harvests timber on Lopez Island in the San Juans on his own claim, Governor Douglas sends word that he must pay taxes to the British Crown. Word of this reaches Ebey as the Collector of Customs for the Port Townsend district in

Washington Territory, which alerts him to the probability of future trouble within the disputed area.

Trouble comes in the form of British Charles Griffin who has over a thousand sheep grazing on the south side of San Juan Island for Hudson Bay Company. Ebey sends a letter to Governor Douglas, telling him that the livestock is "subject to seizure for nonpayment of taxes" to the United States. In response, Douglas appoints his man Griffin as a Justice of the Peace for the San Juan District and tells him to arrest Ebey as a common offender if he comes around.

Ebey *does* come around, of course, on May 2nd to investigate with his friend Captain Henry Webber who assists with navigation on the schooner they charter, the *Sara Stone*. He finds more than sheep on the island. There are cattle, horses, and hogs with a team of Hawaiians tending them. Ebey finds Griffin and introduces himself.

"I have come to seize your livestock for . . . violation of U.S. Revenue laws, for non-payment of American taxes," he says.

Griffin is surprised, remembering that he has been directed to arrest Ebey but wondering how he might manage it. He sends word across the straits to Governor Douglas in Victoria and visits with Ebey and Captain Webber while waiting for a reply.

Ebey would like to avoid an international incident and waits until the next day for word from Douglas. When he sees Douglas's ship *Otter* coming, he and Captain Webber raise the American flag on the nearest hill. Sangster, the Collector of Customs at Victoria, comes ashore from the *Otter* in a small boat and immediately raises the British flag on Griffin's farm.

"Mr. Sangster," Ebey says, extending his hand when the man approaches. He already knows the man, but Sangster does not extend his hand. "I am happy to see you, sir," Ebey says. "Share a whiskey with us, will you?" He raises a bottle in invitation.

"What are you doing on British soil?" Sangster asks, his face serious.

Ebey knows this is not a typical reaction to an offer of whiskey for Sangster. "I am an American on American soil," he says. "Here to confiscate some . . . contraband livestock."

Sangster's face reddens.

"Calm down man," Ebey says. "Why doesn't Governor Douglas come ashore to talk?"

"He would rather that *you* come aboard the *Otter* instead."

Ebey refuses, not wanting to acknowledge any claims Britain might have to the island.

With a clear impasse, Captain Webber agrees to stay on San Juan Island so that Ebey can return home to report the situation. Before leaving, Ebey swears Webber in as Deputy Customs Collector.

From his office in Port Townsend, Ebey describes the situation and sends it with his regular Puget Sound tax report to the Treasury Department:

> *"I have no doubt but Mr. Webber, the Inspector, has been arrested and taken to Vancouver Island as a prisoner. I shall visit San Juan Island in a few days and ascertain his fate. Should I find that Mr. Webber has been kidnapped, I shall place another inspector on the island and call upon the Executive to this Territory to protect him."*

Canadian (British) Customs Collector Sangster does try to arrest Captain Webber, but he is met with Webber's four six-shooters and gives it up. Then Webber goes to the mainland for supplies so that he can set up a permanent camp on San Juan Island. He is in his camp when the Washington Territorial Legislature in Olympia forms the county of Whatcom with boundaries that include the San Juan Islands. By the time the Whatcom County Commissioners instruct their new sheriff to assess Griffin's property and levy a tax, Captain Webber has been there nearly a year and has become friends with Griffin. They have watched out for each other as neighbors do, especially for protection against northern Indians.

Nearly a year after Ebey's first visit to San Juan Island, Whatcom County Representative to the Legislature, Alonzo Poe, along with the chairman of the county commissioners, the county auditor, the coroner, and two others arrive on two vessels to enforce the law by confiscating livestock for failure to pay taxes. Unfortunately, Griffin has hidden his livestock. It is late morning when they begin their search, rowing small boats around the island for hours. Continuing in darkness, they finally find a herd of breeding rams hidden in the woods at 3 a.m. After a wink of sleep, they herd the feisty, bleating rams to the loading dock used by Hudson Bay Company, and despite Griffin's protests, load 34 of the horn-headed rascals onto their two ships. The tide is against them, forcing them to wait, then they run aground and must wait some more. Eventually, they manage to sail away and unload the rams onto mainland United States. Hudson Bay Company files a claim through the British government. U.S. President Pierce writes to Isaac

Stevens, governor of Washington Territory, that he is not to provoke further conflicts, but without conceding any property to Great Britain.

Several months later, Ebey relieves Captain Webber from duty and swears in Oscar Olney as his replacement. Olney looks like he has already been attacked by northern Indians. Part of his scalp and a few fingers are missing, but in truth it happened when a cannon burst near him during a ceremonial salute. Like his predecessor, he becomes friends with Griffin. When more than fifty northern Indians come ashore on San Juan to take five American "Boston heads" including Oscar Olney's, Olney escapes to Port Townsend. Not wanting to risk what is left of his scalp, he resigns his position.

The conflict will continue. When an American farmer kills one of Griffin's pigs in 1859, the military is summoned, and the Pig War begins. The conflict is not settled until 1872 with the United States retaining possession of the San Juan Islands.

{ **39** }

Calista, 1854

People leave their ghosts wherever they go. The earth never forgets us. People who have lived in a spot are in some way still there. —Rina Swentzell, Santa Clara Pueblo

Captain Coupe comes in the door when his wife Maria is plucking a chicken. She wipes a lock of hair away that has escaped her bonnet with the back of her hand and sees his face. "Has someone died?"

Coupe is pale, shaking his head. "We do not have legal claim to all of our land."

"What do you mean!" Maria asks, strangling the chicken for a second time.

He swallows, seeing that her teeth are clenched. "Someone else filed a claim last August. Their property overlaps ours."

"How is that possible, Thomas? We have been living here, right here, under the watchful eye of God Almighty, for Heaven's sake!" Her jaw seems more prominent than before.

"I should have filed the claim to legalize it as soon as you agreed to stay. It just slipped my mind with all the talk about the new house."

Maria raises the iron skillet, amazed at her own strength as she waves it in the air. "You will solve this problem Captain Coupe, and you will solve it immediately! If I can learn to milk a cow, you can certainly do that much!" She slams the skillet back onto the stove with a mighty clang, throws the half-plucked chicken into it and heads for the door. "As you know, I never intended to be a pioneer wife! From now on, milk your own darn cow!"

* * *

Calista Kinney's expression looks expectant, her eyebrows tightly arched over dark eyes. Her light, kinky hair becomes floating wings when it is free from the knot at the back of her head, which is often. At 15, her mischievous shenanigans come to an end as she and her seven siblings attend their mother's funeral in Boston. Their father, Captain Simeon Kinney, previously commander of a passenger clipper ship between Boston, London, China and the East Indies, is currently loading spars at Snakelum Point for San Francisco. When he hears of his wife's death, he sends word that the children must come to San Francisco.

Their trip around Cape Horn takes five months of rationed water and only enough clothing to change every two weeks.

Thank goodness her older sister, Maria, had previously traveled around the world with her father and could help them manage. By the time they arrive in San Francisco in February 1853, they feel and look like sewer rats from Boston. Their father welcomes them to their new home on ship.

Calista admires her father though he seems a bit older, his slight build slightly smaller, his hair beginning to thin. He describes Whidbey Island as a Garden of Eden, and she asks to see it for herself. Though he transports spars on the ship that he commands, the *Burnham,* he continues to conduct himself as the proper captain of a passenger ship, and 16-year-old Calista feels like a special guest. During the two weeks it takes to sail there, she asks for stories of his travels. The one that shows his sense of humor and tolerance for misbehavior is her favorite.

"One time," he says, "I had a lazy young sailor with me who skirted his work on ship. You must keep them busy, you see, Calista, or they get onery, and there is much to do to keep the ship afloat. So I gave the lad a chair in the middle of the deck where he could rest comfortably while he watched his mates work all around him. I even had his pipe delivered to him so he could smoke and enjoy himself. The others thought it was a great joke. But he stayed in the chair for only a few minutes, then he was up with a smile and working alongside them."

"I love that story," she says.

"In truth, I think the young one was a little homesick. When he saw the rest of the crew smiling at him and playing along, he felt like he had a bit of a home on ship, and it made him want to belong."

They arrive at Penn's Cove and the deeper they sail into it, the more unsettled Calista feels. It is lined with Indian villages and canoes. Her father says there is no danger and points to the tall cross on the bluff as they pass, evidence of religious belief. They unload at a little store in Coveland and sail out again.

Just beyond the great cross, they stop at the log cabin of another ship's captain, Thomas and Maria Coupe. To Calista, Maria seems to be loving, reminding her of her mother, with kind eyes. She is also practical, a no-nonsense person. As they sew the first short clothes for Coupe's expected baby, Calista talks about her mother's death and their trip around the Horn. It is the same trip that Maria and her children had endured, causing Maria to immediately consider Calista as part of the family.

Maria confesses to Calista about her recent frustrations with her husband. "Not that there haven't been frustrations with him in the past, mind you," Maria says. "There can be quite a lot when you are married to a sea captain who is gone most of the time. But just last week, he finally filed our claim for this property! After we have been living in this tiny cabin here for over a year! We have a larger house being built on this property for heaven's sake."

Calista looks up from her sewing. "At least he has filed it now . . . hasn't he?"

"Except that our claim was rejected. A Mr. Ivans has a claim on part of it. Mr. Ivans filed last August."

"Oh my!" Calista says, lowering her work to her lap. "And you have your new house started here?"

Maria nods. "Colonel Ebey counseled my husband, told him that he would need to purchase the property from Mr. Ivans." She stabs the needle into the fabric as if it needs to be punished. "Evidently, Mr. Ivans and his wife moved into their cabin last May before they had the roof on it!"

The next day, Calista sails with her father to Camano Island to pick up pilings for San Francisco. She freezes when Indians come on board to see the white woman, especially when they feel her clothing. One Indian woman smiles and pats her on the head, offering to paddle Calista around in a canoe while the men work. They call her Kol-lis-tal-la, "good Indian woman." Calista pays the woman in beads, ship's biscuits and calico fabric.

Having been invited for dinner at the Coup home, they return to the Cove and anchor at Long Point. Calista wears her heavy black silk dress and silk bonnet trimmed in roses. She is helping Maria prepare dinner when her father comes in with Captain Howard Lovejoy and her older brother Thomas who serves as Lovejoy's mate. They have just arrived on the *Chalcedony*. At 48 years old, Lovejoy has a fine-boned, confident face with only a fringe of beard. He is handsome, his blue eyes twinkling with humor, attracting Calista's attention. He is in Penn's Cove to hire Skagit Indians at Snakelum Point and Long Point to help with logging to make spars for San Francisco.

It is a large gathering around the table at Coupe's house for venison and potatoes that evening, sending the children to eat on the floor near the fire. Captain Lovejoy and Calista clearly enjoy each other's company. When he escorts Calista back to her father's ship, he holds his oil skin McIntosh over her shoulders to protect her dress from the rain. The Coupe's look at each other with eyebrows raised, wondering if something will come of it.

In the fall, the top-sail schooner *Jefferson Davis*, the first U.S. revenue cruiser on Puget Sound, anchors in Port Townsend. It is a lovely new ship, and it is in need of a pilot. True to his word to Maria, Coupe becomes its sailing master, which will keep him closer to home.

"Finally," Maria says, "a promise kept."

{ 40 }

Winfield, 1854

Tall prairie grass, wind-swept and burnished gold, whispers with the long-dead voices of all who passed away, disease-ridden and exhausted, on this trail in their dream voyage to Oregon or California. – Warren Gossett, "Ghosts of The Oregon Trail"

The moment that Ebey's mother, Sarah, receives word that Rebecca has passed, she announces to the family that they will, in fact, be leaving Missouri in the spring to move to Whidbey Island. She has grandchildren to care for and nothing will stop her.

Winfield Scott Ebey, the youngest in the family, is anxious to be with his brother. With three siblings already in the ground, having died in their twenties, he knows how precarious life can be. He is 23 years old when they begin the trip, a clean-shaven, handsome young man with an easy smile, a thick mop of black hair, fair skin and clear blue eyes.

In spring, he patriotically attaches a small U.S. flag to the front of their first wagon and hollers "Come Up!" at the oxen to get them headed west. Along with his parents, Jacob and Sarah Ebey, Winfield comes with his older sisters, "Ruth" Elizabeth who is deaf and does not speak, and Mary Ebey Wright who comes without her husband, having separated from him several years before. Mary brings her children Almira "Myra" who is 11 years old and James "Polk" who is two years younger. Also in the group are two cousins, George Ebey and George Beam as well as James Wood, a family friend. They travel in two wagons with ten oxen, eight cows, three horses, a mule and Winfield's long-haired dog of dubious lineage named Lion.

When they approach Indian Territory in Nebraska, they decide to join another train for more security and round up the wagons at night. But their only attack comes in the form of weather. A hailstorm hits in the night, and Winfield bolts out of bed to hold the horses and keep *them* from bolting. He is pummeled by balls of ice until it is three inches deep. Then the wind collapses the tents and blows the covers from the wagons. Bone-cold rain drenches everything. They manage to get the tents back up, and Winfield brings a bucket of smoldering coals into the tent he shares with Beam and James for a little heat. "So this is May on the Oregon Trail," he says, thankful for his India rubber coat.

"I've heard it can be quite an undertaking," James says, chuckling.

Rainwater pours off the brim of Winfield's hat into the coals. "We old timers just shake it off with a chaw and a whiskey."

As the train approaches the shallow Great Platte River, they travel through groves of cottonwood and willow to face a large war party of Sioux on their way to fight the Pawnee. Impressed by their magnificent horses and war paint, Winfield gives them food and beads and they become friends, shooting ducks together in the evening. They tell him that the Sioux have always been friends to the whites. The Pawnee are thieves.

Danger of another sort arrives. James Wood is sick after drinking from a warm pool and gets worse over several days. Winfield rides six miles behind for a doctor and returns with cholera medicine but becomes ill himself that night. His father Jacob is ill as well, barely able to sit on a horse, but he takes over Winfield's duties the next day.

The rain pounds and the train stops. They layer two tents, one over the other, to keep the rain off. James Wood is dying. Winfield's Journal: *"Not a relative stood by his grave, but many friends were there. Men by the thousands have laid their weary bodies to rest in this valley ending hopes of wealth…Here lies a high-hearted son of the West."*

There are more deaths: the only young son of a deaf man named Pepper Box, a baby named Mary King who is buried in a donated trunk that is decorated with wild roses, a man who becomes ill in the morning and dies in the afternoon, the work of cholera. He leaves his wife and six children. Winfield's attention lingers on red and blue blankets that wave from the trees of a Sioux graveyard as they roll on by.

Riding on horseback becomes a luxury. The trail is more rugged than Winfield had imagined. He worries about breaking a tooth as he is jerked and jostled while driving the wagon.

On the North Platte, with rose bushes in full bloom, cattle from other wagon trains cover the hills, and they must swim their cattle across the river to find grazing. When it is time to bring them back, the water is deeper and wider and faster, and Winfield finds himself alone on the wrong side. He has no animal to hang onto for the swim back.

He starts off but is immediately sucked under water, flailing down the river. When his head comes up, he yells "Help!" and he's down again, swallowing water. He comes up, choking, and sees a rope thrown but can't reach it. He thinks he may not make it when someone grabs him by the hair and drags him to shallow water. It's his Pa on his horse, and he keeps ahold of the hair until Winfield fights back, struggling to shore on all fours like a wet dog.

"You've got to keep your head up, son."

Winfield coughs up water. "I imagine it was a manly show of drowning, though."

"You're just lucky you've got a good mop of hair on your head."

Winfield's Journal, July 4th: *"Crowds of Emigrants and loud reports of firearms throughout the day testify that this is the birth Day of American Freedom, and that although here in the wilds of the Rocky Mountains, a thousand miles from our home we are Yet American Citizens. At Devil's Gate, every heart beats high with Patriotic Pride as it welcomes this Glorious Anniversary."*

* * *

On August 4, four days beyond the abandoned Fort Hall, where they must traverse thirty miles of waterless terrain, they become desperate. The oxen are ready to drop from lack of water, and some men can scarcely walk. No one is strong enough to set up the tents. On guard duty, Winfield cannot stay awake in the night among the rocks and wakes with two wolves staring at him. When they finally arrive at a stream, they stay to recover, but their situation is not ideal. The ground is covered in black crickets and two cows drop dead. Even so, Winfield thinks he has never enjoyed himself more. He fishes in Trout Creek and hunts buffalo with the Sioux and Cheyenne, and everyone's health returns.

Two days before Fort Boise, a four-wagon train comes up behind them in a hurry. They've been attacked by Indians. Two of their men are dead and one is dying, shot through his lungs. His wife and four small children ride in horror with him in the back of a wagon as they continue on with Winfield's train. He fights for every painful, bloody breath and dies that evening, the color of ash.

Within a few miles the next morning, a Nez Perce rider comes from Fort Boise to warn them about an Indian attack just ahead that occurred the previous Sunday. It was against the Ward train. All were killed, 18 people. Everyone loads their guns. Winfield's father, Jacob, puts such a stern expression on his hardened face for an all-night watch that his loaded double barrel shotgun seems unnecessary. He says that he would just as soon have a little fight as not. His mother, Sarah, seems more determined than alarmed.

Within two miles, they roll up on the attack site. Six bodies remain partially covered next to the trail. It shakes Winfield to the core, knowing that but for the grace of God, it could have been them, women, children and all. They stay to dig into the ground darkened with blood for a better burial. Winfield finds a gun barrel with its stock broken off and the barrel badly bent, a clear sign of a desperate fight. He leaves a note at the graves to warn others.

Every man now is armed. Even the drivers carry their rifles in one hand and their whip for the oxen in the other. The women and children do not walk, but ride in the wagons. At a river, Winfield wades in and through the timber before moving the train through.

Fort Boise is shabby, recently repaired after a flood, and populated with Nez Perce families. They trade for fresh salmon, new peas and potatoes and are escorted down the trail in safety by the Nez Perce on their fine horses.

Back on the trail, they meet Major Granville Haller with full beard and mustache above a naked chin and an in-charge smile. He leads mounted U.S. Troops in the opposite direction to look for the group of Snake Indians responsible for the Ward Massacre. From Major Haller, Winfield learns that a survivor of the killings was found, a boy who was shot through with an arrow who hid and crawled for days to find help, the arrow protruding from both sides of his body. Behind Haller's troops comes Captain Nathan Olney with a mounted volunteer group to fight Indians for the spoils of war. Winfield hopes that Haller finds them first.

At Umatilla Springs, they come to the Old Emigrant Road that leads to the Dalles while the new trail to Puget's Sound via Walla Walla goes to the right. They go right and reach the mighty Columbia in mid-September where they are able to cross with the help of a ferry. Indians in canoes help them swim the cattle across. The next day, they come in full view of the final barrier, the Cascade Mountain Range, and directly in front of it stands snow-topped Mount Rainier rising up into the clouds. They stop at a Klickitat village where gardens are fenced, and plowing is done with oxen. At the Puyallup River, they see fertile land and Indians living in houses and small farms. They buy more vegetables and fresh salmon.

Finally arriving at Fort Steilacoom, it seems that everyone knows Ebey. They are warmly welcomed and fed and given a letter from Ebey telling them to take the *Major Tompkins* to Whidbey Island. When George Beam agrees to watch over their stock, they board the steamer for the trip up Puget Sound.

On board, a clean-shaven man with a practical smile that is nearly a grimace curls the sides of his mouth up into a wide grin. "You must be Isaac Ebey's family," he says, holding out his hand to Winfield. "I am Alonzo Poe, delighted that happenstance has afforded me the opportunity to share this last leg of your long trip. Isaac will be relieved to see you."

Winfield nearly loses the strength in his legs as he shakes Alonzo's hand with both of his own. He did not know how determined he had been to complete the trip, how it had used up so much of his strength, and now he feels that he has completed it. With no duties to perform, he is suddenly exhausted and finds a spot to sleep as the boat steams north. After several stops, he is enjoying his second day's sleep when Alonzo wakes him.

"We are in Port Townsend Harbor," Alonzo says. "Your brother is coming."

{ **41** }

"Treaties," 1854-55

*Every part of this soil is sacred . . . Even the rocks thrill with mem-
ories of stirring events connected with the lives of my people, and the
very dust upon which you now stand responds more lovingly to their
footsteps than yours, because it is rich with the blood of our ancestors,
and our bare feet are conscious of the sympathetic touch.* –Sealth
(Chief Seattle)

On October 11, Ebey pulls alongside *Major Thompkins* and
climbs the ship's ladder. When he steps on deck, he nearly
drowns in family, and the pain he has felt since Rebecca's death
softens.

On the landing below The Cabins, Eason and Ellison anx-
iously wait for the family to arrive from Port Townsend. They
help their grandmother onto the pier, and she gets her arms
around them, saying, "I've got you now." She sees Mount Rainier

to the South and the Olympic Mountains to the west, including Hurricane Ridge. "What a beautiful home you boys have."

"Yours too now, Grandma," Eason says.

Ebey helps his sister Ruth out of the canoe and hugs her. "Will you like it here?" he signs with his hands.

She smiles and nods. "Beautiful," she signs.

On the dock, his sister Mary sees Lion's long tail wagging so hard that it threatens to knock her son Polk into the water. "Watch your brother, Myra. He hasn't learned to swim yet." Lion sees Rover on shore and trots stiffly to meet him nose to nose and nose to tail.

As they walk up the trail to the house, a schooner leaves Port Townsend, its sails opening in the wind. They stop to watch. "What a sight," Winfield says. "What a beautiful sight." He breathes deeply and Ebey squeezes his shoulder.

"I'm glad you're here, brother," he says, feeling a catch in his throat. He steps back to walk with his father.

Jacob vigorously shakes his hand. "Looks like you've got a nice farm going here, son."

Ebey cannot think of a better compliment. "You're just in time," he says, smiling. "We're in the middle of harvest."

As soon as they are in the house, Ebey's mother Sarah walks briskly through and asks, "Where is Hettie? I want to see my granddaughter."

"She is not well, mother," Ebey says. "She is being cared for at a doctor's home by his wife, Carolyn Kellogg. Her sister Chloe is the one who took care of Rebecca."

Sarah Ebey stands with her hands on hips. "I want to see her. I've waited long enough."

Ebey, his mother and Winfield ride south three miles on horseback beyond Crockett's property to Doc Kellogg's home. Hettie seems weak and thin, scarcely able to stand alone even though she is a year and a half old. They stay for dinner with the Kelloggs while Sarah learns from the doctor about Hettie's care. On the ride home, Hettie sits in front of her Pa, his arm around her to keep her warm and safe. Whenever he holds her, she is like a conduit to Rebecca. *My mother is here now love, she will take charge of Hettie as you wanted.*

Sarah is already thinking of ways to put some weight and muscle on her granddaughter. She blinks at her surroundings. Both she and Jacob had trouble with their eyes on the overland trail and it will take time to clear up. She is only 58 years old, and everything will be fine.

* * *

Michael Simmons and Frank Shaw paddle a canoe and follow Indian trails through the wilderness as the maple and oak trees lose their leaves. Evenings get quite cool now in their portable camp. They have been tasked by Governor Stevens to make sense of the tribes in Puget Sound so that representatives can be selected to sign the treaties that are being written by George Gibbs. Both men are well-known and trusted among the Indian populations, and they understand which groups get along together. Relationships between groups are much more intricate than "tribes," and although leaders might have some influence, they will be reluctant to sign any document that will affect someone else.

The men look for friendly Indians to invite to the treaty signing who have enough wealth and status to have a family and slaves, hoping they will be willing to represent a group. Both men dislike the assignment but know they can do it with the least upset for the Indians. Before they left Olympia, Shaw had been asked if he thought he would be able to get the Indians to sign the treaties. His face had dropped, and he had looked at the ground, "Yeah, I can get the Indians to sign their death warrant." It had made his stomach cramp. He was thankful to Gibbs who had written into the treaties that Indians would continue to have the right to take fish at their usual places and continue with the privilege of hunting, gathering roots and berries, and pasturing their horses on open and unclaimed lands.

Three treaties are created for Puget Sound and are to be signed within one month. Signers represent "tribes, bands and villages." The Medicine Creek treaty at Tumwater is the first, held on December 26, 1854, for the Puyallup, Nisqually, Squaxin and related people. Six hundred and fifty out of 893 attend, though they come with misgivings. Some have heard that if they do not come, the governor will send them on a steamship to a land of never-ending darkness. Others come to give warnings. "Do not sign the white man's paper. We do not know what it says. It is the white man's paper, not ours."

Through Gibbs, Governor Stevens explains that he represents the government in the promise of money, schools, housing, and healthcare and certain land on which to live and the allowance to hunt and fish where they have always done so. Gibbs reads the treaty in Chinook Jargon, a limited language. Each signer's name and tribe are transcribed next to his written X. Seventeen signatures at the end of the document indicate the whites who were there as witnesses.

Leschi, a leader of the Nisqually and Puyallup people who has been a good friend to the settlers, refuses to sign the treaty paper. In fact, he makes a big show of not signing it. He has been working his own large farm and will not give it up. He says he will not sign and stomps away. Somehow, his X appears on the signed treaty document.

Next is the Point Elliot treaty signing at Mukilteo less than a month later on January 22, 1855, to represent the Duwamish, Etakmur, Samish, Skagit, Lummi, Snohomish, Suquamish, Swinomish and related people. It is delayed for a few days to wait for the Snohomish. Their village has been destroyed as punishment for a white man being killed, and they slowly shuffle into camp, afraid of more penalty.

After the governor's short speech, Sealth, a leader of the Duwamish and Suquamish who will become known as Chief Seattle, rises to speak. He rests his hand on the head of the short governor as he begins.

"The white chief says that Big Chief at Washington sends us greetings of friendship and goodwill. This is kind of him for we know he has little need of our friendship in return. His people are many. They are like the grass that covers vast prairies. My people are few. They resemble the scattered trees of a storm-swept plain. The great, and I presume — good, White Chief sends us word that he wishes to buy our land but is willing to allow us enough to live comfortably.

"Every part of the Earth is sacred to my people. Every shining pine needle, every sandy shore, every mist in the dark woods, every clearing and humming insect is holy in the memory and experiences of my people. So when the Great Chief in Washington sends word that he wishes to buy our land, he asks much of us.

"Our good father in Washington—for I presume he is now our father as well as yours, sends us word that if we do as he desires, he will protect us. His brave warriors will be to us a bristling wall of strength, and his wonderful ships of war will fill our harbors, so that our ancient enemies far to the northward will cease to frighten our women, children, and old men.

"I will not mourn at the untimely fate of my people. Tribe follows tribe, and nation follows nation, like the waves of the sea. It is the order of nature, and regret is useless. Your time of decay may be distant, but it will surely come, for even the White Man whose God walked and talked with him as friend to friend, cannot be exempt from the common destiny. We may be brothers after all. We will see."

Patkanim, the prominent leader of the Snohomish and Snoqualmie who had tried to lead a movement against the whites before Ebey came, does not hesitate to sign in front of thousands of his people as witnesses. A sea captain has taken him to San Francisco, and he has seen white people covering the shore and city like a swarm of ants. Also, he is learning that it can be lucrative to be friends to the whites.

The signed Point Elliot treaty at Mukilteo shows 82 signatures indicated by each individual's "X" to represent those communities around Whidbey Island. The X signatures include Snetlum's son and grandson: George (Kwuss-ka-nam) and George Jr. (Hel-mits). Like Leschi, there is some question as to whether they attended the meeting even though their X's appear on the document.

The third signing is the Point No Point treaty that is signed four days later on January 26, 1855, on the northern tip of the Kitsap Peninsula to represent the Chimakum, Klallam, Twana, Skokomish and related people.

The treaties on Puget Sound are not ratified for four years. There are no government payments, no healthcare, no schools. Indians continue to live in their traditional villages, and settlers continue to move in.

{ **42** }

Militia, 1855

At night when the streets of your cities and villages are silent and you think them deserted, they will throng with the returning hosts that once filled them and still love this beautiful land. –Sealth (Chief Seattle)

On Whidbey Island, when word gets out that there is a doctor at Admiralty Head, settlers come who are ill or injured. Men come from sawmills and logging camps, sailors from ships. Doc Kellogg gets around to them by canoe as best he can, earning the name, The Canoe Doctor. Ultimately, he builds a hospital wing to his home where he can care for the more serious cases. Many patients have no money. They help at the hospital according to their physical ability as a way of paying for treatment and board. Still, it all puts extra work on Carolyn Kellogg who has her own newborn to attend, Albert.

Carolyn's days are more than full. Along with patient care, she makes soap, stirring a boiling pot of lye and fat until her arm aches and her hair goes straight. She makes tallow-dipped candles that require hours of work, and there's always the sewing and laundry and the kitchen garden. It's the cooking for patients that is her biggest challenge. The neighbors help by building an outdoor oven in the yard. Sam Hancock provides bricks from his new brick kiln and William Hastie lays the bricks.

* * *

The newly arrived Ebey family claims land above Isaac and build their new home. By spring, Isaac Ebey leaves for the Washington Territorial Convention as a delegate. He hopes to offset the aggressive, military actions of Governor Stevens. Winfield receives a letter from Ebey who is in Olympia: *"I think I have 15 delegates aligned with me while Governor Isaac Stevens has nine. I hope to have at least some political strength in the Territory. The struggle on the Sound will be between the Governor and myself."*

On Sunday, Winfield thinks about Ebey's letter as he waits for church to begin in their new home up from the bluff at Sunnyside. He has always admired his brother's willingness to volunteer, especially when it might help others, and Winfield usually follows his brother's advice. As church begins, Winfield looks at the congregation. He sees only married couples and a few old bachelors who seem to be decaying before their time. Their eyes roam as if searching for something that exists only in their imaginations. He is afraid that he will regret ignoring Ebey's advice to marry before coming west. The memory of a moonlit walk with a young lady on the Oregon Trail brings a few lines from "Porphyria's Lover" by Robert Browning.

"Those raven ringlets dark as night
My foolish heart's enslaving,
The least of which I know would set
Ten poets madly raving."

When Ebey returns from Olympia, he takes his horse cart to the interior of Penn's Cove where the clam shells are several feet deep. The wind is calm here and the morning sun is bright. Happy to be on Whidbey Island rather than anywhere else, he gathers the shells into the cart to take home. He will burn the shells for lime and use the lime to plaster a few walls and to sweeten the outhouse. As he works, he thinks about his family. His mother has reminded him that it has been two years since Rebecca's death. She tells him that it is time for him to find a new wife. He remembers the conversation.

"It is not fair to your boys or to me, for that matter," she says. "You need a wife to take care of your home and family, especially since you are away so much of the time."

"You know how demanding the farm is, mother. How am I to do that and my Customs job in Port Townsend and have time for territorial government obligations as well as a wife?"

"Think of it as a partnership, son. She would be there to help you, not cause more work. Who will watch over them with their studies since you have duties elsewhere?"

It would feel like a betrayal to Rebecca, he thinks to himself, hearing the clunk of shells dropping into the bucket. *What if I cannot be home enough for a wife? What if she becomes ill like Rebecca?*

He had told her that he would try. He empties two more buckets of shells into the cart and thinks about the Indian attacks east of the Cascades that he has heard about. He prays to God that hostilities can be avoided in Puget Sound, but the thought of the governor's military approach to all things, including his thinking that settlers who are friends with Indians are enemies . . . It's a problem.

* * *

At the end of October, Jane Kineth and family, who live between Coupe's and Snakelum Point, are paddled to Olympia for shopping. On their return trip, they are shocked to see settlers' homes on fire, more than one. It is black angry smoke with flames rising through the trees, not the comforting white smoke that is the sign of warmth and hospitality of other settlers. Jane does not believe the rumor she heard about the chance that Lower Skagit Indians, the people she and her children live beside every day, could join hostile northern tribes or inland tribes to get rid of the whites.

"You will stay with me, won't you?" she asks her Skagit paddlers.

"Yes, we will not abandon you," her paddler replies. She sees the worried expression on his face and feels him pull harder through the water.

Encouraged by the Yakamas, a group of Klickitat and Nisqually are attacking white settlers and burning their homes. It is Sunday, October 28, and will be known as the White River Massacre in south King and Thurston Counties. Three families are killed.

News of the attacks comes to Port Townsend the next day on the schooner *Emilie Parker* along with the additional report of Indian rebellion east of the mountains. Regular military forces are dispatched there but defeated, and the Indians are congregated several thousand strong.

* * *

Isaac Ebey is appointed Adjutant General for Jefferson and Island counties for a three-year term and is called to raise a company of one hundred volunteers. He takes the oath of office before Winfield who has recently been admitted to the bar and is serving as a Justice of the Peace. Twenty-five of Ebey's company come from Whidbey Island, saying they will only serve if he is captain, and although some had called him colonel before, now everyone does. They name themselves the Northern Rangers, Company I, First Regiment of Washington Territory Volunteers for a three-month enlistment with Ebey as Captain. Officers include First Lieutenant Samuel Howe and Second Lieutenant James Keymes.

Ebey goes to Snakelum Point to talk with George Snetlum. George agrees that it is time to talk, and they sit at the fire to pass the pipe. The pipe always helps slow down the conversation, encourage thinking. "It has been a long time since we have smoked," George says, passing the pipe.

Ebey draws in the white smoke and exhales. "Yes, George. I hope you and your village have been well."

"Well enough," George says.

"You have heard about the fights between Indians and whites east of the Mountains and in South Puget Sound?"

"Yes, Ebey."

"Your father's hope was that the settlers on this island would keep the Lower Skagit people from being attacked by aggressive Indians."

"We continue to hope that."

"I would like to bring the other Lower Skagit from the Skagit and Snohomish Rivers to the island and keep them safe also. It will separate them from the Upper Skagit and Snohomish who might be influenced by aggressive tribes. It would help keep them out of harm's way if fighting begins."

"Where will they stay?" George asks.

"I will send Lt. Samuel Howe to . . . bring them over from the mainland. Some may want to stay with you, or they may stay on the north side of the Cove. Will you speak with Squi-qui there for me?"

George nods once, and the pipe is passed a few more times while he considers the implications.

* * *

Within ten days, a block house is erected for protection on John Crockett's property, and three Crockett families move there. It is a two-story, single room log building with an interior ladder to reach the second floor, a ladder that can be pulled up. The second level is larger than the first to extend beyond the first-floor wall so that potential intruders on the ground can be seen and shot through holes in the floor around the edges. It is also more difficult for an intruder to get to the second floor from the outside. It is much too cramped to house three families.

John Alexander also builds a blockhouse, and Frances Alexander takes her children to sleep there every night. "Put on your pajamas, children, then your coats and get your bedrolls," she says. "Time for bed." She leads them along the narrow path through the dark trees, every noise along the way terrifying and every shadow moving in the wind looking like an angry Indian. "Hang onto each other," she whispers, carrying her youngest child in one arm and the oil lamp with the other, providing just enough light to see the trail.

After two weeks, she has had enough. "I would rather be killed by Indians in my own home than be frightened to death on the trail," she tells her husband. "Besides, the children need to sleep in their beds." Still, she has the rifle next to her bed every night.

Colonel Ebey helps outfit thirty men, including Winfield, who will serve under Second Lieutenant Keymes to go up the Snohomish River on the 46-foot schooner *A. Y. Trask*. It will be towed by the steamer *Traveler*. The volunteers will establish a fort and a blockade on a narrow bend of the river by anchoring a boom of logs across the water and placing a guard on each bank to prevent aggressive Indians from coming down.

The militia that camp on the Snohomish River to build the fort are far from comfortable, especially the older volunteers. They wake up cold and damp to a lead-gray morning, needing to move to get the ache out. Waves of cold rain visit often at night, and the volunteers lie down in their bedrolls while wet fog rises from the ground. Their rations are similar to those eaten on the Oregon Trail: salt meat, hard tack, potatoes. By mid-November, they have two logs in place on the river and are giving small government flags to friendly Indians for identification. Their fort is built on an island on the Snohomish River, and they name it Fort Ebey.

With white flag in hand, Patkanim goes up the river to see his people. He later comes back down with a group of women and children to evacuate them. "I cannot control my people," he says. "I am afraid of them. I will recruit my own Snohomish Company for defense."

Captain Fay, newly appointed Indian Agent, calls on friendly Indians to come to Whidbey Island for safety. The Lower Skagit from the Skagit River settle on the northern shore of Penn's Cove. Colonel Ebey checks in with them when he can. Nathaniel Hill serves as Indian Agent for the friendly Snoqualmie and adjacent tribes who go to Holmes Harbor. The Lummi, Nooksack, Samish and some additional Lower Skagit people are gathered at Miller's Point north of Penn's Cove. Colonel Simmons supervises 1,700 Snohomish and allied tribes near Skagit Head at the south end of the Island.

By the end of November, Winfield writes in his journal that Ebey's Fort on the Snohomish River is nearly finished. They have begun drills and shooting practice twice a day but have seen no hostile Indians. He is sent to Port Townsend, closer to home. On New Year's Eve, when a few in his group discover a confiscated keg of whiskey in the Customs House, he comes down with a fever and goes to bed. He misses the fun when they tap the keg over a knot in the floor for some sampling and perform a shaman's dance to heal him. Winfield wakes in the morning and reports that a shaman visited his fever dream.

* * *

Tensions continue to be high on Whidbey Island, especially for Calista. Maria Coupe had been right about the attraction between Calista and Captain Lovejoy when they met over her dinner table on a blustery night. Now that Calista is Mrs. Calista Kinney Lovejoy and lives on the island, she brings her new baby girl to visit the Coupes often, especially when Captain Lovejoy is at sea.

"There is nothing to worry about, Calista." Maria puts a reassuring hand on Calista's hand. "These local Indians are completely peace-loving. They would never hurt anyone unless they had to defend themselves."

"I'm more worried about Indians who come to the island who do not belong here," Calista says. She passes the baby to Maria.

"There are defense groups everywhere," Maria says, tucking the baby into her left arm to stir her pot of soup with her right. "Don't you have an Indian boy spending nights with you, so you won't be alone?"

"He's more like a family member. Tom, a son of Squi-qui. My husband took him on a trip to China and India, and he feels he owes us now. He sleeps inside the doorway and if Indians come around, he cries, 'Go away! This is the daughter of Captain Kinney!'" she giggles.

Maria lifts the baby to her shoulder. "He sounds like a good alarm, to me."

{ 43 }

Emily, 1856

I heard the quiet feet of a ghost stirring the fallen leaves, and a sigh echoing in the branches. –Dallas Kenmore, Author

In the beginning of a new year, the *R. B. Potter* lands a small protective force of soldiers north of Partridge Point on Whidbey Island, north of Ebey's. Winfield is home, his three-month enlistment complete, and he is not satisfied. "A lot of good those soldiers will do up there," he says. "Why can't they be in a more populated area?" Since enlisting in the militia, he has imagined himself single-handedly saving the day, constantly strategizing about ways to apprehend those who would attack his community. He wishes his brother was there to manage things. Isaac Ebey has been in Olympia since the end of November and has written that he may be bringing home a wife.

In the dark of early morning, Winfield hears his father's voice, *"Indians! Indians! The yard is full of Indians!"* He jerks on his pants, pulls up his boots, grabs his rifle and runs to the bluff just in time to see two canoes of northern Indians pushing off from the beach. He raises his rifle to shoot, but the click reminds him that it is not loaded. Others without ammunition stand with him while the Indians stop to pick up their friends on shore. Winfield sees them propel themselves away with the sail they have stolen from the tiny Revenue Cutter *Rival.*

Wondering what other damage or injury they've done, Winfield and the others push off in the *Rival,* four spare oars pulling hard to chase after them. The Hill brothers and Bill Engle come in a canoe as well. After several miles, they are just about to give up when the fog clears and they see the culprits. They go harder for another twelve miles with every muscle straining until they catch the thieves, stopping their canoe with Winfield's empty long gun. Grudgingly, the Indians give up the clothes they stole from various clotheslines, Sam Hancock's canoe, sails, oars and the compass from the *Rival,* and a great quantity of potatoes.

A week later, Ebey sails north with his new wife, Emily Palmer Sconce, a 31-year-old widow from The Dalles, with her six-year-old daughter, Anna. They were introduced through mutual friends in Olympia and were married in Portland. As they travel home, Ebey is proud of Emily and a little bit nervous. She is still an attractive woman, even after eight years of being a farmer's wife and a good mother to her daughter Anna, but he is bringing her to the home and family that he shared with Rebecca. He thinks about how the two women are similar in many ways. They are both very practical for one thing, essential for the wives of farmers, but Emily is much more wary of Indians than Rebecca had been. Even though Rebecca had some frightening moments, she knew the local Indians well, and the children had gravitated to her.

He still feels tense about the Indian turmoil that erupted in south Puget Sound. "I blame Governor Stevens," he tells Emily. "It does not need to be this way. Those of us who were first settlers did well with them, even depended on them at times. It is Stevens' treaties that's causing . . . rebellion. Think of how their lives have been changed."

"Why Colonel Ebey," Emily says, turning up the fur collar of her wine-colored coat. The corners of her mouth turn up too as she takes his arm, "we certainly cannot allow them to be killing people or stealing or burning homes."

"That is true my dear." He pats her hand. "It is just so unfortunate and . . . unnecessary."

When they arrive home, Eason and Ellison act a bit shy. Winfield congratulates them on their wedding and tells them they are to come to their parents' home at Sunnyside for dinner. Emily and her daughter Anna meet the entire Ebey clan there as well as Rebecca's brothers: Thomas, John and James Davis. Ebey's parents, Sarah and Jacob, welcome her heartily, hoping that she will move into the family smoothly and be a help to their son.

"Welcome to the island," Jacob says, trying to look pleasant. "Welcome to the family."

"You will be meeting the neighbors over the next few weeks," Sarah says. "Some will invite you to dinner and some will drop by with little welcome gifts. They don't want to overwhelm you with too much all at once. They want you to be able to settle in."

Emily introduces Anna to her new stepsister Hettie. Eason and Ellison are sweet and kind and stand next to Hettie like protective big brothers. Ellison's eyes glisten and he bites his tongue behind his smile while his mother's spirit embraces him. Ebey sees his son's face and feels her too. It takes his breath away.

"Hettie will stay with us," Sarah says. "It was Rebecca's last wish."

Emily nods, thankful to not be responsible for a child that needs extra attention. Sarah wonders if Emily's down-turned mouth shows that she is sad or if it is normal for her.

* * *

Within a few days, the Governor and Mrs. Stevens come to The Cabins on the *Active*. Stevens tells Ebey that the fighting will continue. "I hope you will continue in your role as Captain, Colonel Ebey," he says.

"I am sorry, governor." Ebey clears his throat. "I . . . have served my three-month enlistment and I have a new wife to consider now."

"Well, sir, you still have your three-year responsibility as Adjutant General to keep a functioning militia group."

Most Whidbey Island volunteers say they will not sign up for another enlistment if Isaac Ebey is not their captain. When he refuses, some sign up under Captain Smalley of Company G in Port Townsend, and others form the 2nd Regiment of Company I to serve specifically on Whidbey Island for a six-month enlistment with Samuel Howe as Captain and Isaac Ebey serving as a Private.

Ebey rides across the island to check on Snetlum's people and sees George Snetlum mending a net. "Our people here and those at Holmes Harbor are getting anxious," George says. "We need to get out and hunt and fish, Ebey. We need to feed ourselves."

"I thought you had food saved up for winter," Ebey says.

"Yes, for our own village," George says. "Not for all the people who have come from other villages. Your hardtack is not popular."

"Can hunting be done on this island and fishing not too far from shore? I don't want anyone getting mixed up in a fight they don't start themselves."

"Yes Ebey, but we will run out of potatoes quickly and be hungry for them. I have heard talk of some attacks coming but I do not know what exactly. Tell your people that we will hunt on the island and fish near the shore. They should not shoot us."

* * *

Patkanim takes advantage of opportunities to make money by working with the whites. He and his hundred followers help build forts and block the Snoqualmie Pass to keep back the warring Indians from east of the Cascades. He helps put down a rebellion by Leschi, the Nisqually who refused to sign the treaty paper. He is especially busy when he learns that he can earn $20 for the head of each hostile Indian and $80 for the head of each chief.

Ebey is horrified when he hears about it, bounties for heads. He thinks he knows exactly who came up with that plan and speaks to Winfield about it. "Simmons says that Patkanim is bringing in severed heads for money . . . lots of them. He declares that many of them are the heads of chiefs."

The image of a burlap bag of severed heads dripping with blood flies into Winfield's mind without warning. He looks like he has suffered an attack. "I thought we were supposed to be the civilized ones."

"Simmons thinks that most of the heads are from slaves. Can you imagine the poor auditor of the Territory needing to take possession and then paying for them?"

"Stop, brother," Winfield says. "Just stop. I can't think of it. Couldn't the auditor declare there is no more money? That must be true since I hear there isn't enough for ammunition."

"That should stop it," Ebey says. "I'll send word to the auditor right away, and request that Captain Howe demand ammunition for our militia. Also, you should know that the Indian agent at Bellingham Bay has sent word for help. The Indians have increased their raids. Seventy-six canoes of northern Indians are there, saying they will take Skagit slaves and American 'Boston heads.'"

Winfield grimaces. "Why heads? Why is it always heads?"

* * *

Despite the current fears, settlers long for a moment of peaceful life and tradition. It arrives in the form of a dance. Winfield and the other young bachelors are invited to Alexander's home to introduce two young ladies: Miss Finely and Miss Miller. The fiddler plays and Winfield looks dashing in his Sunday best as he waltzes about the parlor with a young lady on her special day. At first, he remembers the genteel moments that he witnessed in the states, but he cannot focus on the merriment for long. His mind returns to his common daydream of capturing the violent Indians and amazing his neighbors with his heroism. It quickly deteriorates to a vision of severed heads, his new nightmare, and he lets himself out the door.

When he visits The Cabins the next morning, Ebey hands him a paper. "A proclamation by the governor," he says.

Winfield reads it aloud:

> "*Certain evil disposed persons of Pierce County have given aid and comfort to the enemy. They have been placed under arrest and ordered to be tried by a military commission... I proclaim Martial Law and suspend the functions of all civil officers in Pierce County.*"

"Can he do that?" Winfield asks.

"No. Only the territorial legislature has the . . . authority to declare martial law," Ebey says. "Unfortunately, white settlers who are friends of the Indians have already been arrested. He is starting with Pierce County and plans to do the same in Thurston County."

Attorneys George Gibbs and H. A. Goldsborough send a letter to the Secretary of State *denying* that the war situation in Puget Sound is as grave as Governor Stevens declares and that his allegations against the arrested settlers are false. "*The sole object of the governor's proclamation is to get half a dozen obscure individuals into his absolute control and to demonstrate that he can, on the field, enact the part of Napoleon.*"

Territorial Chief Justice Edward Lander demands that the arrested settlers be released. When they are not released, he cites Governor Stevens for contempt of court. So, Governor Stevens has Lander arrested. Judge Francis Chenoweth of Pierce County comes from his sickbed to preside over matters and rules that Stevens has no legal power to declare martial law. The governor releases the prisoners but refuses to pay the contempt of court fine of $50. His friends pay it for him since they know the strength of his stubbornness.

The governor receives a written rebuke from the Washington Territorial Legislature, and President Pierce receives widespread pleas from settlers to remove Stevens from his position of governor. The result is that a letter is sent to Governor Stevens from the U.S. Secretary of State:

"Martial law cannot be justified when it acts against the existing government. Your conduct in that respect does not therefore meet with favorable regard of the President."

* * *

Ebey enjoys the heat of the sun on his back as he walks his fields. He looks toward the water, expecting to see a vessel in the Strait. Instead, he sees twelve large canoes with the tall prow of the northern Indians pull into the landing below his bluff. He watches as some come up the hill, wondering if he should go for his hunting rifle.

They walk directly to the spring for water. When he goes to remind them that they are not to come below the 49th parallel, one produces a paper of permission from Governor Douglas of Vancouver, Canada. In Ebey's mind, a note from Governor Douglas means little. When they leave, Ebey sends word to Major Haller, commander of Fort Townsend, who sends a detachment on the revenue cutter *Jefferson Davis* to ensure that they truly leave, headed north.

On August 10, the "war" in Puget Sound is pronounced over with the capture of Leschi. Leschi is a friend to many settlers, and Ebey feels they will strongly defend him in court.

Winfield hopes his nightmare of severed heads will be gone too.

There is, however, no assurance that the northern Indians will stay in the north.

{ **44** }

Port Gamble, Fall 1856

The dead are not powerless. Dead, did I say? There is no death, only a change of worlds. –Sealth (Chief Seattle)

Ebey is up at Sunnyside to help his father Jacob hew logs for a smokehouse while Emily is home, washing laundry. She turns to see a small group of northern Indians at her door. Her heart stops. She is alone and realizes full-well how vulnerable she is. Remembering Jacob Ebey's advice to never show fear, she acts bravely, though her knees shake. She knows that they usually demand food, so she gives them a loaf of bread and is able to wave them away . . . this time.

Ebey is able to stay close to home for a few days while Emily regains her equilibrium until he must go out to help surveyors on the island and to get the thrashing machine from Bill Engle. In the evening, he continues to read *Dream Life* as he sits with Emily in the parlor. He shakes his head at the author's view of college. "It rather lessens my opinion of the good results flowing from a collegiate education," he tells her. "If it tends to deaden the high moral feelings that are home bred, then its results are less good than I have expected."

"Then it is good that the boys learn their morals at home," Emily says. She shakes out Ellison's pants, having let down the hems.

When Ebey must go to Port Townsend, his sister Mary comes down from Sunnyside to spend the day with Emily, and George Ebey and Winfield spend the night. Emily writes in her journal, *I have two soldiers here. If the Indians come, we will be ready for them.*

When Ebey returns home, he brings sugar and good news of income. "Major Haller at Fort Townsend has ordered two hundred pounds of beef per week for his Company of the Fourth Infantry. We won the bid," he says, then stops and sniffs the air. "What's in the oven?"

"Apple pie," Emily says. She opens the oven door to lift out three pies. "You've brought sugar just in time." Anna hovers near her mother, also interested in pie. "You did say that growing beef would be lucrative, Colonel Ebey. I did not doubt it."

"The U.S. Steamship *Massachusetts* was there in Port Townsend," he says. "I watched it leave on its way to Bellingham Bay. Did you see it?"

"No, I was too busy to look up."

"I hope you see it next time, such an impressive ship, 178 feet long, four cannons . . . quite majestic on the water with its sails open."

He is up early the next morning to kill and butcher a three-year old steer and sends the meat to Port Townsend. Then, with the thrashing machine available, he thrashes his wheat and covers it with straw, predicting it will rain.

Passengers arrive at Ebey's Landing and borrow a horse to go to the Cove where they continue on the steamer *Traveler* to Bellingham Bay. Emily tries to adjust to the unpredictable schedule of people coming and going, but it takes energy. She pulls a second batch of bread out of the oven, wishing for a better stove. Then she begins to prepare the pheasant that Eason shot and a goose gifted from Bill Engle. She thinks about a day when her work will be done and hopes that her husband will be home from Port Townsend in time for dinner.

The next day, Ebey and Eason split a large log on the beach for fence posts and help raise Alexander's second house. Two men come for beef, and Ebey kills the cow and returns with them to Port Townsend to do his Customs work. A windstorm blows in and doubting that Ebey will be able to come home because of it, his sister Mary and her daughter Myra and little Hettie come to stay the night with Emily. As the storm continues the second night, Myra stays to finish a story she is writing about a girl with sky-blue hair and red-green eyes. She is so focused on her story that Emily thinks the roof could fly away and Myra would not notice. Thankfully, Winfield takes Myra's place the following night.

Ebey is cold and wet when he gets home, and Emily hands him a towel. "I started off in my canoe," he says, "but it took on so much water, I had to turn back. Then I got a ride on the sloop *Colonel Ebey*, but we ended up at Point Wilson, two miles north of Port Townsend, still on the other side of the strait. We had to anchor there until morning. Finally, a hard west wind took us across the strait, but we ended up south of here at Doc Kellogg's, and I had to walk the four miles home."

"Tsk, tsk, tsk," she says, "you poor man," lifting a damp lock of hair that has fallen over his forehead.

"Not complaining, mind you. Just letting you know how it was."

"Well, let's hope you do not get my cold. Anna is just getting over hers."

* * *

Ebey returns from a visit to Alexanders where he bought coffee, tobacco and soap and sees three northern Indians pass by the landing, headed north in a hurry. He wonders what has happened.

He learns that Northern Indians have been stealing whatever they can get their hands on around Puget Sound. They were pursued by marines on the *U.S. Massachusetts* and overtaken at Port Gamble. There, they joined a different group of northern Indians who were employed in logging. The employed Indians refused to give up the thieves. Commander Swartout had a brass howitzer on shore and the little steamer *Traveler* drawn up to shore with a mortar on her. The Indians hoisted a red flag and began firing their guns, so the steamer fired a cannon, and the marines on shore charged. Indians hid in the woods while the marines continued to shoot until the next morning when the Indians raised a white flag. Twenty-seven Indians were killed along with at least one leader, 21 wounded, one marine killed, all property including canoes was destroyed. Survivors were forced aboard the *U.S. Massachusetts* and escorted north.

Ebey and Winfield go to Bill Engle and Robert Hill, not wanting to discuss Indian matters in front of Emily. "What do you think about building a stockade?" Ebey asks.

"That's not a bad idea," Bill says. "The northern Indians are relentless . . . and vengeful."

"I suspect the fight at Port Gamble could have been avoided," Ebey says. "Still, we couldn't let them steal whatever they want all over the Sound. They are not supposed to be here at all."

"You know they will retaliate," Hill says. "They won't let 27 deaths be forgotten, especially the death of a leader."

"I'll drive the cattle back from the bluff, so they won't be seen from the water," Winfield says. "Don't want to attract attention to them and have them stolen."

At the request of John Crockett, Ebey speaks with Major Haller at Fort Townsend regarding military protection for the Island. Major Haller writes to Lt. Nugent at Fort Steilacoom on December 3rd.

"A large number of highly respectable citizens who have settled upon Whidbey's Island have accumulated considerable property, stock etc. which with the valuable improvements of their claims would be much exposed to the depredations of the Russian Indians (from Alaska) and British Indians (from Canada) in the event of a descent and might tempt them to plunder the Island. This does not take into consideration the danger to life . . . Should it be convenient for a U. S. Naval Vessel to cruise among the islands north of this place and

occasionally anchor in Penn's Cove, it would not only give a feeling of security to the inhabitants but produce a great moral effect upon those Northern Indians . . ."

* * *

Ebey rides his horse that has not been trained to herd cattle, hoping to be able to sort a beef cow from the herd to supply the weekly order, but the horse does not understand the task. He hadn't imagined how much work it would be when he contracted to supply two hundred pounds of beef to Fort Townsend each week. With his customs work, he needs to be in two places at once, and now that Emily has heard of the Port Gamble incident and is insistent that he be home with her, he must make a change. After enduring the laughter of his Skagit audience resulting from his frustration with his horse, he gives it up. He will ask to use a neighbor's horse, one that has been trained.

He talks with Winfield. "How would you feel about taking over the cultivating of our fields if I move Emily and the children to Port Townsend for the winter?"

"Who will supply the weekly orders for beef then?" Winfield asks.

"You would. I would be in Port Townsend to handle the trade and delivery and to do my Customs work, and Emily would be more at ease. I'm not able to travel whenever I need to in winter because of storms."

"We can try it," Winfield says, "as long as I can hire some help."

"Good," Ebey says. "I will present the plan to Emily. I suspect she will start packing before I finish speaking of it." He chuckles.

He leaves to deliver the butchered meat to Fort Townsend, but does not return for two nights, and Winfield comes to stay with Emily at The Cabins. Snow falls hard and heavy and a violent southeast wind blows. The cattle retreat to the thick woods or gather close together at the fence line.

On the third day, the weather is balmy, the snow melts, and Winfield digs potatoes with his father at Sunnyside. Even though Winfield has been assuring Emily that her husband is fine, he and his father have become concerned. When he receives a letter from Ebey, saying that he has hired the sloop *Colonel Ebey* to take 600 bushels of potatoes from New Dungeness to Bellingham Bay, Winfield is relieved.

Emily is disappointed. She and the children are packed and ready to move to Port Townsend as soon as he returns.

Winfield fills the beef order just before another big storm hits causing mail carriers from Steilacoom to bed down in Ebey's parlor with their blankets on the floor. Everyone hunkers down and the mail carriers are there for nearly a week. Winfield hooks up the horse and wagon to take Ellison and Anna to their grandparents' house for an outing. Then he takes Eason to visit at Alexander's where Emily buys a few small things for the children's Christmas stockings. Winfield continues to spend nights at The Cabins for Emily's sake. She passes the time by sewing a pair of pants for her missing husband. Otherwise, Christmas is not much of an event.

Two Indians come in a very small canoe for the week's beef. Winfield fills their order and asks if they know the whereabouts of Colonel Ebey, but they only shrug. Emily writes in the journal, *"Something has surely happened to the Colonel. We have been expecting him for two weeks."*

Colonel Humpback, 1857

Ghosts can make your thoughts as heavy as branches after a storm.
–Rebecca Maizel, *Infinite Days.*

On New Year's Day, two men come from Bellingham Bay and say they have not seen or heard anything of Colonel Ebey. Immediately, Winfield starts for Port Townsend. He asks the *Jefferson Davis* to go looking for him, but the men aboard say that they saw him on Monday morning among the San Juan Islands. He was fine.

When Winfield returns to Whidbey Island, snow falls to eight inches deep. Emily and the boys are busy keeping fires burning and sweeping snow. Thomas, Rebecca's brother, drives his team down with a load of wood which is needed. He also hauls a load of straw from his house to cover the potatoes. The next day, the freeze hardens water two inches deep. Ebey has been gone for three weeks.

On January 7, they receive word that Colonel Isaac Ebey has not arrived at Bellingham Bay. *"Oh, my Lord!"* Emily writes in the journal. *"Can it be that I am never to see him again?"* She has already been a widow once.

In a panic, Winfield goes home for his gun and blanket, hires a canoe and Indian crew and leaves for Bellingham Bay. In the canal, the tide is too low to continue, and they must wait. Then ice stops them altogether. The Indians sleep while Winfield stays awake to worry and keep the fire going in the frigid cold. He feels certain that the northern Indians either have his brother prisoner or have killed him. The thought twists his stomach as he sits helpless, forced to wait, his imagination turning ugly.

The next day when they get out of the canal, he sees a sail in the distance and waves his handkerchief on a pole. As they get closer, he sees it is a sloop with bits of shredded sail still hanging, "Colonel Ebey" written on the side. Winfield scrambles aboard and finds Ebey, grabbing him into his arms. He is cold as ice, his face wind burnt, his lips shrunk and withered from dehydration. Winfield begins to beat him about the shoulders and back and legs, trying to get the circulation going. The few crew seem to be just as bad.

"Where are we?" Ebey asks, his mouth dry. "Just south of Bellingham Bay?"

"No brother. You are barely beyond the canal. When did you lose your sails?"

"The night of December 21," Ebey says, shivering. "We've been drifting at the mercy of wind and tides ever since, nearly freezing to death. We pulled with oars when the tide was favorable, but we weren't sure where we were."

Winfield wraps him in another blanket and passes around his water. "The crew from *Jefferson Davis* told me that they saw you and everything was fine."

Ebey shakes his head. "We could not make enough signal to alert them."

"I will deliver the potatoes," Winfield says. "You go back to Emily in my canoe. She's fit to be tied."

* * *

After a week of recovery, Ebey takes his family to Port Townsend as promised. Northern Indians still prowl Puget Sound, declaring to take American "Boston heads" in retaliation for the massacre at Port Gamble and the killing of a tyee (leader). They also take Indian slaves, proving their prowess by sneaking undetected onto Whidbey Island and grabbing three Skagit women. The women had been harvesting cedar bark in the forest. The strip of bark that was being pulled up from the base of the tree was discovered hanging at chest height like an open wound.

Governor Stevens is more focused on Indian unrest from east of the Cascade Mountains than from northern Indians. Nevertheless, he comes back to Olympia after hearing of a plan of attack in Puget Sound, thinking he will calm things down by saying that the hostiles will be exterminated. He travels to Alki Beach aboard the *U.S.S. Active* to reassure the settlers there, but Sealth (Chief Seattle) and his family warn the settlers of danger. His message spreads and settlers prepare to hide in blockhouses and behind barricades. Some Whidbey Island residents move off island. Local Natives remain afraid.

With his family happily settled in Port Townsend, Ebey paddles across Admiralty Inlet to attend the Island County Democrat meeting at Coveland to choose delegates for the Democratic Territorial Convention. He is surprised to find a group there who promote Isaac Stevens. Ebey knew Stevens to be a former Whig, a conservative, and feels that Stevens should not influence the Democrats of Island County. In protest, he and the Crockett men leave the meeting, announcing that they will regroup in three days for a rescheduled meeting after they have a chance to talk to people individually. However, in their absence, delegates are elected who will support Stevens for a future run as delegate for Washington Territory to the U.S. House of Representatives. Ebey is frustrated. He is elected Probate Judge, and Winfield is elected Superintendent of Public Schools.

Before he returns to his Customs work and family in Port Townsend, Ebey decides to take the weekly meat order with him. He and Winfield separate a young bull to butcher and load the meat into the wagon to transport down to the beach to his canoe. Ebey stands on the tongue of the wagon as they go. Spring is all around him and he is thinking of how there could still be snow back in Missouri when a deer that had been curled up in the brush bolts in front of the oxen. The oxen shock and run, knocking Ebey down and the wheels of the heavy wooden cart roll over him.

He lies still, trying to breathe through the pain, certain that some ribs are broken, praying that his back is okay. Before he can prop himself up, Winfield's face is next to his. "How badly are you hurt? Should I get Doc Kellogg?"

"Let me lie still a moment. All I know is pain for now." Ebey breathes a little more air with each breath. "Can you get me to the house do you think?"

"Depends on how much pain you can handle, I guess. But I can get you there." Winfield goes slow, helping Ebey sit, then takes an arm over his own neck to pull him to standing, but Ebey wants to stay bent over. He begins to shuffle, not wanting to lift his feet.

"Alright, this is a preview of when you're truly an old man, dear brother," Winfield says, "though you'll never see the sun or blue sky again."

They both begin to chuckle. "What if I lie on my back?" Ebey says, shuffling.

"You'll never see where you're going, either . . . I wonder how long it takes being bent over like that to grow a big hump on your back . . . Colonel Humpback."

They both laugh and Ebey stops shuffling to hold his ribs. "Please . . . stop."

Once Ebey is home, Winfield rides to get Doc Kellogg, and within a few hours, his ribs are wrapped. Against the doctor's advice, Ebey insists that Winfield paddle him home to Port Townsend, along with the meat order. "We don't want that meat to go bad and Emily will be worried sick if I don't return today."

In Port Townsend, Winfield delivers Ebey to his door. "Your husband is so devoted to you that he has risked his health to get home," he says to Emily.

Ebey lifts his head to smile a pained, crooked smile. "You don't mind a bruised husband, do you?"

Emily pulls him inside. "As long as you're in one piece and your heart is still beating, I'll take you."

Though stiff and sore and still bent over from his accident, Ebey feels it his duty to continue his efforts against Governor Stevens. As a resident of Port Townsend now, he travels to Drew's Mill on the Cowlitz River, Lewis County, to attend the Democratic Convention as a delegate from Jefferson County. Once again, Stevens is chosen as delegate. He will eventually be elected as the delegate of Washington Territory to the U.S. House of Representatives despite the protests of settlers.

Ebey thinks that settlers' votes reflect their fears. Some are thankful that Stevens' governorship is over, and his new position is a non-voting one.

* * *

It seems impossible to keep northern Indians out of Puget Sound. The schooner *Phantom* traveling from Port Townsend to Victoria is boarded and robbed. Four Klallams are killed near Port Madison on Bainbridge Island, a half-way point between Whidbey Island and Olympia. Puget Sound Indians are upset. White settlers continue to move away from Whidbey Island.

On May 25, twelve canoes holding 150 northern Indians, half of them women, stop at Ebey's Landing, causing trepidation for Winfield. He wonders if he should go for help or sound an alarm, but they show their white flags indicating that they are friendly, and a few come up to The Cabins to get water from the spring. Winfield speaks to them, and one says he has a paper from Governor Douglas in Victoria. After watching them leave under sail, Winfield lets Captain Coupe know of their presence.

Coupe sends a note to Major Haller at Fort Townsend to tell him to be on the lookout. Major Haller takes a detachment on the *Jefferson Davis* to ensure that they leave the Sound.

In the meantime, Winfield continues to send the beef order to Port Townsend each week. His parents seem unconcerned about Indian aggression. His father Jacob, with his typical scowl, tells him that if they cannot defend their own families and property, then maybe they don't deserve to live in the new territory. But Winfield is worried, still fighting nightmares, and he writes in his journal, *"God only knows what is to become of us. I cannot believe we are to be murdered by them, but we may. We are in His hands to do with us as He wills."*

{ **46** }

Back to The Cabins,
Summer 1857

Certain places are more likely to attract ghostly activity than others. –Joseph A. Citro, Author

On July 25, the Ebey family moves from Port Townsend back to The Cabins on Whidbey Island. His parents at Sunnyside and Hettie are thrilled to have them back. Emily is not as excited. She is still afraid because of the Indian crimes she has heard about, but she understands that Ebey needs to manage his farm. There is much to do.

They have settled in by August 3rd when Judge Chenowith comes for the trial of Private John Reagan for murder. U.S. Marshall George Corliss and his wife Lucretia are at court as well and stay at The Cabins with Ebey who is a prosecutor for the case. After several days of trial and a verdict of guilty, Reagan is sentenced to be hanged, but he escapes.

A week later, the Corliss couple are still there. They come to stay at The Cabins each month on his regular schedule for the county court sessions which are held on the first floor of Cranney's store in Coveland.

Also on the island is the survey crew with their never-ending task of marking new land claims. First thing in the morning, Ebey checks in with them for an update.

"Not much activity here the last few weeks, Colonel, other than us working," the surveyor says. "We did send a group of northern Indians pack'n. They were camped on the beach below the Kellogg claim for several days. Mrs. Kellogg said that she had put up with them long enough. They'd been drinking and hanging around. Then they killed one of her calves. With her husband away, she asked us to get rid of them. They're gone as far as we know."

"I'm glad you were here. I suppose we must always keep an eye out if we want to avoid trouble," Ebey says. He enjoys the clear, warm morning as he walks back to The Cabins, wondering if Marshall Corliss is interested in doing some hunting.

While Ebey and Corliss are out looking for deer, Winfield visits in the parlor with Lucretia Corliss whom he met on the Oregon Trail three years ago. It was before she was married, when she was still Lucretia Judson. Winfield feels a tiny bit of envy for the judge, thinking he should have courted Lucretia when he had the chance . . . except that his future was uncertain then, and he hadn't anything to offer her. They hear the men coming back from their hunt, stomping their feet before coming inside. Ebey carries his old 45-inch German jaeger rifle.

Winfield laughs. "I can't believe you still use that old thing."

"Brought a deer down with it just now," Ebey says, setting the long gun in the corner. "It's the only gun I have. Come and help me hang it to bleed, will you Winfield?"

The next night, August 11, the Ebeys play the card game Faro at the dining table with the Corlisses after the children are in bed. A few northern Indians had come to the door earlier in the day to buy sugar and flour and Ebey had told them they had none for sale. Now Eason and Ellison are asleep in the little bedroom on the porch and Anna is tucked into her bedroll on a pallet in the parlor so that the Corlisses may have the bedroom. The clean laundry flutters on the line outside as the cards are shuffled, and one is turned over. The chips are laid down for bets. When they all begin to yawn and eyelids droop, they turn in for the night, Ebeys in the parlor with Anna.

"I forgot about the laundry," Emily says, putting on her nightgown. "I'm too tired to bring it in now."

"Let it be," Ebey says. "It's probably damp from the night air anyway. We can get it in the morning."

They are asleep when Rover begins running back and forth between Ebey and the door, whining. "What is it boy?" Ebey says, getting up.

Emily wakes up too. "Do you think someone is stealing the laundry?"

"We'd better bring it in, I guess," Ebey says.

They both start down the kitchen steps when Ebey sees Indians standing in the dark. "What do you want?" he asks, pushing Emily back toward the door. Two shots are fired, a bullet striking him in the side of the head. His hand goes to his head as if he does not understand what has happened. He stumbles around the side of the house as Emily slams the door, screaming. She hears him fall heavily against the window and raises the glass, telling him to climb inside, but he is confused and turns to go back. Two more guns are fired.

An Indian who is breaking through the door nearly grabs Eason and Ellison as they scamper away to the bedroom where the Marshall sends the boys out through the window. Lucretia and Eason go out followed by Emily, Anna, and Ellison as Marshall Corliss holds the bedroom door shut and then follows. Outside, a gun is fired at them, sending Lucretia over the yard fence. Emily, who has ahold of Anna, knocks off some pickets to get through. She hears the Indians going through the house, breaking dishes.

As she tears through the brush, Lucretia hears someone behind her, certain it is an Indian in pursuit. She finds a road and runs full out. It takes her to Bill Engle's house. The night explodes as she violently pounds on his door. They see her covered in scratches and brambles, and Bill and the Hill brothers grab their guns. They send an Indian running to spread the message of an attack and then run to The Cabins, calling Ebey's name. They hear the Indians run from the house, tearing pickets off the fence as they go. When they can find no one home in the dark, they decide that everyone must be hiding in the woods.

Winfield and Thomas Hastie arrive to join them in the search, having been alerted by the Indian runner. It is a dark night, two o'clock in the morning, but they find the dislodged yard pickets and rely on their voices in the woods, calling out as they walk, "Corliss . . . Ebey . . ."

There is panic in Winfield's voice, "Ellison . . . Eason." Finally, they hear a response from a cluster of trees, and Winfield runs ahead. It's Corliss. "Your wife is safe," he says.

They find Emily and Anna shivering under a blanket though it is a warm night. Ellison runs to his uncle Winfield and is in his arms, a safe place. "Where is Eason?" Winfield asks.

"We don't know," Emily says. "He went out the window with Lucretia."

Winfield's heart races as he turns with his arms still around Ellison to continue the search. Eason steps out of the brush. "Lucretia was fast," Eason says. "I couldn't keep up."

After Winfield gets ahold of him, he looks to Marshall Corliss. "No Isaac?" he asks quietly.

Corliss shakes his head.

Bill Engle squeezes Winfield's shoulder in the dark. "Lucretia said that your brother had gone outside before the trouble, before she heard gunshots."

Winfield's heart drops into his stomach and he launches a prayer. *Holy Father of All, Please Lord, let us find him alive.*

Bill Engle leads the survivors to his house where Lucretia waits in paralyzing fear. Thomas Hastie and the Hill brothers go with Winfield back to The Cabins to look for Ebey. Winfield's fear of what he might find constricts his breath as he hurries ahead. When they near the house, they are met by Rebecca's brothers, John and Thomas Davis, who were also alerted by the Indian messenger.

John grabs Winfield by both shoulders. "He's dead, brother."

Winfield gasps, his knees buckling. Recovering enough to stand, he wants to go to Ebey, but John holds him back. "You do not want to see it," he says. "They've taken his head."

The Making of a Ghost,
August 11, 1857

"There was something about the old houses at The Cabins that bound my brother to them." –Winfield Ebey

Rebecca's brother, John, pulls Winfield away from the gruesome scene. "Come away, man," he says. "You've got to think of your brother as he was."

Winfield is numb, putting one foot in front of the other, and finds himself at John's cabin, a candle lit, a cup of coffee steaming in front of him.

"Would you rather have a shot of whiskey?" John asks. "I need one."

Winfield moves his head back and forth. "Can't swallow." He is frozen in the chair. "I've got to see my brother."

John pours a whiskey. "Swallow this and take a breath before you pass out. We will go at dawn."

By the beginning of daylight, Winfield has not moved a muscle. His legs are stiff as they walk to The Cabins.

"Are you sure you want to see it, brother?" John asks, walking beside him. "It would be better to remember him as he was. The sight of it could haunt your dreams as it has haunted my thoughts these last hours."

"I have had nightmares of severed heads for months," Winfield says, watching his shoes walk over the ground. "I need to see him."

John leads him to the kitchen porch side of the house where his brother's body lies on his side, Rover curled up at his back. Winfield turns to vomit though there is nothing in his stomach to come up. He had still hoped for an impossible mistake. Sucking air into his lungs, he kneels down and lifts a cold, rigid hand. It is the hand of his brother, absolutely. "They used his own axe!" he cries, seeing the bloody murder weapon on the ground. Winfield stays, sobbing over Ebey's deformed body and petting Rover's head until John's hand is under his arm, lifting him.

Rebecca's other brother, Thomas, is there too. They wrap Isaac's body in a blanket and carry him into the house and lay him on his bed amongst the rubble and broken glass from the windows. "They took everything they could," John says, "and smashed the rest."

"I have seen death," Winfield whispers, "but never so horrible as this . . . If it had been the Lord's will, if he had died in this bed with his family and religion surrounding him, I could give him up, but not like this." He sees Ebey's old rifle lying on the floor in the corner. "That old thing," he says, pointing. "I could never convince him to get a proper gun. He said that was all he needed for hunting, and he could never shoot anyone anyway."

At Sunnyside, Jacob and Sarah Ebey's house, Emily holds Anna while she sleeps. Winfield lies on a bed but is afraid to close his eyes. He knows he will see the bloody tragedy again if he sleeps and decides against it. Most of the house is awake as well. By one o'clock in the afternoon, a crowd has come together. Bill Engle and the Hill brothers have dug a grave next to Rebecca's grave above the bluff near The Cabins. John Crockett has built a coffin, but it is too small. He must add pieces.

Grandma Sarah worries for her grandchildren even though her heart is breaking over the loss of her eldest son. Eason and Ellison remember their mother's death, but death from a long illness is much easier to accept than a brutal murder. She tries to explain to five-year-old Hettie what has occurred. "Your Pa has given up the ghost, darling."

"Given up the ghost, Grandmum?"

"He has gone to Heaven, dear one. His spirit has flown."

"Will he come back?" Hettie asks. "I will miss him if he does not come back."

"We will all miss him, sweetness. I think his spirit will be with us whenever we think of him, but not his body."

"Can we see his spirit?" Hettie asks, looking hopeful.

"I am not sure, dear. Some people say they can see spirits. Usually at night, I think."

Neighbors come somberly from the west side of the island and from Penn's Cove. Young Anna stands in a daze with her mother Emily. Thirteen-year-old Eason and Ellison, age 11, stand on each side of Hettie, being protective brothers as their

Ma and Pa would have wanted. Grandma Sarah and Grandpa Jacob stand behind, and the sisters and cousins and friends are all around: Davises, Crocketts, Alexanders, Coupes, Kelloggs, and every sailing Captain in the vicinity to name a few.

Winfield sees Joseph Smith at the graveside, a resident from the Cove with the background of preacher. As he watches the Crockett men solemnly lower his brother's casket into the ground, he hopes that Smith will preach a funeral. He sees Samuel Crockett visibly shaking. Smith seems too shocked to speak. Everyone is distraught, too stunned to say anything. Winfield manages to say a few words, *"My brother . . . He was only 39 . . . He was never so happy in his life as he was at The Cabins. If I, if we, could have looked upon his face one more time . . . so often I have found encouragement there . . . It is right that he be buried next to Rebecca. After life's fitful fever, they will sleep well, side by side."*

* * *

District Court Judge Chenoweth calls a meeting for protection from "incursions of a savage and foreign foe." Fifty people from Whidbey Island go to Port Townsend and pass a resolution to kill every northern Indian who comes onto the island from that time on. Chenoweth tells Governor Douglas in Victoria to deliver the murderers, not knowing at the time that they came from Russian America (Alaska) rather than British Columbia. Two days later, three large canoes of friendly Indians are sent north by Governor Douglas to hunt the murderers.

In Port Townsend, a captain of the U.S. Revenue Service arrests seven northern Indians from the neighborhood and keeps them in chains. He sends some Indian women to the San Juan

Islands to say that the seven men will be hung at noon on the 15th if the murderers are not turned over to authorities.

Winfield's Journal, August 15: *"Three long, torturous days have passed since my brother's murder. I have been unable to write. My noble high-minded brother is no more. It is like a horrible dream, too dreadful for reality."*

Neighbors stand guard at Ebey's bluff to watch for northern Indians, and in spite of no sleep, Winfield takes his turn with Tom Hastie. "I think I spoke with the Indians who killed your brother," Tom says, "before they did it, that is."

"You would recognize them?"

"Yes, a couple of them, I think. They asked me if Colonel Ebey was an important man," Tom says. "I told them 'yes, a tyee, a very important leader.' Then they wanted to know who all was in the house." Tom's face turns ashen. "I should have suspected something."

Winfield senses a cold pressure and wonders if his brother's spirit is there. "You are not to blame, Tom. You could not have known," Winfield says. He looks left and right down the beach. "I want to send the family out of the country, but they won't go. They say they will move to a blockhouse instead."

Jacob Ebey sends the family to John Crockett's blockhouse at night until their own blockhouses are built. There are two, connected with a 12-foot stockade that surrounds his home. John Crockett builds a second blockhouse and connects it to the first with a stockade, calling it "Fort Whidbey." The Davis brothers, Thomas, John and James, create a blockhouse by adding logs to John's house. Winfield helps when he's not chasing oxen or working at the farm or butchering beef.

The Cabins remain deserted. Winfield and Thomas, Rebecca's younger brother, strip the walls of cloth and paper from the inside to prevent it from falling into the hands of the Indians. Winfield writes in his journal: *The old place looks lonesome, once a place of rescue, comfort and love, now a place of dread. It will be left to ruin and decay.* He continues to fight against sleep, knowing it will be haunted by severed heads, his brother's among them.

Determined to have his brother's killers found and his head returned, he writes letters to territorial officials and meets them face to face, pleading for an investigation, but they have no authority to go out of country. He collects signatures on a petition to make the case that the U.S. Army must act, but it gets no result. His only consolation is that Ebey's friends assure him that they will never stop looking.

Winfield attempts to investigate on his own, going to see George Snetlum at Snakelum Point for information. To George, Winfield seems exhausted, panicked, his spirit fractured, and he asks Winfield to sit, pass the pipe. It isn't until he sees Winfield's body relax that he speaks.

"I am sorry that killers came for Ebey. They were the ones he was hoping to protect *us* from," George says. "You don't look so good."

"I need to find his killers, George, get my brother's remains back." He draws on the pipe and returns it to George. "The memory of his headless body will not leave my sleep until I do."

The smoke from fire and pipe rises to the vent in the roof. "My father, Snetlum, had dreams of heads. It was from his young warrior days when he killed ten who would have killed him."

"How did he manage?"

"It was the Cross," George says. "When he prayed before the Cross, his nightmares were taken away, for a while anyway."

Winfield holds the pipe in mid-air. He realizes that he has been so consumed by sorrow and needing to "fix" things, that he has not thought of asking God to remove the pain or the burden of his nightmares. *Maybe I want to feel the pain,* he thinks.

"You must let Ebey go," George says, "or his Spirit can become attached here." He takes the pipe and pats Winfield's hand. "I will let you know if I learn anything about his killers."

After Winfield leaves, George continues to smoke, thinking of the promise that Ebey made to his father when Snetlum had welcomed settlers who were good people and would protect them from aggressive northern Indians. He is sorry about Ebey's death and wishes him well in the Afterlife. The settlers have told him that since Ebey's death, no northern Indian will ever again set foot on Whidbey Island and live to talk about it, and he knows that Ebey has kept his promise, though it took his life.

* * *

At Sunnyside, Winfield thinks about his brother's great courage that allowed him to leave his home and family to travel across the country, risking his life for the betterment of them all. He is grateful for God's Grace that allowed him to have precious time with his brother, not just on Whidbey Island, but as a young boy looking up to his older brother. He will never stop loving him.

He prays for the ability to see Ebey the way he was in life, to remember him as a whole person full of ideas and hope and strength of character. Finally, Ebey comes in a dream, the picture of health. "Think of me as I was," he says smiling. His voice sounds like he speaks underwater.

Relief washes over Winfield. "Brother . . ." Winfield smiles back. "I miss you."

"I put my heart and soul here. Part of me will always be in this place, here on the prairie, on the beach or bluff, at The Cabins. I will be here if you need me."

Winfield wakes feeling refreshed and hopeful, as if Ebey has given him the encouragement that he has always received from him, as if he has been given permission to end his search, knowing that his brother has everything he needs.

Now and then at dusk, when fog begins to crawl up the bluff, Hettie hurries out to look for her Pa's spirit, lantern in hand. She feels him with her when the fog comes in as if he calls her name. People say that her Ma and Pa are happy together, and she would like to see that, to meet her mother and to see her Pa happy.

$\{\ 48\ \}$

Spirit Place

The land knows you, even when you are lost. –Robin Wall Kimmerer, Braiding Sweetgrass

Whidbey Island lives with memories. The tide still rolls, and the fog climbs up from the water and fades, and tomorrow, the sun will shine down on Ebey's cultivated prairie. In Ebey's Reserve, we hear and see his name everywhere we go and know his story. We are not strangers here, and we are not alone. He is with us still.

The remnant of Snetlum's original Whidbey Cross is contained in glass in front of the Coupeville Museum, changed from its magnificent, twenty-four-foot symbol of faith like a transformation from body to spirit. It has been broken, its cross piece lost, and the upright piece has been used to bear a fence rather than the prayers and joy of the first Christians of Whidbey Island.

Snetlum's great grandson said that every time Snetlum walked by the Cross, he either kissed it or lay down before it. Perhaps Native spirit cherishes it even now, and Snetlum's adoration remains.

I see Snakelum Point from my home. On bright, late afternoons it enlarges, nearly pulsates in the golden warmth of the sun and I can imagine the people there, the longhouse, their homes and children running about. Snetlum's tiny burial space is still protected above the beach on private property. I deliver a tiny pinch of tobacco with a prayer of hope that I have done them justice, as if that is even possible. I've been told that the tiniest things are huge in the spirit world. A normal, loving hug from Spirit can crush a person, and I do not linger, just in case. As I turn to leave, a White Deer hesitates behind a yew tree to see if I am a threat, then moves on.

During an evening visit to Sunnyside Cemetery, I sit to imagine The Cabins where they once were and the activities of long ago. As the sky darkens into night, and the moon comes up full, it brings the scent of freshly baked bread along with the earthy aroma of a newly turned field. The fog begins to climb up over the bluff and across the prairie, and I am enticed to walk down into it toward The Cabins. A young woman stands with her back to me, wearing a long dark dress and light-colored apron. Her hair is tied at the nap of her neck. She leans out toward the water as if searching for something or someone.

Then a man appears beside her, a young virile man. He holds her hand and kisses her cheek. She leans into him, seemingly relieved. As they begin to walk away together, a child, her hair thick and long down her back runs toward them, a lantern in her hand. They turn to embrace her, and I am overwhelmed with a sense of Peace and Joy as they walk away together, Hettie with her parents.

{ 49 }

Epilogue

Beings take the shapes of everything, trees, rocks, people, fish. Their spirits retain intelligence and emotions and partner with individuals to grant them abilities. Humans are the newest beings and have the most to learn. –Traditional Suquamish belief.

Emily and her daughter leave for Olympia on the next available passage after Ebey's death and do not come back.

Carolyn Kellogg realizes that her husband, the doctor, was the northern Indians' first choice to kill rather than Ebey. As a doctor, her husband had the highest status, the equivalent to a Shaman, the correct status to balance the loss of their leader who had been killed at the Port Gamble massacre. They had camped below her home to wait for the Canoe Doctor to come home from Olympia until she'd asked the survey crew to send them away.

The Indians could not leave entirely, they had a job to do and would not be welcome at home until it was done. It was the duty of revenge. They had paddled three miles north and camped in front of The Cabins, then asked Tom Hastie if Ebey was an important man.

In 1858:

John Alexander gets his wooden leg caught in driftwood on the beach and it breaks off. He crawls home in the freezing rain and dies of pneumonia. His son and five Skagit friends hollow out a cedar log the Native American way for his burial at the foot of the giant wooden cross that was erected by Snetlum's people. His wife Frances cooks for the harbor men since there are many ships in the Cove and eventually, she marries Captain Fay.

Leschi is hanged, though settlers defend him. Colonel Granville Haller says that he was convicted by a known liar (a friend of Isaac Stevens).

In 1859:

Ebey's mother Sarah dies of a stroke. George Beam is married and becomes guardian to Ebey's children.

The Puget Sound treaties are ratified (four years after their signing.) Over the next twenty to thirty years, the Skagit people gradually move onto the reservations, either the Swinomish Reservation near LaConner in Skagit County or the Tulalip Reservation near Everett in Snohomish County. Some prefer to live in the mountains of the upper Skagit River.

On December 1, Winfield reads in a Victoria newspaper that his brother's scalp has been retrieved. Captain Charles Dodd of Hudson Bay Company learned that the fleeing Indians had stopped at Smith Island in the San Juans during their escape long enough to scalp the head and bury it on the island, then take the scalp as proof of their completed duty. Dodd learned that the female leader who had been killed at the Port Gamble massacre for whom they needed revenge was from a Tlingit clan on an island in Southeast Alaska. He had attempted to negotiate for the scalp several times and was anchored off the island on the steamer *Labouchere* when in the night, three young Indians came to the ship. They traded Ebey's scalp for six blankets, three pipes, one cotton handkerchief, six heads of tobacco, and some cotton fabric.

In 1860:

Winfield and cousin George Beam build the Ferry House on Ebey's Bluff, naming it The Ebey Inn. It is to be an income for Eason and Ellison, a post office and tavern with overnight rooms.

On April 5, Winfield receives Ebey's scalp delivered by an old friend, Alonzo Poe. Winfield calls his relief *"a sad memento of the past."*

1861, Hettie dies of consumption. She is 7 years old. Before her death, Ellison reminds her to not be afraid, she will finally meet her mother and see her mother and father happy together.

In 1862:

Ebey's father, Jacob, dies in February after a long illness. Ebey's deaf sister, Elizabeth Ruth, falls from Blowers Bluff on the northeast point of Penn's Cove while picking blackberries in September. She dies of her injuries many days later.

Dr. Richard Lansdale moves away. He becomes physician to the Skokomish and later, the Quinault Indians, living to be 87 years old and dying in 1898.

Thomas Davis sells his land claim, half to Charles Terry and half to William Engle and leaves the island.

1865, Winfield dies in California having traveled there to recover from consumption. His sister Mary has his body brought back for burial at Sunnyside. At some point, Ellison has his parents' and Hettie's remains also moved from The Cabins location up to Sunnyside.

In 1866, Major Granville Owen Haller and his wife Henrietta move to Coupeville and build a house on Front Street.

1867, The United States buys Alaska from Russia.

1880, George Snetlum dies. He is 60 years old.

In 1881, Coupeville, named for Captain Thomas Coupe, becomes the county seat for Island County. Thomas and Maria Coupe previously donated land for a school and church.

A great grandson of Snetlum named Charlie continues to live in the longhouse on Snakelum Point until his death in the early 1930s. He was 85 years old.

A granite monument has been placed on the hill above Ebey's Landing, 908 feet northwest of where he was killed August 11, 1857. Photograph courtesy of WA State Secretary of State.

Today, we who take much for granted in the United States might imagine the hopes and dreams that propelled those first Emigrants across this glorious landscape not so long ago. Their new lives were hard-earned, and I hope that we have inherited enough of their strength of character and foresight to continue the dream.

The Native American way of life was entirely changed within a single lifetime against their will. They were eventually forced to give up the practices of their cultures, and it was devastating to them. It is a stain on our history that their treatment was often unfair and harsh.

The Coupeville Museum reports that the most common questions asked by visitors are: *What was life like for the Native Americans? Did they shape the development of Island County?* I think this book gives a partial answer.

I believe that the first settlers on Whidbey Island treated their Native neighbors with respect. They hired local Native Americans for domestic and farm chores as well as travel and mail delivery. The Indians were reimbursed for their potatoes that were ruined by settler's cows. Ebey seems to have protected the Skagit people during the conflict with aggressive tribes when he gathered them together for protection. Rebecca Ebey must have had a good relationship with the Indian children since that is where she gained much of her information. John

Alexander's casket was created the Indian way by his son and his son's four Indian friends who hollowed out a tree.

The Native American practice of burning the fields to keep the trees out and encourage camas bulbs along with the natural prairies attracted early farmers and eventually led to the creation of Ebey's Landing National Historic Reserve.

For more information on Whidbey Island settlers, I recommend Jimmie Jean Cook's book, *A particular friend, PENN'S COVE: A History of the Settlers, Claims and Buildings of Central Whidbey Island.* You will see a map of original land claims and pictures of some of the people in my book as well as other settlers who arrive later. The author was instrumental in preserving the history of Sunnyside Cemetery and in the creation of the Central Whidbey Island National Historical District in 1973.

Some tidbits: I had no idea that I would be spending so much time on the Oregon Trail for this book and that most pioneers were in their 20s when they started out. I had to keep reminding myself that travel was by water, so Whidbey Island was centrally located, close to Port Townsend, Olympia, Bellingham, Camano Island, etc.

My hope is that this book encourages others to share their own family stories that have been carried down through generations. A special thank you to readers, especially those who leave reviews on Amazon and/or Goodreads.

I would love to hear from you: https://victoriaventrisshea.com

Facts and Fiction

This is a work of fiction. Although researched, some information was lacking and occasionally, there were conflicting accounts. First-person journals were used when possible.

Native Americans

For most Native American groups, including from Russian America, maintaining balance in all things was essential, which included a life for a life of equal status. It was also true for those within their own clan. Taking heads was standard procedure for some groups, including for those who killed Ebey.

Snakelum Point is named after Snetlum, whose name changed spellings in the writings of those who met him over the years, beginning with Netlin. Snakelum Point was his home. The story of Snetlum killing ten invaders comes from John Fornsby's recollection of stories told by his grandmother, though the actual account occurred away from home as an act of revenge.

Snetlum's guardian spirits were my guess. Tolo, the nickname for his wife is fiction. Due Ductivid was his only wife according to the priest Blanchet. Either she was special, or he was devout. His great grandson said that Snetlum never passed the big cross without kissing it or lying down in front of it. It is possible that his original burial location was closer to the beach and may have been relocated to its current location.

One source estimates that 1200 Skagit lived around Penn's Cove at one point in time. In 1792, Joseph Whidbey reported that he saw about 600 Native Americans in Penn's Cove. In 1841, Wilkes estimated 400-500. It was summer in both cases, and large numbers were likely away at summer camps for food gathering. Native people were affected by smallpox, malaria, flu, measles, and their original number was cut in half to 300 at the time of Snetlum's death in the winter of 1852.

The legend of the origin of the Skagit people on Whidbey Island was written by A.W. Arnold, Skagit Indian and Whidbey pioneer, for *Island County Times* in 1896. It had been re-told in his family through generations.

Settlers

Washington Territory encompassed what later became the states of Washington, Idaho, and parts of Montana and Wyoming.

White settlers populated Whidbey Island quickly. By the end of 1858, one year after Ebey's death, the white population on the island was reported to be 180. There were 130 meat cattle, 162 hogs, and 64 acres planted in potatoes. One year later, the numbers increased to 257 settlers, 809 meat cattle, 544 hogs, 144 acres of potatoes.

According to Ezra Meeker, Ebey had a "stoppage" in his speech that some interpret as a stutter. Meeker states that his speech seemed comical at first but was quickly forgotten because of his sincerity and intellect. I showed him to be empathetic, even helpful to Snetlum. Ebey used Indian names for places whenever he knew them, showing appreciation of their culture. He did not fear the Indians, did not carry a gun, only had an old 45-inch German jaeger rifle for hunting.

The only letter that I created was in Chapter 23 from Ebey to Rebecca when he learns of her mother's death.

My best guess is that Rebecca charged about $1.50 for room and board at The Cabins.

Today, tiny Ebey Island near Everett on the Snohomish River is the site of the blockhouse/fort built by Winfield Ebey and other volunteers to stop the Upper Skagit and Snohomish from coming down the Snohomish River during the troubles of 1855 (although they never came).

Consumption (tuberculosis) was common and thought to be inherited until the 1880's when it was determined to be contagious. Isaac's and Rebecca's sons, Eason and Ellison, succumb to it in their 40's as well as Ellison's young son.

Ebey was instrumental in convincing the U.S. government to make the territory north of the Columbia River into a separate territory from Oregon Territory. He was representative of Thurston County at the Oregon Territory Legislature in 1852. He helped form the counties of Island, Jefferson, Pierce and King. In 1853, he was appointed as Island County's first Justice of the Peace and probate judge. Also, President Franklin Pierce appointed him as Collector of Customs for the Puget Sound District. In 1855, he was a delegate to the Washington Territorial Convention in Olympia, and was Adjutant General during the Indian unrest, raising a company of a hundred volunteers as militia and serving as Caprain.

Ebey's Landing National Historic Reserve is the first historic reserve in America. It was established in 1978 by Congress to provide a record of Pacific Northwest history. It is 25 square miles in the heart of Whidbey Island. The Ebey's Forever Conference is held each November, featuring lectures, workshops, and field trips by leaders in sustainability, historic preservation, and agriculture.

Location of Original Land Claims

Map of Puget Sound

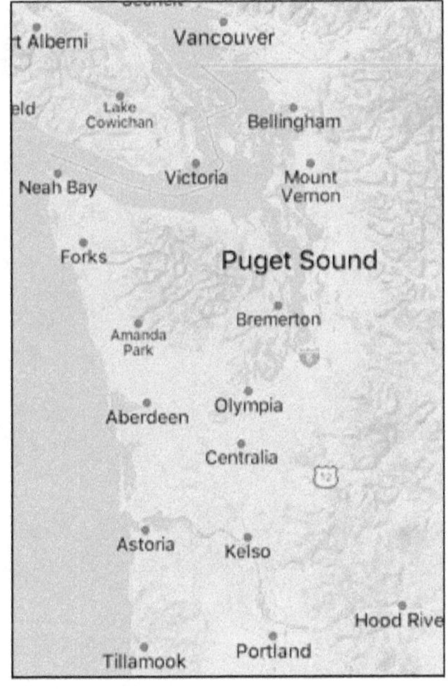

Acknowledgements

A special thank you to Island County Historical Society and Museum in Coupeville. I could not have written this book without Rebecca's and Winfield's journals. Lynn Hyde, Director of Historic Whidbey, gave an informative presentation. The University of Washington Archives provided Ebey family letters.

Also, I appreciate Kellen Diamanti who sent me the "Fornsby chapter" from *Indians of the Urban Northwest*, Columbia University Press, 1949, which contains family stories of Snetlum as passed down through his family members. Kellen is co-author of *Stamp of the Century* about the inverted Jenny stamp and the uncovered stories of those involved.

Thank you to my first editor, my husband, who seemed quite critical with this book: "What does that have to do with the story? Too many characters." His opinions and understanding of history and government were crucial.

Thank you so much to early readers for their feedback: Carol Olsen who always asks questions that cause me to think; to my niece Kim Siner who finds inconsistencies with an eagle eye; to Claudia MacIsaac who focused on the flow and stopped me from publishing before it was ready; and to my niece Ann

Acknowledgements

Burgess, one of my greatest cheerleaders, who traveled part of the Oregon Trail in a covered wagon herself not too long ago.

Finally, thank you to Kingfisher Bookstore in Coupeville for supporting local authors and for keeping my books on the shelf.

Major Resources

(*indicates sources that were especially helpful)

Bennett, Lee Ann. (1972). "Effects of White Contact on Lower Skagit Indians," Washington Archaeological Society: Seattle, WA (Master's Thesis Paper).

Cahail, Alice Kellogg as told to her by her father Albert H. Kellogg, son of the Whidby pioneer, Dr. John Coe Kellogg. (1939). *The Life of Dr. John Coe Kellogg*, Whidbey Island Farm Bureau News: Whidbey Island, WA.

***Cook, Jimmie Jean. (1973). *A particular friend, PENN'S COVE*, Island County Historical Society: Coupeville, WA.

Doyle, Susan Badger and Dykes, Fred W. editors. (1997). *The 1854 Oregon Trail Diary of Winfield Scott Ebey*, Oregon-California Trails Association: Independence, Missouri.

Eckrom, J. A. (1989). *Remembered Drums: A History of the Puget Sound Indian War*, Pioneer Press Books: Walla Walla, WA.

Major Resources

*Eells, Myron and Castile, George Pierre. (1985). *The Indians of Puget Sound: The Notebooks of Myron Eells,* University of Washington Press: Seattle, WA.

*Engle, Flora Augusta Pearson. (2016). *Recollections of Early Days on Whidby Island,* Island County Historical Society: Coupeville, WA. Available at the museum.

Haeberlin, Hermann and Gunther, Erna. (1930). *The Indians of Puget Sound,* University of Washington Press: Seattle, WA.

Hyde, Lynn, Director of Historic Whidbey. (October 2022). "Trade with Salish," and "First Settlers," slide presentations at Coupeville Library. HistoricWhidbey@comcast.net

Island County Museum and Archives, Coupeville, WA, *The Journal of Rebecca Ebey.*

*Kellog, George A. (1934). *A History of Whidbey's Island,* Island County Historical Society: Coupeville, WA.

Kibbe, L. A. (no date given). *Diary of Colonel Isaac N. and Mrs. Emily Ebey 1856-67,* "Kessinger's Legacy Reprints," Kessinger Publishing, Washington State.

Kluger, Richard. (2011). *The Bitter Waters of Medicine Creek: A Tragic Clash Between Whites and Native Americans,* Alfred A. Knoff: NY.

Lynn, Judy and Foss, Kay and the Island County Historical Society and Museum. (2012). *Coupeville: Images of America,* Arcadia Publishing: Charleston, SC.

McDaniel, Nancy L. (2004). *The Snohomish Tribe of Indians: Our Heritage... Our People,* Self-published.

McKay, Kathryn. (1999). Master's Thesis "Recycling the Soul: Death and the Continuity of Life in Coast Salish Burial Practices," University of Victoria: B.C

Meeker, Ezra. (1905). *Pioneer Reminiscences of Puget Sound: The Tragedy of Leschi*, Lowman W. Hanford Stationery & Printing Co.: Seattle, WA.

Monheim, Allee. (2023). Public Service Libraries, Special Collections regarding Ebeys, University of Washington: Seattle, WA.

*Neils, Dorothy. (1989). *By Canoe and Sailing Ship They Came*, Spindthrift Publishing Company:Oak Harbor, WA.

Richardson, David. (1871). *Pig War Islands*. Orcas Publishing Company, Eastsound, WA.

Trebon, T. (2000). "Beyond Isaac Ebey: Tracing the Remnants of Native American Culture on Whidbey," *Columbia*, Vol. 4, No. 3, pages 6-12.

Wollwage, Lance K.; Tasa, Guy; Kramer, Stephenie; (January 2015), "A Partial Stratigraphy of the Snakelum Pt. Site."

https://www.researchgate.net/publication/273449277

https://gsswi.org/documents/seacaptainsofwhidbeyisland.pdf

https://octa-journals.org/merrill-mattes-collection/the-narrative-of-samuel-hancock-1845-1860

About the Author

Victoria Ventris Shea writes historical fiction of the Pacific Northwest. Her goal is to entertain readers by telling stories of the past that focus on real people with families and real problems like ours today. Her books often include interactions between whites and Native Americans when required by the time period and setting of the story.

Although she grew up in the Spokane area of Washington state and taught there for most of her career, she also lived and taught for many years in Sequim on the Olympic Peninsula and one year in Hawaii where she continues to visit. She currently lives on Whidbey Island with her husband, home of Penn Cove mussels. Her adult children and grandbaby live nearby.

She enjoys reading, research, writing, cooking, yoga, Musselfest in March, the Water Festival in May, warm weather, and most of all, her family.

Other Books by Victoria Ventris Shea

SHAGOON

Ana, a Tlingit newborn of Wolf Clan, meant to die in the Alaskan forest, is raised in a California mission. When she is sent back to Alaska on the *Discovery* with British Captain George Vancouver, she sails with Whidbey, Puget and Baker on their regular route, wintering in Hawaii. On ship, she meets a handsome Hawaiian who is returning to his home. Now she must choose between love in Hawaii or duty in Alaska which includes unknown dangers and the chance of meeting her family. The story begins with Ana's mother whose fierce love for her warrior husband launches a change for future generations.

One of the strongest pieces of historical fiction I've encountered. It warrants multiple reads. –Judge, 29th Annual Self-published Books, Writer's Digest.

A wonderfully complete, beautiful picture of a society that was uncompromising and tough. Highly recommended, 5 Star –Grant Leishman, Reader's Favorite.

BRICK, LIME AND MOONSHINE

Inlanders of the Pacific Northwest are resilient during Prohibition from moonshining farms in Palouse to rum-running across the Canadian border and a drinking house on Loon Lake. Based on memoir, family history and oral legend.

--Outstanding historical novel, highly recommended. 5 Star –Reader's Favorite

--The sweet tone fed my soul. –Crystal Eddy, Portland OR